Hans Christian Andersen Fairy Tales

Hans Christian Andersen Fairy Tales

SIRIUS

This edition published in 2019 by Sirius Publishing, a division of Arcturus Publishing Limited,
26/27 Bickels Yard, 151–153 Bermondsey Street,
London SE1 3HA

Copyright © Arcturus Holdings Limited

All rights reserved. No part of this publication may be reproduced, stored in a retrieval system, or transmitted, in any form or by any means, electronic, mechanical, photocopying, recording or otherwise, without prior written permission in accordance with the provisions of the Copyright Act 1956 (as amended). Any person or persons who do any unauthorised act in relation to this publication may be liable to criminal prosecution and civil claims for damages.

ISBN: 978-1-78950-398-2
AD007186UK

Printed in China

CONTENTS

Introduction 7

The Tinder Box. 9

The Little Mermaid. 18

The Flying Trunk 45

The Red Shoes 52

Little Tiny or Thumbelina 59

The Girl who Trod on a Loaf. 72

The Nightingale. 80

The Storks 91

The Garden of Paradise 98

The Snow Queen. 115

What the Moon Saw 153

The Marsh King's Daughter 197

The Travelling Companions 243

The Elfin Hill 265

The Wild Swans 273

The Emperor's New Suit 292

The Swineherd 298

The Shepherdess and the Sweep 304

The Ugly Duckling 310

The Naughty Boy 322

The Princess and the Pea 325

The Brave Tin Soldier 327

Little Claus and Big Claus 333

The Wicked Prince 347

The Phoenix Bird 351

Little Ida's Flowers 353

The Buckwheat 362

Ole-Luk-Oie, The Dream God 365

The Top and Ball 380

The Fir-Tree 383

The Darning-Needle 393

The Little Match-Seller 397

The Shadow 400

The Old House 415

The Happy Family 425

INTRODUCTION

In 1846 *The Athenæum* literary magazine described a collection of stories by Hans Christian Andersen, as 'a book full of life and fancy; a book for grandfathers no less than grandchildren, not a word of which will be skipped by those who have it once in hand', and this is no less true today. Sadly, a life filled with such fancy was not one experienced by Andersen himself.

Hans Christian Andersen was born in April 1805 in Odense, Denmark. He was the only child, of a poor illiterate washerwoman and a father who doted on him. It was his father who introduced him to literature, reading to him *Holberg's Plays* and *Arabian Tales*. After his father's death and his mother's remarriage, he was sent to a school for the poor and had to support himself through an apprenticeship. Deciding this was not the life for him, he thought that he would try his fortune in Copenhagen, where he would put to use his talent for singing.

Andersen's singing was not a success. Soon his voice broke (or was damaged by 'consequence of my being compelled to wear bad shoes through the winter, and having besides no warm underclothes'). He found himself very low, but the kindness of strangers intervened and he soon decided to try his hand at poetry instead.

Through the benevolence of Jonas Collin, the director of the Royal Danish Theatre, Andersen was sent to grammar school. This was partly funded, at Collin's behest, by King Frederick VI, and Andersen was first at school in Slagelse and later Helsingør.

At the latter, Andersen lived with his schoolmaster. Of this time, he said, 'My life in this family furnishes the most evil dreams to my remembrance… my prayer to God every evening was, that he would remove this cup from me and let me die.' Though his schooldays were miserable, his education allowed him to enter the University of Copenhagen.

Hans Christian Andersen began as many fairy and folk tale writers did, producing revised versions of the fairy tales he had heard as a child, the first collection of which was published in 1835. As with many of Andersen's attempts to gain fame and fortune, this was not, initially, a particularly successful venture: 'Several of my friends, whose judgement was of value to me, counselled me entirely to abstain from writing tales for which I had no talent… I would willingly have discontinued writing them, but they forced themselves from me.'

Despite the advice of his friends, Andersen continued to write both interpretations of traditional folklore and his own original tales, and by the third booklet had produced many of the stories now considered classics, such as 'Thumbelina or Little Tiny', 'The Little Mermaid' and 'The Emperor's New Clothes'. Much of his success is attributed to his writing style, which was often styled as the spoken language, but even more so, due to his ability, through his own experience, to identify with the downtrodden, outcast and unfortunate. Though his lowly start and slow ascent to success meant Andersen never felt fully accepted, his famed vanity would surely now be sated by the continued success of his tales. Much like many of Andersen's ventures in life, his tales do not always end happily ever after…

THE TINDER BOX

A soldier came marching along the high road: 'Left, right – left, right.' He had his knapsack on his back, and a sword at his side; he had been to the wars, and was now returning home.

As he walked on, he met a very frightful-looking old witch in the road. Her under-lip hung quite down on her breast, and she stopped and said, 'Good evening, soldier; you have a very fine sword, and a large knapsack, and you are a real soldier; so you shall have as much money as ever you like.'

'Thank you, old witch,' said the soldier.

'Do you see that large tree,' said the witch, pointing to a tree which stood beside them. 'Well, it is quite hollow inside, and you must climb to the top, when you will see a hole, through which you can let yourself down into the tree to a great depth. I will tie a rope round your body, so that I can pull you up again when you call out to me.'

'But what am I to do, down there in the tree?' asked the soldier.

'Get money,' she replied; 'for you must know that when you reach the ground under the tree, you will find yourself in a large hall, lighted up by three hundred lamps; you will then see three doors, which can be easily opened, for the keys are in all the locks. On entering the first of the chambers, to which these doors lead, you will see a large chest, standing in the middle of the floor, and upon it a dog seated, with a pair of eyes as large as teacups. But you need not be at all afraid of him; I will give you my blue checked apron, which you must spread upon the floor, and then boldly seize hold of the dog, and place him upon it. You can then open the chest, and take from it as many pence as you please, they are only copper pence; but if you would rather have silver money, you must go into the second chamber. Here you will find another dog, with eyes as big as mill-wheels; but do not let that trouble you. Place him upon my apron, and then take what money you please. If, however, you like gold best, enter the third chamber, where there is another chest full of it. The dog who sits on this chest is very dreadful; his eyes are as big as a tower, but do not mind him. If he also is placed upon my apron, he cannot hurt you, and you may take from the chest what gold you will.'

'This is not a bad story,' said the soldier; 'but what am I to give you, you old witch? For, of course, you do not mean to tell me all this for nothing.'

'No,' said the witch; 'but I do not ask for a single penny. Only promise to bring me an old tinder-box, which my grandmother left behind the last time she went down there.'

'Very well; I promise. Now tie the rope round my body.'

'Here it is,' replied the witch; 'and here is my blue checked apron.'

As soon as the rope was tied, the soldier climbed up the tree, and let himself down through the hollow to the ground beneath; and here he found, as the witch had told him, a large hall, in which many hundred lamps were all burning. Then he opened the first door. 'Ah!' There sat the dog, with the eyes as large as teacups, staring at him.

'You're a pretty fellow,' said the soldier, seizing him, and placing him on the witch's apron, while he filled his pockets from the chest with as many pieces as they would hold. Then he closed the lid, seated the dog upon it again, and walked into another chamber, And, sure enough, there sat the dog with eyes as big as mill-wheels.

'You had better not look at me in that way,' said the soldier; 'you will make your eyes water.' And then he seated him also upon the apron, and opened the chest. But when he saw what a quantity of silver money it contained, he very quickly threw away all the coppers he had taken, and filled his pockets and his knapsack with nothing but silver.

Then he went into the third room, and there the dog was really hideous; his eyes were, truly, as big as towers, and they turned round and round in his head like wheels.

'Good morning,' said the soldier, touching his cap, for he had never seen such a dog in his life. But after looking at him more closely, he thought he had been civil enough, so he placed him on the floor, and opened the chest. Good gracious, what a quantity of gold there was! Enough to buy all the sugar-sticks of the sweet-stuff women; all the tin soldiers, whips and rocking-horses in the world, or even the whole town itself. There was, indeed, an immense quantity. So the soldier now threw away all the silver money he had taken, and filled his pockets and his knapsack with gold instead; and not only his pockets and his knapsack, but even his cap and boots, so that he could scarcely walk.

He was really rich now; so he replaced the dog on the chest, closed the door, and called up through the tree, 'Now pull me out, you old witch.'

'Have you got the tinder-box?' asked the witch.

'No; I declare I quite forgot it.' So he went back and fetched the tinder-box, and then the witch drew him up out of the tree, and he stood again in the high road, with his pockets, his knapsack, his cap and his boots full of gold.

'What are you going to do with the tinder-box?' asked the soldier.

'That is nothing to you,' replied the witch; 'you have the money, now give me the tinder-box.'

'I tell you what,' said the soldier; 'if you don't tell me what you are going to do with it, I will draw my sword and cut off your head.'

'No,' said the witch.

The soldier immediately cut off her head, and there she lay on the ground. Then he tied up all his money in her apron and slung it on his back like a bundle, put the tinder-box in his pocket, and walked off to the nearest town. It was a very nice town, and he put up at the best inn and ordered a dinner of all his favourite dishes, for now he was rich and had plenty of money.

The servant who cleaned his boots thought they certainly were a shabby pair to be worn by such a rich gentleman, for he had not yet bought any new ones. The next day, however, he procured some good clothes and proper boots, so that our soldier soon became known as a fine gentleman, and the people visited him, and told him all the wonders that were to be seen in the town, and of the king's beautiful daughter, the princess.

'Where can I see her?' asked the soldier.

'She is not to be seen at all,' they said; 'she lives in a large copper castle, surrounded by walls and towers. No one but the king himself can pass in or out, for there has been a prophecy that she will marry a common soldier, and the king cannot bear to think of such a marriage.'

'I should like very much to see her,' thought the soldier; but he could not obtain permission to do so. However, he passed a very pleasant time: went to the theatre, drove in the king's garden, and gave a great deal of money to the poor, which was very good of him; he remembered what it had been in olden times to be without a shilling. Now he was rich, had fine clothes and many friends, who all declared he was a fine fellow and a real gentleman, and all this gratified him exceedingly. But his money would not last forever; and as he spent and gave away a great deal daily, and received none, he found himself at last with only two shillings left. So he was obliged to leave his elegant rooms, and live in a little garret under the roof, where he had to clean his own boots, and even mend them with a large needle. None of his friends came to see him, there were too many stairs to mount up. One dark evening, he had not even a penny to buy a candle; then all at once he remembered that there was a piece of candle stuck in the tinder-box, which he had brought from the old tree, into which the witch had helped him.

He found the tinder-box, but no sooner had he struck a few sparks from the flint and steel, than the door flew open and the dog with eyes as big as teacups, whom he had seen while down in the tree, stood before him, and said, 'What orders, master?'

'Hallo,' said the soldier; 'well this is a pleasant tinderbox, if it brings me all I wish for.'

'Bring me some money,' said he to the dog.

He was gone in a moment, and presently returned, carrying a large bag of coppers in his mouth. The soldier very soon discovered after this the value of the tinder-box. If he struck the flint once, the dog who sat on the chest of copper money made his appearance; if twice, the dog came from the chest of silver; and if three times, the dog with eyes like towers, who watched over the gold. The soldier had now plenty of money; he returned to his elegant rooms, and reappeared in his fine clothes, so that his friends knew him again directly, and made as much of him as before.

After a while he began to think it was very strange that no one could get a look at the princess. 'Everyone says she is very beautiful,' thought he to himself; 'but what is the use of that if she is to be shut up in a copper castle surrounded by so many towers. Can I by any means get to see her. Stop! Where is my tinder-box?' Then he struck a light, and in a moment the dog, with eyes as big as teacups, stood before him.

'It is midnight,' said the soldier, 'yet I should very much like to see the princess, if only for a moment.'

The dog disappeared instantly, and before the soldier could even look round, he returned with the princess. She was lying on the dog's back asleep, and looked so lovely, that everyone who saw her would know she was a real princess. The soldier could not help kissing her, true soldier as he was. Then the dog ran back with the princess; but in the morning, while at breakfast with the king and queen, she told them what a singular dream she had had during the night, of a dog and a soldier, that she had ridden on the dog's back, and been kissed by the soldier.

'That is a very pretty story, indeed,' said the queen. So the next night one of the old ladies of the court was set to watch by the princess's bed, to discover whether it really was a dream, or what else it might be.

The soldier longed very much to see the princess once more, so he sent for the dog again in the night to fetch her, and to run with her as fast as ever he could. But the old lady put on water boots, and ran after him as quickly as he did, and found that he carried the princess into a large house. She thought it would help her to remember the place if she made a large cross on the door with a piece of chalk. Then she went home to bed, and the dog presently returned with the princess. But when he saw that a cross had been made on the door of the house, where the soldier lived, he took another piece of chalk and made crosses on all the doors in the town, so that the lady-in-waiting might not be able to find out the right door.

Early the next morning the king and queen accompanied the lady and all the officers of the household, to see where the princess had been.

'Here it is,' said the king, when they came to the first door with a cross on it.

'No, my dear husband, it must be that one,' said the queen, pointing to a second door having a cross also.

'And here is one, and there is another!' they all exclaimed; for there were crosses on all the doors in every direction.

So they felt it would be useless to search any farther. But the queen was a very clever woman; she could do a great deal more than merely ride in a carriage. She took her large gold scissors, cut a piece of silk into squares, and made a neat little bag. This bag she filled with buckwheat flour, and tied it round the princess's neck; and then she cut a small hole in the bag, so that the flour might be scattered on the ground as the princess went along. During the night, the dog came again and carried the princess on his back, and ran with her to the soldier, who loved her very much, and wished that he had been a prince, so that he might have her for a wife. The dog did not observe how the flour ran out of the bag all the way from the castle wall to the soldier's house, and even up to the window, where he had climbed with the princess. Therefore in the morning the king and queen found out where their daughter had been, and the soldier was taken up and put in prison. Oh, how dark and disagreeable it was as he sat there, and the people said to him, 'Tomorrow you will be hanged.' It was not very pleasant news, and besides, he had left the tinder-box at the inn. In the morning he could see through the iron grating of the little window how the people were hastening out of the town to see him hanged; he heard the drums beating, and saw the soldiers marching. Everyone ran out to look at them and a shoemaker's boy, with a leather apron and slippers on, galloped by so fast that one of his slippers flew off and struck against the wall where the soldier sat looking through the iron grating. 'Hallo, you shoemaker's boy, you need not be in such a hurry,' cried the soldier to him. 'There will be nothing to see till I come; but if you will run to the house where I have been living, and bring me my tinder-box, you shall have four shillings, but you must put your best foot foremost.'

The shoemaker's boy liked the idea of getting the four shillings, so he ran very fast and fetched the tinder-box, and gave it to the soldier. And now we shall see what happened. Outside the town a large gibbet had been erected, round which stood the soldiers and several thousands of people. The king and the queen sat on splendid thrones opposite to the judges and the whole council. The soldier already stood on the ladder; but as they were about to place the rope around his neck, he said that an innocent request was often granted to a poor criminal before he suffered death. He wished very much to smoke a pipe, as it would be the last pipe he should ever smoke in the world. The king could not refuse this request, so the soldier took his tinder-box, and struck fire, once, twice, thrice – and there in a moment stood all the dogs: the one with eyes as big as teacups, the one with eyes as large as mill-wheels, and the third, whose eyes were like towers. 'Help me now, that I may not be hanged,' cried the soldier.

And the dogs fell upon the judges and all the councillors; seized one by the legs, and another by the nose, and tossed them many feet high in the air, so that they fell down and were dashed to pieces.

'I will not be touched,' said the king. But the largest dog seized him, as well as the queen, and threw them after the others. Then the soldiers and all the people were afraid, and cried, 'Good soldier, you shall be our king, and you shall marry the beautiful princess.'

So they placed the soldier in the king's carriage, and the three dogs ran on in front and cried 'Hurrah!' and the little boys whistled through their fingers, and the soldiers presented arms. The princess came out of the copper castle, and became queen, which was very pleasing to her. The wedding festivities lasted a whole week, and the dogs sat at the table, and stared with all their eyes.

THE LITTLE MERMAID

Far out in the ocean, where the water is as blue as the prettiest cornflower, and as clear as crystal, it is very, very deep; so deep, indeed, that no cable could fathom it: many church steeples, piled one upon another, would not reach from the ground beneath to the surface of the water above. There dwell the Sea King and his subjects. We must not imagine that there is nothing at the bottom of the sea but bare yellow sand. No, indeed; the most singular flowers and plants grow there; the leaves and stems of which are so pliant that the slightest agitation of the water causes them to stir as if they had life. Fishes, both large and small, glide between the branches, as birds fly among the trees here upon land. In the deepest spot of all stands the castle of the Sea King. Its walls are built of coral, and the long, gothic windows are of the clearest amber. The roof is formed of shells that open and close as the water flows over them. Their appearance is very beautiful, for in each lies a glittering pearl, which would be fit for the diadem of a queen.

The Sea King had been a widower for many years, and his aged mother kept house for him. She was a very wise woman, and exceedingly proud of her high birth; on that account she wore twelve oysters on her tail; while others, also of high rank, were only allowed to wear six. She was, however, deserving of very great praise, especially for her care of the little sea-princesses, her granddaughters. They were six beautiful children; but the youngest was the prettiest of them all: her skin was as clear and delicate as a rose-leaf, and her eyes as blue as the deepest sea; but, like all the others, she had no feet, and her body ended in a fish's tail. All day long they played in the great halls of the castle, or among the living flowers that grew out of the walls. The large amber windows were open, and the fish swam in, just as the swallows fly into our houses when we open the windows, excepting that the fishes swam up to the princesses, ate out of their hands, and allowed themselves to be stroked. Outside the castle there was a beautiful garden, in which grew bright red and dark blue flowers, and blossoms like flames of fire; the fruit glittered like gold, and the leaves and stems waved to and fro continually. The earth itself was the finest sand, but blue as the flame of burning sulphur. Over everything lay a peculiar blue radiance, as if it were surrounded by the air from above, through which the blue sky shone, instead of the dark depths of the sea. In calm weather the sun could be seen, looking like a purple flower, with the light streaming from the calyx. Each of the young princesses had a little plot of ground in the garden, where she might dig and plant as she pleased. One arranged her flower-bed into the form of a whale; another thought it better to make hers like the figure of a little mermaid; but that of the youngest was round like the sun, and contained flowers as red as his rays at sunset. She was a strange child, quiet and thoughtful; and while her sisters would be delighted with the wonderful things which they obtained from the wrecks of vessels, she cared for nothing but her pretty red flowers, like the sun, excepting a beautiful marble statue. It was the representation of a handsome boy, carved out of pure white stone, which had fallen to the bottom of the sea from a wreck. She planted by the statue a rose-coloured weeping willow. It grew splendidly, and very soon hung its fresh branches over the statue, almost down to the blue sands. The shadow had a violet tint, and waved to and fro like the branches; it seemed as if the crown of the tree and the root were at play, and trying to kiss each other. Nothing gave her so much pleasure as to hear about the world above the sea. She made her old grandmother tell her all she knew of the ships and of the towns, the people and the animals. To her it seemed most wonderful and beautiful to hear that the flowers of the land should have fragrance, and not those below the sea; that the trees of the forest should be green; and that the fishes among the trees could sing so sweetly, that it was quite a pleasure to hear them. Her grandmother called the little birds fishes, or she would not have understood her; for she had never seen birds.

'When you have reached your fifteenth year,' said the grandmother, 'you will have permission to rise up out of the sea, to sit on the rocks in the moonlight, while the great ships are sailing by; and then you will see both forests and towns.'

In the following year, one of the sisters would be fifteen: but as each was a year younger than the other, the youngest would have to wait five years before her turn came to rise up from the bottom of the ocean, and see the earth as we do. However, each promised to tell the others what she saw on her first visit, and what she thought the most beautiful; for their grandmother could not tell them enough; there were so many things on which they wanted information. None of them longed so much for her turn to come as the youngest, she who had the longest time to wait, and who was so quiet and thoughtful. Many nights she stood by the open window, looking up through the dark blue water, and watching the fish as they splashed about with their fins and tails.

She could see the moon and stars shining faintly; but through the water they looked larger than they do to our eyes. When something like a black cloud passed between her and them, she knew that it was either a whale swimming over her head, or a ship full of human beings, who never imagined that a pretty little mermaid was standing beneath them, holding out her white hands towards the keel of their ship.

As soon as the eldest was fifteen, she was allowed to rise to the surface of the ocean. When she came back, she had hundreds of things to talk about; but the most beautiful, she said, was to lie in the moonlight, on a sandbank, in the quiet sea, near the coast, and to gaze on a large town nearby, where the lights were twinkling like hundreds of stars; to listen to the sounds of the music, the noise of carriages and the voices of human beings, and then to hear the merry bells peal out from the church steeples; and because she could not go near to all those wonderful things, she longed for them more than ever. Oh, did not the youngest sister listen eagerly to all these descriptions? And afterwards, when she stood at the open window looking up through the dark blue water, she thought of the great city, with all its bustle and noise, and even fancied she could hear the sound of the church bells, down in the depths of the sea.

In another year the second sister received permission to rise to the surface of the water, and to swim about where she pleased. She rose just as the sun was setting, and this, she said, was the most beautiful sight of all. The whole sky looked like gold, while violet and rose-coloured clouds, which she could not describe, floated over her; and, still more rapidly than the clouds, flew a large flock of wild swans towards the setting sun, looking like a long white veil across the sea. She also swam towards the sun;

but it sunk into the waves, and the rosy tints faded from the clouds and from the sea.

The third sister's turn followed; she was the boldest of them all, and she swam up a broad river that emptied itself into the sea. On the banks she saw green hills covered with beautiful vines; palaces and castles peeped out from amid the proud trees of the forest; she heard the birds singing, and the rays of the sun were so powerful that she was obliged often to dive down under the water to cool her burning face. In a narrow creek she found a whole troop of little human children, quite naked, and sporting about in the water; she wanted to play with them, but they fled in a great fright; and then a little black animal came to the water; it was a dog, but she did not know that, for she had never before seen one. This animal barked at her so terribly that she became frightened, and rushed back to the open sea. But she said she should never forget the beautiful forest, the green hills, and the pretty little children who could swim in the water, although they had not fish's tails.

The fourth sister was more timid; she remained in the midst of the sea, but she said it was quite as beautiful there as nearer the land. She could see for so many miles around her, and the sky above looked like a bell of glass. She had seen the ships, but at such a great distance that they looked like seagulls. The dolphins sported in the waves, and the great whales spouted water from their nostrils till it seemed as if a hundred fountains were playing in every direction.

The fifth sister's birthday occurred in the winter; so when her turn came, she saw what the others had not seen the first time they went up. The sea looked quite green, and large icebergs were floating about, each like a pearl, she said, but larger and loftier than the churches built by men. They were of the most singular shapes, and glittered like diamonds. She had seated herself upon one of the largest, and let the wind play with her long hair, and she remarked that all the ships sailed by rapidly, and steered as far away as they could from the iceberg, as if they were afraid of it. Towards evening, as the sun went down, dark clouds covered the sky, the thunder rolled and the lightning flashed, and the red light glowed on the icebergs as they rocked and tossed on the heaving sea. On all the ships the sails were reefed with fear and trembling, while she sat calmly on the floating iceberg, watching the blue lightning, as it darted its forked flashes into the sea.

When first the sisters had permission to rise to the surface, they were each delighted with the new and beautiful sights they saw; but now, as grown-up girls, they could go when they pleased, and they had become indifferent about it. They wished themselves back again in the water, and after a month had passed they said it was much more beautiful down below, and pleasanter to be at home. Yet often, in the evening hours, the five sisters would twine their arms round each other, and rise to the surface, in a row. They had more beautiful voices than any human being could have; and before the approach of a storm, and when they expected a ship would be lost, they swam before the vessel, and sang sweetly of the delights to be found in the depths of the sea, and begging the sailors not to fear if they sank to the bottom. But the sailors could not understand the song, they took it for the howling of the storm. And these things were never to be beautiful for them; for if the ship sank, the men were drowned, and their dead bodies alone reached the palace of the Sea King.

When the sisters rose, arm-in-arm, through the water in this way, their youngest sister would stand quite alone, looking after them, ready to cry, only that the mermaids have no tears, and therefore they suffer more. 'Oh, were I but fifteen years old,' said she: 'I know that I shall love the world up there, and all the people who live in it.'

At last she reached her fifteenth year. 'Well, now, you are grown up,' said the old dowager, her grandmother; 'so you must let me adorn you like your other sisters;' and she placed a wreath of white lilies in her hair, and every flower leaf was half a pearl. Then the old lady ordered eight great oysters to attach themselves to the tail of the princess to show her high rank.

'But they hurt me so,' said the little mermaid.

'Pride must suffer pain,' replied the old lady. Oh, how gladly she would have shaken off all this grandeur, and laid aside the heavy wreath! The red flowers in her own garden would have suited her much better, but she could not help herself: so she said, 'Farewell,' and rose as lightly as a bubble to the surface of the water.

The sun had just set as she raised her head above the waves; but the clouds were tinted with crimson and gold, and through the glimmering twilight beamed the evening star in all its beauty. The sea was calm, and the air mild and fresh. A large ship, with three masts, lay becalmed on the water, with only one sail set; for not a breeze stiffed, and the sailors sat idle on deck or amongst the rigging. There was music and song on board; and, as darkness came on, a hundred coloured lanterns were lighted, as if the flags of all nations waved in the air. The little mermaid swam close to the cabin windows; and now and then, as the waves lifted her up, she could look in through clear glass window-panes, and see a number of well-dressed people within. Among them was a young prince, the most beautiful of all, with large black eyes; he was sixteen years of age, and his birthday was being kept with much rejoicing. The sailors were dancing on deck, but when the prince came out of the cabin, more than a hundred rockets rose in the air, making it as bright as day. The little mermaid was so startled that she dived under water; and when she again stretched out her head, it appeared as if all the stars of heaven were falling around her, she had never seen such fireworks before. Great suns spurted fire about, splendid fireflies flew into the blue air, and everything was reflected in the clear, calm sea beneath. The ship itself was so brightly illuminated that all the people, and even the smallest rope, could be distinctly and plainly seen. And how handsome the young prince looked, as he pressed the hands of all present and smiled at them, while the music resounded through the clear night air.

It was very late; yet the little mermaid could not take her eyes from the ship, or from the beautiful prince. The coloured lanterns had been extinguished, no more rockets rose in the air, and the cannon had ceased firing; but the sea became restless, and a moaning, grumbling sound could be heard beneath the waves: still the little mermaid remained by the cabin window, rocking up and down on the water, which enabled her to look in. After a while, the sails were quickly unfurled, and the noble ship continued her passage; but soon the waves rose higher, heavy clouds darkened the sky, and lightning appeared in the distance. A dreadful storm was approaching; once more the sails were reefed, and the great ship pursued her flying course over the raging sea. The waves rose mountains high, as if they would have overtopped the mast; but the ship dived like a swan between them, and then rose again on their lofty, foaming crests. To the little mermaid this appeared pleasant sport; not so to the sailors. At length the ship groaned and creaked; the thick planks gave way under the lashing of the sea as it broke over the deck; the mainmast snapped asunder like a reed; the ship lay over on her side; and the water rushed in. The little mermaid now perceived that the crew were in danger; even she herself was obliged to be careful to avoid the beams and planks of the wreck which lay scattered on the water. At one moment it was so pitch dark that she could not see a single object, but a flash of lightning revealed the whole scene; she could see every one who had been on board excepting the prince; when the ship parted, she had seen him sink into the deep waves, and she was glad, for she thought he would now be with her; and then she remembered that human beings could not live in the water, so that when he got down to her father's palace he would be quite dead. But he must not die. So she swam about among the beams and planks which strewed the surface of the sea, forgetting that they could crush her to pieces. Then she dived deeply under the dark waters, rising and falling with the waves, till at length she managed to reach the young prince, who was fast losing the power of swimming in that stormy sea. His limbs were failing him, his beautiful eyes were closed, and he would have died had not the little mermaid come to his assistance. She held his head above the water, and let the waves drift them where they would.

In the morning the storm had ceased; but of the ship not a single fragment could be seen. The sun rose up red and glowing from the water, and its beams brought back the hue of health to the prince's cheeks; but his eyes remained closed. The mermaid kissed his high, smooth forehead, and stroked back his wet hair; he seemed to her like the marble statue in her little garden, and she kissed him again, and wished that he might live. Presently they came in sight of land; she saw lofty blue mountains, on which the white snow rested as if a flock of swans were lying upon them. Near the coast were beautiful green forests, and close by stood a large building, whether a church or a convent she could not tell. Orange and citron trees grew in the garden, and before the door stood lofty palms. The sea here formed a little bay, in which the water was quite still, but very deep; so she swam with the handsome prince to the beach, which was covered with fine, white sand, and there she laid him in the warm sunshine, taking care to raise his head higher than his body. Then bells sounded in the large white building, and a number of young girls came into the garden. The little mermaid swam out farther from the shore and placed herself between some high rocks that rose out of the water; then she covered her head and neck with the foam of the sea so that her little face might not be seen, and watched to see what would become of the poor prince. She did not wait long before she saw a young girl approach the spot where he lay. She seemed frightened at first, but only for a moment; then she fetched a number of people, and the mermaid saw that the prince came to life again, and smiled upon those who stood round him. But to her he sent no smile; he knew not that she had saved him. This made her very unhappy, and when he was led away into the great building, she dived down sorrowfully into the water, and returned to her father's castle. She had always been silent and thoughtful, and now she was more so than ever. Her sisters asked her what she had seen during her first visit to the surface of the water; but she would tell them nothing. Many an evening and morning did she rise to the place where she had left the prince. She saw the fruits in the garden ripen till they were gathered, the snow on the tops of the mountains melt away; but she never saw the prince, and therefore she returned home, always more sorrowful than before. It was her only comfort to sit in her own little garden, and fling her arm round the beautiful marble statue which was like the prince; but she gave up tending her flowers, and they grew in wild confusion over the paths, twining their long leaves and stems round the branches of the trees, so that the whole place became dark and gloomy. At length she could bear it no longer, and told one of her sisters all about it. Then the others heard the secret, and very soon it became known to two mermaids whose intimate friend happened to know who the prince was. She had also seen the festival on board ship, and she told them where the prince came from, and where his palace stood.

'Come, little sister,' said the other princesses; then they entwined their arms and rose up in a long row to the surface of the water, close by the spot where they knew the prince's palace stood. It was built of bright yellow shining stone, with long flights of marble steps, one of which reached quite down to the sea. Splendid gilded cupolas rose over the roof, and between the pillars that surrounded the whole building stood lifelike statues of marble. Through the clear crystal of the lofty windows could be seen noble rooms, with costly silk curtains and hangings of tapestry; while the walls were covered with beautiful paintings which were a pleasure to look at. In the centre of the largest saloon a fountain threw its sparkling jets high up into the glass cupola of the ceiling, through which the sun shone down upon the water and upon the beautiful plants growing round the basin of the fountain. Now that she knew where he lived, she spent many an evening and many a night on the water near the palace. She would swim much nearer the shore than any of the others ventured to do; indeed once she went quite up the narrow channel under the marble balcony, which threw a broad shadow on the water. Here she would sit and watch the young prince, who thought himself quite alone in the bright moonlight. She saw him many times of an evening sailing in a pleasant boat, with music playing and flags waving. She peeped out from among the green rushes, and if the wind caught her long silvery-white veil, those who saw it believed it to be a swan, spreading out its wings. On many a night, too, when the fishermen, with their torches, were out at sea, she heard them relate so many good things about the doings of the young prince, that she was glad she had saved his life when he had been tossed about half-dead on the waves. And she remembered that his head had rested on her bosom, and how heartily she had kissed him; but he knew nothing of all this, and could not even dream of her. She grew more and more fond of human beings, and wished more and more to be able to wander about with those whose world seemed to be so much larger than her own. They could fly over the sea in ships, and mount the high hills which were far above the clouds; and the lands they possessed, their woods and their fields, stretched far away beyond the reach of her sight. There was so much that she wished to know, and her sisters were unable to answer all her questions. Then she applied to her old grandmother, who knew all about the upper world, which she very rightly called the lands above the sea.

'If human beings are not drowned,' asked the little mermaid, 'can they live forever? Do they never die as we do here in the sea?'

'Yes,' replied the old lady, 'they must also die, and their term of life is even shorter than ours. We sometimes live to three hundred years, but when we cease to exist here we only become the foam on the surface of the water, and we have not even a grave down here of those we love. We have not immortal souls, we shall never live again; but, like the green seaweed, when once it has been cut off, we can never flourish more. Human beings, on the contrary, have a soul which lives forever, lives after the body has been turned to dust. It rises up through the clear, pure air beyond the glittering stars. As we rise out of the water, and behold all the land of the earth, so do they rise to unknown and glorious regions which we shall never see.'

'Why have not we an immortal soul?' asked the little mermaid mournfully. 'I would give gladly all the hundreds of years that I have to live, to be a human being only for one day, and to have the hope of knowing the happiness of that glorious world above the stars.'

'You must not think of that,' said the old woman; 'we feel ourselves to be much happier and much better off than human beings.'

'So I shall die,' said the little mermaid, 'and as the foam of the sea I shall be driven about never again to hear the music of the waves, or to see the pretty flowers nor the red sun. Is there anything I can do to win an immortal soul?'

'No,' said the old woman, 'unless a man were to love you so much that you were more to him than his father or mother; and if all his thoughts and all his love were fixed upon you, and the priest placed his right hand in yours, and he promised to be true to you here and hereafter, then his soul would glide into your body and you would obtain a share in the future happiness of mankind. He would give a soul to you and retain his own as well; but this can never happen. Your fish's tail, which amongst us is considered so beautiful, is thought on earth to be quite ugly; they do not know any better, and they think it necessary to have two stout props, which they call legs, in order to be handsome.'

Then the little mermaid sighed, and looked sorrowfully at her fish's tail. 'Let us be happy,' said the old lady, 'and dart and spring about during the three hundred years that we have to live, which is really quite long enough; after that we can rest ourselves all the better. This evening we are going to have a court ball.'

It is one of those splendid sights which we can never see on earth. The walls and the ceiling of the large ballroom were of thick but transparent crystal. Many hundreds of colossal shells, some of a deep red, others of a grass-green, stood on each side in rows, with blue fire in them, which lighted up the whole saloon and shone through the walls, so that the sea was also illuminated. Innumerable fishes, great and small, swam past the crystal walls; on some of them the scales glowed with a purple brilliancy, and on others they shone like silver and gold. Through the halls flowed a broad stream, and in it danced the mermen and the mermaids to the music of their own sweet singing. No one on earth has such a lovely voice as theirs. The little mermaid sang more sweetly than them all. The whole court applauded her with hands and tails; and for a moment her heart felt quite gay, for she knew she had the loveliest voice of any on earth or in the sea. But she soon thought again of the world above her, for she could not forget the charming prince, nor her sorrow that she had not an immortal soul like his; therefore she crept away silently out of her father's palace, and while everything within was gladness and song, she sat in her own little garden sorrowful and alone. Then she heard the bugle sounding through the water, and thought – 'He is certainly sailing above, he on whom my wishes depend, and in whose hands I should like to place the happiness of my life. I will venture all for him, and to win an immortal soul, while my sisters are dancing in my father's palace, I will go to the sea witch, of whom I have always been so much afraid, but she can give me counsel and help.'

And then the little mermaid went out from her garden, and took the road to the foaming whirlpools, behind which the sorceress lived. She had never been that way before: neither flowers nor grass grew there; nothing but bare, grey, sandy ground stretched out to the whirlpool, where the water, like foaming mill-wheels, whirled round everything that it seized, and cast it into the fathomless deep. Through the midst of these crushing whirlpools the little mermaid was obliged to pass, to reach the dominions of the sea witch; and also for a long distance the only road lay right across a quantity of warm, bubbling mire, called by the witch her turfmoor. Beyond this stood her house, in the centre of a strange forest, in which all the trees and flowers were polypi, half animals and half plants; they looked like serpents with a hundred heads growing out of the ground. The branches were long slimy arms, with fingers like flexible worms, moving limb after limb from the root to the top. All that could be reached in the sea they seized upon, and held fast, so that it never escaped from their clutches. The little mermaid was so alarmed at what she saw that she stood still, and her heart beat with fear, and she was very nearly turning back; but she thought of the prince, and of the human soul for which she longed, and her courage returned. She fastened her long flowing hair round her head, so that the polypi might not seize hold of it. She laid her hands together across her bosom, and then she darted forward as a fish shoots through the water, between the supple arms and fingers of the ugly polypi, which were stretched out on each side of her. She saw that each held in its grasp something it had seized with its numerous little arms, as if they were iron bands. The white skeletons of human beings who had perished at sea, and had sunk down into the deep waters, skeletons of land animals, oars, rudders and chests of ships were lying tightly grasped by their clinging arms; even a little mermaid, whom they had caught and strangled; and this seemed the most shocking of all to the little princess.

She now came to a space of marshy ground in the wood, where large, fat water-snakes were rolling in the mire and showing their ugly, drab-coloured bodies. In the midst of this spot stood a house, built with the bones of shipwrecked human beings. There sat the sea witch, allowing a toad to eat from her mouth, just as people sometimes feed a canary with a piece of sugar. She called the ugly water-snakes her little chickens, and allowed them to crawl all over her bosom.

'I know what you want,' said the sea witch; 'it is very stupid of you, but you shall have your way, and it will bring you to sorrow, my pretty princess. You want to get rid of your fish's tail, and to have two supports instead of it, like human beings on earth, so that the young prince may fall in love with you, and that you may have an immortal soul.' And then the witch laughed so loud and disgustingly, that the toad and the snakes fell to the ground, and lay there wriggling about. 'You are but just in time,' said the witch; 'for after sunrise tomorrow I should not be able to help you till the end of another year. I will prepare a draught for you, with which you must swim to land tomorrow before sunrise, and sit down on the shore and drink it. Your tail will then disappear, and shrink up into what mankind calls legs, and you will feel great pain, as if a sword were passing through you. But all who see you will say that you are the prettiest little human being they ever saw. You will still have the same floating gracefulness of movement, and no dancer will ever tread so lightly; but at every step you take it will feel as if you were treading upon sharp knives, and that the blood must flow. If you will bear all this, I will help you.'

'Yes, I will,' said the little princess in a trembling voice, as she thought of the prince and the immortal soul.

'But think again,' said the witch; 'for when once your shape has become like a human being, you can no more be a mermaid. You will never return through the water to your sisters, or to your father's palace again; and if you do not win the love of the prince, so that he is willing to forget his father and mother for your sake, and to love you with his whole soul, and allow the priest to join your hands that you may be man and wife, then you will never have an immortal soul. The first morning after he marries another your heart will break, and you will become foam on the crest of the waves.'

'I will do it,' said the little mermaid, and she became pale as death.

'But I must be paid also,' said the witch, 'and it is not a trifle that I ask. You have the sweetest voice of any who dwell here in the depths of the sea, and you believe that you will be able to charm the prince with it also, but this voice you must give to me; the best thing you possess will I have for the price of my draught. My own blood must be mixed with it that it may be as sharp as a two-edged sword.'

'But if you take away my voice,' said the little mermaid, 'what is left for me?'

'Your beautiful form, your graceful walk, and your expressive eyes; surely with these you can enchain a man's heart. Well, have you lost your courage? Put out your little tongue that I may cut it off as my payment; then you shall have the powerful draught.'

'It shall be,' said the little mermaid.

Then the witch placed her cauldron on the fire, to prepare the magic draught.

'Cleanliness is a good thing,' said she, scouring the vessel with snakes, which she had tied together in a large knot; then she pricked herself in the breast, and let the black blood drop into it. The steam that rose formed itself into such horrible shapes that no one could look at them without fear. Every moment the witch threw something else into the vessel, and when it began to boil, the sound was like the weeping of a crocodile. When at last the magic draught was ready, it looked like the clearest water. 'There it is for you,' said the witch. Then she cut off the mermaid's tongue, so that she became dumb, and would never again speak or sing. 'If the polypi should seize hold of you as you return through the wood,' said the witch, 'throw over them a few drops of the potion, and their fingers will be torn into a thousand pieces.' But the little mermaid had no occasion to do this, for the polypi sprang back in terror when they caught sight of the glittering draught, which shone in her hand like a twinkling star.

So she passed quickly through the wood and the marsh, and between the rushing whirlpools. She saw that in her father's palace the torches in the ballroom were extinguished, and all within asleep; but she did not venture to go in to them, for now she was dumb and going to leave them forever, she felt as if her heart would break. She stole into the garden, took a flower from the flower-beds of each of her sisters, kissed her hand a thousand times towards the palace, and then rose up through the dark blue waters. The sun had not risen when she came in sight of the prince's palace, and approached the beautiful marble steps, but the moon shone clear and bright. Then the little mermaid drank the magic draught, and it seemed as if a two-edged sword went through her delicate body: she fell into a swoon, and lay like one dead. When the sun arose and shone over the sea, she recovered, and felt a sharp pain; but just before her stood the handsome young prince. He fixed his coal-black eyes upon her so earnestly that she cast down her own, and then became aware that her fish's tail was gone, and that she had as pretty a pair of white legs and tiny feet as any little maiden could have; but she had no clothes, so she wrapped herself in her long, thick hair. The prince asked her who she was, and where she came from, and she looked at him mildly and sorrowfully with her deep blue eyes; but she could not speak. Every step she took was as the witch had said it would be, she felt as if treading upon the points of needles or sharp knives; but she bore it willingly, and stepped as lightly by the prince's side as a soap-bubble, so that he and all who saw her wondered at her graceful swaying movements. She was very soon arrayed in costly robes of silk and muslin, and was the most beautiful creature in the palace; but she was dumb, and could neither speak nor sing.

Beautiful female slaves, dressed in silk and gold, stepped forward and sang before the prince and his royal parents: one sang better than all the others, and the prince clapped his hands and smiled at her. This was great sorrow to the little mermaid; she knew how much more sweetly she herself could sing once, and she thought, 'Oh if he could only know that! I have given away my voice forever, to be with him.'

The slaves next performed some pretty fairy-like dances, to the sound of beautiful music. Then the little mermaid raised her lovely white arms, stood on the tips of her toes, and glided over the floor, and danced as no one yet had been able to dance. At each moment her beauty became more revealed, and her expressive eyes appealed more directly to the heart than the songs of the slaves. Everyone was enchanted, especially the prince, who called her his little foundling; and she danced again quite readily, to please him, though each time her foot touched the floor it seemed as if she trod on sharp knives.

The prince said she should remain with him always, and she received permission to sleep at his door, on a velvet cushion. He had a page's dress made for her, that she might accompany him on horseback. They rode together through the sweet-scented woods, where the green boughs touched their shoulders, and the little birds sang among the fresh leaves. She climbed with the prince to the tops of high mountains; and although her tender feet bled so that even her steps were marked, she only laughed, and followed him till they could see the clouds beneath them looking like a flock of birds travelling to distant lands. While at the prince's palace, and when all the household were asleep, she would go and sit on the broad marble steps; for it eased her burning feet to bathe them in the cold sea-water; and then she thought of all those below in the deep.

Once during the night her sisters came up arm-in-arm, singing sorrowfully as they floated on the water. She beckoned to them, and then they recognised her, and told her how she had grieved them. After that, they came to the same place every night; and once she saw in the distance her old grandmother, who had not been to the surface of the sea for many years, and the old Sea King, her father, with his crown on his head. They stretched out their hands towards her, but they did not venture so near the land as her sisters did.

As the days passed, she loved the prince more fondly, and he loved her as he would love a little child, but it never came into his head to make her his wife; yet, unless he married her, she could not receive an immortal soul; and, on the morning after his marriage with another, she would dissolve into the foam of the sea.

'Do you not love me the best of them all?' the eyes of the little mermaid seemed to say, when he took her in his arms, and kissed her fair forehead.

'Yes, you are dear to me,' said the prince; 'for you have the best heart, and you are the most devoted to me; you are like a young maiden whom I once saw, but whom I shall never meet again. I was in a ship that was wrecked, and the waves cast me ashore near a holy temple, where several young maidens performed the service. The youngest of them found me on the shore, and saved my life. I saw her but twice, and she is the only one in the world whom I could love; but you are like her, and you have almost driven her image out of my mind. She belongs to the holy temple, and my good fortune has sent you to me instead of her; and we will never part.'

'Ah, he knows not that it was I who saved his life,' thought the little mermaid. 'I carried him over the sea to the wood where the temple stands: I sat beneath the foam, and watched till the human beings came to help him. I saw the pretty maiden that he loves better than he loves me;' and the mermaid sighed deeply, but she could not shed tears. 'He says the maiden belongs to the holy temple, therefore she will never return to the world. They will meet no more: while I am by his side, and see him every day. I will take care of him, and love him, and give up my life for his sake.'

Very soon it was said that the prince must marry, and that the beautiful daughter of a neighbouring king would be his wife, for a fine ship was being fitted out. Although the prince gave out that he merely intended to pay a visit to the king, it was generally supposed that he really went to see his daughter. A great company were to go with him. The little mermaid smiled, and shook her head. She knew the prince's thoughts better than any of the others.

'I must travel,' he had said to her; 'I must see this beautiful princess; my parents desire it; but they will not oblige me to bring her home as my bride. I cannot love her; she is not like the beautiful maiden in the temple, whom you resemble. If I were forced to choose a bride, I would rather choose you, my dumb foundling, with those expressive eyes.' And then he kissed her rosy mouth, played with her long, waving hair, and laid his head on her heart, while she dreamed of human happiness and an immortal soul. 'You are not afraid of the sea, my dumb child,' said he, as they stood on the deck of the noble ship which was to carry them to the country of the neighbouring king. And then he told her of storm and of calm, of strange fishes in the deep beneath them, and of what the divers had seen there; and she smiled at his descriptions, for she knew better than anyone what wonders were at the bottom of the sea.

In the moonlight, when all on board were asleep, excepting the man at the helm, who was steering, she sat on the deck, gazing down through the clear water. She thought she could distinguish her father's castle, and upon it her aged grandmother, with the silver crown on her head, looking through the rushing tide at the keel of the vessel. Then her sisters came up on the waves, and gazed at her mournfully, wringing their white hands. She beckoned to them, and smiled, and wanted to tell them how happy and well off she was; but the cabin-boy approached, and when her sisters dived down he thought it was only the foam of the sea which he saw.

The next morning the ship sailed into the harbour of a beautiful town belonging to the king whom the prince was going to visit. The church bells were ringing, and from the high towers sounded a flourish of trumpets; and soldiers, with flying colours and glittering bayonets, lined the rocks through which they passed. Every day was a festival; balls and entertainments followed one another.

But the princess had not yet appeared. People said that she was being brought up and educated in a religious house, where she was learning every royal virtue. At last she came. Then the little mermaid, who was very anxious to see whether she was really beautiful, was obliged to acknowledge that she had never seen a more perfect vision of beauty. Her skin was delicately fair, and beneath her long dark eyelashes her laughing blue eyes shone with truth and purity.

'It was you,' said the prince, 'who saved my life when I lay dead on the beach,' and he folded his blushing bride in his arms. 'Oh, I am too happy,' said he to the little mermaid; 'my fondest hopes are all fulfilled. You will rejoice at my happiness; for your devotion to me is great and sincere.'

The little mermaid kissed his hand, and felt as if her heart were already broken. His wedding morning would bring death to her, and she would change into the foam of the sea. All the church bells rung, and the heralds rode about the town proclaiming the betrothal. Perfumed oil was burning in costly silver lamps on every altar. The priests waved the censers, while the bride and bridegroom joined their hands and received the blessing of the bishop. The little mermaid, dressed in silk and gold, held up the bride's train; but her ears heard nothing of the festive music, and her eyes saw not the holy ceremony; she thought of the night of death which was coming to her, and of all she had lost in the world. On the same evening the bride and bridegroom went on board ship; cannons were roaring, flags waving, and in the centre of the ship a costly tent of purple and gold had been erected. It contained elegant couches, for the reception of the bridal pair during the night. The ship, with swelling sails and a favourable wind, glided away smoothly and lightly over the calm sea. When it grew dark a number of coloured lamps were lit, and the sailors danced merrily on the deck. The little mermaid could not help thinking of her first rising out of the sea, when she had seen similar festivities and joys; and she joined in the dance, poised herself in the air as a swallow when he pursues his prey, and all present cheered her with wonder. She had never danced so elegantly before. Her tender feet felt as if cut with sharp knives, but she cared not for it; a sharper pang had pierced through her heart. She knew this was the last evening she should ever see the prince, for whom she had forsaken her kindred and her home; she had given up her beautiful voice, and suffered unheard-of pain daily for him, while he knew nothing of it. This was the last evening that she would breathe the same air with him, or gaze on the starry sky and the deep sea; an eternal night, without a thought or a dream, awaited her: she had no soul and now she could never win one. All was joy and gaiety on board ship till long after midnight; she laughed and danced with the rest, while the thoughts of death were in her heart. The prince kissed his beautiful bride, while she played with his raven hair, till they went arm-in-arm to rest in the splendid tent. Then all became still on board the ship; the helmsman, alone awake, stood at the helm.

The little mermaid leaned her white arms on the edge of the vessel, and looked towards the east for the first blush of morning, for that first ray of dawn that would bring her death. She saw her sisters rising out of the flood: they were as pale as herself; but their long, beautiful hair waved no more in the wind, and had been cut off.

'We have given our hair to the witch,' said they, 'to obtain help for you, that you may not die tonight. She has given us a knife: here it is, see it is very sharp. Before the sun rises you must plunge it into the heart of the prince; when the warm blood falls upon your feet they will grow together again, and form into a fish's tail, and you will be once more a mermaid, and return to us to live out your three hundred years before you die and change into the salt sea foam. Haste, then; he or you must die before sunrise. Our old grandmother moans so for you that her white hair is falling off from sorrow, as ours fell under the witch's scissors. Kill the prince and come back; hasten: do you not see the first red streaks in the sky? In a few minutes the sun will rise, and you must die.' And then they sighed deeply and mournfully, and sank down beneath the waves.

The little mermaid drew back the crimson curtain of the tent, and beheld the fair bride with her head resting on the prince's breast. She bent down and kissed his fair brow, then looked at the sky on which the rosy dawn grew brighter and brighter; then she glanced at the sharp knife, and again fixed her eyes on the prince, who whispered the name of his bride in his dreams. She was in his thoughts, and the knife trembled in the hand of the little mermaid: then she flung it far away from her into the waves; the water turned red where it fell, and the drops that spurted up looked like blood. She cast one more lingering, half-fainting glance at the prince, and then threw herself from the ship into the sea, and thought her body was dissolving into foam. The sun rose above the waves, and its warm rays fell on the cold foam of the little mermaid, who did not feel as if she were dying. She saw the bright sun, and all around her floated hundreds of transparent beautiful beings; she could see through them the white sails of the ship, and the red clouds in the sky; their speech was melodious, but too ethereal to be heard by mortal ears, as they were also unseen by mortal eyes. The little mermaid perceived that she had a body like theirs, and that she continued to rise higher and higher out of the foam. 'Where am I?' asked she, and her voice sounded ethereal, as the voice of those who were with her; no earthly music could imitate it.

'Among the daughters of the air,' answered one of them. 'A mermaid has not an immortal soul, nor can she obtain one unless she wins the love of a human being. On the power of another hangs her eternal destiny. But the daughters of the air, although they do not possess an immortal soul, can, by their good deeds, procure one for themselves. We fly to warm countries, and cool the sultry air that destroys mankind with the pestilence. We carry the perfume of the flowers to spread health and restoration. After we have striven for three hundred years to all the good in our power, we receive an immortal soul and take part in the happiness of mankind. You, poor little mermaid, have tried with your whole heart to do as we are doing; you have suffered and endured and raised yourself to the spirit-world by your good deeds; and now, by striving for three hundred years in the same way, you may obtain an immortal soul.'

The little mermaid lifted her glorified eyes towards the sun, and felt them, for the first time, filling with tears. On the ship, in which she had left the prince, there were life and noise; she saw him and his beautiful bride searching for her; sorrowfully they gazed at the pearly foam, as if they knew she had thrown herself into the waves. Unseen she kissed the forehead of the bride, and fanned the prince, and then mounted with the other children of the air to a rosy cloud that floated through the aether.

'After three hundred years, thus shall we float into the kingdom of heaven,' said she. 'And we may even get there sooner,' whispered one of her companions. 'Unseen we can enter the houses of men, where there are children, and for every day on which we find a good child, who is the joy of his parents and deserves their love, our time of probation is shortened. The child does not know, when we fly through the room, that we smile with joy at his good conduct, for we can count one year less of our three hundred years. But when we see a naughty or a wicked child, we shed tears of sorrow, and for every tear a day is added to our time of trial!'

THE FLYING TRUNK

There was once a merchant who was so rich that he could have paved the whole street with gold, and would even then have had enough for a small alley. But he did not do so; he knew the value of money better than to use it in this way. So clever was he that every shilling he put out brought him a crown; and so he continued till he died. His son inherited his wealth, and he lived a merry life with it; he went to a masquerade every night, made kites out of five-pound notes and threw pieces of gold into the sea instead of stones, making ducks and drakes of them. In this manner he soon lost all his money. At last he had nothing left but a pair of slippers, an old dressing-gown and four shillings. And now all his friends deserted him, they could not walk with him in the streets; but one of them, who was very good-natured, sent him an old trunk with this message, 'Pack up!' 'Yes,' he said, 'it is all very well to say "pack up",' but he had nothing left to pack up, therefore he seated himself in the trunk. It was a very wonderful trunk; no sooner did anyone press on the lock than the trunk could fly. He shut the lid and pressed the lock, when away flew the trunk up the chimney with the merchant's son in it, right up into the clouds. Whenever the bottom of the trunk cracked, he was in a great fright, for if the trunk fell to pieces he would have made a tremendous somersault over the trees. However, he got safely in his trunk to the land of Turkey. He hid the trunk in the wood under some dry leaves, and then went into the town: he could do this very well, for the Turks always go about dressed in dressing-gowns and slippers, as he was himself. He happened to meet a nurse with a little child. 'I say, you Turkish nurse,' cried he, 'what castle is that near the town, with the windows placed so high?'

'The king's daughter lives there,' she replied; 'it has been prophesied that she will be very unhappy about a lover, and therefore no one is allowed to visit her, unless the king and queen are present.'

'Thank you,' said the merchant's son. So he went back to the wood, seated himself in his trunk, flew up to the roof of the castle, and crept through the window into the princess's room. She lay on the sofa asleep, and she was so beautiful that the merchant's son could not help kissing her. Then she awoke, and was very much frightened; but he told her he was a Turkish angel, who had come down through the air to see her, which pleased her very much. He sat down by her side and talked to her: he said her eyes were like beautiful dark lakes, in which the thoughts swam about like little mermaids, and he told her that her forehead was a snowy mountain, which contained splendid halls full of pictures. And then he related to her about the stork who brings the beautiful children from the rivers. These were delightful stories; and when he asked the princess if she would marry him, she consented immediately.

'But you must come on Saturday,' she said; 'for then the king and queen will take tea with me. They will be very proud when they find that I am going to marry a Turkish angel; but you must think of some very pretty stories to tell them, for my parents like to hear stories better than anything. My mother prefers one that is deep and moral; but my father likes something funny, to make him laugh.'

'Very well,' he replied; 'I shall bring you no other marriage portion than a story,' and so they parted. But the princess gave him a sword which was studded with gold coins, and these he could use.

Then he flew away to the town and bought a new dressing-gown, and afterwards returned to the wood, where he composed a story, so as to be ready for Saturday, which was no easy matter. It was ready, however, by Saturday, when he went to see the princess. The king and queen, and the whole court, were at tea with the princess; and he was received with great politeness.

'Will you tell us a story?' said the queen – 'one that is instructive and full of deep learning.'

'Yes, but with something in it to laugh at,' said the king.

'Certainly,' he replied, and commenced at once, asking them to listen attentively. 'There was once a bundle of matches that were exceedingly proud of their high descent. Their genealogical tree, that is, a large pine-tree from which they had been cut, was at one time a large, old tree in the wood. The matches now lay between a tinder-box and an old iron saucepan, and were talking about their youthful days. "Ah! Then we grew on the green boughs, and were as green as they; every morning and evening we were fed with diamond drops of dew. Whenever the sun shone, we felt his warm rays, and the little birds would relate stories to us as they sung. We knew that we were rich, for the other trees only wore their green dress in summer, but our family were able to array themselves in green, summer and winter. But the woodcutter came, like a great revolution, and our family fell under the axe. The head of the house obtained a situation as mainmast in a very fine ship, and can sail round the world when he will. The other branches of the family were taken to different places, and our office now is to kindle a light for common people. This is how such high-born people as we came to be in a kitchen.'"

"'Mine has been a very different fate,' said the iron pot, which stood by the matches; "from my first entrance into the world I have been used to cooking and scouring. I am the first in this house, when anything solid or useful is required. My only pleasure is to be made clean and shining after dinner, and to sit in my place and have a little sensible conversation with my neighbours. All of us, excepting the waterbucket, which is sometimes taken into the courtyard, live here together within these four walls. We get our news from the market-basket, but he sometimes tells us very unpleasant things about the people and the government. Yes, and one day an old pot was so alarmed that he fell down and was broken to pieces. He was a liberal, I can tell you."

"'You are talking too much,' said the tinder-box, and the steel struck against the flint till some sparks flew out, crying, "We want a merry evening, don't we?"

"'Yes, of course,' said the matches, "let us talk about those who are the highest born."

"No, I don't like to be always talking of what we are," remarked the saucepan; "let us think of some other amusement; I will begin. We will tell something that has happened to ourselves; that will be very easy, and interesting as well. On the Baltic Sea, near the Danish shore—"

"'What a pretty commencement!" said the plates; "we shall all like that story, I am sure."

"'Yes; well in my youth, I lived in a quiet family, where the furniture was polished, the floors scoured, and clean curtains put up every fortnight,"

"'What an interesting way you have of relating a story," said the carpet-broom; "it is easy to perceive that you have been a great deal in women's society, there is something so pure runs through what you say."

"'That is quite true," said the waterbucket; and he made a spring with joy, and splashed some water on the floor.

'Then the saucepan went on with his story, and the end was as good as the beginning.

'The plates rattled with pleasure, and the carpet-broom brought some green parsley out of the dust-hole and crowned the saucepan, for he knew it would vex the others; and he thought, "If I crown him today he will crown me tomorrow."

"'Now, let us have a dance," said the fire-tongs; and then how they danced and stuck up one leg in the air. The chair-cushion in the corner burst with laughter when she saw it.

"'Shall I be crowned now?" asked the fire-tongs; so the broom found another wreath for the tongs.

"'They were only common people after all," thought the matches. The tea-urn was now asked to sing, but she said she had a cold, and could not sing without boiling heat. They all thought this was affectation, and because she did not wish to sing excepting in the parlour, when on the table with the grand people.

'In the window sat an old quill-pen, with which the maid generally wrote. There was nothing remarkable about the pen, excepting that it had been dipped too deeply in the ink, but it was proud of that.

"'If the tea-urn won't sing," said the pen, "she can leave it alone; there is a nightingale in a cage who can sing; she has not been taught much, certainly, but we need not say anything this evening about that.'

"'I think it highly improper," said the tea-kettle, who was kitchen singer, and half-brother to the tea-urn, "that a rich foreign bird should be listened to here. Is it patriotic? Let the market-basket decide what is right."

"'I certainly am vexed," said the basket; "inwardly vexed, more than anyone can imagine. Are we spending the evening properly? Would it not be more sensible to put the house in order? If each were in his own place I would lead a game; this would be quite another thing."

"'Let us act a play," said they all. At the same moment the door opened, and the maid came in. Then not one stirred; they all remained quite still; yet, at the same time, there was not a single pot amongst them who had not a high opinion of himself, and of what he could do if he chose.

"'Yes, if we had chosen," they each thought, "we might have spent a very pleasant evening."

'The maid took the matches and lighted them; dear me, how they sputtered and blazed up!

"'Now then," they thought, "everyone will see that we are the first. How we shine; what a light we give!" Even while they spoke their light went out.'

'What a capital story,' said the queen, 'I feel as if I were really in the kitchen, and could see the matches; yes, you shall marry our daughter.'

'Certainly,' said the king, 'thou shalt have our daughter.' The king said thou to him because he was going to be one of the family. The wedding-day was fixed, and, on the evening before, the whole city was illuminated. Cakes and sweetmeats were thrown among the people. The street boys stood on tiptoe and shouted 'hurrah', and whistled between their fingers; altogether it was a very splendid affair.

'I will give them another treat,' said the merchant's son. So he went and bought rockets and crackers, and all sorts of fireworks that could be thought of, packed them in his trunk, and flew up with it into the air. What a whizzing and popping they made as they went off! The Turks, when they saw such a sight in the air, jumped so high that their slippers flew about their ears. It was easy to believe after this that the princess was really going to marry a Turkish angel.

As soon as the merchant's son had come down in his flying trunk to the wood after the fireworks, he thought, 'I will go back into the town now, and hear what they think of the entertainment.' It was very natural that he should wish to know. And what strange things people did say, to be sure! Everyone whom he questioned had a different tale to tell, though they all thought it very beautiful.

'I saw the Turkish angel myself,' said one; 'he had eyes like glittering stars, and a head like foaming water.'

'He flew in a mantle of fire,' cried another, 'and lovely little cherubs peeped out from the folds.'

He heard many more fine things about himself, and that the next day he was to be married. After this he went back to the forest to rest himself in his trunk. It had disappeared! A spark from the fireworks which remained had set it on fire; it was burnt to ashes! So the merchant's son could not fly any more, nor go to meet his bride. She stood all day on the roof waiting for him, and most likely she is waiting there still; while he wanders through the world telling fairy tales, but none of them so amusing as the one he related about the matches.

THE RED SHOES

Once upon a time there was little girl, pretty and dainty. But in summer-time she was obliged to go barefooted because she was poor, and in winter she had to wear large wooden shoes, so that her little instep grew quite red.

In the middle of the village lived an old shoemaker's wife; she sat down and made, as well as she could, a pair of little shoes out of some old pieces of red cloth. They were clumsy, but she meant well, for they were intended for the little girl, whose name was Karen.

Karen received the shoes and wore them for the first time on the day of her mother's funeral. They were certainly not suitable for mourning; but she had no others, and so she put her bare feet into them and walked behind the humble coffin.

Just then a large old carriage came by, and in it sat an old lady; she looked at the little girl, and taking pity on her, said to the clergyman, 'Look here, if you will give me the little girl, I will take care of her.'

Karen believed that this was all on account of the red shoes, but the old lady thought them hideous, and so they were burnt. Karen herself was dressed very neatly and cleanly; she was taught to read and to sew, and people said that she was pretty. But the mirror told her, 'You are more than pretty – you are beautiful.'

One day the queen was travelling through that part of the country, and had her little daughter, who was a princess, with her.

All the people, amongst them Karen too, streamed towards the castle, where the little princess, in fine white clothes, stood before the window and allowed herself to be stared at. She wore neither a train nor a golden crown, but beautiful red morocco shoes; they were indeed much finer than those which the shoemaker's wife had sewn for little Karen. There is really nothing in the world that can be compared to red shoes!

Karen was now old enough to be confirmed; she received some new clothes, and she was also to have some new shoes. The rich shoemaker in the town took the measure of her little foot in his own room, in which there stood great glass cases full of pretty shoes and white slippers. It all looked very lovely, but the old lady could not see very well, and therefore did not get much pleasure out of it. Amongst the shoes stood a pair of red ones, like those which the princess had worn. How beautiful they were! The shoemaker said that they had been made for a count's daughter, but that they had not fitted her.

'I suppose they are of shiny leather?' asked the old lady. 'They shine so.'

'Yes, they do shine,' said Karen. They fitted her, and were bought. But the old lady knew nothing of their being red, for she would never have allowed Karen to be confirmed in red shoes, as she was now to be.

Everybody looked at her feet, and the whole of the way from the church door to the choir it seemed to her as if even the ancient figures on the monuments, in their stiff collars and long black robes, had their eyes fixed on her red shoes. It was only of these that she thought when the clergyman laid his hand upon her head and spoke of the holy baptism, of the covenant with God, and told her that she was now to be a grown-up Christian. The organ pealed forth solemnly, and the sweet children's voices mingled with that of their old leader; but Karen thought only of her red shoes. In the afternoon the old lady heard from everybody that Karen had worn red shoes. She said that it was a shocking thing to do, that it was very improper, and that Karen was always to go to church in future in black shoes, even if they were old.

On the following Sunday there was Communion. Karen looked first at the black shoes, then at the red ones – looked at the red ones again, and put them on.

The sun was shining gloriously, so Karen and the old lady went along the footpath through the corn, where it was rather dusty.

At the church door stood an old crippled soldier leaning on a crutch; he had a wonderfully long beard, more red than white, and he bowed down to the ground and asked the old lady whether he might wipe her shoes. Then Karen put out her little foot too. 'Dear me, what pretty dancing-shoes!' said the soldier. 'Sit fast, when you dance,' said he, addressing the shoes, and slapping the soles with his hand.

The old lady gave the soldier some money and then went with Karen into the church.

And all the people inside looked at Karen's red shoes, and all the figures gazed at them; when Karen knelt before the altar and put the golden goblet to her mouth, she thought only of the red shoes. It seemed to her as though they were swimming about in the goblet, and she forgot to sing the psalm, forgot to say the 'Lord's Prayer'.

Now everyone came out of church, and the old lady stepped into her carriage. But just as Karen was lifting up her foot to get in too, the old soldier said: 'Dear me, what pretty dancing shoes!'

And Karen could not help it, she was obliged to dance a few steps; and when she had once begun, her legs continued to dance. It seemed as if the shoes had got power over them. She danced round the church corner, for she could not stop; the coachman had to run after her and seize her. He lifted her into the carriage, but her feet continued to dance, so that she kicked the good old lady violently. At last they took off her shoes, and her legs were at rest.

At home the shoes were put into the cupboard, but Karen could not help looking at them.

Now the old lady fell ill, and it was said that she would not rise from her bed again. She had to be nursed and waited upon, and this was no one's duty more than Karen's. But there was a grand ball in the town, and Karen was invited. She looked at the red shoes, saying to herself that there was no sin in doing that; she put the red shoes on, thinking there was no harm in that either; and then she went to the ball; and commenced to dance.

But when she wanted to go to the right, the shoes danced to the left, and when she wanted to dance up the room, the shoes danced down the room, down the stairs, through the street and out through the gates of the town. She danced, and was obliged to dance, far out into the dark wood. Suddenly something shone up among the trees, and she believed it was the moon, for it was a face. But it was the old soldier with the red beard; he sat there nodding his head and said: 'Dear me, what pretty dancing shoes!'

She was frightened, and wanted to throw the red shoes away; but they stuck fast. She tore off her stockings, but the shoes had grown fast to her feet. She danced and was obliged to go on dancing over field and meadow, in rain and sunshine, by night and by day – but by night it was most horrible.

She danced out into the open churchyard; but the dead there did not dance. They had something better to do than that. She wanted to sit down on the pauper's grave where the bitter fern grows; but for her there was neither peace nor rest. And as she danced past the open church door she saw an angel there in long white robes, with wings reaching from his shoulders down to the earth; his face was stern and grave, and in his hand he held a broad shining sword.

'Dance you shall,' said he, 'dance in your red shoes till you are pale and cold, till your skin shrivels up and you are a skeleton! Dance you shall, from door to door, and where proud and wicked children live you shall knock, so that they may hear you and fear you! Dance you shall, dance – !'

'Mercy!' cried Karen. But she did not hear what the angel answered, for the shoes carried her through the gate into the fields, along highways and byways, and unceasingly she had to dance.

One morning she danced past a door that she knew well; they were singing a psalm inside, and a coffin was being carried out covered with flowers. Then she knew that she was forsaken by every one and damned by the angel of God.

She danced, and was obliged to go on dancing through the dark night. The shoes bore her away over thorns and stumps till she was all torn and bleeding; she danced away over the heath to a lonely little house. Here, she knew, lived the executioner; and she tapped with her finger at the window and said:

'Come out, come out! I cannot come in, for I must dance.'

And the executioner said: 'I don't suppose you know who I am. I strike off the heads of the wicked, and I notice that my axe is tingling to do so.'

'Don't cut off my head!' said Karen. 'For then I could not repent of my sin. But cut off my feet with the red shoes.'

And then she confessed all her sin, and the executioner struck off her feet with the red shoes; but the shoes danced away with the little feet across the field into the deep forest.

And he carved her a pair of wooden feet and some crutches, and taught her a psalm which is always sung by sinners; she kissed the hand that guided the axe, and went away over the heath.

'Now, I have suffered enough for the red shoes,' she said; 'I will go to church, so that people can see me.' And she went quickly up to the church-door; but when she came there, the red shoes were dancing before her, and she was frightened, and turned back.

During the whole week she was sad and wept many bitter tears, but when Sunday came again she said: 'Now I have suffered and striven enough. I believe I am quite as good as many of those who sit in church and give themselves airs.' And so she went boldly on; but she had not got farther than the churchyard gate when she saw the red shoes dancing along before her. Then she became terrified, and turned back and repented right heartily of her sin.

She went to the parsonage, and begged that she might be taken into service there. She would be industrious, she said, and do everything that she could; she did not mind about the wages as long as she had a roof over her, and was with good people. The pastor's wife had pity on her, and took her into service. And she was industrious and thoughtful. She sat quiet and listened when the pastor read aloud from the Bible in the evening. All the children liked her very much, but when they spoke about dress and grandeur and beauty she would shake her head.

On the following Sunday they all went to church, and she was asked whether she wished to go too; but, with tears in her eyes, she looked sadly at her crutches. And then the others went to hear God's word, but she went alone into her little room; this was only large enough to hold the bed and a chair. Here she sat down with her hymn-book, and as she was reading it with a pious mind, the wind carried the notes of the organ over to her from the church, and in tears she lifted up her face and said: 'O God! Help me!'

Then the sun shone so brightly, and right before her stood an angel of God in white robes; it was the same one whom she had seen that night at the church-door. He no longer carried the sharp sword, but a beautiful green branch, full of roses; with this he touched the ceiling, which rose up very high, and where he had touched it there shone a golden star. He touched the walls, which opened wide apart, and she saw the organ which was pealing forth; she saw the pictures of the old pastors and their wives, and the congregation sitting in the polished chairs and singing from their hymn-books. The church itself had come to the poor girl in her narrow room, or the room had gone to the church. She sat in the pew with the rest of the pastor's household, and when they had finished the hymn and looked up, they nodded and said, 'It was right of you to come, Karen.'

'It was mercy,' said she.

The organ played and the children's voices in the choir sounded soft and lovely. The bright warm sunshine streamed through the window into the pew where Karen sat, and her heart became so filled with it, so filled with peace and joy, that it broke. Her soul flew on the sunbeams to Heaven, and no one was there who asked after the red shoes.

LITTLE TINY OR THUMBELINA

There was once a woman who wished very much to have a little child, but she could not obtain her wish. At last she went to a fairy, and said, 'I should so very much like to have a little child; can you tell me where I can find one?'

'Oh, that can be easily managed,' said the fairy. 'Here is a barleycorn of a different kind to those which grow in the farmer's fields, and which the chickens eat; put it into a flower-pot, and see what will happen.'

'Thank you,' said the woman, and she gave the fairy twelve shillings, which was the price of the barleycorn. Then she went home and planted it, and immediately there grew up a large handsome flower, something like a tulip in appearance, but with its leaves tightly closed as if it were still a bud. 'It is a beautiful flower,' said the woman, and she kissed the red and golden-coloured leaves, and while she did so the flower opened, and she could see that it was a real tulip. Within the flower, upon the green velvet stamens, sat a very delicate and graceful little maiden. She was scarcely half as long as a thumb, and they gave her the name of 'Thumbelina', or Tiny, because she was so small. A walnut-shell, elegantly polished, served her for a cradle; her bed was formed of blue violet-leaves, with a rose-leaf for a counterpane. Here she slept at night, but during the day she amused herself on a table, where the woman had placed a plateful of water. Round this plate were wreaths of flowers with their stems in the water, and upon it floated a large tulip-leaf, which served Tiny for a boat. Here the little maiden sat and rowed herself from side to side, with two oars made of white horsehair. It really was a very pretty sight. Tiny could, also, sing so softly and sweetly that nothing like her singing had ever before been heard. One night, while she lay in her pretty bed, a large, ugly, wet toad crept through a broken pane of glass in the window, and leaped right upon the table where Tiny lay sleeping under her rose-leaf quilt. 'What a pretty little wife this would make for my son,' said the toad, and she took up the walnut-shell in which little Tiny lay asleep, and jumped through the window with it into the garden.

In the swampy margin of a broad stream in the garden lived the toad, with her son. He was uglier even than his mother, and when he saw the pretty little maiden in her elegant bed, he could only cry, 'Croak, croak, croak'.

'Don't speak so loud, or she will wake,' said the toad, 'and then she might run away, for she is as light as swan's down. We will place her on one of the water-lily leaves out in the stream; it will be like an island to her, she is so light and small, and then she cannot escape; and, while she is away, we will make haste and prepare the state-room under the marsh, in which you are to live when you are married.'

Far out in the stream grew a number of water-lilies, with broad green leaves, which seemed to float on the top of the water. The largest of these leaves appeared farther off than the rest, and the old toad swam out to it with the walnut-shell, in which little Tiny lay still asleep. The tiny little creature woke very early in the morning, and began to cry bitterly when she found where she was, for she could see nothing but water on every side of the large green leaf, and no way of reaching the land. Meanwhile the old toad was very busy under the marsh, decking her room with rushes and wild yellow flowers, to make it look pretty for her new daughter-in-law. Then she swam out with her ugly son to the leaf on which she had placed poor little Tiny. She wanted to fetch the pretty bed, that she might put it in the bridal chamber to be ready for her. The old toad bowed low to her in the water, and said, 'Here is my son, he will be your husband, and you will live happily in the marsh by the stream.'

'Croak, croak, croak,' was all her son could say for himself; so the toad took up the elegant little bed, and swam away with it, leaving Tiny all alone on the green leaf, where she sat and wept. She could not bear to think of living with the old toad, and having her ugly son for a husband. The little fishes, who swam about in the water beneath, had seen the toad, and heard what she said, so they lifted their heads above the water to look at the little maiden. As soon as they caught sight of her, they saw she was very pretty, and it made them very sorry to think that she must go and live with the ugly toads. 'No, it must never be!' So they assembled together in the water, round the green stalk which held the leaf on which the little maiden stood, and gnawed it away at the root with their teeth. Then the leaf floated down the stream, carrying Tiny far away out of reach of land.

Tiny sailed past many towns, and the little birds in the bushes saw her, and sang, 'What a lovely little creature'; so the leaf swam away with her farther and farther, till it brought her to other lands. A graceful little white butterfly constantly fluttered round her, and at last alighted on the leaf. Tiny pleased him, and she was glad of it, for now the toad could not possibly reach her, and the country through which she sailed was beautiful, and the sun shone upon the water, till it glittered like liquid gold. She took off her girdle and tied one end of it round the butterfly, and the other end of the ribbon she fastened to the leaf, which now glided on much faster than ever, taking little Tiny with it as she stood. Presently a large cockchafer flew by; the moment he caught sight of her, he seized her round her delicate waist with his claws, and flew with her into a tree. The green leaf floated away on the brook, and the butterfly flew with it, for he was fastened to it, and could not get away.

Oh, how frightened little Tiny felt when the cockchafer flew with her to the tree! But especially was she sorry for the beautiful white butterfly which she had fastened to the leaf, for if he could not free himself he would die of hunger. But the cockchafer did not trouble himself at all about the matter. He seated himself by her side on a large green leaf, gave her some honey from the flowers to eat, and told her she was very pretty, though not in the least like a cockchafer. After a time, all the cockchafers turned up their feelers, and said, 'She has only two legs! How ugly that looks!' 'She has no feelers,' said another. 'Her waist is quite slim. Pooh! She is like a human being.'

'Oh! She is ugly,' said all the lady cockchafers, although Tiny was very pretty. Then the cockchafer who had run away with her believed all the others when they said she was ugly, and would have nothing more to say to her, and told her she might go where she liked. Then he flew down with her from the tree, and placed her on a daisy, and she wept at the thought that she was so ugly that even the cockchafers would have nothing to say to her. And all the while she was really the loveliest creature that one could imagine, and as tender and delicate as a beautiful rose-leaf. During the whole summer poor little Tiny lived quite alone in the wide forest. She wove herself a bed with blades of grass, and hung it up under a broad leaf, to protect herself from the rain. She sucked the honey from the flowers for food, and drank the dew from their leaves every morning. So passed away the summer and the autumn, and then came the winter – the long, cold winter. All the birds who had sung to her so sweetly were flown away, and the trees and the flowers had withered. The large clover leaf under the shelter of which she had lived was now rolled together and shrivelled up, nothing remained but a yellow, withered stalk. She felt dreadfully cold, for her clothes were torn, and she was herself so frail and delicate that poor little Tiny was nearly frozen to death. It began to snow too; and the snow-flakes, as they fell upon her, were like a whole shovelful falling upon one of us, for we are tall, but she was only an inch high. Then she wrapped herself up in a dry leaf, but it cracked in the middle and could not keep her warm, and she shivered with cold. Near the wood in which she had been living lay a corn-field, but the corn had been cut a long time; nothing remained but the bare dry stubble standing up out of the frozen ground. It was to her like struggling through a large wood. Oh, how she shivered with the cold. She came at last to the door of a field-mouse, who had a little den under the corn-stubble. There dwelt the field-mouse in warmth and comfort, with a whole roomful of corn, a kitchen and a beautiful dining room. Poor little Tiny stood before the door just like a little beggar-girl, and begged for a small piece of barley-corn, for she had been without a morsel to eat for two days.

'You poor little creature,' said the field-mouse, who was really a good old field-mouse, 'come into my warm room and dine with me.' She was very pleased with Tiny, so she said, 'You are quite welcome to stay with me all the winter, if you like; but you must keep my rooms clean and neat, and tell me stories, for I shall like to hear them very much.' And Tiny did all the field-mouse asked her, and found herself very comfortable.

'We shall have a visitor soon,' said the field-mouse one day; 'my neighbour pays me a visit once a week. He is better off than I am; he has large rooms, and wears a beautiful black velvet coat. If you could only have him for a husband, you would be well provided for indeed. But he is blind, so you must tell him some of your prettiest stories.'

But Tiny did not feel at all interested about this neighbour, for he was a mole. However, he came and paid his visit dressed in his black velvet coat.

'He is very rich and learned, and his house is twenty times larger than mine,' said the field-mouse.

He was rich and learned, no doubt, but he always spoke slightingly of the sun and the pretty flowers, because he had never seen them. Tiny was obliged to sing to him, 'Ladybird, ladybird, fly away home' and many other pretty songs. And the mole fell in love with her because she had such a sweet voice; but he said nothing yet, for he was very cautious. A short time before, the mole had dug a long passage under the earth, which led from the dwelling of the field-mouse to his own, and here she had permission to walk with Tiny whenever she liked. But he warned them not to be alarmed at the sight of a dead bird which lay in the passage. It was a perfect bird, with a beak and feathers, and could not have been dead long, and was lying just where the mole had made his passage. The mole took a piece of phosphorescent wood in his mouth, and it glittered like fire in the dark; then he went before them to light them through the long, dark passage. When they came to the spot where lay the dead bird, the mole pushed his broad nose through the ceiling, the earth gave way, so that there was a large hole, and the daylight shone into the passage. In the middle of the floor lay a dead swallow, his beautiful wings pulled close to his sides, his feet and his head drawn up under his feathers; the poor bird had evidently died of the cold. It made little Tiny very sad to see it, she did so love the little birds; all the summer they had sung and twittered for her so beautifully. But the mole pushed it aside with his crooked legs, and said, 'He will sing no more now. How miserable it must be to be born a little bird! I am thankful that none of my children will ever be birds, for they can do nothing but cry "tweet, tweet" and always die of hunger in the winter.'

'Yes, you may well say that, as a clever man!' exclaimed the field-mouse. 'What is the use of his twittering, for when winter comes he must either starve or be frozen to death. Still birds are very high-bred.'

Tiny said nothing; but when the two others had turned their backs on the bird, she stooped down and stroked aside the soft feathers which covered the head, and kissed the closed eyelids. 'Perhaps this was the one who sang to me so sweetly in the summer,' she said; 'and how much pleasure it gave me, you dear, pretty bird.'

The mole now stopped up the hole through which the daylight shone, and then accompanied the lady home. But during the night Tiny could not sleep; so she got out of bed and wove a large, beautiful carpet of hay; then she carried it to the dead bird, and spread it over him; with some down from the flowers which she had found in the field-mouse's room. It was as soft as wool, and she spread some of it on each side of the bird, so that he might lie warmly in the cold earth. 'Farewell, you pretty little bird,' said she, 'farewell; thank you for your delightful singing during the summer, when all the trees were green, and the warm sun shone upon us.' Then she laid her head on the bird's breast, but she was alarmed immediately, for it seemed as if something inside the bird went 'thump, thump'. It was the bird's heart; he was not really dead, only benumbed with the cold, and the warmth had restored him to life. In autumn, all the swallows fly away into warm countries, but if one happens to linger, the cold seizes it, it becomes frozen, and falls down as if dead; it remains where it fell, and the cold snow covers it. Tiny trembled very much; she was quite frightened, for the bird was large, a great deal larger than herself – she was only an inch high. But she took courage, laid the wool more thickly over the poor swallow, and then took a leaf which she had used for her own counterpane, and laid it over the head of the poor bird. The next morning she again stole out to see him. He was alive but very weak; he could only open his eyes for a moment to look at Tiny, who stood by holding a piece of decayed wood in her hand, for she had no other lantern. 'Thank you, pretty little maiden,' said the sick swallow; 'I have been so nicely warmed that I shall soon regain my strength, and be able to fly about again in the warm sunshine.'

'Oh,' said she, 'it is cold out of doors now; it snows and freezes. Stay in your warm bed; I will take care of you.'

Then she brought the swallow some water in a flower-leaf, and after he had drank, he told her that he had wounded one of his wings in a thorn-bush, and could not fly as fast as the others, who were soon far away on their journey to warm countries. Then at last he had fallen to the earth, and could remember no more, nor how he came to be where she had found him. The whole winter the swallow remained underground, and Tiny nursed him with care and love. Neither the mole nor the field-mouse knew anything about it, for they did not like swallows. Very soon the springtime came, and the sun warmed the earth. Then the swallow bade farewell to Tiny, and she opened the hole in the ceiling which the mole had made. The sun shone in upon them so beautifully that the swallow asked her if she would go with him; she could sit on his back, he said, and he would fly away with her into the green woods. But Tiny knew it would make the field-mouse very grieved if she left her in that manner, so she said, 'No, I cannot.'

'Farewell, then, farewell, you good, pretty little maiden,' said the swallow; and he flew out into the sunshine.

Tiny looked after him, and the tears rose in her eyes. She was very fond of the poor swallow.

'Tweet, tweet,' sang the bird, as he flew out into the green woods, and Tiny felt very sad. She was not allowed to go out into the warm sunshine. The corn which had been sown in the field over the house of the field-mouse had grown up high into the air, and formed a thick wood to Tiny, who was only an inch in height.

'You are going to be married, Tiny,' said the field-mouse. 'My neighbour has asked for you. What good fortune for a poor child like you. Now we will prepare your wedding clothes. They must be both woollen and linen. Nothing must be wanting when you are the mole's wife.'

Tiny had to turn the spindle, and the field-mouse hired four spiders, who were to weave day and night. Every evening the mole visited her, and was continually speaking of the time when the summer would be over. Then he would keep his wedding-day with Tiny; but now the heat of the sun was so great that it burned the earth, and made it quite hard, like a stone. As soon as the summer was over, the wedding should take place. But Tiny was not at all pleased; for she did not like the tiresome mole. Every morning when the sun rose, and every evening when it went down, she would creep out at the door, and as the wind blew aside the ears of corn, so that she could see the blue sky, she thought how beautiful and bright it seemed out there, and wished so much to see her dear swallow again. But he never returned; for by this time he had flown far away into the lovely green forest.

When autumn arrived, Tiny had her outfit quite ready; and the field-mouse said to her, 'In four weeks the wedding must take place.'

Then Tiny wept, and said she would not marry the disagreeable mole.

'Nonsense,' replied the field-mouse. 'Now don't be obstinate, or I shall bite you with my white teeth. He is a very handsome mole; the queen herself does not wear more beautiful velvets and furs. His kitchen and cellars are quite full. You ought to be very thankful for such good fortune.'

So the wedding-day was fixed, on which the mole was to fetch Tiny away to live with him, deep under the earth, and never again to see the warm sun, because he did not like it. The poor child was very unhappy at the thought of saying farewell to the beautiful sun, and as the field-mouse had given her permission to stand at the door, she went to look at it once more.

'Farewell bright sun,' she cried, stretching out her arm towards it; and then she walked a short distance from the house; for the corn had been cut, and only the dry stubble remained in the fields. 'Farewell, farewell,' she repeated, twining her arm round a little red flower that grew just by her side. 'Greet the little swallow from me, if you should see him again.'

'Tweet, tweet,' sounded over her head suddenly. She looked up, and there was the swallow himself flying close by. As soon as he spied Tiny, he was delighted; and then she told him how unwilling she felt to marry the ugly mole, and to live always beneath the earth, and never to see the bright sun any more. And as she told him she wept.

'Cold winter is coming,' said the swallow, 'and I am going to fly away into warmer countries. Will you go with me? You can sit on my back, and fasten yourself on with your sash. Then we can fly away from the ugly mole and his gloomy rooms, – far away, over the mountains, into warmer countries, where the sun shines more brightly than here; where it is always summer, and the flowers bloom in greater beauty. Fly now with me, dear little Tiny; you saved my life when I lay frozen in that dark passage.'

'Yes, I will go with you,' said Tiny; and she seated herself on the bird's back, with her feet on his outstretched wings, and tied her girdle to one of his strongest feathers.

Then the swallow rose in the air, and flew over forest and over sea, high above the highest mountains, covered with eternal snow. Tiny would have been frozen in the cold air, but she crept under the bird's warm feathers, keeping her little head uncovered, so that she might admire the beautiful lands over which they passed. At length they reached the warm countries, where the sun shines brightly and the sky seems so much higher above the earth. Here, on the hedges and by the wayside, grew purple, green and white grapes; lemons and oranges hung from trees in the woods; and the air was fragrant with myrtles and orange blossoms. Beautiful children ran along the country lanes, playing with large gay butterflies; and as the swallow flew farther and farther, every place appeared still more lovely.

At last they came to a blue lake, and by the side of it, shaded by trees of the deepest green, stood a palace of dazzling white marble, built in the olden times. Vines clustered round its lofty pillars, and at the top were many swallows' nests, and one of these was the home of the swallow who carried Tiny.

'This is my house,' said the swallow; 'but it would not do for you to live there – you would not be comfortable. You must choose for yourself one of those lovely flowers, and I will put you down upon it, and then you shall have everything that you can wish to make you happy.'

'That will be delightful,' she said, and clapped her little hands for joy.

A large marble pillar lay on the ground, which, in falling, had been broken into three pieces. Between these pieces grew the most beautiful large white flowers; so the swallow flew down with Tiny, and placed her on one of the broad leaves. But how surprised she was to see in the middle of the flower a tiny little man, as white and transparent as if he had been made of crystal! He had a gold crown on his head and delicate wings at his shoulders, and was not much larger than Tiny herself. He was the angel of the flower; for a tiny man and a tiny woman dwell in every flower; and this was the king of them all.

'Oh, how beautiful he is!' whispered Tiny to the swallow.

The little prince was at first quite frightened at the bird, who was like a giant compared with such a delicate little creature as himself; but when he saw Tiny, he was delighted, and thought her the prettiest little maiden he had ever seen. He took the gold crown from his head and placed it on hers, and asked her name, and if she would be his wife, and queen over all the flowers.

This certainly was a very different sort of husband to the son of a toad, or the mole with black velvet and fur; so she said, 'Yes,' to the handsome prince. Then all the flowers opened, and out of each came a little lady or a tiny lord, all so pretty it was quite a pleasure to look at them. Each of them brought Tiny a present; but the best gift was a pair of beautiful wings, which had belonged to a large white fly, and they fastened them to Tiny's shoulders, so that she might fly from flower to flower. Then there was much rejoicing, and the little swallow who sat above them, in his nest, was asked to sing a wedding song, which he did as well as he could; but in his heart he felt sad for he was very fond of Tiny, and would have liked never to part from her again.

'You must not be called Tiny any more,' said the spirit of the flowers to her. 'It is an ugly name, and you are so very pretty. We will call you Maia.'

'Farewell, farewell,' said the swallow, with a heavy heart as he left the warm countries to fly back to Denmark. There he had a nest over the window of a house in which dwelt the writer of fairy tales. The swallow sang, 'Tweet, tweet,' and from his song came the whole story.

THE GIRL WHO TROD ON A LOAF

There was once a girl who trod on a loaf to avoid soiling her shoes, and the misfortunes that happened to her in consequence are well known. Her name was Inge; she was a poor child, but proud and presuming, and with a bad and cruel disposition. When quite a little child she would delight in catching flies and tearing off their wings, so as to make creeping things of them. When older, she would take cockchafers and beetles, and stick pins through them. Then she pushed a green leaf, or a little scrap of paper towards their feet, and when the poor creatures would seize it and hold it fast, and turn over and over in their struggles to get free from the pin, she would say, 'The cockchafer is reading; see how he turns over the leaf.' She grew worse instead of better with years and, unfortunately, she was pretty, which caused her to be excused, when she should have been sharply reproved.

'Your headstrong will requires severity to conquer it,' her mother often said to her. 'As a little child you used to trample on my apron, but one day I fear you will trample on my heart.' And, alas, this fear was realized.

Inge was taken to the house of some rich people, who lived at a distance, and who treated her as their own child, and dressed her so fine that her pride and arrogance increased.

When she had been there about a year, her patroness said to her, 'You ought to go, for once, and see your parents, Inge.'

So Inge started to go and visit her parents; but she only wanted to show herself in her native place, that the people might see how fine she was. She reached the entrance of the village, and saw the young labouring men and maidens standing together chatting, and her own mother amongst them. Inge's mother was sitting on a stone to rest, with a fagot of sticks lying before her, which she had picked up in the wood. Then Inge turned back; she who was so finely dressed she felt ashamed of her mother, a poorly clad woman, who picked up wood in the forest. She did not turn back out of pity for her mother's poverty, but from pride.

Another half-year went by, and her mistress said, 'You ought to go home again, and visit your parents, Inge, and I will give you a large wheaten loaf to take to them, they will be glad to see you, I am sure.'

So Inge put on her best clothes and her new shoes, drew her dress up around her, and set out, stepping very carefully, that she might be clean and neat about the feet, and there was nothing wrong in doing so. But when she came to the place where the footpath led across the moor, she found small pools of water and a great deal of mud, so she threw the loaf into the mud, and trod upon it, that she might pass without wetting her feet. But as she stood with one foot on the loaf and the other lifted up to step forward, the loaf began to sink under her, lower and lower, till she disappeared altogether, and only a few bubbles on the surface of the muddy pool remained to show where she had sunk. And this is the story.

But where did Inge go? She sank into the ground, and went down to the Marsh Woman, who is always brewing there.

The Marsh Woman is related to the elf maidens, who are well known, for songs are sung and pictures painted about them. But of the Marsh Woman nothing is known, excepting that when a mist arises from the meadows, in summertime, it is because she is brewing beneath them. To the Marsh Woman's brewery Inge sunk down, to a place which no one can endure for long. A heap of mud is a palace compared with the Marsh Woman's brewery; and as Inge fell she shuddered in every limb, and soon became cold and stiff as marble. Her foot was still fastened to the loaf, which bowed her down as a golden ear of corn bends the stem.

An evil spirit soon took possession of Inge, and carried her to a still worse place, in which she saw crowds of unhappy people, waiting in a state of agony for the gates of mercy to be opened to them, and in every heart was a miserable and eternal feeling of unrest. It would take too much time to describe the various tortures these people suffered, but Inge's punishment consisted in standing there as a statue, with her foot fastened to the loaf. She could move her eyes about, and see all the misery around her, but she could not turn her head; and when she saw the people looking at her she thought they were admiring her pretty face and fine clothes, for she was still vain and proud. But she had forgotten how soiled her clothes had become while in the Marsh Woman's brewery, and that they were covered with mud; a snake had also fastened itself in her hair, and hung down her back, while from each fold in her dress a great toad peeped out and croaked like an asthmatic poodle. Worse than all was the terrible hunger that tormented her, and she could not stoop to break off a piece of the loaf on which she stood. No; her back was too stiff, and her whole body like a pillar of stone. And then came creeping over her face and eyes flies without wings; she winked and blinked, but they could not fly away, for their wings had been pulled off; this, added to the hunger she felt, was horrible torture.

THE GIRL WHO TROD ON A LOAF

'If this lasts much longer,' she said, 'I shall not be able to bear it.' But it did last, and she had to bear it, without being able to help herself.

A tear, followed by many scalding tears, fell upon her head, and rolled over her face and neck, down to the loaf on which she stood. Who could be weeping for Inge? She had a mother in the world still, and the tears of sorrow which a mother sheds for her child will always find their way to the child's heart, but they often increase the torment instead of being a relief. And Inge could hear all that was said about her in the world she had left, and everyone seemed cruel to her. The sin she had committed in treading on the loaf was known on earth, for she had been seen by the cowherd from the hill, when she was crossing the marsh and had disappeared.

When her mother wept and exclaimed, 'Ah, Inge! What grief thou hast caused thy mother,' she would say, 'Oh that I had never been born! My mother's tears are useless now.'

And then the words of the kind people who had adopted her came to her ears, when they said, 'Inge was a sinful girl, who did not value the gifts of God, but trampled them under her feet.'

'Ah,' thought Inge, 'they should have punished me, and driven all my naughty tempers out of me.'

A song was made about 'The girl who trod on a loaf to keep her shoes from being soiled', and this song was sung everywhere. The story of her sin was also told to the little children, and they called her 'wicked Inge', and said she was so naughty that she ought to be punished. Inge heard all this, and her heart became hardened and full of bitterness.

But one day, while hunger and grief were gnawing in her hollow frame, she heard a little, innocent child, while listening to the tale of the vain, haughty Inge, burst into tears and exclaim, 'But will she never come up again?'

And she heard the reply, 'No, she will never come up again.'

'But if she were to say she was sorry, and ask pardon, and promise never to do so again?' asked the little one.

'Yes, then she might come; but she will not beg pardon,' was the answer.

'Oh, I wish she would!' said the child, who was quite unhappy about it. 'I should be so glad. I would give up my doll and all my playthings, if she could only come here again. Poor Inge! It is so dreadful for her.'

These pitying words penetrated to Inge's inmost heart, and seemed to do her good. It was the first time anyone had said 'Poor Inge!' without saying something about her faults. A little innocent child was weeping, and praying for mercy for her. It made her feel quite strange, and she would gladly have wept herself, and it added to her torment to find she could not do so. And while she thus suffered in a place where nothing changed, years passed away on earth, and she heard her name less frequently mentioned. But one day a sigh reached her ear, and the words, 'Inge! Inge! What a grief thou hast been to me! I said it would be so.' It was the last sigh of her dying mother.

After this, Inge heard her kind mistress say, 'Ah, poor Inge! Shall I ever see thee again? Perhaps I may, for we know not what may happen in the future.' But Inge knew right well that her mistress would never come to that dreadful place.

Time passed – a long, bitter time – then Inge heard her name pronounced once more, and saw what seemed two bright stars shining above her. They were two gentle eyes closing on earth. Many years had passed since the little girl had lamented and wept about 'poor Inge'. That child was now an old woman, whom God was taking to Himself. In the last hour of existence the events of a whole life often appear before us; and this hour the old woman remembered how, when a child, she had shed tears over the story of Inge, and she prayed for her now. As the eyes of the old woman closed to earth, the eyes of the soul opened upon the hidden things of eternity, and then she, in whose last thoughts Inge had been so vividly present, saw how deeply the poor girl had sunk. She burst into tears at the sight, and in heaven, as she had done when a little child on earth, she wept and prayed for poor Inge. Her tears and her prayers echoed through the dark void that surrounded the tormented captive soul, and the unexpected mercy was obtained for it through an angel's tears. As in thought Inge seemed to act over again every sin she had committed on earth, she trembled, and tears she had never yet been able to weep rushed to her eyes. It seemed impossible that the gates of mercy could ever be opened to her; but while she acknowledged this in deep penitence, a beam of radiant light shot suddenly into the depths upon her. More powerful than the sunbeam that dissolves the man of snow which the children have raised, more quickly than the snowflake melts and becomes a drop of water on the warm lips of a child, was the stony form of Inge changed, and as a little bird she soared, with the speed of lightning, upward to the world of mortals. A bird that felt timid and shy to all things around it, that seemed to shrink with shame from meeting any living creature, and hurriedly sought to conceal itself in a dark corner of an old ruined wall; there it sat cowering and unable to utter a sound, for it was voiceless. Yet how quickly the little bird discovered the beauty of everything around it. The sweet, fresh air; the soft radiance of the moon, as its light spread over the earth; the fragrance which exhaled from bush and tree, made it feel happy as it sat there clothed in its fresh, bright plumage. All creation seemed to speak of beneficence and love. The bird wanted to give utterance to thoughts that stirred in his breast, as the cuckoo and the nightingale in the spring, but it could not. Yet in heaven can be heard the song of praise, even from a worm; and the notes trembling in the breast of the bird were as audible to heaven even as the psalms of David before they had fashioned themselves into words and song.

Christmas-time drew near, and a peasant who dwelt close by the old wall stuck up a pole with some ears of corn fastened to the top, that the birds of heaven might have feast, and rejoice in the happy, blessed time. And on Christmas morning the sun arose and shone upon the ears of corn, which were quickly surrounded by a number of twittering birds. Then, from a hole in the wall, gushed forth in song the swelling thoughts of the bird as he issued from his hiding place to perform his first good deed on earth – and in heaven it was well known who that bird was.

The winter was very hard; the ponds were covered with ice, and there was very little food for either the beasts of the field or the birds of the air. Our little bird flew away into the public roads, and found here and there, in the ruts of the sledges, a grain of corn, and at the halting places some crumbs. Of these he ate only a few, but he called around him the other birds and the hungry sparrows, that they too might have food. He flew into the towns, and looked about, and wherever a kind hand had strewed bread on the window-sill for the birds, he only ate a single crumb himself, and gave all the rest to the rest of the other birds. In the course of the winter the bird had in this way collected many crumbs and given them to other birds, till they equalled the weight of the loaf on which Inge had trod to keep her shoes clean; and when the last bread-crumb had been found and given, the grey wings of the bird became white, and spread themselves out for flight.

'See, yonder is a seagull!' cried the children, when they saw the white bird, as it dived into the sea, and rose again into the clear sunlight, white and glittering. But no one could tell whither it went then although some declared it flew straight to the sun.

THE NIGHTINGALE

In China, you know, the emperor is a Chinese, and all those about him are Chinamen also. The story I am going to tell you happened a great many years ago, so it is well to hear it now before it is forgotten. The emperor's palace was the most beautiful in the world. It was built entirely of porcelain, and very costly, but so delicate and brittle that whoever touched it was obliged to be careful. In the garden could be seen the most singular flowers, with pretty silver bells tied to them, which tinkled so that every one who passed could not help noticing the flowers. Indeed, everything in the emperor's garden was remarkable, and it extended so far that the gardener himself did not know where it ended. Those who travelled beyond its limits knew that there was a noble forest, with lofty trees, sloping down to the deep blue sea, and the great ships sailed under the shadow of its branches. In one of these trees lived a nightingale, who sang so beautifully that even the poor fishermen, who had so many other things to do, would stop and listen. Sometimes, when they went at night to spread their nets, they would hear her sing, and say, 'Oh, is not that beautiful?' But when they returned to their fishing, they forgot the bird until the next night. Then they would hear it again, and exclaim, 'Oh, how beautiful is the nightingale's song!'

Travellers from every country in the world came to the city of the emperor, which they admired very much, as well as the palace and gardens; but when they heard the nightingale, they all declared it to be the best of all. And the travellers, on their return home, related what they had seen; and learned men wrote books, containing descriptions of the town, the palace and the gardens; but they did not forget the nightingale, which was really the greatest wonder. And those who could write poetry composed beautiful verses about the nightingale who lived in a forest near the deep sea. The books travelled all over the world, and some of them came into the hands of the emperor; and he sat in his golden chair, and, as he read, he nodded his approval every moment, for it pleased him to find such a beautiful description of his city, his palace, and his gardens. But when he came to the words 'the nightingale is the most beautiful of all', he exclaimed, 'What is this? I know nothing of any nightingale. Is there such a bird in my empire? And even in my garden? I have never heard of it. Something, it appears, may be learnt from books.'

Then he called one of his lords-in-waiting, who was so high-bred that when any in an inferior rank to himself spoke to him, or asked him a question, he would answer, 'Pooh,' which means nothing.

'There is a very wonderful bird mentioned here, called a nightingale,' said the emperor; 'they say it is the best thing in my large kingdom. Why have I not been told of it?'

'I have never heard the name,' replied the cavalier; 'she has not been presented at court.'

'It is my pleasure that she shall appear this evening,' said the emperor; 'the whole world knows what I possess better than I do myself.'

'I have never heard of her,' said the cavalier; 'yet I will endeavour to find her.'

But where was the nightingale to be found? The nobleman went upstairs and down, through halls and passages; yet none of those whom he met had heard of the bird. So he returned to the emperor, and said that it must be a fable, invented by those who had written the book. 'Your imperial majesty,' said he, 'cannot believe everything contained in books; sometimes they are only fiction, or what is called the black art.'

'But the book in which I have read this account,' said the emperor, 'was sent to me by the great and mighty emperor of Japan, and therefore it cannot contain a falsehood. I will hear the nightingale, she must be here this evening; she has my highest favour; and if she does not come, the whole court shall be trampled upon after supper is ended.'

'Tsing-pe!' cried the lord-in-waiting, and again he ran up and down stairs, through all the halls and corridors; and half the court ran with him, for they did not like the idea of being trampled upon. There was a great inquiry about this wonderful nightingale, whom all the world knew, but who was unknown to the court.

At last they met with a poor little girl in the kitchen, who said, 'Oh, yes, I know the nightingale quite well; indeed, she can sing. Every evening I have permission to take home to my poor sick mother the scraps from the table; she lives down by the sea-shore, and as I come back I feel tired, and I sit down in the wood to rest, and listen to the nightingale's song. Then the tears come into my eyes, and it is just as if my mother kissed me.'

'Little maiden,' said the lord-in-waiting, 'I will obtain for you constant employment in the kitchen, and you shall have permission to see the emperor dine, if you will lead us to the nightingale; for she is invited for this evening to the palace.' So she went into the wood where the nightingale sang, and half the court followed her. As they went along, a cow began lowing.

'Oh,' said a young courtier, 'now we have found her; what wonderful power for such a small creature; I have certainly heard it before.'

'No, that is only a cow lowing,' said the little girl; 'we are a long way from the place yet.'

Then some frogs began to croak in the marsh.

'Beautiful,' said the young courtier again. 'Now I hear it, tinkling like little church bells.'

'No, those are frogs,' said the little maiden; 'but I think we shall soon hear her now.' And presently the nightingale began to sing.

'Hark, hark! There she is,' said the girl, 'and there she sits,' she added, pointing to a little grey bird who was perched on a bough.

'Is it possible?' said the lord-in-waiting. 'I never imagined it would be a little, plain, simple thing like that. She has certainly changed colour at seeing so many grand people around her.'

'Little nightingale,' cried the girl, raising her voice, 'our most gracious emperor wishes you to sing before him.'

'With the greatest pleasure,' said the nightingale, and began to sing most delightfully.

'It sounds like tiny glass bells,' said the lord-in-waiting, 'and see how her little throat works. It is surprising that we have never heard this before; she will be a great success at court.'

'Shall I sing once more before the emperor?' asked the nightingale, who thought he was present.

'My excellent little nightingale,' said the courtier, 'I have the great pleasure of inviting you to a court festival this evening, where you will gain imperial favour by your charming song.'

'My song sounds best in the green wood,' said the bird; but still she came willingly when she heard the emperor's wish.

The palace was elegantly decorated for the occasion. The walls and floors of porcelain glittered in the light of a thousand lamps. Beautiful flowers, round which little bells were tied, stood in the corridors: what with the running to and fro and the draught, these bells tinkled so loudly that no one could speak to be heard. In the centre of the great hall, a golden perch had been fixed for the nightingale to sit on. The whole court was present, and the little kitchen-maid had received permission to stand by the door. She was not installed as a real court cook. All were in full dress, and every eye was turned to the little grey bird when the emperor nodded to her to begin. The nightingale sang so sweetly that the tears came into the emperor's eyes, and then rolled down his cheeks, as her song became still more touching and went to everyone's heart. The emperor was so delighted that he declared the nightingale should have his gold slipper to wear round her neck, but she declined the honour with thanks: she had been sufficiently rewarded already. 'I have seen tears in an emperor's eyes,' she said, 'that is my richest reward. An emperor's tears have wonderful power, and are quite sufficient honour for me;' and then she sang again more enchantingly than ever.

'That singing is a lovely gift,' said the ladies of the court to each other; and then they took water in their mouths to make them utter the gurgling sounds of the nightingale when they spoke to any one, so that they might fancy themselves nightingales. And the footmen and chambermaids also expressed their satisfaction, which is saying a great deal, for they are very difficult to please. In fact the nightingale's visit was most successful. She was now to remain at court, to have her own cage, with liberty to go out twice a day, and once during the night. Twelve servants were appointed to attend her on these occasions, who each held her by a silken string fastened to her leg. There was certainly not much pleasure in this kind of flying.

The whole city spoke of the wonderful bird, and when two people met, one said 'nightin' and the other said 'gale', and they understood what was meant, for nothing else was talked of. Eleven peddlers' children were named after her, but not one of them could sing a note.

One day the emperor received a large packet on which was written 'The Nightingale'. 'Here is no doubt a new book about our celebrated bird,' said the emperor. But instead of a book, it was a work of art contained in a casket, an artificial nightingale made to look like a living one, and covered all over with diamonds, rubies and sapphires. As soon as the artificial bird was wound up, it could sing like the real one, and could move its tail up and down, which sparkled with silver and gold. Round its neck hung a piece of ribbon, on which was written 'The Emperor of Japan's nightingale is poor compared with that of the Emperor of China's.'

'This is very beautiful,' exclaimed all who saw it, and he who had brought the artificial bird received the title of 'Imperial nightingale-bringer-in-chief'.

'Now they must sing together,' said the court, 'and what a duet it will be.' But they did not get on well, for the real nightingale sang in its own natural way, but the artificial bird sang only waltzes.

'That is not a fault,' said the music-master, 'it is quite perfect to my taste.' So then it had to sing alone, and was as successful as the real bird; besides, it was so much prettier to look at, for it sparkled like bracelets and breast-pins. Three and thirty times did it sing the same tunes without being tired; the people would gladly have heard it again, but the emperor said the living nightingale ought to sing something. But where was she? No one had noticed her when she flew out at the open window, back to her own green woods.

'What strange conduct,' said the emperor, when her flight had been discovered; and all the courtiers blamed her, and said she was a very ungrateful creature.

'But we have the best bird after all,' said one, and then they would have the bird sing again, although it was the thirty-fourth time they had listened to the same piece, and even then they had not learnt it, for it was rather difficult. But the music-master praised the bird in the highest degree, and even asserted that it was better than a real nightingale, not only in its dress and the beautiful diamonds, but also in its musical power. 'For you must perceive, my chief lord and emperor, that with a real nightingale we can never tell what is going to be sung, but with this bird everything is settled. It can be opened and explained, so that people may understand how the waltzes are formed, and why one note follows upon another.'

'This is exactly what we think,' they all replied, and then the music-master received permission to exhibit the bird to the people on the following Sunday, and the emperor commanded that they should be present to hear it sing. When they heard it they were like people intoxicated; however it must have been with drinking tea, which is quite a Chinese custom. They all said 'Oh!' and held up their forefingers and nodded, but a poor fisherman, who had heard the real nightingale, said, 'It sounds prettily enough, and the melodies are all alike; yet there seems something wanting, I cannot exactly tell what.'

And after this the real nightingale was banished from the empire, and the artificial bird placed on a silk cushion close to the emperor's bed. The presents of gold and precious stones which had been received with it were round the bird, and it was now advanced to the title of 'Little Imperial Toilet Singer', and to the rank of No. 1 on the left hand; for the emperor considered the left side, on which the heart lies, as the most noble, and the heart of an emperor is in the same place as that of other people.

The music-master wrote a work, in twenty-five volumes, about the artificial bird, which was very learned and very long, and full of the most difficult Chinese words; yet all the people said they had read it, and understood it, for fear of being thought stupid and having their bodies trampled upon.

So a year passed, and the emperor, the court and all the other Chinese knew every little turn in the artificial bird's song; and for that same reason it pleased them better. They could sing with the bird, which they often did. The street-boys sang, 'Zi-zi-zi, cluck, cluck, cluck,' and the emperor himself could sing it also. It was really most amusing.

One evening, when the artificial bird was singing its best, and the emperor lay in bed listening to it, something inside the bird sounded 'whizz'. Then a spring cracked. 'Whir-r-r-r' went all the wheels, running round, and then the music stopped. The emperor immediately sprang out of bed, and called for his physician; but what could he do? Then they sent for a watchmaker; and, after a great deal of talking and examination, the bird was put into something like order; but he said that it must be used very carefully, as the barrels were worn, and it would be impossible to put in new ones without injuring the music. Now there was great sorrow, as the bird could only be allowed to play once a year; and even that was dangerous for the works inside it. Then the music-master made a little speech, full of hard words, and declared that the bird was as good as ever; and, of course no one contradicted him.

Five years passed, and then a real grief came upon the land. The Chinese really were fond of their emperor, and he now lay so ill that he was not expected to live. Already a new emperor had been chosen and the people who stood in the street asked the lord-in-waiting how the old emperor was; but he only said, 'Pooh!' and shook his head.

Cold and pale lay the emperor in his royal bed; the whole court thought he was dead, and everyone ran away to pay homage to his successor. The chamberlains went out to have a talk on the matter, and the ladies' maids invited company to take coffee. Cloth had been laid down on the halls and passages, so that not a footstep should be heard, and all was silent and still. But the emperor was not yet dead, although he lay white and stiff on his gorgeous bed, with the long velvet curtains and heavy gold tassels. A window stood open, and the moon shone in upon the emperor and the artificial bird. The poor emperor, finding he could scarcely breathe with a strange weight on his chest, opened his eyes, and saw Death sitting there. He had put on the emperor's golden crown, and held in one hand his sword of state, and in the other his beautiful banner. All around the bed and peeping through the long velvet curtains were a number of strange heads, some very ugly, and others lovely and gentle-looking. These were the emperor's good and bad deeds, which stared him in the face now Death sat at his heart.

'Do you remember this?' 'Do you recollect that?' they asked one after another, thus bringing to his remembrance circumstances that made the perspiration stand on his brow.

'I know nothing about it,' said the emperor. 'Music! Music!' he cried. 'The large Chinese drum! That I may not hear what they say.' But they still went on, and Death nodded like a Chinaman to all they said. 'Music! Music!' shouted the emperor. 'You little precious golden bird, sing, pray sing! I have given you gold and costly presents; I have even hung my golden slipper round your neck. Sing! Sing!' But the bird remained silent. There was no one to wind it up, and therefore it could not sing a note.

Death continued to stare at the emperor with his cold, hollow eyes, and the room was fearfully still. Suddenly there came through the open window the sound of sweet music. Outside, on the bough of a tree, sat the living nightingale. She had heard of the emperor's illness, and was therefore come to sing to him of hope and trust. And as she sung, the shadows grew paler and paler; the blood in the emperor's veins flowed more rapidly, and gave life to his weak limbs; and even Death himself listened, and said, 'Go on, little nightingale, go on.'

'Then will you give me the beautiful golden sword and that rich banner? And will you give me the emperor's crown?' said the bird.

So Death gave up each of these treasures for a song; and the nightingale continued her singing. She sung of the quiet churchyard, where the white roses grow, where the elder-tree wafts its perfume on the breeze, and the fresh, sweet grass is moistened by the mourners' tears. Then Death longed to go and see his garden, and floated out through the window in the form of a cold, white mist.

'Thanks, thanks, you heavenly little bird. I know you well. I banished you from my kingdom once, and yet you have charmed away the evil faces from my bed, and banished Death from my heart, with your sweet song. How can I reward you?'

'You have already rewarded me,' said the nightingale. 'I shall never forget that I drew tears from your eyes the first time I sang to you. These are the jewels that rejoice a singer's heart. But now sleep, and grow strong and well again. I will sing to you again.'

And as she sung, the emperor fell into a sweet sleep; and how mild and refreshing that slumber was! When he awoke, strengthened and restored, the sun shone brightly through the window; but not one of his servants had returned – they all believed he was dead; only the nightingale still sat beside him, and sang.

'You must always remain with me,' said the emperor. 'You shall sing only when it pleases you; and I will break the artificial bird into a thousand pieces.'

'No; do not do that,' replied the nightingale; 'the bird did very well as long as it could. Keep it here still. I cannot live in the palace, and build my nest; but let me come when I like. I will sit on a bough outside your window, in the evening, and sing to you, so that you may be happy, and have thoughts full of joy. I will sing to you of those who are happy, and those who suffer; of the good and the evil, who are hidden around you. The little singing bird flies far from you and your court to the home of the fisherman and the peasant's cot. I love your heart better than your crown; and yet something holy lingers round that also. I will come, I will sing to you; but you must promise me one thing.'

'Everything,' said the emperor, who, having dressed himself in his imperial robes, stood with the hand that held the heavy golden sword pressed to his heart.

'I only ask one thing,' she replied; 'let no one know that you have a little bird who tells you everything. It will be best to conceal it.' So saying, the nightingale flew away.

The servants now came in to look after the dead emperor; when, lo, there he stood, and, to their astonishment, said, 'Good morning.'

THE STORKS

On the last house in a little village the storks had built a nest, and the mother stork sat in it with her four young ones, who stretched out their necks and pointed their black beaks, which had not yet turned red like those of the parent birds. A little way off, on the edge of the roof, stood the father stork, quite upright and stiff; not liking to be quite idle, he drew up one leg and stood on the other, so still that it seemed almost as if he were carved in wood. 'It must look very grand,' thought he, 'for my wife to have a sentry guarding her nest. They do not know that I am her husband; they will think I have been commanded to stand here, which is quite aristocratic;' and so he continued standing on one leg.

In the street below were a number of children at play, and when they caught sight of the storks, one of the boldest amongst the boys began to sing a song about them, and very soon he was joined by the rest. These are the words of the song, but each only sang what he could remember of them in his own way.

Stork, stork, fly away,
Stand not on one leg, I pray,
See your wife is in her nest,
With her little ones at rest.
They will hang one,
And fry another;

They will shoot a third,
And roast his brother.

'Just hear what those boys are singing,' said the young storks; 'they say we shall be hanged and roasted.'

'Never mind what they say; you need not listen,' said the mother. 'They can do no harm.'

But the boys went on singing and pointing at the storks, and mocking at them, excepting one of the boys whose name was Peter; he said it was a shame to make fun of animals, and would not join with them at all. The mother stork comforted her young ones, and told them not to mind. 'See,' she said, 'how quiet your father stands, although he is only on one leg.'

'But we are very much frightened,' said the young storks, and they drew back their heads into the nests.

The next day when the children were playing together, and saw the storks, they sang the song again –

They will hang one,
And roast another.

'Shall we be hanged and roasted?' asked the young storks.

'No, certainly not,' said the mother. 'I will teach you to fly, and when you have learnt, we will fly into the meadows, and pay a visit to the frogs, who will bow themselves to us in the water, and cry 'Croak, croak,' and then we shall eat them up; that will be fun.'

'And what next?' asked the young storks.

'Then,' replied the mother, 'all the storks in the country will assemble together, and go through their autumn manoeuvres, so that it is very important for every one to know how to fly properly. If they do not, the general will thrust them through with his beak, and kill them. Therefore you must take pains and learn, so as to be ready when the drilling begins.'

'Then we may be killed after all, as the boys say; and hark! They are singing again.'

'Listen to me, and not to them,' said the mother stork. 'After the great review is over, we shall fly away to warm countries far from hence, where there are mountains and forests. To Egypt, where we shall see three-cornered houses built of stone, with pointed tops that reach nearly to the clouds. They are called pyramids, and are older than a stork could imagine; and in that country, there is a river that overflows its banks, and then goes back, leaving nothing but mire; there we can walk about, and eat frogs in abundance.'

'Oh, oh!' cried the young storks.

'Yes, it is a delightful place; there is nothing to do all day long but eat, and while we are so well off out there, in this country there will not be a single green leaf on the trees, and the weather will be so cold that the clouds will freeze, and fall on the earth in little white rags.' The stork meant snow, but she could not explain it in any other way.

'Will the naughty boys freeze and fall in pieces?' asked the young storks.

'No, they will not freeze and fall into pieces,' said the mother, 'but they will be very cold, and be obliged to sit all day in a dark, gloomy room, while we shall be flying about in foreign lands, where there are blooming flowers and warm sunshine.'

Time passed on, and the young storks grew so large that they could stand upright in the nest and look about them. The father brought them, every day, beautiful frogs, little snakes and all kinds of stork-dainties that he could find. And then, how funny it was to see the tricks he would perform to amuse them. He would lay his head quite round over his tail, and clatter with his beak, as if it had been a rattle; and then he would tell them stories all about the marshes and fens.

'Come,' said the mother one day, 'now you must learn to fly.' And all the four young ones were obliged to come out on the top of the roof. Oh, how they tottered at first, and were obliged to balance themselves with their wings, or they would have fallen to the ground below.

'Look at me,' said the mother, 'you must hold your heads in this way, and place your feet so. Once, twice, once, twice – that is it. Now you will be able to take care of yourselves in the world.'

Then she flew a little distance from them, and the young ones made a spring to follow her; but down they fell plump, for their bodies were still too heavy.

'I don't want to fly,' said one of the young storks, creeping back into the nest. 'I don't care about going to warm countries.'

'Would you like to stay here and freeze when the winter comes?' said the mother. 'Or till the boys come to hang you, or to roast you? – Well then, I'll call them.'

'Oh no, no,' said the young stork, jumping out on the roof with the others; and now they were all attentive, and by the third day could fly a little. Then they began to fancy they could soar, so they tried to do so, resting on their wings, but they soon found themselves falling, and had to flap their wings as quickly as possible. The boys came again in the street singing their song: –

'Stork, stork, fly away.'

'Shall we fly down, and pick their eyes out?' asked the young storks.

'No; leave them alone,' said the mother. 'Listen to me; that is much more important. Now then. One-two-three. Now to the right. One-two-three. Now to the left, round the chimney. There now, that was very good. That last flap of the wings was so easy and graceful that I shall give you permission to fly with me tomorrow to the marshes. There will be a number of very superior storks there with their families, and I expect you to show them that my children are the best brought up of any who may be present. You must strut about proudly – it will look well and make you respected.'

'But may we not punish those naughty boys?' asked the young storks.

'No; let them scream away as much as they like. You can fly from them now up high amid the clouds, and will be in the land of the pyramids when they are freezing, and have not a green leaf on the trees or an apple to eat.'

'We will revenge ourselves,' whispered the young storks to each other, as they again joined the exercising.

Of all the boys in the street who sang the mocking song about the storks, not one was so determined to go on with it as he who first began it. Yet he was a little fellow not more than six years old. To the young storks he appeared at least a hundred, for he was so much bigger than their father and mother. To be sure, storks cannot be expected to know how old children and grown-up people are. So they determined to have their revenge on this boy, because he began the song first and would keep on with it. The young storks were very angry, and grew worse as they grew older; so at last their mother was obliged to promise that they should be revenged, but not until the day of their departure.

'We must see first how you acquit yourselves at the grand review,' said she. 'If you get on badly there, the general will thrust his beak through you, and you will be killed, as the boys said, though not exactly in the same manner. So we must wait and see.'

'You shall see,' said the young birds, and then they took such pains and practised so well every day that at last it was quite a pleasure to see them fly so lightly and prettily. As soon as the autumn arrived, all the storks began to assemble together before taking their departure for warm countries during the winter. Then the review commenced. They flew over forests and villages to show what they could do, for they had a long journey before them. The young storks performed their part so well that they received a mark of honour, with frogs and snakes as a present. These presents were the best part of the affair, for they could eat the frogs and snakes, which they very quickly did.

'Now let us have our revenge,' they cried.

'Yes, certainly,' cried the mother stork. 'I have thought upon the best way to be revenged. I know the pond in which all the little children lie, waiting till the storks come to take them to their parents. The prettiest little babies lie there dreaming more sweetly than they will ever dream in the time to come. All parents are glad to have a little child, and children are so pleased with a little brother or sister. Now we will fly to the pond and fetch a little baby for each of the children who did not sing that naughty song to make game of the storks.'

'But the naughty boy, who began the song first, what shall we do to him?' cried the young storks.

'There lies in the pond a little dead baby who has dreamed itself to death,' said the mother. 'We will take it to the naughty boy, and he will cry because we have brought him a little dead brother. But you have not forgotten the good boy who said it was a shame to laugh at animals: we will take him a little brother and sister too, because he was good. He is called Peter, and you shall all be called Peter in future.'

So they all did what their mother had arranged, and from that day, even till now, all the storks have been called Peter.

THE GARDEN OF PARADISE

There was once a king's son who had a larger and more beautiful collection of books than anyone else in the world, and full of splendid copper-plate engravings. He could read and obtain information respecting every people of every land; but not a word could he find to explain the situation of the garden of paradise, and this was just what he most wished to know. His grandmother had told him when he was quite a little boy, just old enough to go to school, that each flower in the garden of paradise was a sweet cake, that the pistils were full of rich wine, that on one flower history was written, on another geography or tables; so those who wished to learn their lessons had only to eat some of the cakes, and the more they ate, the more history, geography or tables they knew. He believed it all then; but as he grew older, and learnt more and more, he became wise enough to understand that the splendour of the garden of paradise must be very different to all this. 'Oh, why did Eve pluck the fruit from the tree of knowledge? Why did Adam eat the forbidden fruit?' thought the king's son. 'If I had been there it would never have happened, and there would have been no sin in the world.' The garden of paradise occupied all his thoughts till he reached his seventeenth year.

One day he was walking alone in the wood, which was his greatest pleasure, when evening came on. The clouds gathered, and the rain poured down as if the sky had been a waterspout;

and it was as dark as the bottom of a well at midnight; sometimes he slipped over the smooth grass, or fell over stones that projected out of the rocky ground. Everything was dripping with moisture, and the poor prince had not a dry thread about him. He was obliged at last to climb over great blocks of stone, with water spurting from the thick moss. He began to feel quite faint, when he heard a most singular rushing noise, and saw before him a large cave, from which came a blaze of light. In the middle of the cave an immense fire was burning, and a noble stag, with its branching horns, was placed on a spit between the trunks of two pine-trees. It was turning slowly before the fire, and an elderly woman, as large and strong as if she had been a man in disguise, sat by, throwing one piece of wood after another into the flames.

'Come in,' she said to the prince; 'sit down by the fire and dry yourself.'

'There is a great draught here,' said the prince, as he seated himself on the ground.

'It will be worse when my sons come home,' replied the woman; 'you are now in the cavern of the Winds, and my sons are the four Winds of heaven: can you understand that?'

'Where are your sons?' asked the prince.

'It is difficult to answer stupid questions,' said the woman. 'My sons have plenty of business on hand; they are playing at shuttlecock with the clouds up yonder in the king's hall,' and she pointed upwards.

'Oh, indeed,' said the prince; 'but you speak more roughly and harshly and are not so gentle as the women I am used to.'

'Yes, that is because they have nothing else to do; but I am obliged to be harsh, to keep my boys in order, and I can do it, although they are so headstrong. Do you see those four sacks hanging on the wall? Well, they are just as much afraid of those sacks as you used to be of the rat behind the looking-glass. I can bend the boys together, and put them in the sacks without any resistance on their parts, I can tell you. There they stay, and dare not attempt to come out until I allow them to do so. And here comes one of them.'

It was the North Wind who came in, bringing with him a cold, piercing blast; large hailstones rattled on the floor, and snowflakes were scattered around in all directions. He wore a bearskin dress and cloak. His sealskin cap was drawn over his ears, long icicles hung from his beard, and one hailstone after another rolled from the collar of his jacket.

'Don't go too near the fire,' said the prince, 'or your hands and face will be frost-bitten.'

'Frost-bitten!' said the North Wind, with a loud laugh. 'Why, frost is my greatest delight. What sort of a little snip are you, and how did you find your way to the cavern of the Winds?'

'He is my guest,' said the old woman, 'and if you are not satisfied with that explanation you can go into the sack. Do you understand me?'

That settled the matter. So the North Wind began to relate his adventures, whence he came, and where he had been for a whole month. 'I come from the polar seas,' he said; 'I have been on the Bear's Island with the Russian walrus-hunters. I sat and slept at the helm of their ship, as they sailed away from North Cape. Sometimes when I woke, the storm-birds would fly about my legs. They are curious birds; they give one flap with their wings, and then on their outstretched pinions soar far away.'

'Don't make such a long story of it,' said the mother of the winds; 'what sort of a place is Bear's Island?'

'A very beautiful place, with a floor for dancing as smooth and flat as a plate. Half-melted snow, partly covered with moss, sharp stones and skeletons of walruses and polar bears, lie all about, their gigantic limbs in a state of green decay. It would seem as if the sun never shone there. I blew gently, to clear away the mist, and then I saw a little hut, which had been built from the wood of a wreck, and was covered with the skins of the walrus, the fleshy side outwards; it looked green and red, and on the roof sat a growling bear. Then I went to the sea-shore, to look for birds' nests, and saw the unfledged nestlings opening their mouths and screaming for food. I blew into the thousand little throats, and quickly stopped their screaming. Farther on were the walruses with pig's heads and teeth a yard long, rolling about like great worms.'

'You relate your adventures very well, my son,' said the mother, 'it makes my mouth water to hear you.

'After that,' continued the North Wind, 'the hunting commenced. The harpoon was flung into the breast of the walrus, so that a smoking stream of blood spurted forth like a fountain, and besprinkled the ice. Then I thought of my own game; I began to blow, and set my own ships, the great icebergs sailing, so that they might crush the boats. Oh, how the sailors howled and cried out! but I howled louder than they. They were obliged to unload their cargo, and throw their chests and the dead walruses on the ice. Then I sprinkled snow over them, and left them in their crushed boats to drift southward, and to taste salt water. They will never return to Bear's Island.'

'So you have done mischief,' said the mother of the Winds.

'I shall leave others to tell the good I have done,' he replied. 'But here comes my brother from the West; I like him best of all, for he has the smell of the sea about him, and brings in a cold, fresh air as he enters.'

'Is that the little Zephyr?' asked the prince.

'Yes, it is the little Zephyr,' said the old woman; 'but he is not little now. In years gone by he was a beautiful boy; now that is all past.'

He came in, looking like a wild man, and he wore a slouched hat to protect his head from injury. In his hand he carried a club, cut from a mahogany tree in the American forests, not a trifle to carry.

'Whence do you come?' asked the mother.

'I come from the wilds of the forests, where the thorny brambles form thick hedges between the trees; where the water-snake lies in the wet grass, and mankind seem to be unknown.'

'What were you doing there?'

'I looked into the deep river, and saw it rushing down from the rocks. The water drops mounted to the clouds and glittered in the rainbow. I saw the wild buffalo swimming in the river, but the strong tide carried him away amidst a flock of wild ducks, which flew into the air as the waters dashed onwards, leaving the buffalo to be hurled over the waterfall. This pleased me; so I raised a storm, which rooted up old trees, and sent them floating down the river.'

'And what else have you done?' asked the old woman.

'I have rushed wildly across the savannahs; I have stroked the wild horses, and shaken the cocoa-nuts from the trees. Yes, I have many stories to relate; but I need not tell everything I know. You know it all very well, don't you, old lady?' And he kissed his mother so roughly that she nearly fell backwards. Oh, he was, indeed, a wild fellow.

Now in came the South Wind, with a turban and a flowing Bedouin cloak.

'How cold it is here!' said he, throwing more wood on the fire. 'It is easy to feel that the North Wind has arrived here before me.'

'Why it is hot enough here to roast a bear,' said the North Wind.

'You are a bear yourself,' said the other.

'Do you want to be put in the sack, both of you?' said the old woman. 'Sit down, now, on that stone, yonder, and tell me where you have been.'

'In Africa, mother. I went out with the Hottentots, who were lion-hunting in the Kaffir land, where the plains are covered with grass the colour of a green olive; and here I ran races with the ostrich, but I soon outstripped him in swiftness. At last I came to the desert, in which lie the golden sands, looking like the bottom of the sea. Here I met a caravan, and the travellers had just killed their last camel, to obtain water; there was very little for them, and they continued their painful journey beneath the burning sun, and over the hot sands, which stretched before them a vast, boundless desert. Then I rolled myself in the loose sand, and whirled it in burning columns over their heads. The dromedaries stood still in terror, while the merchants drew their caftans over their heads, and threw themselves on the ground before me, as they do before Allah, their god. Then I buried them beneath a pyramid of sand, which covers them all. When I blow that away on my next visit, the sun will bleach their bones, and travellers will see that others have been there before them; otherwise, in such a wild desert, they might not believe it possible.'

'So you have done nothing but evil,' said the mother. 'Into the sack with you;' and, before he was aware, she had seized the

South Wind round the body, and popped him into the bag. He rolled about on the floor, till she sat herself upon him to keep him still.

'These boys of yours are very lively,' said the prince.

'Yes,' she replied, 'but I know how to correct them, when necessary; and here comes the fourth.' In came the East Wind, dressed like a Chinese.

'Oh, you come from that quarter, do you?' said she. 'I thought you had been to the garden of paradise.'

'I am going there tomorrow,' he replied; 'I have not been there for a hundred years. I have just come from China, where I danced round the porcelain tower till all the bells jingled again. In the streets an official flogging was taking place, and bamboo canes were being broken on the shoulders of men of every high position, from the first to the ninth grade. They cried, 'Many thanks, my fatherly benefactor;' but I am sure the words did not come from their hearts, so I rang the bells till they sounded, 'ding, ding-dong'.

'You are a wild boy,' said the old woman; 'it is well for you that you are going tomorrow to the garden of paradise; you always get improved in your education there. Drink deeply from the fountain of wisdom while you are there, and bring home a bottleful for me.'

'That I will,' said the East Wind; 'but why have you put my brother South in a bag? Let him out; for I want him to tell me about the phoenix-bird. The princess always wants to hear of this bird when I pay her my visit every hundred years. If you will open the sack, sweetest mother, I will give you two pocketfuls of tea, green and fresh as when I gathered it from the spot where it grew.'

'Well, for the sake of the tea, and because you are my own boy, I will open the bag.'

She did so, and the South Wind crept out, looking quite cast down, because the prince had seen his disgrace.

'There is a palm-leaf for the princess,' he said. 'The old phoenix, the only one in the world, gave it to me himself. He has scratched on it with his beak the whole of his history during the hundred years he has lived. She can there read how the old phoenix set fire to his own nest, and sat upon it while it was burning, like a Hindoo widow. The dry twigs around the nest crackled and smoked till the flames burst forth and consumed the phoenix to ashes. Amidst the fire lay an egg, red-hot, which presently burst with a loud report, and out flew a young bird. He is the only phoenix in the world, and the king over all the other birds. He has bitten a hole in the leaf which I give you, and that is his greeting to the princess.'

'Now let us have something to eat,' said the mother of the Winds. So they all sat down to feast on the roasted stag; and as the prince sat by the side of the East Wind, they soon became good friends.

'Pray tell me,' said the prince, 'who is that princess of whom you have been talking? And where lies the garden of paradise?'

'Ho! Ho!' said the East Wind. 'Would you like to go there? Well, you can fly off with me tomorrow; but I must tell you one thing – no human being has been there since the time of Adam and Eve. I suppose you have read of them in your Bible.'

'Of course I have,' said the prince.

'Well,' continued the East Wind, 'when they were driven out of the garden of paradise, it sunk into the earth; but it retained its warm sunshine, its balmy air and all its splendour. The fairy queen lives there, in the island of happiness, where death never comes, and all is beautiful. I can manage to take you there tomorrow, if you will sit on my back. But now don't talk any more, for I want to go to sleep;' and then they all slept.

When the prince awoke in the early morning, he was not a little surprised at finding himself high up above the clouds. He was seated on the back of the East Wind, who held him faithfully; and they were so high in the air that woods and fields, rivers and lakes, as they lay beneath them, looked like a painted map.

'Good morning,' said the East Wind. 'You might have slept on a while; for there is very little to see in the flat country over which we are passing unless you like to count the churches; they look like spots of chalk on a green board.' The green board was the name he gave to the green fields and meadows.

'It was very rude of me not to say good-bye to your mother and your brothers,' said the prince.

'They will excuse you, as you were asleep,' said the East Wind; and then they flew on faster than ever.

The leaves and branches of the trees rustled as they passed. When they flew over seas and lakes, the waves rose higher, and the large ships dipped into the water like diving swans. As darkness came on, towards evening, the great towns looked charming; lights were sparkling, now seen now hidden, just as the sparks go out one after another on a piece of burnt paper. The prince clapped his hands with pleasure; but the East Wind advised him not to express his admiration in that manner, or he might fall down, and find himself hanging on a church steeple. The eagle in the dark forests flies swiftly; but faster than he flew the East Wind. The Cossack, on his small horse, rides lightly o'er the plains; but lighter still passed the prince on the winds of the wind.

'There are the Himalayas, the highest mountains in Asia,' said the East Wind. 'We shall soon reach the garden of paradise now.'

Then, they turned southward, and the air became fragrant with the perfume of spices and flowers. Here figs and pomegranates grew wild, and the vines were covered with clusters of blue and purple grapes. Here they both descended to the earth, and stretched themselves on the soft grass, while the flowers bowed to the breath of the wind as if to welcome it. 'Are we now in the garden of paradise?' asked the prince.

'No, indeed,' replied the East Wind; 'but we shall be there very soon. Do you see that wall of rocks, and the cavern beneath it, over which the grape vines hang like a green curtain? Through that cavern we must pass. Wrap your cloak round you; for while the sun scorches you here, a few steps farther it will be icy cold. The bird flying past the entrance to the cavern feels as if one wing were in the region of summer, and the other in the depths of winter.'

'So this then is the way to the garden of paradise?' asked the prince, as they entered the cavern. It was indeed cold; but the cold soon passed, for the East Wind spread his wings, and they gleamed like the brightest fire. As they passed on through this wonderful cave, the prince could see great blocks of stone, from which water trickled, hanging over their heads in fantastic shapes. Sometimes it was so narrow that they had to creep on their hands and knees, while at other times it was lofty and wide, like the free air. It had the appearance of a chapel for the dead, with petrified organs and silent pipes. 'We seem to be passing through the valley of death to the garden of paradise,' said the prince.

But the East Wind answered not a word, only pointed forwards to a lovely blue light which gleamed in the distance. The blocks of stone assumed a misty appearance, till at last they looked like white clouds in moonlight. The air was fresh and balmy, like a breeze from the mountains perfumed with flowers from a valley of roses. A river, clear as the air itself, sparkled at their feet, while in its clear depths could be seen gold and silver fish sporting in the bright water, and purple eels emitting sparks of fire at every moment, while the broad leaves of the water-lilies, that floated on its surface, flickered with all the colours of the rainbow. The flower in its colour of flame seemed to receive its nourishment from the water, as a lamp is sustained by oil. A marble bridge, of such exquisite workmanship that it appeared as if formed of lace and pearls, led to the island of happiness, in which bloomed the garden of paradise. The East Wind took the prince in his arms, and carried him over, while the flowers and the leaves sang the sweet songs of his childhood in tones so full and soft that no human voice could venture to imitate. Within the garden grew large trees, full of sap; but whether they were palm-trees or gigantic water-plants, the prince knew not. The climbing plants hung in garlands of green and gold, like the illuminations on the margins of old missals or twined among the initial letters. Birds, flowers, and festoons appeared intermingled in seeming confusion. Close by, on the grass, stood a group of peacocks, with radiant tails outspread to the sun. The prince touched them, and found, to his surprise, that they were not really birds, but the leaves of the burdock tree, which shone with the colours of a peacock's tail. The lion and the tiger, gentle and tame, were springing about like playful cats among the green bushes, whose perfume was like the fragrant blossom of the olive. The plumage of the wood-pigeon glistened like pearls as it struck the lion's mane with its wings; while the antelope, usually so shy, stood near, nodding its head as if it wished to join in the frolic. The fairy of paradise next made her appearance. Her raiment shone like the sun, and her serene countenance beamed with happiness like that of a mother rejoicing over her child. She was young and beautiful, and a train of lovely maidens followed her, each wearing a bright star in her hair. The East Wind gave her the palm-leaf, on which was written the history of the phoenix; and her eyes sparkled with joy. She then took the prince by the hand, and led him into her palace, the walls of which were richly coloured, like a tulip-leaf when it is turned to the sun. The roof had the appearance of an inverted flower, and the colours grew deeper and brighter to the gazer. The prince walked to a window, and saw what appeared to be the tree of knowledge of good and evil, with Adam and Eve standing by, and the serpent near them. 'I thought they were banished from paradise,' he said.

The princess smiled, and told him that time had engraved each event on a window-pane in the form of a picture; but, unlike other pictures, all that it represented lived and moved – the leaves rustled, and the persons went and came, as in a looking-glass. He looked through another pane, and saw the ladder in Jacob's dream, on which the angels were ascending and descending with outspread wings. All that had ever happened in the world here lived and moved on the panes of glass, in pictures such as time alone could produce. The fairy now led the prince into a large, lofty room with transparent walls, through which the light shone. Here were portraits, each one appearing more beautiful than the other – millions of happy beings, whose laughter and song mingled in one sweet melody: some of these were in such an elevated position that they appeared smaller than the smallest rosebud, or like pencil dots on paper. In the centre of the hall stood a tree, with drooping branches, from which hung golden apples, both great and small, looking like oranges amid the green leaves. It was the tree of knowledge of good and evil, from which Adam and Eve had plucked and eaten the forbidden fruit, and from each leaf trickled a bright red dewdrop, as if the tree were weeping tears of blood for their sin. 'Let us now take the boat,' said the fairy: 'a sail on the cool waters will refresh us. But we shall not move from the spot, although the boat may rock on the swelling water; the countries of the world will glide before us, but we shall remain still.'

It was indeed wonderful to behold. First came the lofty Alps, snow-clad, and covered with clouds and dark pines. The horn resounded, and the shepherds sang merrily in the valleys. The banana-trees bent their drooping branches over the boat, black swans floated on the water, and singular animals and flowers appeared on the distant shore. New Holland, the fifth division of the world, now glided by, with mountains in the background, looking blue in the distance. They heard the song of the priests, and saw the wild dance of the savage to the sound of the drums and trumpets of bone; the pyramids of Egypt rising to the clouds; columns and sphinxes, overthrown and buried in the sand, followed in their turn; while the northern lights flashed out over the extinguished volcanoes of the north, in fireworks none could imitate.

The prince was delighted, and yet he saw hundreds of other wonderful things more than can be described. 'Can I stay here forever?' asked he.

'That depends upon yourself,' replied the fairy. 'If you do not, like Adam, long for what is forbidden, you can remain here always.'

'I should not touch the fruit on the tree of knowledge,' said the prince; 'there is abundance of fruit equally beautiful.'

'Examine your own heart,' said the princess, 'and if you do not feel sure of its strength, return with the East Wind who brought you. He is about to fly back, and will not return here for a hundred years. The time will not seem to you more than a hundred hours, yet even that is a long time for temptation and resistance. Every evening, when I leave you, I shall be obliged to say, "Come with me," and to beckon to you with my hand. But you must not listen, nor move from your place to follow me; for with every step you will find your power to resist weaker. If once you attempted to follow me, you would soon find yourself in the hall, where grows the tree of knowledge, for I sleep beneath its perfumed branches. If you stooped over me, I should be forced to smile. If you then kissed my lips, the garden of paradise would sink into the earth, and to you it would be lost. A keen wind from the desert would howl around you; cold rain fall on your head, and sorrow and woe be your future lot.'

'I will remain,' said the prince.

So the East Wind kissed him on the forehead, and said, 'Be firm; then shall we meet again when a hundred years have passed. Farewell, farewell.' Then the East Wind spread his broad pinions, which shone like the lightning in harvest, or as the northern lights in a cold winter.

'Farewell, farewell,' echoed the trees and the flowers.

Storks and pelicans flew after him in feathery bands, to accompany him to the boundaries of the garden.

'Now we will commence dancing,' said the fairy; 'and when it is nearly over at sunset, while I am dancing with you, I shall make a sign, and ask you to follow me: but do not obey. I shall be obliged to repeat the same thing for a hundred years; and each time, when the trial is past, if you resist, you will gain strength, till resistance becomes easy, and at last the temptation will be quite overcome. This evening, as it will be the first time, I have warned you.'

After this the fairy led him into a large hall, filled with transparent lilies. The yellow stamina of each flower formed a tiny golden harp, from which came forth strains of music like the mingled tones of flute and lyre. Beautiful maidens, slender and graceful in form and robed in transparent gauze, floated through the dance, and sang of the happy life in the garden of paradise, where death never entered, and where all would bloom forever in immortal youth. As the sun went down, the whole heavens became crimson and gold, and tinted the lilies with the hue of roses. Then the beautiful maidens offered to the prince sparkling wine; and when he had drank, he felt happiness greater than he had ever known before. Presently the background of the hall opened and the tree of knowledge appeared, surrounded by a halo of glory that almost blinded him. Voices, soft and lovely as his mother's sounded in his ears, as if she were singing to him, 'My child, my beloved child.' Then the fairy beckoned to him, and said in sweet accents, 'Come with me, come with me.' Forgetting his promise, forgetting it even on the very first evening, he rushed towards her, while she continued to beckon to him and to smile. The fragrance around him overpowered his senses, the music from the harps sounded more entrancing, while around the tree appeared millions of smiling faces, nodding and singing. 'Man should know everything; man is the lord of the earth.' The tree of knowledge no longer wept tears of blood, for the dewdrops shone like glittering stars.

'Come, come,' continued that thrilling voice, and the prince followed the call. At every step his cheeks glowed, and the blood rushed wildly through his veins. 'I must follow,' he cried; 'it is not a sin, it cannot be, to follow beauty and joy. I only want to see her sleep, and nothing will happen unless I kiss her, and that I will not do, for I have strength to resist, and a determined will.'

The fairy threw off her dazzling attire, bent back the boughs, and in another moment was hidden among them.

'I have not sinned yet,' said the prince, 'and I will not;' and then he pushed aside the boughs to follow the princess. She was lying already asleep, beautiful as only a fairy in the garden of paradise could be. She smiled as he bent over her, and he saw tears trembling out of her beautiful eyelashes. 'Do you weep for me?' he whispered. 'Oh weep not, thou loveliest of women. Now do I begin to understand the happiness of paradise; I feel it to my inmost soul, in every thought. A new life is born within me. One moment of such happiness is worth an eternity of darkness and woe.' He stooped and kissed the tears from her eyes, and touched her lips with his.

A clap of thunder, loud and awful, resounded through the trembling air. All around him fell into ruin. The lovely fairy, the beautiful garden, sunk deeper and deeper. The prince saw it sinking down in the dark night till it shone only like a star in the distance beneath him. Then he felt a coldness, like death, creeping over him; his eyes closed, and he became insensible.

When he recovered, a chilling rain was beating upon him, and a sharp wind blew on his head. 'Alas! What have I done?' he sighed; 'I have sinned like Adam, and the garden of paradise has sunk into the earth.' He opened his eyes, and saw the star in the distance, but it was the morning star in heaven which glittered in the darkness.

Presently he stood up and found himself in the depths of the forest, close to the cavern of the Winds, and the mother of the

Winds sat by his side. She looked angry, and raised her arm in the air as she spoke. 'The very first evening!' she said. 'Well, I expected it! If you were my son, you should go into the sack.'

'And there he will have to go at last,' said a strong old man, with large black wings, and a scythe in his hand, whose name was Death. 'He shall be laid in his coffin, but not yet. I will allow him to wander about the world for a while, to atone for his sin, and to give him time to become better. But I shall return when he least expects me. I shall lay him in a black coffin, place it on my head, and fly away with it beyond the stars. There also blooms a garden of paradise, and if he is good and pious he will be admitted; but if his thoughts are bad, and his heart is full of sin, he will sink with his coffin deeper than the garden of paradise has sunk. Once in every thousand years I shall go and fetch him, when he will either be condemned to sink still deeper, or be raised to a happier life in the world beyond the stars.'

THE SNOW QUEEN

STORY THE FIRST,
WHICH DESCRIBES A LOOKING-GLASS
AND THE BROKEN FRAGMENTS.

You must attend to the commencement of this story, for when we get to the end we shall know more than we do now about a very wicked hobgoblin; he was one of the very worst, for he was a real demon. One day, when he was in a merry mood, he made a looking-glass which had the power of making everything good or beautiful that was reflected in it almost shrink to nothing, while everything that was worthless and bad looked increased in size and worse than ever. The most lovely landscapes appeared like boiled spinach, and the people became hideous, and looked as if they stood on their heads and had no bodies. Their countenances were so distorted that no one could recognise them, and even one freckle on the face appeared to spread over the whole of the nose and mouth. The demon said this was very amusing. When a good or pious thought passed through the mind of anyone it was misrepresented in the glass; and then how the demon laughed at his cunning invention. All who went to the demon's school – for he kept a school – talked everywhere of the wonders they had seen, and declared that people could now, for the first time, see what the world and mankind were really like. They carried the glass about everywhere, till at last there was not a land nor a people who had not been looked at through this distorted mirror. They wanted even to fly with it up to heaven to see the angels, but the higher they flew the more slippery the glass became, and they could scarcely hold it, till at last it slipped from their hands, fell to the earth, and was broken into millions of pieces. But now the looking-glass caused more unhappiness than ever, for some of the fragments were not so large as a grain of sand, and they flew about the world into every country. When one of these tiny atoms flew into a person's eye, it stuck there unknown to him, and from that moment he saw everything through a distorted medium, or could see only the worst side of what he looked at, for even the smallest fragment retained the same power which had belonged to the whole mirror. Some few persons even got a fragment of the looking-glass in their hearts, and this was very terrible, for their hearts became cold like a lump of ice. A few of the pieces were so large that they could be used as window-panes; it would have been a sad thing to look at our friends through them. Other pieces were made into spectacles; this was dreadful for those who wore them, for they could see nothing either rightly or justly. At all this the wicked demon laughed till his sides shook – it tickled him so to see the mischief he had done. There were still a number of these little fragments of glass floating about in the air, and now you shall hear what happened with one of them.

SECOND STORY:
A LITTLE BOY AND A LITTLE GIRL

In a large town, full of houses and people, there is not room for everybody to have even a little garden, therefore they are obliged to be satisfied with a few flowers in flower-pots. In one of these large towns lived two poor children who had a garden something larger and better than a few flower-pots. They were not brother and sister, but they loved each other almost as much as if they had been. Their parents lived opposite to each other in two garrets, where the roofs of neighbouring houses projected out towards each other and the water-pipe ran between them. In each house was a little window, so that anyone could step across the gutter from one window to the other. The parents of these children had each a large wooden box in which they cultivated kitchen herbs for their own use, and a little rose-bush in each box, which grew splendidly. Now after a while the parents decided to place these two boxes across the water-pipe, so that they reached from one window to the other and looked like two banks of flowers. Sweet-peas drooped over the boxes, and the rose-bushes shot forth long branches, which were trained round the windows and clustered together almost like a triumphal arch of leaves and flowers. The boxes were very high, and the children knew they must not climb upon them, without permission, but they were often, however, allowed to step out together and sit upon their little stools under the rose-bushes, or play quietly. In winter all this pleasure came to an end, for the windows were sometimes quite frozen over. But then they would warm copper pennies on the stove, and hold the warm pennies against the frozen pane; there would be very soon a little round hole through which they could peep, and the soft bright eyes of the little boy and girl would beam through the hole at each window as they looked at each other. Their names were Kay and Gerda. In summer they could be together with one jump from the window, but in winter they had to go up and down the long staircase, and out through the snow before they could meet.

'See there are the white bees swarming,' said Kay's old grandmother one day when it was snowing.

'Have they a queen bee?' asked the little boy, for he knew that the real bees had a queen.

'To be sure they have,' said the grandmother. 'She is flying there where the swarm is thickest. She is the largest of them all, and never remains on the earth, but flies up to the dark clouds. Often at midnight she flies through the streets of the town, and looks in at the windows, then the ice freezes on the panes into wonderful shapes, that look like flowers and castles.'

'Yes, I have seen them,' said both the children, and they knew it must be true.

'Can the Snow Queen come in here?' asked the little girl.

'Only let her come,' said the boy, 'I'll set her on the stove and then she'll melt.'

Then the grandmother smoothed his hair and told him some more tales. One evening, when little Kay was at home, half undressed, he climbed on a chair by the window and peeped out through the little hole. A few flakes of snow were falling, and one of them, rather larger than the rest, alighted on the edge of one of the flower boxes. This snow-flake grew larger and larger, till at last it became the figure of a woman, dressed in garments of white gauze, which looked like millions of starry snow-flakes linked together. She was fair and beautiful, but made of ice –

shining and glittering ice. Still she was alive and her eyes sparkled like bright stars, but there was neither peace nor rest in their glance. She nodded towards the window and waved her hand. The little boy was frightened and sprang from the chair; at the same moment it seemed as if a large bird flew by the window. On the following day there was a clear frost, and very soon came the spring. The sun shone; the young green leaves burst forth; the swallows built their nests; windows were opened, and the children sat once more in the garden on the roof, high above all the other rooms. How beautifully the roses blossomed this summer. The little girl had learnt a hymn in which roses were spoken of, and then she thought of their own roses, and she sang the hymn to the little boy, and he sang too: –

'Roses bloom and cease to be,
But we shall the Christ-child see.'

Then the little ones held each other by the hand, and kissed the roses, and looked at the bright sunshine, and spoke to it as if the Christ-child were there. Those were splendid summer days. How beautiful and fresh it was out among the rose-bushes, which seemed as if they would never leave off blooming. One day Kay and Gerda sat looking at a book full of pictures of animals and birds, and then just as the clock in the church tower struck twelve, Kay said, 'Oh, something has struck my heart!' And soon after, 'There is something in my eye.'

The little girl put her arm round his neck, and looked into his eye, but she could see nothing.

'I think it is gone,' he said. But it was not gone; it was one of those bits of the looking-glass – that magic mirror, of which we have spoken – the ugly glass which made everything great and good appear small and ugly, while all that was wicked and bad became more visible, and every little fault could be plainly seen. Poor little Kay had also received a small grain in his heart, which very quickly turned to a lump of ice. He felt no more pain, but the glass was there still. 'Why do you cry?' said he at last; 'it makes you look ugly. There is nothing the matter with me now. Oh, see!' he cried suddenly, 'that rose is worm-eaten, and this one is quite crooked. After all they are ugly roses, just like the box in which they stand,' and then he kicked the boxes with his foot, and pulled off the two roses.

'Kay, what are you doing?' cried the little girl; and then, when he saw how frightened she was, he tore off another rose, and jumped through his own window away from little Gerda.

When she afterwards brought out the picture book, he said, 'It was only fit for babies in long clothes,' and when grandmother told any stories, he would interrupt her with 'but'; or, when he could manage it, he would get behind her chair, put on a pair of spectacles, and imitate her very cleverly, to make people laugh. By-and-by he began to mimic the speech and gait of persons in the street. All that was peculiar or disagreeable in a person he would imitate directly, and people said, 'That boy will be very clever; he has a remarkable genius.' But it was the piece of glass in his eye, and the coldness in his heart, that made him act like this. He would even tease little Gerda, who loved him with all her heart. His games, too, were quite different; they were not so childish. One winter's day, when it snowed, he brought out a burning-glass, then he held out the tail of his blue coat, and let the snow-flakes fall upon it. 'Look in this glass, Gerda,' said he; and she saw how every flake of snow was magnified, and looked like a beautiful flower or a glittering star. 'Is it not clever?' said Kay. 'And much more interesting than looking at real flowers. There is not a single fault in it, and the snow-flakes are quite perfect till they begin to melt.'

Soon after Kay made his appearance in large thick gloves, and with his sledge at his back. He called up stairs to Gerda, 'I've got to leave to go into the great square, where the other boys play and ride.' And away he went.

In the great square, the boldest among the boys would often tie their sledges to the country people's carts, and go with them a good way. This was capital. But while they were all amusing themselves, and Kay with them, a great sledge came by; it was painted white, and in it sat someone wrapped in a rough white fur, and wearing a white cap. The sledge drove twice round the square, and Kay fastened his own little sledge to it, so that when it went away, he followed with it. It went faster and faster right through the next street, and then the person who drove turned round and nodded pleasantly to Kay, just as if they were acquainted with each other, but whenever Kay wished to loosen his little sledge the driver nodded again, so Kay sat still, and they drove out through the town gate. Then the snow began to fall so heavily that the little boy could not see a hand's breadth before him, but still they drove on; then he suddenly loosened the cord so that the large sled might go on without him, but it was of no use, his little carriage held fast, and away they went like the wind. Then he called out loudly, but nobody heard him, while the snow beat upon him, and the sledge flew onwards. Every now and then it gave a jump as if it were going over hedges and ditches. The boy was frightened, and tried to say a prayer, but he could remember nothing but the multiplication table.

The snow-flakes became larger and larger, till they appeared like great white chickens. All at once they sprang on one side, the great sledge stopped, and the person who had driven it rose up. The fur and the cap, which were made entirely of snow, fell off, and he saw a lady, tall and white: it was the Snow Queen.

'We have driven well,' said she, 'but why do you tremble? Here, creep into my warm fur.' Then she seated him beside her in the sledge, and as she wrapped the fur round him he felt as if he were sinking into a snow-drift.

'Are you still cold?' she asked, as she kissed him on the forehead. The kiss was colder than ice; it went quite through to his heart, which was already almost a lump of ice; he felt as if he were going to die, but only for a moment; he soon seemed quite well again, and did not notice the cold around him.

'My sledge! Don't forget my sledge,' was his first thought, and then he looked and saw that it was bound fast to one of the white chickens, which flew behind him with the sledge at its back. The Snow Queen kissed little Kay again, and by this time he had forgotten little Gerda, his grandmother and all at home.

'Now you must have no more kisses,' she said, 'or I should kiss you to death.'

Kay looked at her, and saw that she was so beautiful, he could not imagine a more lovely and intelligent face; she did not now seem to be made of ice, as when he had seen her through his window, and she had nodded to him. In his eyes she was perfect, and he did not feel at all afraid. He told her he could do mental arithmetic, as far as fractions, and that he knew the number of square miles and the number of inhabitants in the country. And she always smiled so that he thought he did not know enough yet, and she looked round the vast expanse as she flew higher and higher with him upon a black cloud, while the storm blew and howled as if it were singing old songs. They flew over woods and lakes, over sea and land; below them roared the wild wind; the wolves howled and the snow crackled; over them flew the black screaming crows, and above all shone the moon, clear and bright – and so Kay passed through the long winter's night, and by day he slept at the feet of the Snow Queen.

THIRD STORY:
THE FLOWER GARDEN OF THE WOMAN WHO COULD CONJURE

But how fared little Gerda during Kay's absence? What had become of him, no one knew, nor could any one give the slightest information, excepting the boys, who said that he had tied his sledge to another very large one, which had driven through the street, and out at the town gate. Nobody knew where it went; many tears were shed for him, and little Gerda wept bitterly for a long time. She said she knew he must be dead; that he was drowned in the river which flowed close by the school. Oh, indeed those long winter days were very dreary. But at last spring came, with warm sunshine. 'Kay is dead and gone,' said little Gerda.

'I don't believe it,' said the sunshine.

'He is dead and gone,' she said to the sparrows.

'We don't believe it,' they replied; and at last little Gerda began to doubt it herself. 'I will put on my new red shoes,' she said one morning, 'those that Kay has never seen, and then I will go down to the river, and ask for him.' It was quite early when she kissed her old grandmother, who was still asleep; then she put on her red shoes, and went quite alone out of the town gates toward the river. 'Is it true that you have taken my little playmate away from me?' said she to the river. 'I will give you my red shoes if you will give him back to me.' And it seemed as if the waves nodded to her in a strange manner. Then she took off her red shoes, which she liked better than anything else, and threw them both into the river, but they fell near the bank, and the little waves carried them back to the land, just as if the river would not take from her what she loved best, because they could not give her back little Kay. But she thought the shoes had not been thrown out far enough. Then she crept into a boat that lay among the reeds, and threw the shoes again from the farther end of the boat into the water, but it was not fastened. And her movement sent it gliding away from the land. When she saw this she hastened to reach the end of the boat, but before she could so it was more than a yard from the bank, and drifting away faster than ever. Then little Gerda was very much frightened, and began to cry, but no one heard her except the sparrows, and they could not carry her to land, but they flew along by the shore, and sang, as if to comfort her, 'Here we are! Here we are!' The boat floated with the stream; little Gerda sat quite still with only her stockings on her feet; the red shoes floated after her, but she could not reach them because the boat kept so much in advance. The banks on each side of the river were very pretty. There were beautiful flowers, old trees, sloping fields, in which cows and sheep were grazing, but not a man to be seen. Perhaps the river will carry me to little Kay, thought Gerda, and then she became more cheerful and raised her head and looked at the beautiful green banks; and so the boat sailed on for hours. At length she came to a large cherry orchard, in which stood a small red house with strange red and blue windows. It had also a thatched roof, and outside were two wooden soldiers that presented arms to her as she sailed past. Gerda called out to them, for she thought they were alive, but of course they did not answer; and as the boat drifted nearer to the shore, she saw what they really were. Then Gerda called still louder, and there came a very old woman out of the house, leaning on a crutch. She wore a large hat to shade her from the sun, and on it were painted all sorts of pretty flowers. 'You poor little child,' said the old woman, 'how did you manage to come all this distance into the wide world on such a rapid rolling stream?' And then the old woman walked in the water, seized the boat with her crutch, drew it to land, and lifted Gerda out. And Gerda was glad to feel herself on dry ground, although she was rather afraid of the strange old woman. 'Come and tell me who you are,' said she, 'and how came you here.'

Then Gerda told her everything, while the old woman shook her head, and said, 'Hem-hem;' and when she had finished, Gerda asked if she had not seen little Kay, and the old woman told her he had not passed by that way, but he very likely would come. So she told Gerda not to be sorrowful, but to taste the cherries and look at the flowers; they were better than any picture-book, for each of them could tell a story. Then she took Gerda by the hand and led her into the little house, and the old woman closed the door. The windows were very high, and as the panes were red, blue and yellow, the daylight shone through them in all sorts of singular colours. On the table stood beautiful cherries, and Gerda had permission to eat as many as she would. While she was eating them the old woman combed out her long flaxen ringlets with a golden comb, and the glossy curls hung down on each side of the little round pleasant face, which looked fresh and blooming as a rose. 'I have long been wishing for a dear little maiden like you,' said the old woman, 'and now you must stay with me, and see how happily we shall live together.' And while she went on combing little Gerda's hair, she thought less and less about her adopted brother Kay, for the old woman could conjure, although she was not a wicked witch; she conjured only a little for her own amusement, and now, because she wanted to keep Gerda. Therefore she went into the garden, and stretched out her crutch towards all the rose-trees, beautiful though they were; and they immediately sunk into the dark earth, so that no one could tell where they had once stood. The old woman was afraid that if little Gerda saw roses she would think of those at home, and then remember little Kay, and run away. Then she took Gerda into the flower-garden. How fragrant and beautiful it was! Every flower that could be thought of for every season of the year was here in full bloom; no picture-book could have more beautiful colours. Gerda jumped for joy, and played till the sun went down behind the tall cherry-trees; then she slept in an elegant bed with red silk pillows, embroidered with coloured violets; and then she dreamed as pleasantly as a queen on her wedding day. The next day, and for many days after, Gerda played with the flowers in the warm sunshine. She knew every flower, and yet, although there were so many of them, it seemed as if one were missing, but which it was she could not tell. One day, however, as she sat looking at the old woman's hat with the painted flowers on it, she saw that the prettiest of them all was a rose. The old woman had forgotten to take it from her hat when she made all the roses sink into the earth. But it is difficult to keep the thoughts together in everything; one little mistake upsets all our arrangements.

'What, are there no roses here?' cried Gerda; and she ran out into the garden, and examined all the beds, and searched and searched. There was not one to be found. Then she sat down and wept, and her tears fell just on the place where one of the rose-trees had sunk down. The warm tears moistened the earth, and the rose-tree sprouted up at once, as blooming as when it had sunk; and Gerda embraced it and kissed the roses, and thought of the beautiful roses at home, and, with them, of little Kay.

'Oh, how I have been detained!' said the little maiden, 'I wanted to seek for little Kay. Do you know where he is?' she asked the roses. 'Do you think he is dead?'

And the roses answered, 'No, he is not dead. We have been in the ground where all the dead lie; but Kay is not there.'

'Thank you,' said little Gerda, and then she went to the other flowers, and looked into their little cups, and asked, 'Do you know where little Kay is?' But each flower, as it stood in the sunshine, dreamed only of its own little fairy tale of history. Not one knew anything of Kay. Gerda heard many stories from the flowers, as she asked them one after another about him.

And what said the tiger-lily? 'Hark, do you hear the drum? – "turn, turn" – there are only two notes, always, "turn, turn". Listen to the women's song of mourning! Hear the cry of the priest! In her long red robe stands the Hindoo widow by the funeral pile. The flames rise around her as she places herself on the dead body of her husband; but the Hindoo woman is thinking of the living one in that circle; of him, her son, who lighted those flames. Those shining eyes trouble her heart more painfully than the flames which will soon consume her body to ashes. Can the fire of the heart be extinguished in the flames of the funeral pile?'

'I don't understand that at all,' said little Gerda.

'That is my story,' said the tiger-lily.

What says the convolvulus? 'Near yonder narrow road stands an old knight's castle; thick ivy creeps over the old ruined walls, leaf over leaf, even to the balcony, in which stands a beautiful maiden. She bends over the balustrades, and looks up the road. No rose on its stem is fresher than she; no apple-blossom, wafted by the wind, floats more lightly than she moves. Her rich silk rustles as she bends over and exclaims, "Will he not come?"'

'Is it Kay you mean?' asked Gerda.

'I am only speaking of a story of my dream,' replied the flower.

What said the little snow-drop? 'Between two trees a rope is hanging; there is a piece of board upon it; it is a swing. Two pretty little girls, in dresses white as snow, and with long green ribbons fluttering from their hats, are sitting upon it swinging. Their brother who is taller than they are, stands in the swing; he has one arm round the rope, to steady himself; in one hand he holds a little bowl, and in the other a clay pipe; he is blowing bubbles. As the swing goes on, the bubbles fly upward, reflecting the most beautiful varying colours. The last still hangs from the bowl of the pipe, and sways in the wind. On goes the swing; and then a little black dog comes running up. He is almost as light as the bubble, and he raises himself on his hind legs, and wants to be taken into the swing; but it does not stop, and the dog falls; then he barks and gets angry. The children stoop towards him, and the bubble bursts. A swinging plank, a light sparkling foam picture – that is my story.'

'It may be all very pretty what you are telling me,' said little Gerda, 'but you speak so mournfully, and you do not mention little Kay at all.'

What do the hyacinths say? 'There were three beautiful sisters, fair and delicate. The dress of one was red, of the second blue and of the third pure white. Hand in hand they danced in the bright moonlight, by the calm lake; but they were human beings, not fairy elves. The sweet fragrance attracted them, and they disappeared in the wood; here the fragrance became stronger. Three coffins, in which lay the three beautiful maidens, glided from the thickest part of the forest across the lake. The fire-flies flew lightly over them, like little floating torches. Do the dancing maidens sleep, or are they dead? The scent of the flower says that they are corpses. The evening bell tolls their knell.'

'You make me quite sorrowful,' said little Gerda; 'your perfume is so strong, you make me think of the dead maidens. Ah! Is little Kay really dead then? The roses have been in the earth, and they say no.'

'Cling, clang,' tolled the hyacinth bells. 'We are not tolling for little Kay; we do not know him. We sing our song, the only one we know.'

Then Gerda went to the buttercups that were glittering amongst the bright green leaves.

'You are little bright suns,' said Gerda; 'tell me if you know where I can find my playfellow.'

And the buttercups sparkled gaily, and looked again at Gerda. What song could the buttercups sing? It was not about Kay.

'The bright warm sun shone on a little court, on the first warm day of spring. His bright beams rested on the white walls of the neighbouring house; and close by bloomed the first yellow flower of the season, glittering like gold in the sun's warm ray. An old woman sat in her armchair at the house door, and her granddaughter, a poor and pretty servant-maid came to see her for a short visit. When she kissed her grandmother there was gold everywhere: the gold of the heart in that holy kiss; it was a golden morning; there was gold in the beaming sunlight, gold in the leaves of the lowly flower, and on the lips of the maiden. There, that is my story,' said the buttercup.

'My poor old grandmother!' sighed Gerda. 'She is longing to see me, and grieving for me as she did for little Kay; but I shall soon go home now, and take little Kay with me. It is no use asking the flowers; they know only their own songs, and can give me no information.'

And then she tucked up her little dress, that she might run faster, but the narcissus caught her by the leg as she was jumping over it; so she stopped and looked at the tall yellow flower, and said, 'Perhaps you may know something.'

Then she stooped down quite close to the flower, and listened; and what did he say?

'I can see myself, I can see myself,' said the narcissus. 'Oh, how sweet is my perfume! Up in a little room with a bow window, stands a little dancing girl, half undressed; she stands sometimes on one leg, and sometimes on both, and looks as if she would tread the whole world under her feet. She is nothing but a delusion. She is pouring water out of a teapot on a piece of stuff which she holds in her hand; it is her bodice. 'Cleanliness is a good thing,' she says. Her white dress hangs on a peg; it has also been washed in the teapot, and dried on the roof. She puts it on, and ties a saffron-coloured handkerchief round her neck, which makes the dress look whiter. See how she stretches out her legs, as if she were showing off on a stem. I can see myself, I can see myself.'

'What do I care for all that,' said Gerda, 'you need not tell me such stuff.' And then she ran to the other end of the garden. The door was fastened, but she pressed against the rusty latch, and it gave way. The door sprang open, and little Gerda ran out with bare feet into the wide world. She looked back three times, but no one seemed to be following her. At last she could run no longer, so she sat down to rest on a great stone, and when she looked round she saw that the summer was over, and autumn very far advanced. She had known nothing of this in the beautiful garden, where the sun shone and the flowers grew all the year round.

'Oh, how I have wasted my time?' said little Gerda. 'It is autumn. I must not rest any longer,' and she rose up to go on. But her little feet were wounded and sore, and everything around her looked so cold and bleak. The long willow-leaves were quite yellow. The dew-drops fell like water, leaf after leaf dropped from the trees, the sloe-thorn alone still bore fruit, but the sloes were sour, and set the teeth on edge. Oh, how dark and weary the whole world appeared!

FOURTH STORY:
THE PRINCE AND PRINCESS

Gerda was obliged to rest again, and just opposite the place where she sat, she saw a great crow come hopping across the snow toward her. He stood looking at her for some time, and then he wagged his head and said, 'Caw, caw; good-day, good-day.' He pronounced the words as plainly as he could, because he meant to be kind to the little girl; and then he asked her where she was going all alone in the wide world.

The word alone Gerda understood very well, and knew how much it expressed. So then she told the crow the whole story of her life and adventures, and asked him if he had seen little Kay.

The crow nodded his head very gravely, and said, 'Perhaps I have – it may be.'

'No! Do you think you have?' cried little Gerda, and she kissed the crow, and hugged him almost to death with joy.

'Gently, gently,' said the crow. 'I believe I know. I think it may be little Kay; but he has certainly forgotten you by this time for the princess.'

'Does he live with a princess?' asked Gerda.

'Yes, listen,' replied the crow, 'but it is so difficult to speak your language. If you understand the crows' language then I can explain it better. Do you?'

'No, I have never learnt it,' said Gerda, 'but my grandmother understands it, and used to speak it to me. I wish I had learnt it.'

'It does not matter,' answered the crow; 'I will explain as well as I can, although it will be very badly done;' and he told her what he had heard. 'In this kingdom where we now are,' said he, 'there lives a princess, who is so wonderfully clever that she has read all the newspapers in the world, and forgotten them too, although she is so clever. A short time ago, as she was sitting on her throne, which people say is not such an agreeable seat as is often supposed, she began to sing a song which commences in these words:

'Why should I not be married?'

'Why not indeed?' said she, and so she determined to marry if she could find a husband who knew what to say when he was spoken to, and not one who could only look grand, for that was so tiresome. Then she assembled all her court ladies together at the beat of the drum, and when they heard of her intentions they were very much pleased. 'We are so glad to hear it,' said they, 'we were talking about it ourselves the other day.' You may believe that every word I tell you is true,' said the crow, 'for I have a tame sweetheart who goes freely about the palace, and she told me all this.'

Of course his sweetheart was a crow, for 'birds of a feather flock together', and one crow always chooses another crow.

'Newspapers were published immediately, with a border of hearts, and the initials of the princess among them. They gave notice that every young man who was handsome was free to visit the castle and speak with the princess; and those who could reply loud enough to be heard when spoken to were to make themselves quite at home at the palace; but the one who spoke best would be chosen as a husband for the princess. Yes, yes, you may believe me, it is all as true as I sit here,' said the crow. 'The people came in crowds. There was a great deal of crushing and running about, but no one succeeded either on the first or second day. They could all speak very well while they were outside in the streets, but when they entered the palace gates, and saw the guards in silver uniforms, and the footmen in their golden livery on the staircase, and the great halls lighted up, they became quite confused. And when they stood before the throne on which the princess sat, they could do nothing but repeat the last words she had said; and she had no particular wish to hear her own words over again. It was just as if they had all taken something to make them sleepy while they were in the palace, for they did not recover themselves nor speak till they got back again into the street. There was quite a long line of them reaching from the town-gate to the palace. I went myself to see them,' said the crow. 'They were hungry and thirsty, for at the palace they did not get even a glass of water. Some of the wisest had taken a few slices of bread and butter with them, but they did not share it with their neighbours; they thought if they went in to the princess looking hungry, there would be a better chance for themselves.'

'But Kay! tell me about little Kay!' said Gerda, 'was he amongst the crowd?'

'Stop a bit, we are just coming to him. It was on the third day, there came marching cheerfully along to the palace a little personage, without horses or carriage, his eyes sparkling like yours; he had beautiful long hair, but his clothes were very poor.'

'That was Kay!' said Gerda joyfully. 'Oh, then I have found him;' and she clapped her hands.

'He had a little knapsack on his back,' added the crow.

'No, it must have been his sledge,' said Gerda; 'for he went away with it.'

'It may have been so,' said the crow; 'I did not look at it very closely. But I know from my tame sweetheart that he passed through the palace gates, saw the guards in their silver uniform and the servants in their liveries of gold on the stairs, but he was not in the least embarrassed. "It must be very tiresome to stand on the stairs," he said. "I prefer to go in." The rooms were blazing with light. Councillors and ambassadors walked about with bare feet, carrying golden vessels; it was enough to make anyone feel serious. His boots creaked loudly as he walked, and yet he was not at all uneasy.'

'It must be Kay,' said Gerda, 'I know he had new boots on, I have heard them creak in grandmother's room.'

'They really did creak,' said the crow, 'yet he went boldly up to the princess herself, who was sitting on a pearl as large as a spinning wheel, and all the ladies of the court were present with their maids, and all the cavaliers with their servants; and each of the maids had another maid to wait upon her, and the cavaliers' servants had their own servants, as well as a page each. They all stood in circles round the princess, and the nearer they stood to the door, the prouder they looked. The servants' pages, who always wore slippers, could hardly be looked at, they held themselves up so proudly by the door.'

'It must be quite awful,' said little Gerda, 'but did Kay win the princess?'

'If I had not been a crow,' said he, 'I would have married her myself, although I am engaged. He spoke just as well as I do, when I speak the crows' language, so I heard from my tame sweetheart. He was quite free and agreeable and said he had not come to woo the princess, but to hear her wisdom; and he was as pleased with her as she was with him.'

'Oh, certainly that was Kay,' said Gerda, 'he was so clever; he could work mental arithmetic and fractions. Oh, will you take me to the palace?'

'It is very easy to ask that,' replied the crow, 'but how are we to manage it? However, I will speak about it to my tame sweetheart, and ask her advice; for I must tell you it will be very difficult to gain permission for a little girl like you to enter the palace.'

'Oh, yes; but I shall gain permission easily,' said Gerda, 'for when Kay hears that I am here, he will come out and fetch me in immediately.'

'Wait for me here by the palings,' said the crow, wagging his head as he flew away.

It was late in the evening before the crow returned. 'Caw, caw,' he said, 'she sends you greeting, and here is a little roll which she took from the kitchen for you; there is plenty of bread there, and she thinks you must be hungry. It is not possible for you to enter the palace by the front entrance. The guards in silver uniform and the servants in gold livery would not allow it. But do not cry, we will manage to get you in; my sweetheart knows a little back-staircase that leads to the sleeping apartments, and she knows where to find the key.'

Then they went into the garden through the great avenue, where the leaves were falling one after another, and they could see the light in the palace being put out in the same manner. And the crow led little Gerda to the back door, which stood ajar. Oh! How little Gerda's heart beat with anxiety and longing; it was just as if she were going to do something wrong, and yet she only wanted to know where little Kay was. 'It must be he,' she thought, 'with those clear eyes, and that long hair.' She could fancy she saw him smiling at her, as he used to at home, when they sat among the roses. He would certainly be glad to see her, and to hear what a long distance she had come for his sake, and to know how sorry they had been at home because he did not come back. Oh what joy and yet fear she felt! They were now on the stairs, and in a small closet at the top a lamp was burning. In the middle of the floor stood the tame crow, turning her head from side to side, and gazing at Gerda, who curtseyed as her grandmother had taught her to do.

'My betrothed has spoken so very highly of you, my little lady,' said the tame crow, 'your life-history, *vita*, as it may be called, is very touching. If you will take the lamp I will walk before you. We will go straight along this way, then we shall meet no one.'

'It seems to me as if somebody were behind us,' said Gerda, as something rushed by her like a shadow on the wall, and then horses with flying manes and thin legs, hunters, ladies and gentlemen on horseback, glided by her, like shadows on the wall.

'They are only dreams,' said the crow, 'they are coming to fetch the thoughts of the great people out hunting.'

'All the better, for we shall be able to look at them in their beds more safely. I hope that when you rise to honour and favour, you will show a grateful heart.'

'You may be quite sure of that,' said the crow from the forest.

They now came into the first hall, the walls of which were hung with rose-coloured satin, embroidered with artificial flowers. Here the dreams again flitted by them but so quickly that Gerda could not distinguish the royal persons. Each hall appeared more splendid than the last, it was enough to bewilder any one. At length they reached a bedroom. The ceiling was like a great palm-tree, with glass leaves of the most costly crystal, and over the centre of the floor two beds, each resembling a lily, hung from a stem of gold. One, in which the princess lay, was white, the other was red; and in this Gerda had to seek for little Kay. She pushed one of the red leaves aside, and saw a little brown neck. Oh, that must be Kay! She called his name out quite loud, and held the lamp over him. The dreams rushed back into the room on horseback. He woke, and turned his head round, it was not little Kay! The prince was only like him in the neck, still he was young and pretty. Then the princess peeped out of her white-lily bed, and asked what was the matter. Then little Gerda wept and told her story, and all that the crows had done to help her.

'You poor child,' said the prince and princess; then they praised the crows, and said they were not angry for what they had done, but that it must not happen again, and this time they should be rewarded.

'Would you like to have your freedom?' asked the princess, 'or would you prefer to be raised to the position of court crows, with all that is left in the kitchen for yourselves?'

Then both the crows bowed, and begged to have a fixed appointment, for they thought of their old age, and said it would be so comfortable to feel that they had provision for their old days, as they called it. And then the prince got out of his bed, and gave it up to Gerda – he could do no more; and she lay down. She folded her little hands, and thought, 'How good everyone is to me, men and animals too;' then she closed her eyes and fell into a sweet sleep. All the dreams came flying back again to her, and they looked like angels, and one of them drew a little sledge, on which sat Kay, and nodded to her. But all this was only a dream, and vanished as soon as she awoke.

The following day she was dressed from head to foot in silk and velvet, and they invited her to stay at the palace for a few days, and enjoy herself, but she only begged for a pair of boots, and a little carriage and a horse to draw it, so that she might go into the wide world to seek for Kay. And she obtained not only boots, but also a muff, and she was neatly dressed; and when she was ready to go, there, at the door, she found a coach made of pure gold, with the coat-of-arms of the prince and princess shining upon it like a star, and the coachman, footman and outriders all wearing golden crowns on their heads. The prince and princess themselves helped her into the coach, and wished her success. The forest crow, who was now married, accompanied her for the first three miles; he sat by Gerda's side, as he could not bear riding backwards. The tame crow stood in the doorway flapping her wings. She could not go with them, because she had been suffering from headache ever since the new appointment, no doubt from eating too much. The coach was well stored with sweet cakes, and under the seat were fruit and gingerbread nuts. 'Farewell, farewell,' cried the prince and princess, and little Gerda wept, and the crow wept; and then, after a few miles, the crow also said, 'Farewell,' and this was the saddest parting. However, he flew to a tree, and stood flapping his black wings as long as he could see the coach, which glittered in the bright sunshine.

FIFTH STORY:
LITTLE ROBBER-GIRL

The coach drove on through a thick forest, where it lighted up the way like a torch, and dazzled the eyes of some robbers, who could not bear to let it pass them unmolested.

'It is gold! It is gold!' cried they, rushing forward, and seizing the horses. Then they struck the little jockeys, the coachman, and the footman dead, and pulled little Gerda out of the carriage.

'She is fat and pretty, and she has been fed with the kernels of nuts,' said the old robber-woman, who had a long beard and eyebrows that hung over her eyes. 'She is as good as a little lamb; how nice she will taste!' And as she said this, she drew forth a shining knife, that glittered horribly. 'Oh!' screamed the old woman the same moment; for her own daughter, who held her back, had bitten her in the ear. She was a wild and naughty girl, and the mother called her an ugly thing, and had not time to kill Gerda.

'She shall play with me,' said the little robber-girl; 'she shall give me her muff and her pretty dress, and sleep with me in my bed.' And then she bit her mother again, and made her spring in the air, and jump about; and all the robbers laughed, and said, 'See how she is dancing with her young cub.'

'I will have a ride in the coach,' said the little robber-girl; and she would have her own way; for she was so self-willed and obstinate.

She and Gerda seated themselves in the coach, and drove away, over stumps and stones, into the depths of the forest. The little robber-girl was about the same size as Gerda, but stronger; she had broader shoulders and a darker skin; her eyes were quite black, and she had a mournful look. She clasped little Gerda round the waist, and said, –

'They shall not kill you as long as you don't make us vexed with you. I suppose you are a princess.'

'No,' said Gerda; and then she told her all her history, and how fond she was of little Kay.

The robber-girl looked earnestly at her, nodded her head slightly, and said, 'They shan't kill you, even if I do get angry with you; for I will do it myself.' And then she wiped Gerda's eyes, and stuck her own hands in the beautiful muff which was so soft and warm.

The coach stopped in the courtyard of a robber's castle, the walls of which were cracked from top to bottom. Ravens and crows flew in and out of the holes and crevices, while great bull-dogs, either of which looked as if it could swallow a man, were jumping about; but they were not allowed to bark. In the large and smoky hall a bright fire was burning on the stone floor. There was no chimney; so the smoke went up to the ceiling, and found a way out for itself. Soup was boiling in a large cauldron, and hares and rabbits were roasting on the spit.

'You shall sleep with me and all my little animals tonight,' said the robber-girl, after they had had something to eat and drink. So she took Gerda to a corner of the hall, where some straw and carpets were laid down. Above them, on laths and perches, were more than a hundred pigeons, who all seemed to be asleep, although they moved slightly when the two little girls came near them. 'These all belong to me,' said the robber-girl; and she seized the nearest to her, held it by the feet, and shook it till it flapped its wings. 'Kiss it,' cried she, flapping it in Gerda's face. 'There sit the wood-pigeons,' continued she, pointing to a number of laths and a cage which had been fixed into the walls, near one of the openings. 'Both rascals would fly away directly, if they were not closely locked up. And here is my old sweetheart "Ba";' and she dragged out a reindeer by the horn; he wore a bright copper ring round his neck, and was tied up. 'We are obliged to hold him tight too, or else he would run away from us also. I tickle his neck every evening with my sharp knife, which frightens him very much.' And then the robber-girl drew a long knife from a chink in the wall, and let it slide gently over the reindeer's neck. The poor animal began to kick, and the little robber-girl laughed, and pulled down Gerda into bed with her.

'Will you have that knife with you while you are asleep?' asked Gerda, looking at it in great fright.

'I always sleep with the knife by me,' said the robber-girl. 'No one knows what may happen. But now tell me again all about little Kay, and why you went out into the world.'

Then Gerda repeated her story over again, while the wood-pigeons in the cage over her cooed, and the other pigeons slept. The little robber-girl put one arm across Gerda's neck, and held the knife in the other, and was soon fast asleep and snoring. But Gerda could not close her eyes at all; she knew not whether she was to live or die. The robbers sat round the fire, singing and drinking, and the old woman stumbled about. It was a terrible sight for a little girl to witness.

Then the wood-pigeons said, 'Coo, coo; we have seen little Kay. A white fowl carried his sledge, and he sat in the carriage of the Snow Queen, which drove through the wood while we were lying in our nest. She blew upon us, and all the young ones died excepting us two. Coo, coo.'

'What are you saying up there?' cried Gerda. 'Where was the Snow Queen going? Do you know anything about it?'

'She was most likely travelling to Lapland, where there is always snow and ice. Ask the reindeer that is fastened up there with a rope.'

'Yes, there is always snow and ice,' said the reindeer; 'and it is a glorious place; you can leap and run about freely on the sparkling ice plains. The Snow Queen has her summer tent there, but her strong castle is at the North Pole, on an island called Spitzbergen.'

'Oh, Kay, little Kay!' sighed Gerda.

'Lie still,' said the robber-girl, 'or I shall run my knife into your body.'

In the morning Gerda told her all that the wood-pigeons had said; and the little robber-girl looked quite serious, and nodded her head, and said, 'That is all talk, that is all talk. Do you know where Lapland is?' she asked the reindeer.

'Who should know better than I do?' said the animal, while his eyes sparkled. 'I was born and brought up there, and used to run about the snow-covered plains.'

'Now listen,' said the robber-girl; 'all our men are gone away – only mother is here, and here she will stay; but at noon she always drinks out of a great bottle, and afterwards sleeps for a little while; and then, I'll do something for you.' Then she jumped out of bed, clasped her mother round the neck, and pulled her by the beard, crying, 'My own little nanny goat, good morning.' Then

THE SNOW QUEEN

her mother filliped her nose till it was quite red; yet she did it all for love.

When the mother had drunk out of the bottle, and was gone to sleep, the little robber-maiden went to the reindeer, and said, 'I should like very much to tickle your neck a few times more with my knife, for it makes you look so funny; but never mind – I will untie your cord, and set you free, so that you may run away to Lapland; but you must make good use of your legs, and carry this little maiden to the castle of the Snow Queen, where her play-fellow is. You have heard what she told me, for she spoke loud enough, and you were listening.'

Then the reindeer jumped for joy; and the little robber-girl lifted Gerda on his back, and had the forethought to tie her on, and even to give her her own little cushion to sit on.

'Here are your fur boots for you,' said she; 'for it will be very cold; but I must keep the muff; it is so pretty. However, you shall not be frozen for the want of it; here are my mother's large warm mittens; they will reach up to your elbows. Let me put them on. There, now your hands look just like my mother's.'

But Gerda wept for joy.

'I don't like to see you fret,' said the little robber-girl; 'you ought to look quite happy now; and here are two loaves and a ham, so that you need not starve.' These were fastened on the reindeer, and then the little robber-maiden opened the door, coaxed in all the great dogs, and then cut the string with which the reindeer was fastened, with her sharp knife, and said, 'Now run, but mind you take good care of the little girl.' And then Gerda stretched out her hand, with the great mitten on it, towards the little robber-girl, and said, 'Farewell,' and away flew the reindeer, over stumps and stones, through the great forest, over marshes and plains, as quickly as he could. The wolves howled, and the ravens screamed; while up in the sky quivered red lights like flames of fire. 'There are my old northern lights,' said the reindeer; 'see how they flash.' And he ran on day and night still faster and faster, but the loaves and the ham were all eaten by the time they reached Lapland.

SIXTH STORY:
THE LAPLAND WOMAN AND THE FINLAND WOMAN

They stopped at a little hut; it was very mean-looking; the roof sloped nearly down to the ground, and the door was so low that the family had to creep in on their hands and knees, when they went in and out. There was no one at home but an old Lapland woman, who was cooking fish by the light of a train-oil lamp. The reindeer told her all about Gerda's story, after having first told his own, which seemed to him the most important, but Gerda was so pinched with the cold that she could not speak. 'Oh, you poor things,' said the Lapland woman, 'you have a long way to go yet. You must travel more than a hundred miles farther, to Finland. The Snow Queen lives there now, and she burns Bengal lights every evening. I will write a few words on a dried stock-fish, for I have no paper, and you can take it from me to the Finland woman who lives there; she can give you better information than I can.' So when Gerda was warmed, and had taken something to eat and drink, the woman wrote a few words on the dried fish, and told Gerda to take great care of it. Then she tied her again on the reindeer, and he set off at full speed. Flash, flash went the beautiful blue northern lights in the air the whole night long. And at length they reached Finland, and knocked at the chimney of the Finland woman's hut, for it had no door above the ground. They crept in, but it was so terribly hot inside that that woman wore scarcely any clothes; she was small and very dirty looking. She loosened little Gerda's dress, and took off the fur boots and the mittens, or Gerda would have been unable to bear the heat; and then she placed a piece of ice on the reindeer's head, and read what was written on the dried fish. After she had read it three times, she knew it by heart, so she popped the fish into the soup saucepan, as she knew it was good to eat, and she never wasted anything. The reindeer told his own story first, and then little Gerda's, and the Finlander twinkled with her clever eyes, but she said nothing. 'You are so clever,' said the reindeer; 'I know you can tie all the winds of the world with a piece of twine. If a sailor unties one knot, he has a fair wind; when he unties the second, it blows hard; but if the third and fourth are loosened, then comes a storm, which will root up whole forests. Cannot you give this little maiden something which will make her as strong as twelve men, to overcome the Snow Queen?'

'The Power of twelve men!' said the Finland woman. 'That would be of very little use.' But she went to a shelf and took down and unrolled a large skin, on which were inscribed wonderful characters, and she read till the perspiration ran down from her forehead. But the reindeer begged so hard for little Gerda, and Gerda looked at the Finland woman with such beseeching tearful eyes, that her own eyes began to twinkle again; so she drew the reindeer into a corner, and whispered to him while she laid a fresh piece of ice on his head, 'Little Kay is really with the Snow Queen, but he finds everything there so much to his taste and his liking that he believes it is the finest place in the world; but this is because he has a piece of broken glass in his heart, and a little piece of glass in his eye. These must be taken out, or he will never be a human being again, and the Snow Queen will retain her power over him.'

'But can you not give little Gerda something to help her to conquer this power?'

'I can give her no greater power than she has already,' said the woman; 'don't you see how strong that is? How men and animals are obliged to serve her, and how well she has got through the world, barefooted as she is. She cannot receive any power from me greater than she now has, which consists in her own purity and innocence of heart. If she cannot herself obtain access to the Snow Queen, and remove the glass fragments from little Kay, we can do nothing to help her. Two miles from here the Snow Queen's garden begins; you can carry the little girl so far, and set her down by the large bush which stands in the snow, covered with red berries. Do not stay gossiping, but come back here as quickly as you can.' Then the Finland woman lifted little Gerda upon the reindeer, and he ran away with her as quickly as he could.

'Oh, I have forgotten my boots and my mittens,' cried little Gerda, as soon as she felt the cutting cold, but the reindeer dared not stop, so he ran on till he reached the bush with the red berries; here he set Gerda down, and he kissed her, and the great bright tears trickled over the animal's cheeks; then he left her and ran back as fast as he could.

There stood poor Gerda, without shoes, without gloves, in the midst of cold, dreary, ice-bound Finland. She ran forwards as quickly as she could, when a whole regiment of snow-flakes came round her; they did not, however, fall from the sky, which was quite clear and glittering with the northern lights. The snow-flakes ran along the ground, and the nearer they came to her, the larger they appeared. Gerda remembered how large and beautiful they looked through the burning-glass. But these were really larger, and much more terrible, for they were alive, and were the guards of the Snow Queen, and had the strangest shapes. Some were like great porcupines, others like twisted serpents with their heads stretching out, and some few were like little fat bears with their hair bristled; but all were dazzlingly white, and all were living snow-flakes. Then little Gerda repeated the Lord's Prayer, and the cold was so great that she could see her own breath come out of her mouth like steam as she uttered the words. The steam appeared to increase, as she continued her prayer, till it took the shape of little angels who grew larger the moment they touched the earth. They all wore helmets on their heads, and carried spears and shields. Their number continued to increase more and more; and by the time Gerda had finished her prayers, a whole legion stood round her. They thrust their spears into the terrible snow-flakes, so that they shivered into a hundred pieces, and little Gerda could go forward with courage and safety. The angels stroked her hands and feet, so that she felt the cold less, and she hastened on to the Snow Queen's castle.

But now we must see what Kay is doing. In truth he thought not of little Gerda, and never supposed she could be standing in the front of the palace.

SEVENTH STORY:
OF THE PALACE OF THE SNOW QUEEN AND WHAT HAPPENED THERE AT LAST

The walls of the palace were formed of drifted snow, and the windows and doors of the cutting winds. There were more than a hundred rooms in it, all as if they had been formed with snow blown together. The largest of them extended for several miles; they were all lighted up by the vivid light of the aurora, and they were so large and empty, so icy-cold and glittering! There were no amusements here, not even a little bear's ball, when the storm might have been the music, and the bears could have danced on their hind legs, and shown their good manners. There were no pleasant games of snap-dragon, or touch, or even a gossip over the tea-table, for the young-lady foxes. Empty, vast and cold were the halls of the Snow Queen. The flickering flame of the northern lights could be plainly seen, whether they rose high or low in the heavens, from every part of the castle. In the midst of its empty, endless hall of snow was a frozen lake, broken on its surface into a thousand forms; each piece resembled another, from being in itself perfect as a work of art, and in the centre of this lake sat the Snow Queen, when she was at home. She called the lake 'The Mirror of Reason', and said that it was the best, and indeed the only one in the world.

Little Kay was quite blue with cold, indeed almost black, but he did not feel it; for the Snow Queen had kissed away the icy shiverings, and his heart was already a lump of ice. He dragged some sharp, flat pieces of ice to and fro, and placed them together in all kinds of positions, as if he wished to make something out of them; just as we try to form various figures with little tablets of wood which we call 'a Chinese puzzle'. Kay's fingers were very artistic; it was the icy game of reason at which he played, and in his eyes the figures were very remarkable, and of the highest importance; this opinion was owing to the piece of glass still sticking in his eye. He composed many complete figures, forming different words, but there was one word he never could manage to form, although he wished it very much. It was the word 'Eternity'. The

Snow Queen had said to him, 'When you can find out this, you shall be your own master, and I will give you the whole world and a new pair of skates.' But he could not accomplish it.

'Now I must hasten away to warmer countries,' said the Snow Queen. 'I will go and look into the black craters of the tops of the burning mountains, Etna and Vesuvius, as they are called – I shall make them look white, which will be good for them, and for the lemons and the grapes.' And away flew the Snow Queen, leaving little Kay quite alone in the great hall which was so many miles in length; so he sat and looked at his pieces of ice, and was thinking so deeply, and sat so still, that any one might have supposed he was frozen.

Just at this moment it happened that little Gerda came through the great door of the castle. Cutting winds were raging around her, but she offered up a prayer and the winds sank down as if they were going to sleep; and she went on till she came to the large empty hall, and caught sight of Kay; she knew him directly; she flew to him and threw her arms round his neck, and held him fast, while she exclaimed, 'Kay, dear little Kay, I have found you at last.'

But he sat quite still, stiff and cold.

Then little Gerda wept hot tears, which fell on his breast, and penetrated into his heart, and thawed the lump of ice, and washed away the little piece of glass which had stuck there. Then he looked at her, and she sang –

'Roses bloom and cease to be,
But we shall the Christ-child see.'

Then Kay burst into tears, and he wept so that the splinter of glass swam out of his eye. Then he recognized Gerda, and said, joyfully, 'Gerda, dear little Gerda, where have you been all this time, and where have I been?' And he looked all around him, and said, 'How cold it is, and how large and empty it all looks,' and he clung to Gerda, and she laughed and wept for joy. It was so pleasing to see them that the pieces of ice even danced about; and when they were tired and went to lie down, they formed themselves into the letters of the word which the Snow Queen had said he must find out before he could be his own master, and have the whole world and a pair of new skates. Then Gerda kissed his cheeks, and they became blooming; and she kissed his eyes, and they shone like her own; she kissed his hands and his feet, and then he became quite healthy and cheerful. The Snow Queen might come home now when she pleased, for there stood his certainty of freedom, in the word she wanted, written in shining letters of ice.

Then they took each other by the hand, and went forth from the great palace of ice. They spoke of the grandmother, and of the roses on the roof, and as they went on the winds were at rest, and the sun burst forth. When they arrived at the bush with red berries, there stood the reindeer waiting for them, and he had brought another young reindeer with him, whose udders were full, and the children drank her warm milk and kissed her on the mouth. Then they carried Kay and Gerda first to the Finland woman, where they warmed themselves thoroughly in the hot room, and she gave them directions about their journey home. Next they went to the Lapland woman, who had made some new clothes for them, and put their sleighs in order. Both the reindeer ran by their side, and followed them as far as the boundaries of the country, where the first green leaves were budding. And here they took leave of the two reindeer and the Lapland woman, and all said farewell. Then the birds began to twitter, and the forest too was full of green young leaves; and out of it came a beautiful horse, which Gerda remembered, for it was one which had drawn the golden coach. A young girl was riding upon it, with a shining red cap on her head, and pistols in her belt. It was the little robber-maiden, who had got tired of staying at home; she was going first to the north, and if that did not suit her, she meant to try some other part of the world. She knew Gerda directly, and Gerda remembered her: it was a joyful meeting.

'You are a fine fellow to go gadding about in this way,' said she to little Kay, 'I should like to know whether you deserve that any one should go to the end of the world to find you.'

But Gerda patted her cheeks, and asked after the prince and princess.

'They are gone to foreign countries,' said the robber-girl.

'And the crow?' asked Gerda.

'Oh, the crow is dead,' she replied; 'his tame sweetheart is now a widow, and wears a bit of black worsted round her leg. She mourns very pitifully, but it is all stuff. But now tell me how you managed to get him back.'

Then Gerda and Kay told her all about it.

'Snip, snap, snare! It's all right at last,' said the robber-girl.

Then she took both their hands, and promised that if ever she should pass through the town, she would call and pay them a visit. And then she rode away into the wide world. But Gerda and Kay went hand-in-hand towards home; and as they advanced, spring appeared more lovely with its green verdure and its beautiful flowers. Very soon they recognised the large town where they lived, and the tall steeples of the churches, in which the sweet bells were ringing a merry peal as they entered it, and found their way to their grandmother's door. They went upstairs into the little room, where all looked just as it used to do. The old clock was going 'tick, tick', and the hands pointed to the time of day, but as they passed through the door into the room they perceived that they were both grown up, and become a man and woman. The roses out on the roof were in full bloom, and peeped in at the window; and there stood the little chairs, on which they had sat when children; and Kay and Gerda seated themselves each on their own chair, and held each other by the hand, while the cold empty grandeur of the Snow Queen's palace vanished from their memories like a painful dream. The grandmother sat in God's bright sunshine, and she read aloud from the Bible, 'Except ye become as little children, ye shall in no wise enter into the kingdom of God.' And Kay and Gerda looked into each other's eyes, and all at once understood the words of the old song,

'Roses bloom and cease to be,
But we shall the Christ-child see.'

And they both sat there, grown up, yet children at heart; and it was summer – warm, beautiful summer.

WHAT THE MOON SAW

INTRODUCTION

It is a strange thing, when I feel most fervently and most deeply, my hands and my tongue seem alike tied, so that I cannot rightly describe or accurately portray the thoughts that are rising within me; and yet I am a painter; my eye tells me as much as that, and all my friends who have seen my sketches and fancies say the same.

I am a poor lad, and live in one of the narrowest of lanes; but I do not want for light, as my room is high up in the house, with an extensive prospect over the neighbouring roofs. During the first few days I went to live in the town, I felt low-spirited and solitary enough. Instead of the forest and the green hills of former days, I had here only a forest of chimney-pots to look out upon. And then I had not a single friend; not one familiar face greeted me.

So one evening I sat at the window, in a desponding mood; and presently I opened the casement and looked out. Oh, how my heart leaped up with joy! Here was a well-known face at last – a round, friendly countenance, the face of a good friend I had known at home. In fact, it was the MOON that looked in upon me. He was quite unchanged, the dear old Moon, and had the same face exactly that he used to show when he peered down upon me through the willow trees on the moor. I kissed my hand to him over and over again, as he shone far into my little room; and he, for his part, promised me that every evening, when he came abroad, he would look in upon me for a few moments. This promise he has faithfully kept. It is a pity that he can only stay such a short time when he comes. Whenever he appears, he tells me of one thing or another that he has seen on the previous night, or on that same evening. 'Just paint the scenes I describe to you' – this is what he said to me – 'and you will have a very pretty picture-book.' I have followed his injunction for many evenings. I could make up a new *Thousand and One Nights*, in my own way, out of these pictures, but the number might be too great, after all. The pictures I have here given have not been chosen at random, but follow in their proper order, just as they were described to me. Some great gifted painter, or some poet or musician, may make something more of them if he likes; what I have given here are only hasty sketches, hurriedly put upon the paper, with some of my own thoughts, interspersed; for the Moon did not come to me every evening – a cloud sometimes hid his face from me.

FIRST EVENING

'Last night' – I am quoting the Moon's own words – 'last night I was gliding through the cloudless Indian sky. My face was mirrored in the waters of the Ganges, and my beams strove to pierce through the thick intertwining boughs of the bananas, arching beneath me like the tortoise's shell. Forth from the thicket tripped a Hindoo maid, light as a gazelle, beautiful as Eve. Airy and ethereal as a vision, and yet sharply defined amid the surrounding shadows, stood this daughter of Hindustan: I could read on her delicate brow the thought that had brought her hither. The thorny creeping plants tore her sandals, but for all that she came rapidly forward. The deer that had come down to the river to quench her thirst sprang by with a startled bound, for in her hand the maiden bore a lighted lamp. I could see the blood in her delicate finger tips, as she spread them for a screen before the dancing flame. She came down to the stream, and set the lamp upon the water, and let it float away. The flame flickered to and fro, and seemed ready to expire; but still the lamp burned on, and the girl's black sparkling eyes, half veiled behind their long silken lashes, followed it with a gaze of earnest intensity. She knew that if the lamp continued to burn so long as she could keep it in sight, her betrothed was still alive; but if the lamp was suddenly extinguished, he was dead. And the lamp burned bravely on, and she fell on her knees and prayed. Near her in the grass lay a speckled snake, but she heeded it not – she thought only of Bramah and of her betrothed. "He lives!" she shouted joyfully. "He lives!" And from the mountains the echo came back upon her, "He lives!"'

SECOND EVENING

'Yesterday,' said the Moon to me, 'I looked down upon a small courtyard surrounded on all sides by houses. In the courtyard sat a clucking hen with eleven chickens; and a pretty little girl was running and jumping around them. The hen was frightened, and screamed, and spread out her wings over the little brood. Then the girl's father came out and scolded her; and I glided away and thought no more of the matter.

'But this evening, only a few minutes ago, I looked down into the same courtyard. Everything was quiet. But presently the little girl came forth again, crept quietly to the hen-house, pushed back the bolt, and slipped into the apartment of the hen and chickens. They cried out loudly, and came fluttering down from their perches, and ran about in dismay, and the little girl ran after them. I saw it quite plainly, for I looked through a hole in the hen-house wall. I was angry with the willful child, and felt glad when her father came out and scolded her more violently than yesterday, holding her roughly by the arm; she held down her head, and her blue eyes were full of large tears. "What are you about here?" he asked. She wept and said, "I wanted to kiss the hen and beg her pardon for frightening her yesterday; but I was afraid to tell you."

'And the father kissed the innocent child's forehead, and I kissed her on the mouth and eyes.'

THIRD EVENING

'In the narrow street round the corner yonder – it is so narrow that my beams can only glide for a minute along the walls of the house, but in that minute I see enough to learn what the world is made of – in that narrow street I saw a woman. Sixteen years ago that woman was a child, playing in the garden of the old parsonage, in the country. The hedges of rose-bush were old, and the flowers were faded. They straggled wild over the paths, and the ragged branches grew up among the boughs of the apple trees; here and there were a few roses still in bloom – not so fair as the queen of flowers generally appears, but still they had colour and scent too. The clergyman's little daughter appeared to me a far lovelier rose, as she sat on her stool under the straggling hedge, hugging and caressing her doll with the battered pasteboard cheeks.

'Ten years afterwards I saw her again. I beheld her in a splendid ballroom: she was the beautiful bride of a rich merchant. I rejoiced at her happiness, and sought her on calm quiet evenings – ah, nobody thinks of my clear eye and my silent glance! Alas! My rose ran wild, like the rose bushes in the garden of the parsonage. There are tragedies in everyday life, and tonight I saw the last act of one.

'She was lying in bed in a house in that narrow street: she was sick unto death, and the cruel landlord came up, and tore away the thin coverlet, her only protection against the cold. "Get up!" said he; "your face is enough to frighten one. Get up and dress yourself, give me money, or I'll turn you out into the street! Quick – get up!" She answered, "Alas! Death is gnawing at my heart. Let me rest." But he forced her to get up and bathe her face, and put a wreath of roses in her hair; and he placed her in a chair at the window, with a candle burning beside her, and went away.

'I looked at her, and she was sitting motionless, with her hands in her lap. The wind caught the open window and shut it with a crash, so that a pane came clattering down in fragments; but still she never moved. The curtain caught fire, and the flames played about her face; and I saw that she was dead. There at the open window sat the dead woman, preaching a sermon against sin – my poor faded rose out of the parsonage garden!'

FOURTH EVENING

'This evening I saw a German play acted,' said the Moon. 'It was in a little town. A stable had been turned into a theatre; that is to say, the stable had been left standing, and had been turned into private boxes, and all the timber work had been covered with coloured paper. A little iron chandelier hung beneath the ceiling, and that it might be made to disappear into the ceiling, as it does in great theatres, when the ting-ting of the prompter's bell is heard, a great inverted tub has been placed just above it.

'"Ting-ting!" and the little iron chandelier suddenly rose at least half a yard and disappeared in the tub; and that was the sign that the play was going to begin. A young nobleman and his lady, who happened to be passing through the little town, were present at the performance, and consequently the house was crowded. But under the chandelier was a vacant space like a little crater: not a single soul sat there, for the tallow was dropping, drip, drip! I saw everything, for it was so warm in there that every loophole had been opened. The male and female servants stood outside, peeping through the chinks, although a real policeman was inside, threatening them with a stick. Close by the orchestra could be seen the noble young couple in two old armchairs, which were usually occupied by his worship the mayor and his lady; but these latter were today obliged to content themselves with wooden forms, just as if they had been ordinary citizens; and the lady observed quietly to herself, "One sees, now, that there is rank above rank;" and this incident gave an air of extra festivity to the whole proceedings. The chandelier gave little leaps, the crowd got their knuckles rapped, and I, the Moon, was present at the performance from beginning to end.'

FIFTH EVENING

'Yesterday,' began the Moon, 'I looked down upon the turmoil of Paris. My eye penetrated into an apartment of the Louvre. An old grandmother, poorly clad – she belonged to the working class – was following one of the under-servants into the great empty throne-room, for this was the apartment she wanted to see – that she was resolved to see; it had cost her many a little sacrifice, and many a coaxing word, to penetrate thus far. She folded her thin hands, and looked round with an air of reverence, as if she had been in a church.

'"Here it was!" she said. "Here!" And she approached the throne, from which hung the rich velvet fringed with gold lace. "There," she exclaimed, "there!" And she knelt and kissed the purple carpet. I think she was actually weeping.

'"But it was not this very velvet!" observed the footman, and a smile played about his mouth. "True, but it was this very place," replied the woman, "and it must have looked just like this." "It looked so, and yet it did not," observed the man: "the windows were beaten in, and the doors were off their hinges, and there was blood upon the floor." "But for all that you can say, my grandson died upon the throne of France. Died!" mournfully repeated the old woman. I do not think another word was spoken, and they soon quitted the hall. The evening twilight faded and my light shone doubly vivid upon the rich velvet that covered the throne of France.

'Now who do you think this poor woman was? Listen, I will tell you a story.

'It happened, in the Revolution of July, on the evening of the most brilliantly victorious day, when every house was a fortress, every window a breastwork. The people stormed the Tuileries. Even women and children were to be found among the combatants. They penetrated into the apartments and halls of the palace. A poor half-grown boy in a ragged blouse fought among the older insurgents. Mortally wounded with several bayonet thrusts, he sank down. This happened in the throne-room. They laid the bleeding youth upon the throne of France, wrapped the velvet around his wounds, and his blood streamed forth upon the imperial purple. There was a picture! The splendid hall, the fighting groups! A torn flag upon the ground, the tricolour was waving above the bayonets, and on the throne lay the poor lad with the pale glorified countenance, his eyes turned towards the sky, his limbs writhing in the death agony, his breast bare, and his poor tattered clothing half hidden by the rich velvet embroidered with silver lilies. At the boy's cradle a prophecy had been spoken: "He will die on the throne of France!" The mother's heart dreamt of a second Napoleon.

'My beams have kissed the wreath of immortelles on his grave, and this night they kissed the forehead of the old grandame, while in a dream the picture floated before her which thou mayest draw – the poor boy on the throne of France.'

SIXTH EVENING

'I've been in Uppsala,' said the Moon: 'I looked down upon the great plain covered with coarse grass, and upon the barren fields. I mirrored my face in the Tyris river, while the steamboat drove the fish into the rushes. Beneath me floated the waves, throwing long shadows on the so-called graves of Odin, Thor and Friga. In the scanty turf that covers the hillside names have been cut. There is no monument here, no memorial on which the traveller can have his name carved, no rocky wall on whose surface he can get it painted; so visitors have the turf cut away for that purpose. The naked earth peers through in the form of great letters and names; these form a network over the whole hill. Here is an immortality, which lasts till the fresh turf grows!

'Up on the hill stood a man, a poet. He emptied the mead horn with the broad silver rim, and murmured a name. He begged the winds not to betray him, but I heard the name. I knew it. A count's coronet sparkles above it, and therefore he did not speak it out. I smiled, for I knew that a poet's crown adorns his own name. The nobility of Eleanora d'Este is attached to the name of Tasso. And I also know where the Rose of Beauty blooms!'

Thus spake the Moon, and a cloud came between us. May no cloud separate the poet from the rose!

SEVENTH EVENING

'Along the margin of the shore stretches a forest of firs and beeches, and fresh and fragrant is this wood; hundreds of nightingales visit it every spring. Close beside it is the sea, the ever-changing sea, and between the two is placed the broad highroad. One carriage after another rolls over it; but I did not follow them, for my eye loves best to rest upon one point. A Hun's grave lies there, and the sloe and blackthorn grow luxuriantly among the stones. Here is true poetry in nature.

'And how do you think men appreciate this poetry? I will tell you what I heard there last evening and during the night.

'First, two rich landed proprietors came driving by. "Those are glorious trees!" said the first. "Certainly; there are ten loads of firewood in each," observed the other: "it will be a hard winter, and last year we got fourteen dollars a load" – and they were gone. "The road here is wretched," observed another man who drove past. "That's the fault of those horrible trees," replied his neighbour; "there is no free current of air; the wind can only come from the sea" – and they were gone. The stage coach went rattling past. All the passengers were asleep at this beautiful spot. The postillion blew his horn, but he only thought, "I can play capitally. It sounds well here. I wonder if those in there like it?" – and the stage coach vanished. Then two young fellows came galloping up on horseback. There's youth and spirit in the blood here, thought I; and, indeed, they looked with a smile at the moss-grown hill and thick forest. "I should not dislike a walk here with the miller's Christine," said one – and they flew past.

'The flowers scented the air; every breath of air was hushed; it seemed as if the sea were a part of the sky that stretched above the deep valley. A carriage rolled by. Six people were sitting in it. Four of them were asleep; the fifth was thinking of his new summer coat, which would suit him admirably; the sixth turned to the coachman and asked him if there were anything remarkable connected with yonder heap of stones. "No," replied the coachman, "it's only a heap of stones; but the trees are remarkable." "How so?" "Why I'll tell you how they are very remarkable. You see, in winter, when the snow lies very deep, and has hidden the whole road so that nothing is to be seen, those trees serve me for a landmark. I steer by them, so as not to drive into the sea; and you see that is why the trees are remarkable."

'Now came a painter. He spoke not a word, but his eyes sparkled. He began to whistle. At this the nightingales sang louder than ever. "Hold your tongues!" he cried testily; and he made accurate notes of all the colours and transitions – blue, and lilac, and dark brown. "That will make a beautiful picture," he said. He took it in just as a mirror takes in a view; and as he worked he whistled a march of Rossini. And last of all came a poor girl. She laid aside the burden she carried, and sat down to rest upon the Hun's grave. Her pale handsome face was bent in a listening attitude towards the forest. Her eyes brightened, she gazed earnestly at the sea and the sky, her hands were folded, and I think she prayed, "Our Father." She herself could not understand the feeling that swept through her, but I know that this minute, and the beautiful natural scene, will live within her memory for years, far more vividly and more truly than the painter could portray it with his colours on paper. My rays followed her till the morning dawn kissed her brow.'

EIGHTH EVENING

Heavy clouds obscured the sky, and the Moon did not make his appearance at all. I stood in my little room, more lonely than ever, and looked up at the sky where he ought to have shown himself. My thoughts flew far away, up to my great friend, who every evening told me such pretty tales, and showed me pictures. Yes, he has had an experience indeed. He glided over the waters of the Deluge, and smiled on Noah's ark just as he lately glanced down upon me, and brought comfort and promise of a new world that was to spring forth from the old. When the Children of Israel sat weeping by the waters of Babylon, he glanced mournfully upon the willows where hung the silent harps. When Romeo climbed the balcony, and the promise of true love fluttered like a cherub toward heaven, the round Moon hung, half hidden among the dark cypresses, in the lucid air. He saw the captive giant at St Helena, looking from the lonely rock across the wide ocean, while great thoughts swept through his soul. Ah! What tales the Moon can tell. Human life is like a story to him. Tonight I shall not see thee again, old friend. Tonight I can draw no picture of the memories of thy visit. And, as I looked dreamily towards the clouds, the sky became bright. There was a glancing light, and a beam from the Moon fell upon me. It vanished again, and dark clouds flew past: but still it was a greeting, a friendly good-night offered to me by the Moon.

NINTH EVENING

The air was clear again. Several evenings had passed, and the Moon was in the first quarter. Again he gave me an outline for a sketch. Listen to what he told me.

'I have followed the polar bird and the swimming whale to the eastern coast of Greenland. Gaunt ice-covered rocks and dark clouds hung over a valley, where dwarf willows and barberry bushes stood clothed in green. The blooming lychnis exhaled sweet odours. My light was faint, my face pale as the water lily that, torn from its stem, has been drifting for weeks with the tide. The crown-shaped

Northern Light burned fiercely in the sky. Its ring was broad, and from its circumference the rays shot like whirling shafts of fire across the whole sky, flashing in changing radiance from green to red. The inhabitants of that icy region were assembling for dance and festivity; but, accustomed to this glorious spectacle, they scarcely deigned to glance at it. "Let us leave the soul of the dead to their ball-play with the heads of the walruses," they thought in their superstition, and they turned their whole attention to the song and dance. In the midst of the circle, and divested of his furry cloak, stood a Greenlander, with a small pipe, and he played and sang a song about catching the seal, and the chorus around chimed in with, 'Eia, Eia, Ah.' And in their white furs they danced about in the circle, till you might fancy it was a polar bear's ball.

'And now a Court of Judgment was opened. Those Greenlanders who had quarrelled stepped forward, and the offended person chanted forth the faults of his adversary in an extempore song, turning them sharply into ridicule, to the sound of the pipe and the measure of the dance. The defendant replied with satire as keen, while the audience laughed, and gave their verdict. The rocks heaved, the glaciers melted, and great masses of ice and snow came crashing down, shivering to fragments as they fall; it was a glorious Greenland summer night. A hundred paces away, under the open tent of hides, lay a sick man. Life still flowed through his warm blood, but still he was to die – he himself felt it, and all who stood round him knew it also; therefore his wife was already sewing round him the shroud of furs, that she might not afterwards be obliged to touch the dead body. And she asked, "Wilt thou be buried on the rock, in the firm snow? I will deck the spot with thy kayak, and thy arrows, and the *angekokk* shall dance over it. Or wouldst thou rather be buried in the sea?" "In the sea," he whispered, and nodded with a mournful smile. "Yes, it is a pleasant summer tent, the sea," observed the wife. "Thousands of seals sport there, the walrus shall lie at thy feet, and the hunt will be safe and merry!" And the yelling children tore the outspread hide from the window-hole, that the dead man might be carried to the ocean, the billowy ocean, that had given him food in life, and that now, in death, was to afford him a place of rest. For his monument, he had the floating, ever-changing icebergs, whereon the seal sleeps, while the storm bird flies round their gleaming summits!'

TENTH EVENING

'I knew an old maid,' said the Moon. 'Every winter she wore a wrapper of yellow satin, and it always remained new, and was the only fashion she followed. In summer she always wore the same straw hat, and I verily believe the very same grey-blue dress.

'She never went out, except across the street to an old female friend; and in later years she did not even take this walk, for the old friend was dead. In her solitude my old maid was always busy at the window, which was adorned in summer with pretty flowers, and in winter with cress, grown upon felt. During the last months I saw her no more at the window, but she was still alive. I knew that, for I had not yet seen her begin the "long journey", of which she often spoke with her friend. "Yes, yes," she was in the habit of saying, "when I come to die I shall take a longer journey than I have made my whole life long. Our family vault is six miles from here. I shall be carried there, and shall sleep there among my family and relatives." Last night a van stopped at the house. A coffin was carried out, and then I knew that she was dead. They placed straw round the coffin, and the van drove away. There slept the quiet old lady, who had not gone out of her house once for the last year. The van rolled out through the town-gate as briskly as if it were going for a pleasant excursion. On the high-road the pace was quicker yet. The coachman looked nervously round every now and then – I fancy he half expected to see her sitting on the coffin, in her yellow satin wrapper. And because he was startled, he foolishly lashed his horses, while he held the reins so tightly that the poor beasts were in a foam: they were young and fiery. A hare jumped across the road and startled them, and they fairly ran away. The old sober maiden, who had for years and years moved quietly round and round in a dull circle, was now, in death, rattled over stock and stone on the public highway. The coffin in its covering of straw tumbled out of the van, and was left on the high-road, while horses, coachman and carriage flew past in wild career. The lark rose up carolling from the field, twittering her morning lay over the coffin, and presently perched upon it, picking with her beak at the straw covering, as though she would tear it up. The lark rose up again, singing gaily, and I withdrew behind the red morning clouds.'

ELEVENTH EVENING

'I will give you a picture of Pompeii,' said the Moon. 'I was in the suburb in the Street of Tombs, as they call it, where the fair monuments stand, in the spot where, ages ago, the merry youths, their temples bound with rosy wreaths, danced with the fair sisters of Lais. Now, the stillness of death reigned around. German mercenaries, in the Neapolitan service, kept guard, played cards and diced; and a troop of strangers from beyond the mountains came into the town, accompanied by a sentry. They wanted to see the city that had risen from the grave illumined by my beams; and I showed them the wheel-ruts in the streets paved with broad lava slabs; I showed them the names on the doors, and the signs that hung there yet: they saw in the little courtyard the basins of the fountains, ornamented with shells; but no jet of water gushed upwards, no songs sounded forth from the richly painted chambers, where the bronze dog kept the door.

'It was the City of the Dead; only Vesuvius thundered forth his everlasting hymn, each separate verse of which is called by men an eruption. We went to the temple of Venus, built of snow-white marble, with its high altar in front of the broad steps, and the weeping willows sprouting freshly forth among the pillars. The air was transparent and blue, and black Vesuvius formed the background, with fire ever shooting forth from it, like the stem of the pine tree. Above it stretched the smoky cloud in the silence of the night, like the crown of the pine, but in a blood-red illumination. Among the company was a lady singer, a real and great singer. I have witnessed the homage paid to her in the greatest cities of Europe. When they came to the tragic theatre, they all sat down on the amphitheatre steps, and thus a small part of the house was occupied by an audience, as it had been many centuries ago. The stage still stood unchanged, with its walled side-scenes, and the two arches in the background, through which the beholders saw the same scene that had been exhibited in the old times – a scene painted by nature herself, namely, the mountains between Sorento and Amalfi. The singer gaily mounted the ancient stage, and sang. The place inspired her, and she reminded me of a wild Arab horse that rushes headlong on with snorting nostrils and flying mane – her song was so light and yet so firm. Anon I thought of the mourning mother beneath the cross at Golgotha, so deep was the expression of pain. And, just as it had done thousands of years ago, the sound of applause and delight now filled the theatre. "Happy, gifted creature!" all the hearers exclaimed. Five minutes more, and the stage was empty, the company had vanished, and not a sound more was heard – all were gone. But the ruins stood unchanged, as they will stand when centuries shall have gone by, and when none shall know of the momentary applause and of the triumph of the fair songstress; when all will be forgotten and gone, and even for me this hour will be but a dream of the past.'

TWELFTH EVENING

'I looked through the windows of an editor's house,' said the Moon. 'It was somewhere in Germany. I saw handsome furniture, many books and a chaos of newspapers. Several young men were present: the editor himself stood at his desk, and two little books, both by young authors, were to be noticed. "This one has been sent to me," said he. "I have not read it yet; what think you of the contents?" "Oh," said the person addressed – he was a poet himself – "it is good enough; a little broad, certainly; but, you see, the author is still young. The verses might be better, to be sure; the thoughts are sound, though there is certainly a good deal of common-place among them. But what will you have? You can't be always getting something new. That he'll turn out anything great I don't believe, but you may safely praise him. He is well read, a remarkable Oriental scholar, and has a good judgment. It was he who wrote that nice review of my *Reflections on Domestic Life*. We must be lenient towards the young man."

"'But he is a complete hack!' objected another of the gentlemen. "Nothing worse in poetry than mediocrity, and he certainly does not go beyond this."

"'Poor fellow,' observed a third, 'and his aunt is so happy about him. It was she, Mr. Editor, who got together so many subscribers for your last translation.'

"'Ah, the good woman! Well, I have noticed the book briefly. Undoubted talent – a welcome offering – a flower in the garden of poetry – prettily brought out – and so on. But this other book – I suppose the author expects me to purchase it? I hear it is praised. He has genius, certainly: don't you think so?"

"'Yes, all the world declares as much,' replied the poet, "but it has turned out rather wildly. The punctuation of the book, in particular, is very eccentric."

"'It will be good for him if we pull him to pieces, and anger him a little, otherwise he will get too good an opinion of himself.'

"'But that would be unfair,' objected the fourth. "Let us not carp at little faults, but rejoice over the real and abundant good that we find here: he surpasses all the rest."

"'Not so. If he is a true genius, he can bear the sharp voice of censure. There are people enough to praise him. Don't let us quite turn his head."

"'Decided talent,' wrote the editor, "with the usual carelessness. that he can write incorrect verses may be seen in page 25, where there are two false quantities. We recommend him to study the ancients, etc."

'I went away,' continued the Moon, 'and looked through the windows in the aunt's house. There sat the be-praised poet, the tame one; all the guests paid homage to him, and he was happy.

'I sought the other poet out, the wild one; him also I found in a great assembly at his patron's, where the tame poet's book was being discussed.

'"I shall read yours also," said Maecenas; "but to speak honestly – you know I never hide my opinion from you – I don't expect much from it, for you are much too wild, too fantastic. But it must be allowed that, as a man, you are highly respectable."

'A young girl sat in a corner; and she read in a book these words:

In the dust lies genius and glory,
But ev'ryday talent will pay.
It's only the old, old story,
But the piece is repeated each day.

THIRTEENTH EVENING

The Moon said, 'Beside the woodland path there are two small farm-houses. The doors are low, and some of the windows are placed quite high, and others close to the ground; and whitethorn and barberry bushes grow around them. The roof of each house is overgrown with moss and with yellow flowers and houseleek. Cabbage and potatoes are the only plants cultivated in the gardens, but out of the hedge there grows a willow tree, and under this willow tree sat a little girl, and she sat with her eyes fixed upon the old oak tree between the two huts.

'It was an old withered stem. It had been sawn off at the top, and a stork had built his nest upon it; and he stood in this nest clapping with his beak. A little boy came and stood by the girl's side: they were brother and sister.

'"What are you looking at?" he asked.

'"I'm watching the stork," she replied: "our neighbours told me that he would bring us a little brother or sister today; let us watch to see it come!"

'"The stork brings no such things," the boy declared, "you may be sure of that. Our neighbour told me the same thing, but she laughed when she said it, and so I asked her if she could say 'On my honour,' and she could not; and I know by that the story about the storks is not true, and that they only tell it to us children for fun."

'"But where do babies come from, then?" asked the girl.

'"Why, an angel from heaven brings them under his cloak, but no man can see him; and that's why we never know when he brings them."

'At that moment there was a rustling in the branches of the willow tree, and the children folded their hands and looked at one another: it was certainly the angel coming with the baby. They took each other's hand, and at that moment the door of one of the houses opened, and the neighbour appeared.

'"Come in, you two," she said. "See what the stork has brought. It is a little brother."

'And the children nodded gravely at one another, for they had felt quite sure already that the baby was come.'

FOURTEENTH EVENING

'I was gliding over the Luneburg Heath,' the Moon said. 'A lonely hut stood by the wayside, a few scanty bushes grew near it, and a nightingale who had lost his way sang sweetly. He died in the coldness of the night: it was his farewell song that I heard.

'The morning dawn came glimmering red. I saw a caravan of emigrant peasant families who were bound to Hamburg, there to take ship for America, where they fancied prosperity would bloom for them. The mothers carried their little children at their backs, the elder ones tottered by their sides, and a poor starved horse tugged at a cart that bore their scanty effects. The cold wind whistled, and therefore the little girl nestled closer to the mother, who, looking up at my decreasing disc, thought of the bitter want at home, and spoke of the heavy taxes they had not been able to raise. The whole caravan thought of the same thing; therefore, the rising dawn seemed to them a message from the sun, of fortune that was to gleam brightly upon them. They heard the dying nightingale sing; it was no false prophet, but a harbinger of fortune. The wind whistled, therefore they did not understand that the nightingale sung, "Far away over the sea! Thou hast paid the long passage with all that was thine, and poor and helpless shalt thou enter Canaan. Thou must sell thyself, thy wife, and thy children. But your griefs shall not last long. Behind the broad fragrant leaves lurks the goddess of Death, and her welcome kiss shall breathe fever into thy blood. Far away, far away, over the heaving billows." And the caravan listened well pleased to the song of the nightingale, which seemed to promise good fortune. Day broke through the light clouds; country people went across the heath to church; the black-gowned women with their white head-dresses looked like ghosts that had stepped forth from the church pictures. All around lay a wide dead plain, covered with faded brown heath, and black charred spaces between the white sand hills. The women carried hymn books, and walked into the church. Oh, pray, pray for those who are wandering to find graves beyond the foaming billows.'

FIFTEENTH EVENING

'I know a Pulcinella,' the Moon told me. 'The public applaud vociferously directly they see him. Every one of his movements is comic, and is sure to throw the house into convulsions of laughter; and yet there is no art in it all – it is complete nature. When he was yet a little boy, playing about with other boys, he was already Punch. Nature had intended him for it, and had provided him with a hump on his back, and another on his breast; but his inward man, his mind, on the contrary, was richly furnished. No one could surpass him in depth of feeling or in readiness of intellect. The theatre was his ideal world. If he had possessed a slender well-shaped figure, he might have been the first tragedian on any stage; the heroic, the great, filled his soul; and yet he had to become a Pulcinella. His very sorrow and melancholy did but increase the comic dryness of his sharply-cut features, and increased the laughter of the audience, who showered plaudits on their favourite. The lovely Columbine was indeed kind and cordial to him; but she preferred to marry the Harlequin. It would have been too ridiculous if beauty and ugliness had in reality paired together.

'When Pulcinella was in very bad spirits, she was the only one who could force a hearty burst of laughter, or even a smile from him: first she would be melancholy with him, then quieter, and at last quite cheerful and happy. "I know very well what is the matter with you," she said; "yes, you're in love!" And he could not help laughing. "I and Love," he cried, "that would have an absurd look. How the public would shout!" "Certainly, you are in love," she continued; and added with a comic pathos, "and I am the person you are in love with." You see, such a thing may be said when it is quite out of the question – and, indeed, Pulcinella burst out laughing, and gave a leap into the air, and his melancholy was forgotten.

'And yet she had only spoken the truth. He did love her, love her adoringly, as he loved what was great and lofty in art. At her wedding he was the merriest among the guests, but in the stillness of night he wept: if the public had seen his distorted face then, they would have applauded rapturously.

'And a few days ago, Columbine died. On the day of the funeral, Harlequin was not required to show himself on the boards, for he was a disconsolate widower. The director had to give a very merry piece, that the public might not too painfully miss the pretty Columbine and the agile Harlequin. Therefore Pulcinella had to be more boisterous and extravagant than ever; and he danced and capered, with despair in his heart; and the audience yelled, and shouted "bravo, bravissimo!" Pulcinella was actually called before the curtain. He was pronounced inimitable.

'But last night the hideous little fellow went out of the town, quite alone, to the deserted churchyard. The wreath of flowers on Columbine's grave was already faded, and he sat down there. It was a study for a painter. As he sat with his chin on his hands, his eyes turned up towards me, he looked like a grotesque monument – a Punch on a grave – peculiar and whimsical! If the people could have seen their favourite, they would have cried as usual, "Bravo, Pulcinella; bravo, bravissimo!"'

SIXTEENTH EVENING

Hear what the Moon told me. 'I have seen the cadet who had just been made an officer put on his handsome uniform for the first time; I have seen the young bride in her wedding dress, and the princess girl-wife happy in her gorgeous robes; but never have I seen a felicity equal to that of a little girl of four years old, whom I watched this evening. She had received a new blue dress, and a new pink hat, the splendid attire had just been put on, and all were calling for a candle, for my rays, shining in through the windows of the room, were not bright enough for the occasion, and further illumination was required. There stood the little maid, stiff and upright as a doll, her arms stretched painfully straight out away from the dress, and her fingers apart; and oh, what happiness beamed from her eyes, and from her whole countenance! "Tomorrow you shall go out in your new clothes," said her mother; and the little one looked up at her hat, and down at her frock, and smiled brightly. "Mother," she cried, "what will the little dogs think, when they see me in these splendid new things?"'

SEVENTEENTH EVENING

'I have spoken to you of Pompeii,' said the Moon; 'that corpse of a city, exposed in the view of living towns: I know another sight still more strange, and this is not the corpse, but the spectre of a city. Whenever the jetty fountains splash into the marble basins, they seem to me to be telling the story of the floating city. Yes, the spouting water may tell of her, the waves of the sea may sing of her fame! On the surface of the ocean a mist often rests, and that is her widow's veil. The bridegroom of the sea is dead, his palace and his city are his mausoleum! Dost thou know this city? She has never heard the rolling of wheels or the hoof-tread of horses in her streets, through which the fish swim, while the black gondola glides spectrally over the green water. I will show you the place,' continued the Moon, 'the largest square in it, and you will fancy yourself transported into the city of a fairy tale. The grass grows rank among the broad flagstones, and in the morning twilight thousands of tame pigeons flutter around the solitary lofty tower. On three sides you find yourself surrounded by cloistered walks. In these the silent Turk sits smoking his long pipe, the handsome Greek leans against the pillar and gazes at the upraised trophies and lofty masts, memorials of power that is gone. The flags hang down like mourning scarves. A girl rests there: she has put down her heavy pails filled with water, the yoke with which she has carried them rests on one of her shoulders, and she leans against the mast of victory. That is not a fairy palace you see before you yonder, but a church: the gilded domes and shining orbs flash back my beams; the glorious bronze horses up yonder have made journeys, like the bronze horse in the fairy tale: they have come hither, and gone hence, and have returned again. Do you notice the variegated splendour of the walls and windows? It looks as if Genius had followed the caprices of a child, in the adornment of these singular temples. Do you see the winged lion on the pillar? The gold glitters still, but his wings are tied – the lion is dead, for the king of the sea is dead; the great halls stand desolate, and where gorgeous paintings hung of yore, the naked wall now peers through. The lazzarone sleeps under the arcade, whose pavement in old times was to be trodden only by the feet of high nobility. From the deep wells, and perhaps from the prisons by the Bridge of Sighs, rise the accents of woe, as at the time when the tambourine was heard in the gay gondolas, and the golden ring was cast from the Bucentaur to Adria, the queen of the seas. Adria! Shroud thyself in mists; let the veil of thy widowhood shroud thy form, and clothe in the weeds of woe the mausoleum of thy bridegroom – the marble, spectral Venice.'

EIGHTEENTH EVENING

'I looked down upon a great theatre,' said the Moon. 'The house was crowded, for a new actor was to make his first appearance that night. My rays glided over a little window in the wall, and I saw a painted face with the forehead pressed against the panes. It was the hero of the evening. The knightly beard curled crisply about the chin; but there were tears in the man's eyes, for he had been hissed off, and indeed with reason. The poor Incapable! But Incapables cannot be admitted into the empire of Art. He had deep feeling, and loved his art enthusiastically, but the art loved not him. The prompter's bell sounded; "the hero enters with a determined air," so ran the stage direction in his part, and he had to appear before an audience who turned him into ridicule. When the piece was over, I saw a form wrapped in a mantle, creeping down the steps: it was the vanquished knight of the evening. The scene-shifters whispered to one another, and I followed the poor fellow home to his room. To hang one's self is to die a mean death, and poison is not always at hand, I know; but he thought of both. I saw how he looked at his pale face in the glass, with eyes half closed, to see if he should look well as a corpse. A man may be very unhappy, and yet exceedingly affected. He thought of death, of suicide; I believe he pitied himself, for he wept bitterly, and when a man has had his cry out he doesn't kill himself.

'Since that time a year had rolled by. Again a play was to be acted, but in a little theatre, and by a poor strolling company. Again I saw the well-remembered face, with the painted cheeks and the crisp beard. He looked up at me and smiled; and yet he had been hissed off only a minute before – hissed off from a wretched theatre, by a miserable audience. And tonight a shabby hearse rolled out of the town-gate. It was a suicide – our painted, despised hero. The driver of the hearse was the only person present, for no one followed except my beams. In a corner of the churchyard the corpse of the suicide was shovelled into the earth, and nettles will soon be growing rankly over his grave, and the sexton will throw thorns and weeds from the other graves upon it.'

NINETEENTH EVENING

'I come from Rome,' said the Moon. 'In the midst of the city, upon one of the seven hills, lie the ruins of the imperial palace. The wild fig tree grows in the clefts of the wall, and covers the nakedness thereof with its broad grey-green leaves; trampling among heaps of rubbish, the ass treads upon green laurels, and rejoices over the rank thistles. From this spot, whence the eagles of Rome once flew abroad, whence they "came, saw, and conquered", our door leads into a little mean house, built of clay between two pillars; the wild vine hangs like a mourning garland over the crooked window. An old woman and her little granddaughter live there: they rule now in the palace of the Caesars, and show to strangers the remains of its past glories. Of the splendid throne-hall only a naked wall yet stands, and a black cypress throws its dark shadow on the spot where the throne once stood. The dust lies several feet deep on the broken pavement; and the little maiden, now the daughter of the imperial palace, often sits there on her stool when the evening bells ring. The keyhole of the door close by she calls her turret window; through this she can see half Rome, as far as the mighty cupola of St Peter's.

'On this evening, as usual, stillness reigned around; and in the full beam of my light came the little granddaughter. On her head she carried an earthen pitcher of antique shape filled with water. Her feet were bare, her short frock and her white sleeves were torn. I kissed her pretty round shoulders, her dark eyes and black shining hair. She mounted the stairs; they were steep, having been made up of rough blocks of broken marble and the capital of a fallen pillar. The coloured lizards slipped away, startled, from before her feet, but she was not frightened at them. Already she lifted her hand to pull the door-bell – a hare's foot fastened to a string formed the bell-handle of the imperial palace. She paused for a moment – of what might she be thinking? Perhaps of the beautiful Christ-child, dressed in gold and silver, which was down below in the chapel, where the silver candlesticks gleamed so bright, and where her little friends sung the hymns in which she also could join? I know not. Presently she moved again – she stumbled: the earthen vessel fell from her head, and broke on the marble steps. She burst into tears. The beautiful daughter of the imperial palace wept over the worthless broken pitcher; with her bare feet she stood there weeping; and dared not pull the string, the bell-rope of the imperial palace!'

TWENTIETH EVENING

It was more than a fortnight since the Moon had shone. Now he stood once more, round and bright, above the clouds, moving slowly onward. Hear what the Moon told me.

'From a town in Fezzan I followed a caravan. On the margin of the sandy desert, in a salt plain, that shone like a frozen lake, and was only covered in spots with light drifting sand, a halt was made. The eldest of the company – the water gourd hung at his girdle, and on his head was a little bag of unleavened bread – drew a square in the sand with his staff, and wrote in it a few words out of the Koran, and then the whole caravan passed over the consecrated spot. A young merchant, a child of the East, as I could tell by his eye and his figure, rode pensively forward on his white snorting steed. Was he thinking, perchance, of his fair young wife? It was only two days ago that the camel, adorned with furs and with costly shawls, had carried her, the beauteous bride, round the walls of the city, while drums and cymbals had sounded, the women sang, and festive shots, of which the bridegroom fired the greatest number, resounded round the camel; and now he was journeying with the caravan across the desert.

'For many nights I followed the train. I saw them rest by the well-side among the stunted palms; they thrust the knife into the breast of the camel that had fallen, and roasted its flesh by the fire. My beams cooled the glowing sands, and showed them the black rocks, dead islands in the immense ocean of sand. No hostile tribes met them in their pathless route, no storms arose, no columns of sand whirled destruction over the journeying caravan. At home the beautiful wife prayed for her husband and her father. "Are they dead?" she asked of my golden crescent; "Are they dead?" she cried to my full disc. Now the desert lies behind them. This evening they sit beneath the lofty palm trees, where the crane flutters round them with its long wings, and the pelican watches them from the branches of the mimosa. The luxuriant herbage is trampled down, crushed by the feet of elephants. A troop of negroes are returning from a market in the interior of the land: the women, with copper buttons in their black hair, and decked out in clothes dyed with indigo, drive the heavily laden oxen, on whose backs slumber the naked black children. A negro leads a young lion which he has brought, by a string. They approach the caravan; the young merchant sits pensive and motionless, thinking of his beautiful wife, dreaming, in the land of the blacks, of his white lily beyond the desert. He raises his head, and – ' But at this moment a cloud passed before the Moon, and then another. I heard nothing more from him this evening.

TWENTY-FIRST EVENING

'I saw a little girl weeping,' said the Moon; 'she was weeping over the depravity of the world. She had received a most beautiful doll as a present. Oh, that was a glorious doll, so fair and delicate! She did not seem created for the sorrows of this world. But the brothers of the little girl, those great naughty boys, had set the doll high up in the branches of a tree and had run away.

'The little girl could not reach up to the doll, and could not help her down, and that is why she was crying. The doll must certainly have been crying too, for she stretched out her arms among the green branches, and looked quite mournful. Yes, these are the troubles of life of which the little girl had often heard tell. Alas, poor doll! It began to grow dark already; and suppose night were to come on completely! Was she to be left sitting on the bough all night long? No, the little maid could not make up her mind to that. "I'll stay with you," she said, although she felt anything but happy in her mind. She could almost fancy she distinctly saw little gnomes, with their high-crowned hats, sitting in the bushes; and further back in the long walk, tall spectres appeared to be dancing. They came nearer and nearer, and stretched out their hands towards the tree on which the doll sat; they laughed scornfully, and pointed at her with their fingers. Oh, how frightened the little maid was! "But if one has not done anything wrong," she thought, "nothing evil can harm one. I wonder if I have done anything wrong?" And she considered. "Oh, yes! I laughed at the poor duck with the red rag on her leg; she limped along so funnily, I could not help laughing; but it's a sin to laugh at animals." And she looked up at the doll. "Did you laugh at the duck too?" she asked; and it seemed as if the doll shook her head.'

TWENTY-SECOND EVENING

'I looked down upon Tyrol,' said the Moon, 'and my beams caused the dark pines to throw long shadows upon the rocks. I looked at the pictures of St Christopher carrying the Infant Jesus that are painted there upon the walls of the houses, colossal figures reaching from the ground to the roof. St Florian was represented pouring water on the burning house, and the Lord hung bleeding on the great cross by the wayside. To the present generation these are old pictures, but I saw when they were put up, and marked how one followed the other. On the brow of the mountain yonder is perched, like a swallow's nest, a lonely convent of nuns. Two of the sisters stood up in the tower tolling the bell; they were both young, and therefore their glances flew over the mountain out into the world. A travelling coach passed by below, the postillion wound his horn, and the poor nuns looked after the carriage for a moment with a mournful glance, and a tear gleamed in the eyes of the younger one. And the horn sounded faint and more faintly, and the convent bell drowned its expiring echoes.'

TWENTY-THIRD EVENING

Hear what the Moon told me. 'Some years ago, here in Copenhagen, I looked through the window of a mean little room. The father and mother slept, but the little son was not asleep. I saw the flowered cotton curtains of the bed move, and the child peep forth. At first I thought he was looking at the great clock, which was gaily painted in red and green. At the top sat a cuckoo, below hung the heavy leaden weights, and the pendulum with the polished disc of metal went to and fro, and said "tick, tick". But no, he was not looking at the clock, but at his mother's spinning wheel, that stood just underneath it. That was the boy's favourite piece of furniture, but he dared not touch it, for if he meddled with it he got a rap on the knuckles. For hours together, when his mother was spinning, he would sit quietly by her side, watching the murmuring spindle and the revolving wheel, and as he sat he thought of many things. Oh, if he might only turn the wheel himself! Father and mother were asleep; he looked at them, and looked at the spinning wheel, and presently a little naked foot peered out of the bed, and then a second foot, and then two little white legs. There he stood. He looked round once more, to see if father and mother were still asleep – yes, they slept; and now he crept softly, softly, in his short little nightgown, to the spinning wheel, and began to spin. The thread flew from the wheel, and the wheel whirled faster and faster. I kissed his fair hair and his blue eyes, it was such a pretty picture.

'At that moment the mother awoke. The curtain shook, she looked forth, and fancied she saw a gnome or some other kind of little spectre. "In Heaven's name!" she cried, and aroused her husband in a frightened way. He opened his eyes, rubbed them with his hands, and looked at the brisk little lad. "Why, that is Bertel," said he. And my eye quitted the poor room, for I have so much to see. At the same moment I looked at the halls of the Vatican, where the marble gods are enthroned. I shone upon the group of the Laocoon; the stone seemed to sigh. I pressed a silent kiss on the lips of the Muses, and they seemed to stir and move. But my rays lingered longest about the Nile group with the colossal god. Leaning against the Sphinx, he lies there thoughtful and meditative, as if he were thinking on the rolling centuries; and little love-gods sport with him and with the crocodiles. In the horn of plenty sat with folded arms a little tiny love-god, contemplating the great solemn river-god, a true picture of the boy at the spinning wheel – the features were exactly the same. Charming and life-like stood the little marble form, and yet the wheel of the year has turned more than a thousand times since the time when it sprang forth from the stone. Just as often as the boy in the little room turned the spinning wheel had the great wheel murmured, before the age could again call forth marble gods equal to those he afterwards formed.

'Years have passed since all this happened,' the Moon went on to say. 'Yesterday I looked upon a bay on the eastern coast of Denmark. Glorious woods are there, and high trees, an old knightly castle with red walls, swans floating in the ponds, and in the background appears, among orchards, a little town with a church. Many boats, the crews all furnished with torches, glided over the silent expanse – but these fires had not been kindled for catching fish, for everything had a festive look. Music sounded, a song was sung, and in one of the boats the man stood erect to whom homage was paid by the rest, a tall sturdy man, wrapped in a cloak. He had blue eyes and long white hair. I knew him, and thought of the Vatican, and of the group of the Nile, and the old marble gods. I thought of the simple little room where little Bertel sat in his night-shirt by the spinning wheel. The wheel of time has turned, and new gods have come forth from the stone. From the boats there arose a shout: "Hurrah, hurrah for Bertel Thorwaldsen!"'

TWENTY-FOURTH EVENING

'I will now give you a picture from Frankfort,' said the Moon. 'I especially noticed one building there. It was not the house in which Goethe was born, nor the old Council House, through whose grated windows peered the horns of the oxen that were roasted and given to the people when the emperors were crowned. No, it was a private house, plain in appearance, and painted green. It stood near the old Jews' Street. It was Rothschild's house.

'I looked through the open door. The staircase was brilliantly lighted: servants carrying wax candles in massive silver candlesticks stood there, and bowed low before an old woman, who was being brought downstairs in a litter. The proprietor of the house stood bare-headed, and respectfully imprinted a kiss on the hand of the old woman. She was his mother. She nodded in a friendly manner to him and to the servants, and they carried her into the dark narrow street, into a little house, that was her dwelling. Here her children had been born, from hence the fortune of the family had arisen. If she deserted the despised street and the little house, fortune would also desert her children. That was her firm belief.'

The Moon told me no more; his visit this evening was far too short. But I thought of the old woman in the narrow despised street. It would have cost her but a word, and a brilliant house would have arisen for her on the banks of the Thames – a word, and a villa would have been prepared in the Bay of Naples.

'If I deserted the lowly house, where the fortunes of my sons first began to bloom, fortune would desert them!' It was a superstition, but a superstition of such a class, that he who knows the story and has seen this picture need have only two words placed under the picture to make him understand it; and these two words are: 'a mother'.

TWENTY-FIFTH EVENING

'It was yesterday, in the morning twilight' – these are the words the Moon told me – 'in the great city no chimney was yet smoking – and it was just at the chimneys that I was looking. Suddenly a little head emerged from one of them, and then half a body, the arms resting on the rim of the chimney-pot. "Ya-hip! Ya-hip!" cried a voice. It was the little chimney-sweeper, who had for the first time in his life crept through a chimney, and stuck out his head at the top. "Ya-hip! Ya-hip!" Yes, certainly that was a very different thing to creeping about in the dark narrow chimneys! The air blew so fresh, and he could look over the whole city towards the green wood. The sun was just rising. It shone round and great, just in his face, that beamed with triumph, though it was very prettily blacked with soot.

'"The whole town can see me now," he exclaimed, "and the moon can see me now, and the sun too. Ya-hip! Ya-hip!" And he flourished his broom in triumph.'

TWENTY-SIXTH EVENING

'Last night I looked down upon a town in China,' said the Moon. 'My beams irradiated the naked walls that form the streets there. Now and then, certainly, a door is seen; but it is locked, for what does the Chinaman care about the outer world? Close wooden shutters covered the windows behind the walls of the houses; but through the windows of the temple a faint light glimmered. I looked in, and saw the quaint decorations within. From the floor to the ceiling pictures are painted, in the most glaring colours, and richly gilt – pictures representing the deeds of the gods here on earth. In each niche statues are placed, but they are almost entirely hidden by the coloured drapery and the banners that hang down. Before each idol (and they are all made of tin) stood a little altar of holy water, with flowers and burning wax lights on it. Above all the rest stood Fo, the chief deity, clad in a garment of yellow silk, for yellow is here the sacred colour. At the foot of the altar sat a living being, a young priest. He appeared to be praying, but in the midst of his prayer he seemed to fall into deep thought, and this must have been wrong, for his cheeks glowed and he held down his head. Poor Soui-Hong! Was he, perhaps, dreaming of working in the little flower garden behind the high street wall? And did that occupation seem more agreeable to him than watching the wax lights in the temple? Or did he wish to sit at the rich feast, wiping his mouth with silver paper between each course? Or was his sin so great that, if he dared utter it, the Celestial Empire would punish it with death? Had his thoughts ventured to fly with the ships of the barbarians, to their homes in far distant England? No, his thoughts did not fly so far, and yet they were sinful, sinful as thoughts born of young hearts, sinful here in the temple, in the presence of Fo and the other holy gods.

'I know whither his thoughts had strayed. At the farther end of the city, on the flat roof paved with porcelain, on which stood the handsome vases covered with painted flowers, sat the beauteous Pu, of the little roguish eyes, of the full lips, and of the tiny feet. The tight shoe pained her, but her heart pained her still more. She lifted her graceful round arm, and her satin dress rustled. Before her stood a glass bowl containing four goldfish. She stirred the bowl carefully with a slender lacquered stick, very slowly, for she, too, was lost in thought. Was she thinking, perchance, how the fishes were richly clothed in gold, how they lived calmly and peacefully in their crystal world, how they were regularly fed, and yet how much happier they might be if they were free? Yes, that she could well understand, the beautiful Pu. Her thoughts wandered away from her home, wandered to the temple, but not for the sake of holy things. Poor Pu! Poor Soui-hong!

'Their earthly thoughts met, but my cold beam lay between the two, like the sword of the cherub.'

TWENTY-SEVENTH EVENING

'The air was calm,' said the Moon; 'the water was transparent as the purest ether through which I was gliding, and deep below the surface I could see the strange plants that stretched up their long arms towards me like the gigantic trees of the forest. The fishes swam to and fro above their tops. High in the air a flight of wild swans were winging their way, one of which sank lower and lower, with wearied pinions, his eyes following the airy caravan, that melted farther and farther into the distance. With outspread wings he sank slowly, as a soap bubble sinks in the still air, till he touched the water. At length his head lay back between his wings, and silently he lay there, like a white lotus flower upon the quiet lake. And a gentle wind arose, and crisped the quiet surface, which gleamed like the clouds that poured along in great broad waves; and the swan raised his head, and the glowing water splashed like blue fire over his breast and back. The morning dawn illuminated the red clouds, the swan rose strengthened, and flew towards the rising sun, towards the bluish coast whither the caravan had gone; but he flew alone, with a longing in his breast. Lonely he flew over the blue swelling billows.'

TWENTY-EIGHTH EVENING

'I will give you another picture of Sweden,' said the Moon. 'Among dark pine woods, near the melancholy banks of the Stoxen, lies the old convent church of Wreta. My rays glided through the grating into the roomy vaults, where kings sleep tranquilly in great stone coffins. On the wall, above the grave of each, is placed the emblem of earthly grandeur, a kingly crown; but it is made only of wood, painted and gilt, and is hung on a wooden peg driven into the wall. The worms have gnawed the gilded wood, the spider has spun her web from the crown down to the sand, like a mourning banner, frail and transient as the grief of mortals. How quietly they sleep! I can remember them quite plainly. I still see the bold smile on their lips, that so strongly and plainly expressed joy or grief. When the steamboat winds along like a magic snail over the lakes, a stranger often comes to the church, and visits the burial vault; he asks the names of the kings, and they have a dead and forgotten sound. He glances with a smile at the worm-eaten crowns, and if he happens to be a pious, thoughtful man, something of melancholy mingles with the smile. Slumber on, ye dead ones! The Moon thinks of you, the Moon at night sends down his rays into your silent kingdom, over which hangs the crown of pine wood.'

TWENTY-NINTH EVENING

'Close by the high-road,' said the Moon, 'is an inn, and opposite to it is a great waggon-shed, whose straw roof was just being re-thatched. I looked down between the bare rafters and through the open loft into the comfortless space below. The turkey-cock slept on the beam, and the saddle rested in the empty crib. In the middle of the shed stood a travelling carriage; the proprietor was inside, fast asleep, while the horses were being watered. The coachman stretched himself, though I am very sure that he had been most comfortably asleep half the last stage. The door of the servants' room stood open, and the bed looked as if it had been turned over and over; the candle stood on the floor, and had burnt deep down into the socket. The wind blew cold through the shed: it was nearer to the dawn than to midnight. In the wooden frame on the ground slept a wandering family of musicians. The father and mother seemed to be dreaming of the burning liquor that remained in the bottle. The little pale daughter was dreaming too, for her eyes were wet with tears. The harp stood at their heads, and the dog lay stretched at their feet.'

THIRTIETH EVENING

'It was in a little provincial town,' the Moon said; 'it certainly happened last year, but that has nothing to do with the matter. I saw it quite plainly. Today I read about it in the papers, but there it was not half so clearly expressed. In the taproom of the little inn sat the bear leader, eating his supper; the bear was tied up outside, behind the wood pile – poor Bruin, who did nobody any harm, though he looked grim enough. Up in the garret three little children were playing by the light of my beams; the eldest was perhaps six years old, the youngest certainly not more than two. "Tramp, tramp" – somebody was coming upstairs: who might it be? The door was thrust open – it was Bruin, the great, shaggy Bruin! He had got tired of waiting down in the courtyard, and had found his way to the stairs. I saw it all,' said the Moon. 'The children were very much frightened at first at the great shaggy animal; each of them crept into a corner, but he found them all out, and smelt at them, but did them no harm. "This must be a great dog," they said, and began to stroke him. He lay down upon the ground, the youngest boy clambered on his back, and bending down a little head of golden curls, played at hiding in the beast's shaggy skin. Presently the eldest boy took his drum, and beat upon it till it rattled again; the bear rose upon his hind legs, and began to dance. It was a charming sight to behold. Each boy now took his gun, and the bear was obliged to have one too, and he held it up quite properly. Here was a capital playmate they had found; and they began marching – one, two; one, two.

'Suddenly someone came to the door, which opened, and the mother of the children appeared. You should have seen her in her dumb terror, with her face as white as chalk, her mouth half open, and her eyes fixed in a horrified stare. But the youngest boy nodded to her in great glee, and called out in his infantile prattle, "We're playing at soldiers." And then the bear leader came running up.'

THIRTY-FIRST EVENING

The wind blew stormy and cold, the clouds flew hurriedly past; only for a moment now and then did the Moon become visible. He said, 'I looked down from the silent sky upon the driving clouds, and saw the great shadows chasing each other across the earth. I looked upon a prison. A closed carriage stood before it; a prisoner was to be carried away. My rays pierced through the grated window towards the wall; the prisoner was scratching a few lines upon it, as a parting token; but he did not write words, but a melody, the outpouring of his heart. The door was opened, and he was led forth, and fixed his eyes upon my round disc. Clouds passed between us, as if he were not to see his face, nor I his. He stepped into the carriage, the door was closed, the whip cracked, and the horses galloped off into the thick forest, whither my rays were not able to follow him; but as I glanced through the grated window, my rays glided over the notes, his last farewell engraved on the prison wall – where words fail, sounds can often speak. My rays could only light up isolated notes, so the greater part of what was written there will ever remain dark to me. Was it the death-hymn he wrote there? Were these the glad notes of joy? Did he drive away to meet death, or hasten to the embraces of his beloved? The rays of the Moon do not read all that is written by mortals.'

THIRTY-SECOND EVENING

'I love the children,' said the Moon, 'especially the quite little ones – they are so droll. Sometimes I peep into the room, between the curtain and the window frame, when they are not thinking of me. It gives me pleasure to see them dressing and undressing. First, the little round naked shoulder comes creeping out of the frock, then the arm; or I see how the stocking is drawn off, and a plump little white leg makes its appearance, and a white little foot that is fit to be kissed, and I kiss it too.

'But about what I was going to tell you. This evening I looked through a window, before which no curtain was drawn, for nobody lives opposite. I saw a whole troop of little ones, all of one family, and among them was a little sister. She is only four years old, but can say her prayers as well as any of the rest. The mother sits by her bed every evening, and hears her say her prayers; and then she has a kiss, and the mother sits by the bed till the little one has gone to sleep, which generally happens as soon as ever she can close her eyes.

'This evening the two elder children were a little boisterous. One of them hopped about on one leg in his long white nightgown, and the other stood on a chair surrounded by the clothes of all the children, and declared he was acting Grecian statues. The third and fourth laid the clean linen carefully in the box, for that is a thing that has to be done; and the mother sat by the bed of the youngest, and announced to all the rest that they were to be quiet, for little sister was going to say her prayers.

'I looked in, over the lamp, into the little maiden's bed, where she lay under the neat white coverlet, her hands folded demurely and her little face quite grave and serious. She was praying the

Lord's Prayer aloud. But her mother interrupted her in the middle of her prayer. "How is it," she asked, "that when you have prayed for daily bread, you always add something I cannot understand? You must tell me what that is." The little one lay silent, and looked at her mother in embarrassment. "What is it you say after our daily bread?" "Dear mother, don't be angry: I only said, and plenty of butter on it.'"

THE MARSH KING'S DAUGHTER

The storks relate to their little ones a great many stories, and they are all about moors and reed banks, and suited to their age and capacity. The youngest of them are quite satisfied with 'kribble, krabble' or such nonsense, and think it very grand; but the elder ones want something with a deeper meaning, or at least something about their own family.

We are only acquainted with one of the two longest and oldest stories which the storks relate – it is about Moses, who was exposed by his mother on the banks of the Nile, and was found by the king's daughter, who gave him a good education, and he afterwards became a great man; but where he was buried is still unknown.

Everyone knows this story, but not the second; very likely because it is quite an inland story. It has been repeated from mouth to mouth, from one stork-mamma to another, for thousands of years; and each has told it better than the last; and now we mean to tell it better than all.

The first stork pair who related it lived at the time it happened, and had their summer residence on the rafters of the Viking's house, which stood near the wild moorlands of Wendsyssell; that is, to speak more correctly, the great moorheath, high up in the north of Jutland, by the Skjagen peak. This wilderness is still an immense wild heath of marshy ground, about which we can read in the 'Official Directory'. It is said that in olden times the place was a lake, the ground of which had heaved up from beneath, and now the moorland extends for miles in every direction, and is surrounded by damp meadows, trembling, undulating swamps, and marshy ground covered with turf, on which grow bilberry bushes and stunted trees. Mists are almost always hovering over this region, which, seventy years ago, was overrun with wolves. It may well be called the Wild Moor; and one can easily imagine, with such a wild expanse of marsh and lake, how lonely and dreary it must have been a thousand years ago. Many things may be noticed now that existed then. The reeds grow to the same height, and bear the same kind of long, purple-brown leaves, with their feathery tips. There still stands the birch, with its white bark and its delicate, loosely hanging leaves; and with regard to the living beings who frequented this spot, the fly still wears a gauzy dress of the same cut, and the favourite colours of the stork are white, with black and red for stockings. The people, certainly, in those days, wore very different dresses to those they now wear, but if any of them, be he huntsman or squire, master or servant, ventured on the wavering, undulating, marshy ground of the moor, they met with the same fate a thousand years ago as they would now. The wanderer sank, and went down to the Marsh King, as he is named, who rules in the great moorland empire beneath. They also called him 'Gunkel King', but we like the name of 'Marsh King' better, and we will give him that name as the storks do. Very little is known of the Marsh King's rule, but that, perhaps, is a good thing.

In the neighbourhood of the moorlands, and not far from the great arm of the North Sea and the Cattegat which is called the Lumfjorden, lay the castle of the Viking, with its water-tight stone cellars, its tower and its three projecting storeys. On the ridge of the roof the stork had built his nest, and there the stork-mamma sat on her eggs and felt sure her hatching would come to something.

One evening, stork-papa stayed out rather late, and when he came home he seemed quite busy, bustling, and important. 'I have something very dreadful to tell you,' said he to the stork-mamma.

'Keep it to yourself then,' she replied. 'Remember that I am hatching eggs; it may agitate me, and will affect them.'

'You must know it at once,' said he. 'The daughter of our host in Egypt has arrived here. She has ventured to take this journey, and now she is lost.'

'She who sprung from the race of the fairies, is it?' cried the mother stork. 'Oh, tell me all about it; you know I cannot bear to be kept waiting at a time when I am hatching eggs.'

'Well, you see, mother,' he replied, 'she believed what the doctors said, and what I have heard you state also, that the moor-flowers which grow about here would heal her sick father; and she has flown to the north in swan's plumage, in company with some other swan-princesses, who come to these parts every year to renew their youth. She came, and where is she now!'

'You enter into particulars too much,' said the mamma stork, 'and the eggs may take cold; I cannot bear such suspense as this.'

'Well,' said he, 'I have kept watch; and this evening I went among the rushes where I thought the marshy ground would bear me, and while I was there three swans came. Something in their manner of flying seemed to say to me, "Look carefully now; there is one not all swan, only swan's feathers." You know, mother, you have the same intuitive feeling that I have; you know whether a thing is right or not immediately.'

'Yes, of course,' said she; 'but tell me about the princess; I am tired of hearing about the swan's feathers.'

'Well, you know that in the middle of the moor there is something like a lake,' said the stork-papa. 'You can see the edge of it if you raise yourself a little. Just there, by the reeds and the green banks, lay the trunk of an elder-tree; upon this the three swans stood flapping their wings, and looking about them; one of them threw off her plumage, and I immediately recognised her as one of the princesses of our home in Egypt. There she sat, without any covering but her long, black hair. I heard her tell the two others to take great care of the swan's plumage, while she dipped down into the water to pluck the flowers which she fancied she saw there. The others nodded, and picked up the feather dress, and took possession of it. I wonder what will become of it, thought I, and she most likely asked herself the same question. If so, she received an answer, a very practical one; for the two swans rose up and flew away with her swan's plumage. 'Dive down now!' they cried. 'Thou shalt never more fly in the swan's plumage, thou shalt never again see Egypt; here, on the moor, thou wilt remain.' So saying, they tore the swan's plumage into a thousand pieces, the feathers drifted about like a snow-shower, and then the two deceitful princesses flew away.'

'Why, that is terrible,' said the stork-mamma; 'I feel as if I could hardly bear to hear any more, but you must tell me what happened next.'

'The princess wept and lamented aloud; her tears moistened the elder stump, which was really not an elder stump but the Marsh King himself, he who in marshy ground lives and rules. I saw myself how the stump of the tree turned round, and was a tree no more, while long, clammy branches like arms, were extended from it. Then the poor child was terribly frightened, and started up to run away. She hastened to cross the green, slimy ground; but it will not bear any weight, much less hers. She quickly sank, and the elder stump dived immediately after her; in fact, it was he who drew her down. Great black bubbles rose up out of the moor-slime, and with these every trace of the two vanished. And now the princess is buried in the wild marsh, she will never now carry flowers to Egypt to cure her father. It would have broken your heart, mother, had you seen it.'

'You ought not to have told me,' said she, 'at such a time as this; the eggs might suffer. But I think the princess will soon find help; someone will rise up to help her. Ah! If it had been you or I, or one of our people, it would have been all over with us.'

'I mean to go every day,' said he, 'to see if anything comes to pass;' and so he did.

A long time went by, but at last he saw a green stalk shooting up out of the deep, marshy ground. As it reached the surface of the marsh, a leaf spread out, and unfolded itself broader and broader, and close to it came forth a bud.

One morning, when the stork-papa was flying over the stem, he saw that the power of the sun's rays had caused the bud to open, and in the cup of the flower lay a charming child – a little maiden, looking as if she had just come out of a bath. The little one was so like the Egyptian princess, that the stork, at the first moment, thought it must be the princess herself, but after a little reflection he decided that it was much more likely to be the daughter of the princess and the Marsh King; and this explained also her being placed in the cup of a water-lily. 'But she cannot be left to lie here,' thought the stork, 'and in my nest there are already so many. But stay, I have thought of something: the wife of the Viking has no children, and how often she has wished for a little one. People always say the stork brings the little ones; I will do so in earnest this time. I shall fly with the child to the Viking's wife; what rejoicing there will be!'

And then the stork lifted the little girl out of the flower-cup, flew to the castle, picked a hole with his beak in the bladder-covered window, and laid the beautiful child in the bosom of the Viking's wife. Then he flew back quickly to the stork-mamma and told her what he had seen and done; and the little storks listened to it all, for they were then quite old enough to do so. 'So you see,' he continued, 'that the princess is not dead, for she must have sent her little one up here; and now I have found a home for her.'

'Ah, I said it would be so from the first,' replied the stork-mamma; 'but now think a little of your own family. Our travelling time draws near, and I sometimes feel a little irritation already under the wings. The cuckoos and the nightingale are already gone, and I heard the quails say they should go too as soon as the wind was favourable. Our youngsters will go through all the manoeuvres at the review very well, or I am much mistaken in them.'

The Viking's wife was above measure delighted when she awoke the next morning and found the beautiful little child lying in her bosom. She kissed it and caressed it; but it cried terribly, and struck out with its arms and legs, and did not seem to be pleased at all. At last it cried itself to sleep; and as it lay there so still and quiet, it was a most beautiful sight to see. The Viking's wife was so delighted, that body and soul were full of joy. Her heart felt so light within her, that it seemed as if her husband and his soldiers, who were absent, must come home as suddenly and unexpectedly as the little child had done. She and her whole household therefore busied themselves in preparing everything for the reception of her lord. The long, coloured tapestry, on which she and her maidens had worked pictures of their idols, Odin, Thor and Friga, was hung up. The slaves polished the old shields that served as ornaments; cushions were placed on the seats, and dry wood laid on the fireplaces in the centre of the hall, so that the flames might be fanned up at a moment's notice. The Viking's wife herself assisted in the work, so that at night she felt very tired, and quickly fell into a sound sleep. When she awoke, just before morning, she was terribly alarmed to find that the infant had vanished. She sprang from her couch, lighted a pine-chip, and searched all round the room, when, at last, in that part of the bed where her feet had been, lay, not the child, but a great, ugly frog. She was quite disgusted at this sight, and seized a heavy stick to kill the frog; but the creature looked at her with such strange, mournful eyes, that she was unable to strike the blow. Once more she searched round the room; then she started at hearing the frog utter a low, painful croak. She sprang from the couch and opened the window hastily; at the same moment the sun rose, and threw its beams through the window, till it rested on the couch where the great frog lay. Suddenly it appeared as if the frog's broad mouth contracted, and became small and red. The limbs moved and stretched out and extended themselves till they took a beautiful shape; and behold there was the pretty child lying before her, and the ugly frog was gone. 'How is this?' she cried, 'have I had a wicked dream? Is it not my own lovely cherub that lies there.' Then she kissed it and fondled it; but the child struggled and fought, and bit as if she had been a little wild cat.

The Viking did not return on that day, nor the next; he was, however, on the way home; but the wind, so favourable to the storks, was against him; for it blew towards the south. A wind in favour of one is often against another.

After two or three days had passed, it became clear to the Viking's wife how matters stood with the child; it was under the influence of a powerful sorcerer. By day it was charming in appearance as an angel of light, but with a temper wicked and wild; while at night, in the form of an ugly frog, it was quiet and mournful, with eyes full of sorrow. Here were two natures, changing inwardly and outwardly with the absence and return of sunlight. And so it happened that by day the child, with the actual form of its mother, possessed the fierce disposition of its father; at night, on the contrary, its outward appearance plainly showed its descent on the father's side, while inwardly it had the heart and mind of its mother. Who would be able to loosen this wicked charm which the sorcerer had worked upon it? The wife of the Viking lived in constant pain and sorrow about it. Her heart clung to the little creature, but she could not explain to her husband the circumstances in which it was placed. He was expected to return shortly; and were she to tell him, he would very likely, as was the custom at that time, expose the poor child in the public highway, and let any one take it away who would. The good wife of the Viking could not let that happen, and she therefore resolved that the Viking should never see the child excepting by daylight.

One morning there sounded a rushing of storks' wings over the roof. More than a hundred pair of storks had rested there during the night, to recover themselves after their excursion; and now they soared aloft, and prepared for the journey southward.

'All the husbands are here, and ready!' they cried. 'Wives and children also!'

'How light we are!' screamed the young storks in chorus. 'Something pleasant seems creeping over us, even down to our toes, as if we were full of live frogs. Ah, how delightful it is to travel into foreign lands!'

'Hold yourselves properly in the line with us,' cried papa and mamma. 'Do not use your beaks so much; it tries the lungs.' And then the storks flew away.

About the same time sounded the clang of the warriors' trumpets across the heath. The Viking had landed with his men. They were returning home, richly laden with spoil from the Gallic coast, where the people, as did also the inhabitants of Britain, often cried in alarm, 'Deliver us from the wild northmen.'

Life and noisy pleasure came with them into the castle of the Viking on the moorland. A great cask of mead was drawn into the hall, piles of wood blazed, cattle were slain and served up, that they might feast in reality, The priest who offered the sacrifice sprinkled the devoted parishioners with the warm blood; the fire crackled, and the smoke rolled along beneath the roof; the soot fell upon them from the beams; but they were used to all these things. Guests were invited, and received handsome presents. All wrongs and unfaithfulness were forgotten. They drank deeply, and threw in each other's faces the bones that were left, which was looked upon as a sign of good feeling amongst them. A bard, who was a kind of musician as well as warrior, and who had been with the Viking in his expedition, and knew what to sing about, gave them one of his best songs, in which they heard all their warlike deeds praised, and every wonderful action brought forward with honour. Every verse ended with this refrain, –

Gold and possessions will flee away,
Friends and foes must die one day;

Every man on earth must die,
But a famous name will never die.

And with that they beat upon their shields, and hammered upon the table with knives and bones, in a most outrageous manner.

The Viking's wife sat upon a raised cross seat in the open hall. She wore a silk dress, golden bracelets and large amber beads. She was in costly attire, and the bard named her in his song, and spoke of the rich treasure of gold which she had brought to her husband. Her husband had already seen the wonderfully beautiful child in the daytime, and was delighted with her beauty; even her wild ways pleased him. He said the little maiden would grow up to be a heroine, with the strong will and determination of a man. She would never wink her eyes, even if, in joke, an expert hand should attempt to cut off her eye-brows with a sharp sword.

The full cask of mead soon became empty, and a fresh one was brought in; for these were people who liked plenty to eat and drink. The old proverb, which every one knows, says that 'the cattle know when to leave their pasture, but a foolish man knows not the measure of his own appetite'. Yes, they all knew this; but men may know what is right, and yet often do wrong. They also knew 'that even the welcome guest becomes wearisome when he sits too long in the house'. But there they remained; for pork and mead are good things. And so at the Viking's house they stayed, and enjoyed themselves; and at night the bondmen slept in the ashes, and dipped their fingers in the fat, and licked them. Oh, it was a delightful time!

Once more in the same year the Viking went forth, though the storms of autumn had already commenced to roar. He went with his warriors to the coast of Britain; he said that it was but an excursion of pleasure across the water, so his wife remained at home with the little girl. After a while, it is quite certain the foster-mother began to love the poor frog, with its gentle eyes and its deep sighs, even better than the little beauty who bit and fought with all around her.

The heavy, damp mists of autumn, which destroy the leaves of the wood, had already fallen upon forest and heath. Feathers of plucked birds, as they call the snow, flew about in thick showers, and winter was coming. The sparrows took possession of the stork's nest, and conversed about the absent owners in their own fashion; and they, the stork pair and all their young ones, where were they staying now? The storks might have been found in the land of Egypt, where the sun's rays shone forth bright and warm, as it does here at midsummer. Tamarinds and acacias were in full bloom all over the country, the crescent of Mahomet glittered brightly from the cupolas of the mosques, and on the slender pinnacles sat many of the storks, resting after their long journey. Swarms of them took divided possession of the nests – nests which lay close to each other between the venerable columns, and crowded the arches of temples in forgotten cities. The date and the palm lifted themselves as a screen or as a sun-shade over them. The grey pyramids looked like broken shadows in the clear air and the far-off desert, where the ostrich wheels his rapid flight, and the lion, with his subtle eyes, gazes at the marble sphinx which lies half buried in sand. The waters of the Nile had retreated, and the whole bed of the river was covered with frogs, which was a most acceptable prospect for the stork families. The young storks thought their eyes deceived them, everything around appeared so beautiful.

'It is always like this here, and this is how we live in our warm country,' said the stork-mamma; and the thought made the young ones almost beside themselves with pleasure.

'Is there anything more to see?' they asked. 'Are we going farther into the country?'

'There is nothing further for us to see,' answered the stork-mamma. 'Beyond this delightful region there are immense forests, where the branches of the trees entwine round each other, while prickly, creeping plants cover the paths, and only an elephant could force a passage for himself with his great feet. The snakes are too large, and the lizards too lively for us to catch. Then there is the desert; if you went there, your eyes would soon be full of sand with the lightest breeze, and if it should blow great guns, you would most likely find yourself in a sand-drift. Here is the best place for you, where there are frogs and locusts; here I shall remain, and so must you.' And so they stayed.

The parents sat in the nest on the slender minaret, and rested, yet still were busily employed in cleaning and smoothing their feathers, and in sharpening their beaks against their red stockings; then they would stretch out their necks, salute each other, and gravely raise their heads with the high-polished forehead, and soft, smooth feathers, while their brown eyes shone with intelligence. The female young ones strutted about amid the moist rushes, glancing at the other young storks and making acquaintances, and swallowing a frog at every third step, or tossing a little snake about with their beaks, in a way they considered very becoming, and besides it tasted very good. The young male storks soon began to quarrel; they struck at each other with their wings, and pecked with their beaks till the blood came. And in this manner many of the young ladies and gentlemen were betrothed to each other: it was, of course, what they wanted, and indeed what they lived for. Then they returned to a nest, and there the quarrelling began afresh; for in hot countries people are almost all violent and passionate. But for all that it was pleasant, especially for the old people, who watched them with great joy: all that their young ones did suited them. Every day here there was sunshine, plenty to eat, and nothing to think of but pleasure. But in the rich castle of their Egyptian host, as they called him, pleasure was not to be found. The rich and mighty lord of the castle lay on his couch, in the midst of the great hall, with its many coloured walls looking like the centre of a great tulip; but he was stiff and powerless in all his limbs, and lay stretched out like a mummy. His family and servants stood round him; he was not dead, although he could scarcely be said to live. The healing moor-flower from the north, which was to have been found and brought to him by her who loved him so well, had not arrived. His young and beautiful daughter who, in swan's plumage, had flown over land and seas to the distant north, had never returned. She is dead, so the two swan-maidens had said when they came home; and they made up quite a story about her, and this is what they told:

'We three flew away together through the air,' said they: 'a hunter caught sight of us, and shot at us with an arrow. The arrow struck our young friend and sister, and slowly singing her farewell song she sank down, a dying swan, into the forest lake. On the shores of the lake, under a spreading birch-tree, we laid her in the cold earth. We had our revenge; we bound fire under the wings of a swallow, who had a nest on the thatched roof of the huntsman. The house took fire, and burst into flames; the hunter was burnt with the house, and the light was reflected over the sea as far as the spreading birch, beneath which we laid her sleeping dust. She will never return to the land of Egypt.' And then they both wept. And stork-papa, who heard the story, snapped with his beak so that it might be heard a long way off.

'Deceit and lies!' cried he. 'I should like to run my beak deep into their chests.'

'And perhaps break it off,' said the mamma stork, 'then what a sight you would be. Think first of yourself, and then of your family; all others are nothing to us.'

'Yes, I know,' said the stork-papa; 'but tomorrow I can easily place myself on the edge of the open cupola, when the learned and wise men assemble to consult on the state of the sick man; perhaps they may come a little nearer to the truth.' And the learned and wise men assembled together, and talked a great deal on every point; but the stork could make no sense out of anything they said; neither were there any good results from their consultations, either for the sick man, or for his daughter in the marshy heath. When we listen to what people say in this world, we shall hear a great deal; but it is an advantage to know what has been said and done before, when we listen to a conversation. The stork did, and we know at least as much as he, the stork.

'Love is a life-giver. The highest love produces the highest life. Only through love can the sick man be cured.' This had been said by many, and even the learned men acknowledged that it was a wise saying.

'What a beautiful thought!' exclaimed the papa stork immediately.

'I don't quite understand it,' said the mamma stork, when her husband repeated it; 'however, it is not my fault, but the fault of the thought; whatever it may be, I have something else to think of.'

Now the learned men had spoken also of love between this one and that one; of the difference of the love which we have for our neighbour to the love that exists between parents and children; of the love of the plant for the light, and how the germ springs forth when the sunbeam kisses the ground. All these things were so elaborately and learnedly explained that it was impossible for stork-papa to follow it, much less to talk about it. His thoughts on the subject quite weighed him down; he stood the whole of the following day on one leg, with half-shut eyes, thinking deeply. So much learning was quite a heavy weight for him to carry. One thing, however, the papa stork could understand. Everyone, high and low, had from their inmost hearts expressed their opinion that it was a great misfortune for so many thousands of people – the whole country indeed – to have this man so sick, with no hopes of his recovery. And what joy and blessing it would spread around if he could by any means be cured! But where bloomed the flower that could bring him health? They had searched for it everywhere; in learned writings, in the shining stars, in the weather and wind. Inquiries had been made in every by-way that could be thought of, until at last the wise and learned men has asserted, as we have been already told, that 'love, the life-giver, could alone give new life to a father;' and in saying this, they had overdone it, and said more than they understood themselves. They repeated it, and wrote it down as a recipe, 'Love is a life-giver.' But how could such a recipe be prepared – that was a difficulty they could not overcome. At last it was decided that help could only come from the princess herself, whose whole soul was wrapped up in her father, especially as a plan had been adopted by her to enable her to obtain a remedy.

More than a year had passed since the princess had set out at night, when the light of the young moon was soon lost beneath the horizon. She had gone to the marble sphinx in the desert, shaking the sand from her sandals, and then passed through the long passage, which leads to the centre of one of the great pyramids, where the mighty kings of antiquity, surrounded with pomp and splendour, lie veiled in the form of mummies. She had been told by the wise men, that if she laid her head on the breast of one of them, from the head she would learn where to find life and recovery for her father. She had performed all this, and in a dream had learnt that she must bring home to her father the lotus flower, which grows in the deep sea, near the moors and heath in the Danish land. The very place and situation had been pointed out to her, and she was told that the flower would restore her father to health and strength. And, therefore, she had gone forth from the land of Egypt, flying over to the open marsh and the wild moor in the plumage of a swan.

The papa and mamma storks knew all this, and we also know it now. We know, too, that the Marsh King has drawn her down to himself, and that to the loved ones at home she is forever dead. One of the wisest of them said, as the stork-mamma also said, 'That in some way she would, after all, manage to succeed;' and so at last they comforted themselves with this hope, and would wait patiently; in fact, they could do nothing better.

'I should like to get away the swan's feathers from those two treacherous princesses,' said the papa stork; 'then, at least, they would not be able to fly over again to the wild moor, and do more wickedness. I can hide the two suits of feathers over yonder, till we find some use for them.'

'But where will you put them?' asked the mamma stork.

'In our nest on the moor. I and the young ones will carry them by turns during our flight across; and as we return, should they prove too heavy for us, we shall be sure to find plenty of places on the way in which we can conceal them till our next journey. Certainly one suit of swan's feathers would be enough for the princess, but two are always better. In those northern countries no one can have too many travelling wrappers.'

'No one will thank you for it,' said stork-mamma; 'but you are master; and, excepting at breeding time, I have nothing to say.'

In the Viking's castle on the wild moor, to which the storks directed their flight in the following spring, the little maiden still remained. They had named her Helga, which was rather too soft a name for a child with a temper like hers, although her form was still beautiful. Every month this temper showed itself in sharper outlines; and in the course of years, while the storks still made the same journeys in autumn to the hill, and in spring to the moors, the child grew to be almost a woman, and before any one seemed aware of it, she was a wonderfully beautiful maiden of sixteen. The casket was splendid, but the contents were worthless. She was, indeed, wild and savage even in those hard, uncultivated times. It was a pleasure to her to splash about with her white hands in the warm blood of the horse which had been slain for sacrifice. In one of her wild moods she bit off the head of the black cock, which the priest was about to slay for the sacrifice. To her foster-father she said one day, 'If thine enemy were to pull down thine house about thy ears, and thou shouldest be sleeping in unconscious security, I would not wake thee; even if I had the power I would never do it, for my ears still tingle with the blow that thou gavest me years ago. I have never forgotten it.' But the Viking treated her words as a joke; he was, like every one else, bewitched with her beauty, and knew nothing of the change in the form and temper of Helga at night. Without a saddle, she would sit on a horse as if she were a part of it, while it rushed along at full speed; nor would she spring from its back, even when it quarrelled with other horses and bit them. She would often leap from the high shore into the sea with all her clothes on, and swim to meet the Viking, when his boat was steering home towards the shore. She once cut off a long lock of her beautiful hair, and twisted it into a string for her bow. 'If a thing is to be done well,' said she, 'I must do it myself.'

The Viking's wife was, for the time in which she lived, a woman of strong character and will; but, compared to her daughter, she was a gentle, timid woman, and she knew that a wicked sorcerer had the terrible child in his power. It was sometimes as if Helga acted from sheer wickedness; for often when her mother stood on the threshold of the door, or stepped into the yard, she would seat herself on the brink of the well, wave her arms and legs in the air, and suddenly fall right in. Here she was able, from her frog nature, to dip and dive about in the water of the deep well, until at last she would climb forth like a cat, and come back into the hall dripping with water, so that the green leaves that were strewed on the floor were whirled round, and carried away by the streams that flowed from her.

But there was one time of the day which placed a check upon Helga. It was the evening twilight; when this hour arrived she became quiet and thoughtful, and allowed herself to be advised and led; then also a secret feeling seemed to draw her towards her mother. And as usual, when the sun set, and the transformation took place, both in body and mind, inwards and outwards, she would remain quiet and mournful, with her form shrunk together in the shape of a frog. Her body was much larger than those animals ever are, and on this account it was much more hideous in appearance; for she looked like a wretched dwarf, with a frog's head, and webbed fingers. Her eyes had a most piteous expression; she was without a voice, excepting a hollow, croaking sound, like the smothered sobs of a dreaming child.

Then the Viking's wife took her on her lap, and forgot the ugly form, as she looked into the mournful eyes, and often said, 'I could wish that thou wouldst always remain my dumb frog child, for thou art too terrible when thou art clothed in a form of beauty.' And the Viking woman wrote Runic characters against sorcery and spells of sickness, and threw them over the wretched child; but they did no good.

'One can scarcely believe that she was ever small enough to lie in the cup of the water-lily,' said the papa stork; 'and now she is grown up, and the image of her Egyptian mother, especially about the eyes. Ah, we shall never see her again; perhaps she has not discovered how to help herself, as you and the wise men said she would. Year after year have I flown across and across the moor, but there was no sign of her being still alive. Yes, and I may as well tell you that you that each year, when I arrived a few days before you to repair the nest, and put everything in its place, I have spent a whole night flying here and there over the marshy lake, as if I had been an owl or a bat, but all to no purpose. The two suit of swan's plumage, which I and the young ones dragged over here from the land of the Nile, are of no use; trouble enough it was to us to bring them here in three journeys, and now they are lying at the bottom of the nest; and if a fire should happen to break out, and the wooden house be burnt down, they would be destroyed.'

'And our good nest would be destroyed, too,' said the mamma stork; 'but you think less of that than of your plumage stuff and your moor-princess. Go and stay with her in the marsh if you like. You are a bad father to your own children, as I have told you already, when I hatched my first brood. I only hope neither we nor our children may have an arrow sent through our wings, owing to that wild girl. Helga does not know in the least what she is about. We have lived in this house longer than she has, she should think of that, and we have never forgotten our duty. We have paid every year our toll of a feather, an egg and a young one, as it is only right we should do. You don't suppose I can wander about the courtyard, or go everywhere as I used to do in old times. I can do it in Egypt, where I can be a companion of the people, without forgetting myself. But here I cannot go and peep into the pots and kettles as I do there. No, I can only sit up here and feel angry with that girl, the little wretch; and I am angry with you, too; you should have left her lying in the water lily, then no one would have known anything about her.'

'You are far better than your conversation,' said the papa stork; 'I know you better than you know yourself.' And with that he gave a hop, and flapped his wings twice, proudly; then he stretched his neck and flew, or rather soared away, without moving his outspread wings. He went on for some distance, and then he gave a great flap with his wings and flew on his course at a rapid rate, his head and neck bending proudly before him, while the sun's rays fell on his glossy plumage.

'He is the handsomest of them all,' said the mamma stork, as she watched him; 'but I won't tell him so.'

Early in the autumn, the Viking again returned home laden with spoil, and bringing prisoners with him. Among them was a young Christian priest, one of those who contemned the gods of the north. Often lately there had been, both in hall and chamber, a talk of the new faith which was spreading far and wide in the south, and which, through the means of the holy Ansgarius, had already reached as far as Hedeby on the Schlei. Even Helga had heard of this belief in the teachings of One who was named Christ, and who for the love of mankind, and for their redemption, had given up His life. But to her all this had, as it were, gone in one ear and out the other. It seemed that she only understood the meaning of the word 'love' when in the form of a miserable frog she crouched together in the corner of the sleeping chamber; but the Viking's wife had listened to the wonderful story, and had felt herself strangely moved by it.

On their return, after this voyage, the men spoke of the beautiful temples built of polished stone, which had been raised for the public worship of this holy love. Some vessels, curiously formed of massive gold, had been brought home among the booty. There was a peculiar fragrance about them all, for they were incense vessels, which had been swung before the altars in the temples by the Christian priests. In the deep stony cellars of the castle, the young Christian priest was immured, and his hands and feet tied together with strips of bark. The Viking's wife considered him as beautiful as Baldur, and his distress raised her pity; but Helga said he ought to have ropes fastened to his heels, and be tied to the tails of wild animals.

'I would let the dogs loose after him' she said; 'over the moor and across the heath. Hurrah! That would be a spectacle for the gods, and better still to follow in its course.'

But the Viking would not allow him to die such a death as that, especially as he was the disowned and despiser of the high gods. In a few days, he had decided to have him offered as a sacrifice on the blood-stone in the grove. For the first time, a man was to be sacrificed here. Helga begged to be allowed to sprinkle the assembled people with the blood of the priest. She sharpened her glittering knife; and when one of the great, savage dogs, who were running about the Viking's castle in great numbers, sprang towards her, she thrust the knife into his side, merely, as she said, to prove its sharpness.

The Viking's wife looked at the wild, badly disposed girl, with great sorrow; and when night came on, and her daughter's beautiful form and disposition were changed, she spoke in eloquent words to Helga of the sorrow and deep grief that was in her heart. The ugly frog, in its monstrous shape, stood before her, and raised its brown mournful eyes to her face, listening to her words, and seeming to understand them with the intelligence of a human being.

'Never once to my lord and husband has a word passed my lips of what I have to suffer through you; my heart is full of grief about you,' said the Viking's wife. 'The love of a mother is greater and more powerful than I ever imagined. But love never entered thy heart; it is cold and clammy, like the plants on the moor.'

Then the miserable form trembled; it was as if these words had touched an invisible bond between body and soul, for great tears stood in the eyes.

'A bitter time will come for thee at last,' continued the Viking's wife; 'and it will be terrible for me too. It had been better for thee if thou hadst been left on the high-road, with the cold night wind to lull thee to sleep.' And the Viking's wife shed bitter tears, and went away in anger and sorrow, passing under the partition of furs, which hung loose over the beam and divided the hall.

The shrivelled frog still sat in the corner alone. Deep silence reigned around. At intervals, a half-stifled sigh was heard from its inmost soul; it was the soul of Helga. It seemed in pain, as if a new life were arising in her heart. Then she took a step forward and listened; then stepped again forward, and seized with her clumsy hands the heavy bar which was laid across the door. Gently, and with much trouble, she pushed back the bar, as silently lifted the latch, and then took up the glimmering lamp which stood in the ante-chamber of the hall. It seemed as if a stronger will than her own gave her strength. She removed the iron bolt from the closed cellar-door, and slipped in to the prisoner. He was slumbering. She touched him with her cold, moist hand, and as he awoke and caught sight of the hideous form, he shuddered as if he beheld a wicked apparition. She drew her knife, cut through the bonds which confined his hands and feet, and beckoned to him to follow her. He uttered some holy names and made the sign of the cross, while the form remained motionless by his side.

'Who art thou,' he asked, 'whose outward appearance is that of an animal, while thou willingly performest acts of mercy?'

The frog-figure beckoned to him to follow her, and led him through a long gallery concealed by hanging drapery to the stables, and then pointed to a horse. He mounted upon it, and she sprang up also before him, and held tightly by the animal's mane. The prisoner understood her, and they rode on at a rapid trot, by a road which he would never have found by himself, across the open heath. He forgot her ugly form, and only thought how the mercy and loving-kindness of the Almighty was acting through this hideous apparition. As he offered pious prayers and sang holy songs of praise, she trembled. Was it the effect of prayer and praise that caused this? or, was she shuddering in the cold morning air at the thought of approaching twilight? What were her feelings? She raised herself up, and wanted to stop the horse and spring off, but the Christian priest held her back with all his might, and then sang a pious song, as if this could loosen the wicked charm that had changed her into the semblance of a frog.

And the horse galloped on more wildly than before. The sky painted itself red, the first sunbeam pierced through the clouds, and in the clear flood of sunlight the frog became changed. It was Helga again, young and beautiful, but with a wicked demoniac spirit. He held now a beautiful young woman in his arms, and he was horrified at the sight. He stopped the horse, and sprang from its back. He imagined that some new sorcery was at work. But Helga also leaped from the horse and stood on the ground. The child's short garment reached only to her knee. She snatched the sharp knife from her girdle, and rushed like lightning at the astonished priest. 'Let me get at thee!' she cried. 'Let me get at thee, that I may plunge this knife into thy body. Thou art pale as ashes, thou beardless slave.' She pressed in upon him. They struggled with each other in heavy combat, but it was as if an invisible power had been given to the Christian in the struggle. He held her fast, and the old oak under which they stood seemed to help him, for the loosened roots on the ground became entangled in the maiden's feet, and held them fast. Close by rose a bubbling spring, and he sprinkled Helga's face and neck with the water, commanded the unclean spirit to come forth, and pronounced upon her a Christian blessing. But the water of faith has no power unless the well-spring of faith flows within. And yet even here its power was shown; something more than the mere strength of a man opposed itself, through his means, against the evil which struggled within her. His holy action seemed to overpower her. She dropped her arms, glanced at him with pale cheeks and looks of amazement. He appeared to her a mighty magician skilled in secret arts; his language was the darkest magic to her, and the movements of his hands in the air were as the secret signs of a magician's wand. She would not have blinked had he waved over her head a sharp knife or a glittering axe; but she shrunk from him as he signed her with the sign of the cross on her forehead and breast, and sat before him like a tame bird, with her head bowed down. Then he spoke to her, in gentle words, of the deed of love she had performed for him during the night, when she had come to him in the form of an ugly frog, to loosen his bonds, and to lead him forth to life and light; and he told her that she was bound in closer fetters than he had been, and that she could recover also life and light by his means. He would take her to Hedeby to St. Ansgarius, and there, in that Christian town, the spell of the sorcerer would be removed. But he would not let her sit before him on the horse, though of her own free will she wished to do so. 'Thou must sit behind me, not before me,' said he. 'Thy magic beauty has a magic power which comes from an evil origin, and I fear it; still I am sure to overcome through my faith in Christ.' Then he knelt down, and prayed with pious fervor. It was as if the quiet woodland were a holy church consecrated by his worship. The birds sang as if they were also of this new congregation; and the fragrance of the wild flowers was as the ambrosial perfume of incense; while, above all, sounded the words of Scripture, 'A light to them that sit in darkness and in the shadow of death, to guide their feet into the way of peace.' And he spoke these words with the deep longing of his whole nature.

Meanwhile, the horse that had carried them in wild career stood quietly by, plucking at the tall bramble-bushes, till the ripe young berries fell down upon Helga's hands, as if inviting her to eat. Patiently she allowed herself to be lifted on the horse, and sat there like a somnambulist – as one who walked in his sleep. The Christian bound two branches together with bark, in the form of a cross, and held it on high as they rode through the forest. The way gradually grew thicker of brushwood, as they rode along, till at last it became a trackless wilderness. Bushes of the wild sloe here and there blocked up the path, so that they had to ride over them. The bubbling spring formed not a stream, but a marsh, round which also they were obliged to guide the horse; still there were strength and refreshment in the cool forest breeze, and no trifling power in the gentle words spoken in faith and Christian love by the young priest, whose inmost heart yearned to lead this poor lost one into the way of light and life. It is said that rain-drops can make a hollow in the hardest stone, and the waves of the sea can smooth and round the rough edges of the rocks; so did the dew of mercy fall upon Helga, softening what was hard, and smoothing what was rough in her character. These effects did not yet appear; she was not herself aware of them; neither does the seed in the lap of earth know, when the refreshing dew and the warm sunbeams fall upon it, that it contains within itself power by which it will flourish and bloom. The song of the mother sinks into the heart of the child, and the little one prattles the words after her, without understanding their meaning; but after a time the thoughts expand, and what has been heard in childhood seems to the mind clear and bright. So now the 'Word', which is all-powerful to create, was working in the heart of Helga.

They rode forth from the thick forest, crossed the heath, and again entered a pathless wood. Here, towards evening, they met with robbers.

'Where hast thou stolen that beauteous maiden?' cried the robbers, seizing the horse by the bridle, and dragging the two riders from its back.

The priest had nothing to defend himself with, but the knife he had taken from Helga, and with this he struck out right and left. One of the robbers raised his axe against him; but the young priest sprang on one side, and avoided the blow, which fell with great force on the horse's neck, so that the blood gushed forth, and the animal sunk to the ground. Then Helga seemed suddenly to awake from her long, deep reverie; she threw herself hastily upon the dying animal. The priest placed himself before her, to defend and shelter her; but one of the robbers swung his iron axe against the Christian's head with such force that it was dashed to pieces, the blood and brains were scattered about, and he fell dead upon the ground. Then the robbers seized beautiful Helga by her white arms and slender waist; but at that moment the sun went down, and as its last ray disappeared, she was changed into the form of a frog. A greenish white mouth spread half over her face; her arms became thin and slimy; while broad hands, with webbed fingers, spread themselves out like fans. Then the robbers, in terror, let her go, and she stood among them, a hideous monster; and as is the nature of frogs to do, she hopped up as high as her own size, and disappeared in the thicket. Then the robbers knew that this must be the work of an evil spirit or some secret sorcery, and, in a terrible fright, they ran hastily from the spot.

The full moon had already risen, and was shining in all her radiant splendour over the earth, when from the thicket, in the form of a frog, crept poor Helga. She stood still by the corpse of the Christian priest, and the carcase of the dead horse. She looked at them with eyes that seemed to weep, and from the frog's head came forth a croaking sound, as when a child bursts into tears. She threw herself first upon one, and then upon the other; brought water in her hand, which, from being webbed, was large and hollow, and poured it over them; but they were dead, and dead they would remain. She understood that at last. Soon wild animals would come and tear their dead bodies; but no, that must not happen. Then she dug up the earth, as deep as she was able, that she might prepare a grave for them. She had nothing but a branch of a tree and her two hands, between the fingers of which the webbed skin stretched, and they were torn by the work, while the blood ran down her hands. She saw at last that her work would be useless, more than she could accomplish; so she fetched more water, and washed the face of the dead, and then covered it with fresh green leaves; she also brought large boughs and spread over him, and scattered dried leaves between the branches. Then she brought the heaviest stones that she could carry, and laid them over the dead body, filling up the crevices with moss, till she thought she had fenced in his resting-place strongly enough. The difficult task had employed her the whole night; and as the sun broke forth, there stood the beautiful Helga in all her loveliness, with her bleeding hands, and, for the first time, with tears on her maiden cheeks. It was, in this transformation, as if two natures were striving together within her; her whole frame trembled, and she looked around her as if she had just awoke from a painful dream. She leaned for support against the trunk of a slender tree, and at last climbed to the topmost branches, like a cat, and seated herself firmly upon them.

THE MARSH KING'S DAUGHTER

She remained there the whole day, sitting alone, like a frightened squirrel, in the silent solitude of the wood, where the rest and stillness is as the calm of death.

Butterflies fluttered around her, and close by were several ant-hills, each with its hundreds of busy little creatures moving quickly to and fro. In the air, danced myriads of gnats, swarm upon swarm, troops of buzzing flies, ladybirds, dragon-flies with golden wings, and other little winged creatures. The worm crawled forth from the moist ground, and the moles crept out; but, excepting these, all around had the stillness of death: but when people say this, they do not quite understand themselves what they mean. None noticed Helga but a flock of magpies, which flew chattering round the top of the tree on which she sat. These birds hopped close to her on the branches with bold curiosity. A glance from her eyes was a signal to frighten them away, and they were not clever enough to find out who she was; indeed she hardly knew herself.

When the sun was near setting, and the evening's twilight about to commence, the approaching transformation aroused her to fresh exertion. She let herself down gently from the tree, and, as the last sunbeam vanished, she stood again in the wrinkled form of a frog, with the torn, webbed skin on her hands, but her eyes now gleamed with more radiant beauty than they had ever possessed in her most beautiful form of loveliness; they were now pure, mild maidenly eyes that shone forth in the face of a frog. They showed the existence of deep feeling and a human heart, and the beauteous eyes overflowed with tears, weeping precious drops that lightened the heart.

On the raised mound which she had made as a grave for the dead priest, she found the cross made of the branches of a tree, the last work of him who now lay dead and cold beneath it. A sudden thought came to Helga, and she lifted up the cross and planted it upon the grave, between the stones that covered him and the dead horse. The sad recollection brought the tears to her eyes, and in this gentle spirit she traced the same sign in the sand round the grave; and as she formed, with both her hands, the sign of the cross, the web skin fell from them like a torn glove. She washed her hands in the water of the spring, and gazed with astonishment at their delicate whiteness. Again she made the holy sign in the air, between herself and the dead man; her lips trembled, her tongue moved, and the name which she in her ride through the forest had so often heard spoken, rose to her lips, and she uttered the words 'Jesus Christ'. Then the frog skin fell from her; she was once more a lovely maiden. Her head bent wearily, her tired limbs required rest, and then she slept.

Her sleep, however, was short. Towards midnight, she awoke; before her stood the dead horse, prancing and full of life, which shone forth from his eyes and from his wounded neck. Close by his side appeared the murdered Christian priest, more beautiful than Baldur, as the Viking's wife had said; but now he came as if in a flame of fire. Such gravity, such stern justice, such a piercing glance shone from his large, gentle eyes, that it seemed to penetrate into every corner of her heart. Beautiful Helga trembled at the look, and her memory returned with a power as if it had been the day of judgment. Every good deed that had been done for her, every loving word that had been said, were vividly before her mind. She understood now that love had kept her here during the day of her trial; while the creature formed of dust and clay, soul and spirit, had wrestled and struggled with evil. She acknowledged that she had only followed the impulses of an evil disposition, that she had done nothing to cure herself; everything had been given her, and all had happened as it were by the ordination of Providence. She bowed herself humbly, confessed her great imperfections in the sight of Him who can read every fault of the heart, and then the priest spoke. 'Daughter of the moorland, thou hast come from the swamp and the marshy earth, but from this thou shalt arise. The sunlight shining into thy inmost soul proves the origin from which thou hast really sprung, and has restored the body to its natural form. I am come to thee from the land of the dead, and thou also must pass through the valley to reach the holy mountains where mercy and perfection dwell. I cannot lead thee to Hedeby that thou mayst receive Christian baptism, for first thou must remove the thick veil with which the waters of the moorland are shrouded, and bring forth from its depths the living author of thy being and thy life. Till this is done, thou canst not receive consecration.'

Then he lifted her on the horse and gave her a golden censer, similar to those she had already seen at the Viking's house. A sweet perfume arose from it, while the open wound in the forehead of the slain priest, shone with the rays of a diamond. He took the cross from the grave, and held it aloft, and now they rode through the air over the rustling trees, over the hills where warriors lay buried each by his dead war-horse; and the brazen monumental figures rose up and galloped forth, and stationed themselves on the summits of the hills. The golden crescent on their foreheads, fastened with golden knots, glittered in the moonlight, and their mantles floated in the wind. The dragon that guards buried treasure lifted his head and gazed after them. The goblins and the satyrs peeped out from beneath the hills, and flitted to and fro in the fields, waving blue, red, and green torches, like the glowing sparks in burning paper. Over woodland and heath, flood and fen, they flew on, till they reached the wild moor, over which they hovered in broad circles. The Christian priest held the cross aloft, and it glittered like gold, while from his lips sounded pious prayers. Beautiful Helga's voice joined with his in the hymns he sung, as a child joins in her mother's song. She swung the censer, and a wonderful fragrance of incense arose from it; so powerful, that the reeds and rushes of the moor burst forth into blossom. Each germ came forth from the deep ground: all that had life raised itself. Blooming water-lilies spread themselves forth like a carpet of wrought flowers, and upon them lay a slumbering woman, young and beautiful. Helga fancied that it was her own image she saw reflected in the still water. But it was her mother she beheld, the wife of the Marsh King, the princess from the land of the Nile.

The dead Christian priest desired that the sleeping woman should be lifted on the horse, but the horse sank beneath the load, as if he had been a funeral pall fluttering in the wind. But the sign of the cross made the airy phantom strong, and then the three rode away from the marsh to firm ground.

At the same moment the cock crew in the Viking's castle, and the dream figures dissolved and floated away in the air, but mother and daughter stood opposite to each other.

'Am I looking at my own image in the deep water?' said the mother.

'Is it myself that I see represented on a white shield?' cried the daughter.

Then they came nearer to each other in a fond embrace. The mother's heart beat quickly, and she understood the quickened pulses. 'My child!' she exclaimed, 'the flower of my heart – my lotus flower of the deep water!' And she embraced her child again and wept, and the tears were as a baptism of new life and love for Helga. 'In swan's plumage I came here,' said the mother, 'and here I threw off my feather dress. Then I sank down through the wavering ground, deep into the marsh beneath, which closed like a wall around me; I found myself after a while in fresher water; still a power drew me down deeper and deeper. I felt the weight of sleep upon my eyelids. Then I slept, and dreams hovered round me. It seemed to me as if I were again in the pyramids of Egypt, and yet the waving elder trunk that had frightened me on the moor stood ever before me. I observed the clefts and wrinkles in the stem; they shone forth in strange colours, and took the form of hieroglyphics. It was the mummy case on which I gazed. At last it burst, and forth stepped the thousand-years'-old king, the mummy form, black as pitch, black as the shining wood-snail or the slimy mud of the swamp. Whether it was really the mummy or the Marsh King I know not. He seized me in his arms, and I felt as if I must die. When I recovered myself, I found in my bosom a little bird, flapping its wings, twittering and fluttering. The bird flew away from my bosom, upwards towards the dark, heavy canopy above me, but a long, green band kept it fastened to me. I heard and understood the tenor of its longings. Freedom! Sunlight! To my father! Then I thought of my father, and the sunny land of my birth, my life, and my love. Then I loosened the band, and let the bird fly away to its home – to a father. Since that hour I have ceased to dream; my sleep has been long and heavy, till in this very hour, harmony and fragrance awoke me, and set me free.'

The green band which fastened the wings of the bird to the mother's heart, where did it flutter now? Whither had it been wafted? The stork only had seen it. The band was the green stalk, the cup of the flower the cradle in which lay the child, that now in blooming beauty had been folded to the mother's heart.

And while the two were resting in each other's arms, the old stork flew round and round them in narrowing circles, till at length he flew away swiftly to his nest, and fetched away the two suits of swan's feathers, which he had preserved there for many years. Then he returned to the mother and daughter, and threw the swan's plumage over them; the feathers immediately closed around them, and they rose up from the earth in the form of two white swans.

'And now we can converse with pleasure,' said the stork-papa; 'we can understand one another, although the beaks of birds are so different in shape. It is very fortunate that you came tonight. Tomorrow we should have been gone. The mother, myself and the little ones, we're about to fly to the south. Look at me now: I am an old friend from the Nile, and a mother's heart contains more than her beak. She always said that the princess would know how to help herself. I and the young ones carried the swan's feathers over here, and I am glad of it now, and how lucky it is that I am here still. When the day dawns we shall start with a great company of other storks. We'll fly first, and you can follow in our track, so that you cannot miss your way. I and the young ones will have an eye upon you.'

'And the lotus-flower which I was to take with me,' said the Egyptian princess, 'is flying here by my side, clothed in swan's feathers. The flower of my heart will travel with me; and so the riddle is solved. Now for home! Now for home!'

But Helga said she could not leave the Danish land without once more seeing her foster-mother, the loving wife of the Viking.

Each pleasing recollection, each kind word, every tear from the heart which her foster-mother had wept for her, rose in her mind, and at that moment she felt as if she loved this mother the best.

'Yes, we must go to the Viking's castle,' said the stork; 'mother and the young ones are waiting for me there. How they will open their eyes and flap their wings! My wife, you see, does not say much; she is short and abrupt in her manner; but she means well, for all that. I will flap my wings at once, that they may hear us coming.' Then stork-papa flapped his wings in first-rate style, and he and the swans flew away to the Viking's castle.

In the castle, every one was in a deep sleep. It had been late in the evening before the Viking's wife retired to rest. She was anxious about Helga, who, three days before, had vanished with the Christian priest. Helga must have helped him in his flight, for it was her horse that was missed from the stable; but by what power had all this been accomplished? The Viking's wife thought of it with wonder, thought on the miracles which they said could be performed by those who believed in the Christian faith, and followed its teachings. These passing thoughts formed themselves into a vivid dream, and it seemed to her that she was still lying awake on her couch, while without darkness reigned. A storm arose; she heard the lake dashing and rolling from east and west, like the waves of the North Sea or the Cattegat. The monstrous snake which, it is said, surrounds the earth in the depths of the ocean, was trembling in spasmodic convulsions. The night of the fall of the gods was come, 'Ragnarok,' as the heathens call the judgment-day, when everything shall pass away, even the high gods themselves. The war trumpet sounded; riding upon the rainbow, came the gods, clad in steel, to fight their last battle on the last battle-field. Before them flew the winged vampires, and the dead warriors closed up the train. The whole firmament was ablaze with the northern lights, and yet the darkness triumphed. It was a terrible hour. And, close to the terrified woman, Helga seemed to be seated on the floor, in the hideous form of a frog, yet trembling, and clinging to her foster-mother, who took her on her lap, and lovingly caressed her, hideous and frog-like as she was. The air was filled with the clashing of arms and the hissing of arrows, as if a storm of hail was descending upon the earth. It seemed to her the hour when earth and sky would burst asunder, and all things be swallowed up in Saturn's fiery lake; but she knew that a new heaven and a new earth would arise, and that corn-fields would wave where now the lake rolled over desolate sands, and the ineffable God reign. Then she saw rising from the region of the dead Baldur the gentle, the loving, and as the Viking's wife gazed upon him, she recognised his countenance. It was the captive Christian priest. 'White Christian!' she exclaimed aloud, and with the words, she pressed a kiss on the forehead of the hideous frog-child. Then the frog-skin fell off, and Helga stood before her in all her beauty, more lovely and gentle-looking, and with eyes beaming with love. She kissed the hands of her foster-mother, blessed her for all her fostering love and care during the days of her trial and misery, for the thoughts she had suggested and awoke in her heart, and for naming the Name which she now repeated. Then beautiful Helga rose as a mighty swan, and spread her wings with the rushing sound of troops of birds of passage flying through the air.

Then the Viking's wife awoke, but she still heard the rushing sound without. She knew it was the time for the storks to depart, and that it must be their wings which she heard. She felt she should like to see them once more, and bid them farewell. She rose from her couch, stepped out on the threshold, and beheld, on the ridge of the roof, a party of storks ranged side by side. Troops of the birds were flying in circles over the castle and the highest trees; but just before her, as she stood on the threshold and close to the well where Helga had so often sat and alarmed her with her wildness, now stood two swans, gazing at her with intelligent eyes. Then she remembered her dream, which still appeared to her as a reality. She thought of Helga in the form of a swan. She thought of a Christian priest, and suddenly a wonderful joy arose in her heart. The swans flapped their wings and arched their necks as if to offer her a greeting, and the Viking's wife spread out her arms towards them, as if she accepted it, and smiled through her tears. She was roused from deep thought by a rustling of wings and snapping of beaks; all the storks arose, and started on their journey towards the south.

'We will not wait for the swans,' said the mamma stork; 'if they want to go with us, let them come now; we can't sit here till the plovers start. It is a fine thing after all to travel in families, not like the finches and the partridges. There the male and the female birds fly in separate flocks, which, to speak candidly, I consider very unbecoming.'

'What are those swans flapping their wings for?'

'Well, every one flies in his own fashion,' said the papa stork. 'The swans fly in an oblique line; the cranes, in the form of a triangle; and the plovers, in a curved line like a snake.'

'Don't talk about snakes while we are flying up here,' said stork-mamma. 'It puts ideas into the children's heads that can not be realised.'

'Are those the high mountains I have heard spoken of?' asked Helga, in the swan's plumage.

'They are storm-clouds driving along beneath us,' replied her mother.

'What are yonder white clouds that rise so high?' again inquired Helga.

'Those are mountains covered with perpetual snows, that you see yonder,' said her mother. And then they flew across the Alps towards the blue Mediterranean.

'Africa's land! Egyptia's strand!' sang the daughter of the Nile, in her swan's plumage, as from the upper air she caught sight of her native land, a narrow, golden, wavy strip on the shores of the Nile; the other birds espied it also and hastened their flight.

'I can smell the Nile mud and the wet frogs,' said the stork-mamma, 'and I begin to feel quite hungry. Yes, now you shall taste something nice, and you will see the marabout bird, and the ibis, and the crane. They all belong to our family, but they are not nearly so handsome as we are. They give themselves great airs, especially the ibis. The Egyptians have spoilt him. They make a mummy of him, and stuff him with spices. I would rather be stuffed with live frogs, and so would you, and so you shall. Better have something in your inside while you are alive, than to be made a parade of after you are dead. That is my opinion, and I am always right.'

'The storks are come,' was said in the great house on the banks of the Nile, where the lord lay in the hall on his downy cushions, covered with a leopard skin, scarcely alive, yet not dead, waiting and hoping for the lotus-flower from the deep moorland in the far north. Relatives and servants were standing by his couch, when the two beautiful swans who had come with the storks flew into the hall. They threw off their soft white plumage, and two lovely female forms approached the pale, sick old man, and threw back their long hair, and when Helga bent over her grandfather, redness came back to his cheeks, his eyes brightened, and life returned to his benumbed limbs. The old man rose up with health and energy renewed; daughter and grandchild welcomed him as joyfully as if with a morning greeting after a long and troubled dream.

Joy reigned through the whole house, as well as in the stork's nest; although there the chief cause was really the good food, especially the quantities of frogs, which seemed to spring out of the ground in swarms.

Then the learned men hastened to note down, in flying characters, the story of the two princesses, and spoke of the arrival of the health-giving flower as a mighty event, which had been a blessing to the house and the land. Meanwhile, the stork-papa told the story to his family in his own way; but not till they had eaten and were satisfied; otherwise they would have had something else to do than to listen to stories.

'Well,' said the stork-mamma, when she had heard it, 'you will be made something of at last; I suppose they can do nothing less.'

'What could I be made?' said stork-papa. 'What have I done? – Just nothing.'

'You have done more than all the rest,' she replied. 'But for you and the youngsters the two young princesses would never have seen Egypt again, and the recovery of the old man would not have been effected. You will become something. They must certainly give you a doctor's hood, and our young ones will inherit it, and their children after them, and so on. You already look like an Egyptian doctor, at least in my eyes.'

'I cannot quite remember the words I heard when I listened on the roof,' said stork-papa, while relating the story to his family;

'all I know is, that what the wise men said was so complicated and so learned that they received not only rank, but presents; even the head cook at the great house was honoured with a mark of distinction, most likely for the soup.'

'And what did you receive?' said the stork-mamma. 'They certainly ought not to forget the most important person in the affair, as you really are. The learned men have done nothing at all but use their tongues. Surely they will not overlook you.'

Late in the night, while the gentle sleep of peace rested on the now happy house, there was still one watcher. It was not stork-papa, who, although he stood on guard on one leg, could sleep soundly. Helga alone was awake. She leaned over the balcony, gazing at the sparkling stars that shone clearer and brighter in the pure air than they had done in the north, and yet they were the same stars. She thought of the Viking's wife in the wild moorland, of the gentle eyes of her foster-mother, and of the tears she had shed over the poor frog-child that now lived in splendour and starry beauty by the waters of the Nile, with air balmy and sweet as spring. She thought of the love that dwelt in the breast of the heathen woman, love that had been shown to a wretched creature, hateful as a human being, and hideous when in the form of an animal. She looked at the glittering stars, and thought of the radiance that had shone forth on the forehead of the dead man, as she had fled with him over the woodland and moor. Tones were awakened in her memory; words which she had heard him speak as they rode onward, when she was carried, wondering and trembling, through the air; words from the great Fountain of love, the highest love that embraces all the human race. What had not been won and achieved by this love?

Day and night beautiful Helga was absorbed in the contemplation of the great amount of her happiness, and lost herself in the contemplation, like a child who turns hurriedly from the giver to examine the beautiful gifts. She was over-powered with her good fortune, which seemed always increasing, and therefore what might it become in the future? Had she not been brought by a wonderful miracle to all this joy and happiness? And in these thoughts she indulged, until at last she thought no more of the Giver. It was the over-abundance of youthful spirits unfolding its wings for a daring flight. Her eyes sparkled with energy, when suddenly arose a loud noise in the court below, and the daring thought vanished. She looked down, and saw two large ostriches running round quickly in narrow circles; she had never seen these creatures before – great, coarse, clumsy-looking birds with curious wings that looked as if they had been clipped, and the birds themselves had the appearance of having been roughly used. She inquired about them, and for the first time heard the legend which the Egyptians relate respecting the ostrich.

Once, say they, the ostriches were a beautiful and glorious race of birds, with large, strong wings. One evening the other large birds of the forest said to the ostrich, 'Brother, shall we fly to the river tomorrow morning to drink, God willing?' and the ostrich answered, 'I will.'

With the break of day, therefore, they commenced their flight; first rising high in the air, towards the sun, which is the eye of God; still higher and higher the ostrich flew, far above the other birds, proudly approaching the light, trusting in its own strength, and thinking not of the Giver, or saying, 'if God will.' When suddenly the avenging angel drew back the veil from the flaming ocean of sunlight, and in a moment the wings of the proud bird were scorched and shrivelled, and they sunk miserably to the earth. Since that time the ostrich and his race have never been able to rise in the air; they can only fly terror-stricken along the ground, or run round and round in narrow circles. It is a warning to mankind, that in all our thoughts and schemes, and in every action we undertake, we should say, 'if God will'.

Then Helga bowed her head thoughtfully and seriously, and looked at the circling ostrich, as with timid fear and simple pleasure it glanced at its own great shadow on the sunlit walls. And the story of the ostrich sunk deeply into the heart and mind of Helga: a life of happiness, both in the present and in the future, seemed secure for her, and what was yet to come might be the best of all, God willing.

Early in the spring, when the storks were again about to journey northward, beautiful Helga took off her golden bracelets, scratched her name on them, and beckoned to the stork-father. He came to her, and she placed the golden circlet round his neck, and begged him to deliver it safely to the Viking's wife, so that she might know that her foster-daughter still lived, was happy, and had not forgotten her.

'It is rather heavy to carry,' thought stork-papa, when he had it on his neck; 'but gold and honour are not to be flung into the street. The stork brings good fortune – they'll be obliged to acknowledge that at last.'

'You lay gold, and I lay eggs,' said stork-mamma; 'with you it is only once in a way, I lay eggs every year. But no one appreciates what we do; I call it very mortifying.'

'But then we have a consciousness of our own worth, mother,' replied stork-papa.

'What good will that do you?' retorted stork-mamma. 'It will neither bring you a fair wind, nor a good meal.'

'The little nightingale, who is singing yonder in the tamarind grove, will soon be going north, too.' Helga said she had often heard her singing on the wild moor, so she determined to send a message by her. While flying in the swan's plumage she had learnt the bird language; she had often conversed with the stork and the swallow, and she knew that the nightingale would understand. So she begged the nightingale to fly to the beechwood, on the peninsula of Jutland, where a mound of stone and twigs had been raised to form the grave, and she begged the nightingale to persuade all the other little birds to build their nests round the place, so that evermore should resound over that grave music and song. And the nightingale flew away, and time flew away also.

In the autumn, an eagle, standing upon a pyramid, saw a stately train of richly laden camels, and men attired in armour on foaming Arabian steeds, whose glossy skins shone like silver, their nostrils were pink, and their thick, flowing manes hung almost to their slender legs. A royal prince of Arabia, handsome as a prince should be, and accompanied by distinguished guests, was on his way to the stately house, on the roof of which the storks' empty nests might be seen. They were away now in the far north, but expected to return very soon. And, indeed, they returned on a day that was rich in joy and gladness.

A marriage was being celebrated, in which the beautiful Helga, glittering in silk and jewels, was the bride, and the bridegroom the young Arab prince. Bride and bridegroom sat at the upper end of the table, between the bride's mother and grandfather. But her gaze was not on the bridegroom, with his manly, sunburnt face, round which curled a black beard, and whose dark fiery eyes were fixed upon her; but away from him, at a twinkling star, that shone down upon her from the sky. Then was heard the sound of rushing wings beating the air. The storks were coming home; and the old stork pair, although tired with the journey and requiring rest, did not fail to fly down at once to the balustrades of the verandah, for they knew already what feast was being celebrated. They had heard of it on the borders of the land, and also that Helga had caused their figures to be represented on the walls, for they belonged to her history.

'I call that very sensible and pretty,' said stork-papa.

'Yes, but it is very little,' said mamma stork; 'they could not possibly have done less.'

But, when Helga saw them, she rose and went out into the verandah to stroke the backs of the storks. The old stork pair bowed their heads, and curved their necks, and even the youngest among the young ones felt honoured by this reception.

Helga continued to gaze upon the glittering star, which seemed to glow brighter and purer in its light; then between herself and the star floated a form, purer than the air, and visible through it. It floated quite near to her, and she saw that it was the dead Christian priest, who also was coming to her wedding feast – coming from the heavenly kingdom.

'The glory and brightness, yonder, outshines all that is known on earth,' said he.

Then Helga the fair prayed more gently, and more earnestly, than she had ever prayed in her life before, that she might be permitted to gaze, if only for a single moment, at the glory and brightness of the heavenly kingdom. Then she felt herself lifted up, as it were, above the earth, through a sea of sound and thought; not only around her, but within her, was there light and song, such as words cannot express.

'Now we must return;' he said; 'you will be missed.'

'Only one more look,' she begged; 'but one short moment more.'

'We must return to earth; the guests will have all departed. Only one more look! – The last!'

Then Helga stood again in the verandah. But the marriage lamps in the festive hall had been all extinguished, and the torches outside had vanished. The storks were gone; not a guest could be seen; no bridegroom – all in those few short moments seemed to have died. Then a great dread fell upon her. She stepped from the verandah through the empty hall into the next chamber, where slept strange warriors. She opened a side door, which once led into her own apartment, but now, as she passed through, she found herself suddenly in a garden which she had never before seen here, the sky blushed red, it was the dawn of morning. Three minutes only in heaven, and a whole night on earth had passed away! Then she saw the storks, and called to them in their own language.

Then stork-papa turned his head towards her, listened to her words, and drew near. 'You speak our language,' said he, 'what do you wish? Why do you appear – you – a strange woman?'

'It is I – it is Helga! Dost thou not know me? Three minutes ago we were speaking together yonder in the verandah.'

'That is a mistake,' said the stork, 'you must have dreamed all this.'

'No, no,' she exclaimed. Then she reminded him of the Viking's castle, of the great lake, and of the journey across the ocean.

Then stork-papa winked his eyes, and said, 'Why that's an old story which happened in the time of my grandfather. There certainly was a princess of that kind here in Egypt once, who came from the Danish land, but she vanished on the evening of her wedding day, many hundred years ago, and never came back.

You may read about it yourself yonder, on a monument in the garden. There you will find swans and storks sculptured, and on the top is a figure of the princess Helga, in marble.'

And so it was; Helga understood it all now, and sank on her knees. The sun burst forth in all its glory, and, as in olden times, the form of the frog vanished in his beams, and the beautiful form stood forth in all its loveliness; so now, bathed in light, rose a beautiful form, purer, clearer than air – a ray of brightness – from the Source of light Himself. The body crumbled into dust, and a faded lotus-flower lay on the spot on which Helga had stood.

'Now that is a new ending to the story,' said stork-papa; 'I really never expected it would end in this way, but it seems a very good ending.'

'And what will the young ones say to it, I wonder?' said stork-mamma.

'Ah, that is a very important question,' replied the stork.

THE TRAVELLING COMPANIONS

Poor John was very sad; for his father was so ill, he had no hope of his recovery. John sat alone with the sick man in the little room, and the lamp had nearly burnt out; for it was late in the night.

'You have been a good son, John,' said the sick father, 'and God will help you on in the world.' He looked at him, as he spoke, with mild, earnest eyes, drew a deep sigh, and died; yet it appeared as if he still slept.

John wept bitterly. He had no one in the wide world now; neither father, mother, brother, nor sister. Poor John! He knelt down by the bed, kissed his dead father's hand, and wept many, many bitter tears. But at last his eyes closed, and he fell asleep with his head resting against the hard bedpost. Then he dreamed a strange dream; he thought he saw the sun shining upon him, and his father alive and well, and even heard him laughing as he used to do when he was very happy. A beautiful girl, with a golden crown on her head, and long, shining hair, gave him her hand; and his father said, 'See what a bride you have won. She is the loveliest maiden on the whole earth.' Then he awoke, and all the beautiful things vanished before his eyes, his father lay dead on the bed, and he was all alone. Poor John!

During the following week the dead man was buried. The son walked behind the coffin which contained his father, whom he so dearly loved, and would never again behold. He heard the earth fall on the coffin-lid, and watched it till only a corner remained in sight, and at last that also disappeared. He felt as if his heart would break with its weight of sorrow, till those who stood round the grave sang a psalm, and the sweet, holy tones brought tears into his eyes, which relieved him. The sun shone brightly down on the green trees, as if it would say, 'You must not be so sorrowful, John. Do you see the beautiful blue sky above you? Your father is up there, and he prays to the loving Father of all, that you may do well in the future.'

'I will always be good,' said John, 'and then I shall go to be with my father in heaven. What joy it will be when we see each other again! How much I shall have to relate to him, and how many things he will be able to explain to me of the delights of heaven, and teach me as he once did on earth. Oh, what joy it will be!'

He pictured it all so plainly to himself that he smiled even while the tears ran down his cheeks.

The little birds in the chestnut-trees twittered, 'Tweet, tweet'; they were so happy, although they had seen the funeral; but they seemed as if they knew that the dead man was now in heaven, and that he had wings much larger and more beautiful than their own; and he was happy now, because he had been good here on earth, and they were glad of it. John saw them fly away out of the green trees into the wide world, and he longed to fly with them; but first he cut out a large wooden cross, to place on his father's grave; and when he brought it there in the evening, he found the grave decked out with gravel and flowers. Strangers had done this; they who had known the good old father who was now dead, and who had loved him very much.

Early the next morning, John packed up his little bundle of clothes, and placed all his money, which consisted of fifty dollars and a few shillings, in his girdle; with this he determined to try his fortune in the world. But first he went into the churchyard; and, by his father's grave, he offered up a prayer, and said, 'Farewell.'

As he passed through the fields, all the flowers looked fresh and beautiful in the warm sunshine, and nodded in the wind, as if they wished to say, 'Welcome to the green wood, where all is fresh and bright.'

Then John turned to have one more look at the old church, in which he had been christened in his infancy, and where his father had taken him every Sunday to hear the service and join in singing the psalms. As he looked at the old tower, he espied the ringer standing at one of the narrow openings, with his little pointed red cap on his head, and shading his eyes from the sun with his bent arm. John nodded farewell to him, and the little ringer waved his red cap, laid his hand on his heart, and kissed his hand to him a great many times, to show that he felt kindly towards him, and wished him a prosperous journey.

John continued his journey, and thought of all the wonderful things he should see in the large, beautiful world, till he found himself farther away from home than ever he had been before. He did not even know the names of the places he passed through, and could scarcely understand the language of the people he met, for he was far away, in a strange land. The first night he slept on a haystack, out in the fields, for there was no other bed for him; but it seemed to him so nice and comfortable that even a king need not wish for a better. The field, the brook, the haystack, with the blue sky above, formed a beautiful sleeping-room. The green grass, with the little red and white flowers, was the carpet; the elder-bushes and the hedges of wild roses looked like garlands on the walls; and for a bath he could have the clear, fresh water of the brook; while the rushes bowed their heads to him, to wish him good morning and good evening. The moon, like a large lamp, hung high up in the blue ceiling, and he had no fear of its setting fire to his curtains. John slept here quite safely all night; and when he awoke, the sun was up, and all the little birds were singing round him, 'Good morning, good morning. Are you not up yet?'

It was Sunday, and the bells were ringing for church. As the people went in, John followed them; he heard God's word, joined in singing the psalms, and listened to the preacher. It seemed to him just as if he were in his own church, where he had been christened, and had sung the psalms with his father. Out in the churchyard were several graves, and on some of them the grass had grown very high. John thought of his father's grave, which he knew at last would look like these, as he was not there to weed and attend to it. Then he set to work, pulled up the high grass, raised the wooden crosses which had fallen down, and replaced the wreaths which had been blown away from their places by the wind, thinking all the time, 'Perhaps someone is doing the same for my father's grave, as I am not there to do it.'

Outside the church door stood an old beggar, leaning on his crutch. John gave him his silver shillings, and then he continued his journey, feeling lighter and happier than ever. Towards evening, the weather became very stormy, and he hastened on as quickly as he could, to get shelter; but it was quite dark by the time he reached a little lonely church which stood on a hill. 'I will go in here,' he said, 'and sit down in a corner; for I am quite tired, and want rest.'

So he went in, and seated himself; then he folded his hands, and offered up his evening prayer, and was soon fast asleep and dreaming, while the thunder rolled and the lightning flashed without. When he awoke, it was still night; but the storm had ceased, and the moon shone in upon him through the windows. Then he saw an open coffin standing in the centre of the church, which contained a dead man, waiting for burial. John was not at all timid; he had a good conscience, and he knew also that the dead can never injure any one. It is living wicked men who do harm to others. Two such wicked persons stood now by the dead man, who had been brought to the church to be buried. Their evil intentions were to throw the poor dead body outside the church door, and not leave him to rest in his coffin.

'Why do you do this?' asked John, when he saw what they were going to do. 'It is very wicked. Leave him to rest in peace, in Christ's name.'

'Nonsense,' replied the two dreadful men. 'He has cheated us; he owed us money which he could not pay, and now he is dead we shall not get a penny; so we mean to have our revenge, and let him lie like a dog outside the church door.'

'I have only fifty dollars,' said John, 'it is all I possess in the world, but I will give it to you if you will promise me faithfully to leave the dead man in peace. I shall be able to get on without the money; I have strong and healthy limbs, and God will always help me.'

'Why, of course,' said the horrid men, 'if you will pay his debt we will both promise not to touch him. You may depend upon that;' and then they took the money he offered them, laughed at him for his good nature, and went their way.

Then he laid the dead body back in the coffin, folded the hands, and took leave of it; and went away contentedly through the great forest. All around him he could see the prettiest little elves dancing in the moonlight, which shone through the trees. They were not disturbed by his appearance, for they knew he was good and harmless among men. They are wicked people only who can never obtain a glimpse of fairies. Some of them were not taller than the breadth of a finger, and they wore golden combs in their long, yellow hair. They were rocking themselves two together on the large dew-drops with which the leaves and the high grass were sprinkled. Sometimes the dew-drops would roll away, and then they fell down between the stems of the long grass, and caused a great deal of laughing and noise among the other little people. It was quite charming to watch them at play. Then they sang songs, and John remembered that he had learnt those pretty songs when he was a little boy. Large speckled spiders, with silver crowns on their heads, were employed to spin suspension bridges and palaces from one hedge to another, and when the tiny drops fell upon them, they glittered in the moonlight like shining glass. This continued till sunrise. Then the little elves crept into the flower-buds, and the wind seized the bridges and palaces, and fluttered them in the air like cobwebs.

As John left the wood, a strong man's voice called after him, 'Hello, comrade, where are you travelling?'

'Into the wide world,' he replied; 'I am only a poor lad, I have neither father nor mother, but God will help me.'

'I am going into the wide world also,' replied the stranger; 'shall we keep each other company?'

'With all my heart,' he said, and so they went on together. Soon they began to like each other very much, for they were both good; but John found out that the stranger was much more clever than himself. He had travelled all over the world, and could describe almost everything. The sun was high in the heavens when they seated themselves under a large tree to eat their breakfast, and at the same moment an old woman came towards them. She was very old and almost bent double. She leaned upon a stick and carried on her back a bundle of firewood, which she had collected in the forest; her apron was tied round it, and John saw three great stems of fern and some willow twigs peeping out. Just as she came close up to them, her foot slipped and she fell to the ground screaming loudly; poor old woman, she had broken her leg! John proposed directly that they should carry the old woman home to her cottage; but the stranger opened his knapsack and took out a box, in which he said he had a salve that would quickly make her leg well and strong again, so that she would be able to walk home herself, as if her leg had never been broken. And all that he would ask in return was the three fern stems which she carried in her apron.

'That is rather too high a price,' said the old woman, nodding her head quite strangely. She did not seem at all inclined to part with the fern stems. However, it was not very agreeable to lie there with a broken leg, so she gave them to him; and such was the power of the ointment that no sooner had he rubbed her leg with it than the old mother rose up and walked even better than she had done before. But then this wonderful ointment could not be bought at a chemist's.

'What can you want with those three fern rods?' asked John of his fellow-traveller.

'Oh, they will make capital brooms,' said he; 'and I like them because I have strange whims sometimes.' Then they walked on together for a long distance.

'How dark the sky is becoming,' said John; 'and look at those thick, heavy clouds.'

'Those are not clouds,' replied his fellow-traveller; 'they are mountains – large lofty mountains – on the tops of which we should be above the clouds, in the pure, free air. Believe me, it is delightful to ascend so high, tomorrow we shall be there.' But the mountains were not so near as they appeared; they had to travel a whole day before they reached them, and pass through black forests and piles of rock as large as a town. The journey had been so fatiguing that John and his fellow-traveller stopped to rest at a roadside inn, so that they might gain strength for their journey on the morrow. In the large public room of the inn a great many persons were assembled to see a comedy performed by dolls. The showman had just erected his little theatre, and the people were sitting round the room to witness the performance. Right in front, in the very best place, sat a stout butcher, with a great bulldog by his side who seemed very much inclined to bite. He sat staring with all his eyes, and so indeed did everyone else in the room. And then the play began. It was a pretty piece, with a king and a queen in it, who sat on a beautiful throne, and had gold crowns on their heads. The trains to their dresses were very long, according to the fashion; while the prettiest of wooden dolls, with glass eyes and large moustaches, stood at the doors, and opened and shut them, that the fresh air might come into the room. It was a very pleasant play, not at all mournful; but just as the queen stood up and walked across the stage, the great bull-dog, who should have been held back by his master, made a spring forward, and caught the queen in the teeth by the slender wrist, so that it snapped in two. This was a very dreadful disaster. The poor man, who was exhibiting the dolls, was much annoyed, and quite sad about his queen; she was the prettiest doll he had, and the bulldog had broken her head and shoulders off. But after all the people were gone away, the stranger, who came with John, said that he could soon set her to rights. And then he brought out his box and rubbed the doll with some of the salve with which he had cured the old woman when she broke her leg. As soon as this was done the doll's back became quite right again; her head and shoulders were fixed on, and she could even move her limbs herself: there was now no occasion to pull the wires, for the doll acted just like a living creature, excepting that she could not speak. The man to whom the show belonged was quite delighted at having a doll who could dance of herself without being pulled by the wires; none of the other dolls could do this.

During the night, when all the people at the inn were gone to bed, some one was heard to sigh so deeply and painfully, and the sighing continued for so long a time, that every one got up to see what could be the matter. The showman went at once to his little theatre and found that it proceeded from the dolls, who all lay on the floor sighing piteously, and staring with their glass eyes; they all wanted to be rubbed with the ointment, so that, like the queen, they might be able to move of themselves. The queen threw herself on her knees, took off her beautiful crown, and, holding it in her hand, cried, 'Take this from me, but do rub my husband and his courtiers.'

The poor man who owned the theatre could scarcely refrain from weeping; he was so sorry that he could not help them. Then he immediately spoke to John's comrade, and promised him all the money he might receive at the next evening's performance, if he would only rub the ointment on four or five of his dolls. But the fellow-traveller said he did not require anything in return, excepting the sword which the showman wore by his side. As soon as he received the sword he anointed six of the dolls with the ointment, and they were able immediately to dance so gracefully that all the living girls in the room could not help joining in the dance. The coachman danced with the cook, and the waiters with the chambermaids, and all the strangers joined; even the tongs and the fire-shovel made an attempt, but they fell down after the first jump. So after all it was a very merry night. The next morning John and his companion left the inn to continue their journey through the great pine-forests and over the high mountains. They arrived at last at such a great height that towns and villages lay beneath them, and the church steeples looked like little specks between the green trees. They could see for miles round, far away to places they had never visited, and John saw more of the beautiful world than he had ever known before. The sun shone brightly in the blue firmament above, and through the clear mountain air came the sound of the huntsman's horn, and the soft, sweet notes brought tears into his eyes, and he could not help exclaiming, 'How good and loving God is to give us all this beauty and loveliness in the world to make us happy!'

His fellow-traveller stood by with folded hands, gazing on the dark wood and the towns bathed in the warm sunshine. At this moment there sounded over their heads sweet music. They looked up, and discovered a large white swan hovering in the air, and singing as never bird sang before. But the song soon became weaker and weaker, the bird's head drooped, and he sunk slowly down, and lay dead at their feet.

'It is a beautiful bird,' said the traveller, 'and these large white wings are worth a great deal of money. I will take them with me. You see now that a sword will be very useful.'

So he cut off the wings of the dead swan with one blow, and carried them away with him.

They now continued their journey over the mountains for many miles, till they at length reached a large city, containing hundreds of towers, that shone in the sunshine like silver. In the midst of the city stood a splendid marble palace, roofed with pure red gold, in which dwelt the king. John and his companion would not go into the town immediately; so they stopped at an inn outside the town, to change their clothes; for they wished to appear respectable as they walked through the streets. The landlord told them that the king was a very good man, who never injured anyone: but as to his daughter, 'Heaven defend us!'

She was indeed a wicked princess. She possessed beauty enough – nobody could be more elegant or prettier than she was; but what of that? For she was a wicked witch; and in consequence of her conduct many noble young princes had lost their lives. Any one was at liberty to make her an offer; were he a prince or a beggar, it mattered not to her. She would ask him to guess three things which she had just thought of, and if he succeed, he was to marry her, and be king over all the land when her father died; but if he could not guess these three things, then she ordered him to be hanged or to have his head cut off. The old king, her father, was very much grieved at her conduct, but he could not prevent her from being so wicked, because he once said he would have nothing more to do with her lovers; she might do as she pleased. Each prince who came and tried the three guesses, so that he might marry the princess, had been unable to find them out, and had been hanged or beheaded. They had all been warned in time, and might have left her alone, if they would. The old king became at last so distressed at all these dreadful circumstances, that for a whole day every year he and his soldiers knelt and prayed that the princess might become good; but she continued as wicked as ever. The old women who drank brandy would colour it quite black before they drank it, to show how they mourned; and what more could they do?

'What a horrible princess!' said John. 'She ought to be well flogged. If I were the old king, I would have her punished in some way.'

Just then they heard the people outside shouting, 'Hurrah!' and, looking out, they saw the princess passing by; and she was really so beautiful that everybody forgot her wickedness, and shouted 'Hurrah!'. Twelve lovely maidens in white silk dresses, holding golden tulips in their hands, rode by her side on coal-black horses. The princess herself had a snow-white steed, decked with diamonds and rubies. Her dress was of cloth of gold, and the whip she held in her hand looked like a sunbeam. The golden crown on her head glittered like the stars of heaven, and her mantle was formed of thousands of butterflies' wings sewn together. Yet she herself was more beautiful than all.

When John saw her, his face became as red as a drop of blood, and he could scarcely utter a word. The princess looked exactly like the beautiful lady with the golden crown, of whom he had dreamed on the night his father died. She appeared to him so lovely that he could not help loving her.

'It could not be true,' he thought, 'that she was really a wicked witch, who ordered people to be hanged or beheaded, if they could not guess her thoughts. Every one has permission to go and ask her hand, even the poorest beggar. I shall pay a visit to the palace,' he said; 'I must go, for I cannot help myself.'

Then they all advised him not to attempt it; for he would be sure to share the same fate as the rest. His fellow-traveller also tried to persuade him against it; but John seemed quite sure of success. He brushed his shoes and his coat, washed his face and his hands, combed his soft flaxen hair, and then went out alone into the town, and walked to the palace.

'Come in,' said the king, as John knocked at the door. John opened it, and the old king, in a dressing gown and embroidered slippers, came towards him. He had the crown on his head, carried his sceptre in one hand, and the orb in the other. 'Wait a bit,' said he, and he placed the orb under his arm, so that he could offer the other hand to John; but when he found that John was another suitor, he began to weep so violently, that both the sceptre and the orb fell to the floor, and he was obliged to wipe his eyes with his dressing gown. Poor old king! 'Let her alone,' he said; 'you will fare as badly as all the others. Come, I will show you.' Then he led him out into the princess's pleasure gardens, and there he saw a frightful sight. On every tree hung three or four king's sons who had wooed the princess, but had not been able to guess the riddles she gave them. Their skeletons rattled in every breeze, so that the terrified birds never dared to venture into the garden. All the flowers were supported by human bones instead of sticks, and human skulls in the flower-pots grinned horribly. It was really a doleful garden for a princess. 'Do you see all this?' said the old king. 'Your fate will be the same as those who are here, therefore do not attempt it. You really make me very unhappy – I take these things to heart so very much.'

John kissed the good old king's hand, and said he was sure it would be all right, for he was quite enchanted with the beautiful princess. Then the princess herself came riding into the palace yard with all her ladies, and he wished her 'Good morning'. She looked wonderfully fair and lovely when she offered her hand to John, and he loved her more than ever. How could she be a wicked witch, as all the people asserted? He accompanied her into the hall, and the little pages offered them gingerbread nuts and sweetmeats, but the old king was so unhappy he could eat nothing, and besides, gingerbread nuts were too hard for him. It was decided that John should come to the palace the next day, when the judges and the whole of the counsellors would be present, to try if he could guess the first riddle. If he succeeded, he would have to come a second time; but if not, he would lose his life – and no one had ever been able to guess even one. However, John was not at all anxious about the result of his trial; on the contrary, he was very merry. He thought only of the beautiful princess, and believed that in some way he should have help, but how he knew not, and did not like to think about it; so he danced along the high-road as he went back to the inn, where he had left his fellow-traveller waiting for him. John could not refrain from telling him how gracious the princess had been, and how beautiful she looked. He longed for the next day so much, that he might go to the palace and try his luck at guessing the riddles. But his comrade shook his head, and looked very mournful. 'I do so wish you to do well,' said he; 'we might have continued together much longer, and now I am likely to lose you; you poor dear John! I could shed tears, but I will not make you unhappy on the last night we may be together. We will be merry, really merry this evening; tomorrow, after you are gone, I shall be able to weep undisturbed.'

It was very quickly known among the inhabitants of the town that another suitor had arrived for the princess, and there was great sorrow in consequence. The theatre remained closed, the women who sold sweetmeats tied crape round the sugar-sticks, and the king and the priests were on their knees in the church.

There was a great lamentation, for no one expected John to succeed better than those who had been suitors before.

In the evening John's comrade prepared a large bowl of punch, and said, 'Now let us be merry, and drink to the health of the princess.' But after drinking two glasses, John became so sleepy that he could not keep his eyes open, and fell fast asleep. Then his fellow-traveller lifted him gently out of his chair, and laid him on the bed; and as soon as it was quite dark, he took the two large wings which he had cut from the dead swan, and tied them firmly to his own shoulders. Then he put into his pocket the largest of the three rods which he had obtained from the old woman who had fallen and broken her leg. After this he opened the window, and flew away over the town, straight towards the palace, and seated himself in a corner, under the window which looked into the bedroom of the princess.

The town was perfectly still when the clocks struck a quarter to twelve. Presently the window opened, and the princess, who had large black wings to her shoulders, and a long white mantle, flew away over the city towards a high mountain. The fellow-traveller, who had made himself invisible, so that she could not possibly see him, flew after her through the air, and whipped the princess with his rod, so that the blood came whenever he struck her. Ah, it was a strange flight through the air! The wind caught her mantle, so that it spread out on all sides, like the large sail of a ship, and the moon shone through it. 'How it hails, to be sure!' said the princess, at each blow she received from the rod; and it served her right to be whipped.

At last she reached the side of the mountain, and knocked. The mountain opened with a noise like the roll of thunder, and the princess went in. The traveller followed her; no one could see him, as he had made himself invisible. They went through a long, wide passage. A thousand gleaming spiders ran here and there on the walls, causing them to glitter as if they were illuminated with fire. They next entered a large hall built of silver and gold. Large red and blue flowers shone on the walls, looking like sunflowers in size, but no one could dare to pluck them, for the stems were hideous poisonous snakes, and the flowers were flames of fire, darting out of their jaws. Shining glow-worms covered the ceiling, and sky-blue bats flapped their transparent wings. Altogether the place had a frightful appearance. In the middle of the floor stood a throne supported by four skeleton horses, whose harness had been made by fiery-red spiders. The throne itself was made of milk-white glass, and the cushions were little black mice, each biting the other's tail. Over it hung a canopy of rose-coloured spider's webs, spotted with the prettiest little green flies, which sparkled like precious stones. On the throne sat an old magician with a crown on his ugly head, and a sceptre in his hand. He kissed the princess on the forehead, seated her by his side on the splendid throne, and then the music commenced. Great black grasshoppers played the mouth organ, and the owl struck herself on the body instead of a drum. It was altogether a ridiculous concert. Little black goblins with false lights in their caps danced about the hall; but no one could see the traveller, and he had placed himself just behind the throne where he could see and hear everything. The courtiers who came in afterwards looked noble and grand; but any one with common sense could see what they really were, only broomsticks, with cabbages for heads. The magician had given them life, and dressed them in embroidered robes. It answered very well, as they were only wanted for show. After there had been a little dancing, the princess told the magician that she had a new suitor, and asked him what she could think of for the suitor to guess when he came to the castle the next morning.

'Listen to what I say,' said the magician, 'you must choose something very easy, he is less likely to guess it then. Think of one of your shoes, he will never imagine it is that. Then cut his head off; and mind you do not forget to bring his eyes with you tomorrow night, that I may eat them.'

The princess curtsied low, and said she would not forget the eyes.

The magician then opened the mountain and she flew home again, but the traveller followed and flogged her so much with the rod, that she sighed quite deeply about the heavy hail-storm, and made as much haste as she could to get back to her bedroom through the window. The traveller then returned to the inn where John still slept, took off his wings and laid down on the bed, for he was very tired. Early in the morning John awoke, and when his fellow-traveller got up, he said that he had a very wonderful dream about the princess and her shoe, he therefore advised John to ask her if she had not thought of her shoe. Of course the traveller knew this from what the magician in the mountain had said.

'I may as well say that as anything,' said John. 'Perhaps your dream may come true; still I will say farewell, for if I guess wrong I shall never see you again.'

Then they embraced each other, and John went into the town and walked to the palace. The great hall was full of people, and the judges sat in arm-chairs, with eider-down cushions to rest their heads upon, because they had so much to think of. The old king stood near, wiping his eyes with his white pocket-handkerchief. When the princess entered, she looked even more beautiful than she had appeared the day before, and greeted everyone present most gracefully; but to John she gave her hand, and said, 'Good morning to you.'

Now came the time for John to guess what she was thinking of; and oh, how kindly she looked at him as she spoke. But when he uttered the single word shoe, she turned as pale as a ghost; all her wisdom could not help her, for he had guessed rightly. Oh, how pleased the old king was! It was quite amusing to see how he capered about. All the people clapped their hands, both on his account and John's, who had guessed rightly the first time. His fellow-traveller was glad also, when he heard how successful John had been. But John folded his hands, and thanked God, who, he felt quite sure, would help him again; and he knew he had to guess twice more. The evening passed pleasantly like the one preceding. While John slept, his companion flew behind the princess to the mountain, and flogged her even harder than before; this time he had taken two rods with him. No one saw him go in with her, and he heard all that was said. The princess this time was to think of a glove, and he told John as if he had again heard it in a dream. The next day, therefore, he was able to guess correctly the second time, and it caused great rejoicing at the palace. The whole court jumped about as they had seen the king do the day before, but the princess lay on the sofa, and would not say a single word. All now depended upon John. If he only guessed rightly the third time, he would marry the princess, and reign over the kingdom after the death of the old king: but if he failed, he would lose his life, and the magician would have his beautiful blue eyes. That evening John said his prayers and went to bed very early, and soon fell asleep calmly. But his companion tied on his wings to his shoulders, took three rods, and, with his sword at his side, flew to the palace. It was a very dark night, and so stormy that the tiles flew from the roofs of the houses, and the trees in the garden upon which the skeletons hung bent themselves like reeds before the wind. The lightning flashed, and the thunder rolled in one long-continued peal all night. The window of the castle opened, and the princess flew out. She was pale as death, but she laughed at the storm as if it were not bad enough. Her white mantle fluttered in the wind like a large sail, and the traveller flogged her with the three rods till the blood trickled down, and at last she could scarcely fly; she contrived, however, to reach the mountain. 'What a hail-storm!' she said, as she entered; 'I have never been out in such weather as this.'

'Yes, there may be too much of a good thing sometimes,' said the magician.

Then the princess told him that John had guessed rightly the second time, and if he succeeded the next morning, he would win, and she could never come to the mountain again, or practise magic as she had done, and therefore she was quite unhappy. 'I will find out something for you to think of which he will never guess, unless he is a greater conjuror than myself. But now let us be merry.'

Then he took the princess by both hands, and they danced with all the little goblins and Jack-o'-lanterns in the room. The red spiders sprang here and there on the walls quite as merrily, and the flowers of fire appeared as if they were throwing out sparks. The owl beat the drum, the crickets whistled and the grasshoppers played the mouth-organ. It was a very ridiculous ball. After they had danced enough, the princess was obliged to go home, for fear she should be missed at the palace. The magician offered to go with her, that they might be company to each other on the way. Then they flew away through the bad weather, and the traveller followed them, and broke his three rods across their shoulders. The magician had never been out in such a hailstorm as this. Just by the palace the magician stopped to wish the princess farewell, and to whisper in her ear, 'Tomorrow think of my head.'

But the traveller heard it, and just as the princess slipped through the window into her bedroom, and the magician turned round to fly back to the mountain, he seized him by the long black beard, and with his sabre cut off the wicked conjuror's head just behind the shoulders, so that he could not even see who it was. He threw the body into the sea to the fishes, and after dipping the head into the water, he tied it up in a silk handkerchief, took it with him to the inn, and then went to bed. The next morning he gave John the handkerchief, and told him not to untie it till the princess asked him what she was thinking of. There were so many people in the great hall of the palace that they stood as thick as radishes tied together in a bundle. The council sat in their arm-chairs with the white cushions. The old king wore new robes, and the golden crown and sceptre had been polished up so that he looked quite smart. But the princess was very pale, and wore a black dress as if she were going to a funeral.

'What have I thought of?' asked the princess, of John. He immediately untied the handkerchief, and was himself quite frightened when he saw the head of the ugly magician. Everyone shuddered, for it was terrible to look at; but the princess sat like a statue, and could not utter a single word. At length she rose and gave John her hand, for he had guessed rightly.

She looked at no one, but sighed deeply, and said, 'You are my master now; this evening our marriage must take place.'

'I am very pleased to hear it,' said the old king. 'It is just what I wish.'

Then all the people shouted 'Hurrah'. The band played music in the streets, the bells rang, and the cake-women took the black crape off the sugar-sticks. There was universal joy. Three oxen, stuffed with ducks and chickens, were roasted whole in the market-place, where every one might help himself to a slice. The fountains spouted forth the most delicious wine, and whoever bought a penny loaf at the baker's received six large buns, full of raisins, as a present. In the evening the whole town was illuminated. The soldiers fired off cannons, and the boys let off crackers. There was eating and drinking, dancing and jumping everywhere. In the palace, the high-born gentlemen and beautiful ladies danced with each other, and they could be heard at a great distance singing the following song: –

Here are maidens, young and fair,
Dancing in the summer air;
Like two spinning-wheels at play,
Pretty maidens dance away –
Dance the spring and summer through
Till the sole falls from your shoe.

But the princess was still a witch, and she could not love John. His fellow-traveller had thought of that, so he gave John three feathers out of the swan's wings, and a little bottle with a few drops in it. He told him to place a large bath full of water by the princess's bed, and put the feathers and the drops into it. Then, at the moment she was about to get into bed, he must give her a little push, so that she might fall into the water, and then dip her three times. This would destroy the power of the magician, and she would love him very much. John did all that his companion told him to do. The princess shrieked aloud when he dipped her under the water the first time, and struggled under his hands in the form of a great black swan with fiery eyes. As she rose the second time from the water, the swan had become white, with a black ring round its neck. John allowed the water to close once more over the bird, and at the same time it changed into a most beautiful princess. She was more lovely even than before, and thanked him, while her eyes sparkled with tears, for having broken the spell of the magician. The next day, the king came with the whole court to offer their congratulations, and stayed till quite late. Last of all came the travelling companion; he had his staff in his hand and his knapsack on his back. John kissed him many times and told him he must not go, he must remain with him, for he was the cause of all his good fortune. But the traveller shook his head, and said gently and kindly, 'No: my time is up now; I have only paid my debt to you. Do you remember the dead man whom the bad people wished to throw out of his coffin? You gave all you possessed that he might rest in his grave; I am that man.' As he said this, he vanished.

The wedding festivities lasted a whole month. John and his princess loved each other dearly, and the old king lived to see many a happy day, when he took their little children on his knees and let them play with his sceptre. And John became king over the whole country.

THE ELFIN HILL

Few large lizards were running nimbly about in the clefts of an old tree; they could understand one another very well, for they spoke the lizard language.

'What a buzzing and a rumbling there is in the elfin hill,' said one of the lizards; 'I have not been able to close my eyes for two nights on account of the noise; I might just as well have had the toothache, for that always keeps me awake.'

'There is something going on within there,' said the other lizard; 'they propped up the top of the hill with four red posts, till cock-crow this morning, so that it is thoroughly aired, and the elfin girls have learnt new dances; there is something.'

'I spoke about it to an earth-worm of my acquaintance,' said a third lizard; 'the earth-worm had just come from the elfin hill, where he has been groping about in the earth day and night. He has heard a great deal; although he cannot see, poor miserable creature, yet he understands very well how to wriggle and lurk about. They expect friends in the elfin hill, grand company, too; but who they are the earth-worm would not say, or, perhaps, he really did not know. All the will-o'-the-wisps are ordered to be there to hold a torch dance, as it is called. The silver and gold which is plentiful in the hill will be polished and placed out in the moonlight.'

'Who can the strangers be?' asked the lizards; 'what can the matter be? Hark, what a buzzing and humming there is!'

Just at this moment the elfin hill opened, and an old elfin maiden, hollow behind, came tripping out; she was the old elf king's housekeeper, and a distant relative of the family; therefore she wore an amber heart on the middle of her forehead. Her feet moved very fast, 'trip, trip'; good gracious, how she could trip right down to the sea to the night-raven.

'You are invited to the elf hill for this evening,' said she; 'but will you do me a great favour and undertake the invitations? You ought to do something, for you have no housekeeping to attend to as I have. We are going to have some very grand people, conjurors, who have always something to say; and therefore the old elf king wishes to make a great display.'

'Who is to be invited?' asked the raven.

'All the world may come to the great ball, even human beings, if they can only talk in their sleep, or do something after our fashion. But for the feast the company must be carefully selected; we can only admit persons of high rank; I have had a dispute myself with the elf king, as he thought we could not admit ghosts. The merman and his daughter must be invited first, although it may not be agreeable to them to remain so long on dry land, but they shall have a wet stone to sit on, or perhaps something better; so I think they will not refuse this time. We must have all the old demons of the first class, with tails, and the hobgoblins and imps; and then I think we ought not to leave out the death-horse, or the grave-pig, or even the church dwarf, although they do belong to the clergy, and are not reckoned among our people; but that is merely their office, they are nearly related to us, and visit us very frequently.'

'Croak,' said the night-raven as he flew away with the invitations.

The elfin maidens were already dancing on the elf hill, and they danced in shawls woven from moonshine and mist, which look very pretty to those who like such things. The large hall within the elf hill was splendidly decorated; the floor had been washed with moonshine, and the walls had been rubbed with magic ointment, so that they glowed like tulip-leaves in the light. In the kitchen were frogs roasting on the spit, and dishes preparing of snail skins, with children's fingers in them, salad of mushroom seed, hemlock, noses and marrow of mice, beer from the marsh woman's brewery, and sparkling salt-petre wine from the grave cellars. These were all substantial food. Rusty nails and church-window glass formed the dessert. The old elf king had his gold crown polished up with powdered slate-pencil; it was like that used by the first form, and very difficult for an elf king to obtain. In the bedrooms, curtains were hung up and fastened with the slime of snails; there was, indeed, a buzzing and humming everywhere.

'Now we must fumigate the place with burnt horse-hair and pig's bristles, and then I think I shall have done my part,' said the elf man-servant.

'Father, dear,' said the youngest daughter, 'may I now hear who our high-born visitors are?'

'Well, I suppose I must tell you now,' he replied; 'two of my daughters must prepare themselves to be married, for the marriages certainly will take place. The old goblin from Norway, who lives in the ancient Dovre mountains, and who possesses many castles built of rock and freestone, besides a gold mine, which is better than all, so it is thought, is coming with his two sons, who are both seeking a wife. The old goblin is a true-hearted, honest, old Norwegian greybeard; cheerful and straightforward. I knew him formerly, when we used to drink together to our good fellowship: he came here once to fetch his wife, she is dead now. She was the daughter of the king of the chalk-hills at Moen. They say he took his wife from chalk; I shall be delighted to see him again. It is said that the boys are ill-bred, forward lads, but perhaps that is not quite correct, and they will become better as they grow older. Let me see that you know how to teach them good manners.'

'And when are they coming?' asked the daughter.

'That depends upon wind and weather,' said the elf king; 'they travel economically. They will come when there is the chance of a ship. I wanted them to come over to Sweden, but the old man was not inclined to take my advice. He does not go forward with the times, and that I do not like.'

Two will-o'-the-wisps came jumping in, one quicker than the other, so of course, one arrived first. 'They are coming! They are coming!' he cried.

'Give me my crown,' said the elf king, 'and let me stand in the moonshine.'

The daughters drew on their shawls and bowed down to the ground. There stood the old goblin from the Dovre mountains, with his crown of hardened ice and polished fir-cones. Besides this, he wore a bear-skin, and great, warm boots, while his sons went with their throats bare and wore no braces, for they were strong men.

'Is that a hill?' said the youngest of the boys, pointing to the elf hill, 'we should call it a hole in Norway.'

'Boys,' said the old man, 'a hole goes in, and a hill stands out; have you no eyes in your heads?'

Another thing they wondered at was that they were able without trouble to understand the language.

'Take care,' said the old man, 'or people will think you have not been well brought up.'

Then they entered the elfin hill, where the select and grand company were assembled, and so quickly had they appeared that they seemed to have been blown together. But for each guest the neatest and pleasantest arrangement had been made. The sea folks sat at table in great water-tubs, and they said it was just like being at home. All behaved themselves properly excepting the two young northern goblins; they put their legs on the table and thought they were all right.

'Feet off the table-cloth!' said the old goblin. They obeyed, but not immediately. Then they tickled the ladies who waited at table, with the fir-cones, which they carried in their pockets. They took off their boots, that they might be more at ease, and gave them to the ladies to hold. But their father, the old goblin, was very different; he talked pleasantly about the stately Norwegian rocks, and told fine tales of the waterfalls which dashed over them with a clattering noise like thunder or the sound of an organ, spreading their white foam on every side. He told of the salmon that leaps in the rushing waters, while the water-god plays on his golden harp. He spoke of the bright winter nights, when the sledge bells are ringing, and the boys run with burning torches across the smooth ice, which is so transparent that they can see the fishes dart forward beneath their feet. He described everything so clearly that those who listened could see it all; they could see the saw-mills going, the men-servants and the maidens singing songs, and dancing a rattling dance – when all at once the old goblin gave the old elfin maiden a kiss, such a tremendous kiss, and yet they were almost strangers to each other.

Then the elfin girls had to dance, first in the usual way, and then with stamping feet, which they performed very well; then followed the artistic and solo dance. Dear me, how they did throw their legs about! No one could tell where the dance began or where it ended, nor indeed which were legs and which were arms, for they were all flying about together, like the shavings in a saw-pit! And then they spun round so quickly that the death-horse and the grave-pig became sick and giddy, and were obliged to leave the table.

'Stop!' cried the old goblin. 'Is that the only house-keeping they can perform? Can they do anything more than dance and throw about their legs, and make a whirlwind?'

'You shall soon see what they can do,' said the elf king. And then he called his youngest daughter to him. She was slender and fair as moonlight, and the most graceful of all the sisters. She took a white chip in her mouth, and vanished instantly; this was her accomplishment. But the old goblin said he should not like his wife to have such an accomplishment, and thought his boys would have the same objection. Another daughter could make a figure like herself follow her, as if she had a shadow, which none of the goblin folk ever had. The third was of quite a different sort; she had learnt in the brew-house of the moor witch how to lard elfin puddings with glow-worms.

'She will make a good housewife,' said the old goblin, and then saluted her with his eyes instead of drinking her health; for he did not drink much.

Now came the fourth daughter, with a large harp to play upon; and when she struck the first chord, every one lifted up the left leg (for the goblins are left-legged), and at the second chord they found they must all do just what she wanted.

'That is a dangerous woman,' said the old goblin; and the two sons walked out of the hill; they had had enough of it. 'And what can the next daughter do?' asked the old goblin.

'I have learnt everything that is Norwegian,' said she; 'and I will never marry, unless I can go to Norway.'

Then her youngest sister whispered to the old goblin, 'That is only because she has heard, in a Norwegian song, that when the world shall decay, the cliffs of Norway will remain standing like monuments; and she wants to get there, that she may be safe; for she is so afraid of sinking.'

'Ho! Ho!' said the old goblin. 'Is that what she means? Well, what can the seventh and last do?'

'The sixth comes before the seventh,' said the elf king, for he could reckon; but the sixth would not come forward.

'I can only tell people the truth,' said she. 'No one cares for me, nor troubles himself about me; and I have enough to do to sew my grave clothes.'

So the seventh and last came; and what could she do? Why, she could tell stories, as many as you liked, on any subject.

'Here are my five fingers,' said the old goblin; 'now tell me a story for each of them.'

So she took him by the wrist, and he laughed till he nearly choked; and when she came to the fourth finger, there was a gold ring on it, as if it knew there was to be a betrothal. Then the old goblin said, 'Hold fast what you have: this hand is yours; for I will have you for a wife myself.'

Then the elfin girl said that the stories about the ring-finger and little Peter Playman had not yet been told.

'We will hear them in the winter,' said the old goblin, 'and also about the fir and the birch-trees, and the ghost stories, and of the tingling frost. You shall tell your tales, for no one over there can do it so well; and we will sit in the stone rooms, where the pine logs are burning, and drink mead out of the golden drinking-horn of the old Norwegian kings. The water-god has given me two; and when we sit there, Nix comes to pay us a visit, and will sing you all the songs of the mountain shepherd-esses. How merry we shall be! The salmon will be leaping in the waterfalls, and dashing against the stone walls, but he will not be able to come in. It is indeed very pleasant to live in old Norway. But where are the lads?'

Where indeed were they? Why, running about the fields, and blowing out the will-o'-the-wisps, who so good-naturedly came and brought their torches.

'What tricks have you been playing?' said the old goblin. 'I have taken a mother for you, and now you may take one of your aunts.'

But the youngsters said they would rather make a speech and drink to their good fellowship; they had no wish to marry. Then they made speeches and drank toasts, and tipped their glasses, to show that they were empty. Then they took off their coats, and lay down on the table to sleep; for they made themselves quite at home. But the old goblin danced about the room with his young bride, and exchanged boots with her, which is more fashionable than exchanging rings.

'The cock is crowing,' said the old elfin maiden who acted as housekeeper; 'now we must close the shutters, that the sun may not scorch us.'

Then the hill closed up. But the lizards continued to run up and down the riven tree; and one said to the other, 'Oh, how much I was pleased with the old goblin!'

'The boys pleased me better,' said the earth-worm. But then the poor miserable creature could not see.

THE WILD SWANS

Far away in the land to which the swallows fly when it is winter, dwelt a king who had eleven sons, and one daughter, named Eliza. The eleven brothers were princes, and each went to school with a star on his breast, and a sword by his side. They wrote with diamond pencils on gold slates, and learnt their lessons so quickly and read so easily that everyone might know they were princes. Their sister Eliza sat on a little stool of plate-glass, and had a book full of pictures, which had cost as much as half a kingdom. Oh, these children were indeed happy, but it was not to remain so always. Their father, who was king of the country, married a very wicked queen, who did not love the poor children at all. They knew this from the very first day after the wedding. In the palace there were great festivities, and the children played at receiving company; but instead of having, as usual, all the cakes and apples that were left, she gave them some sand in a tea-cup, and told them to pretend it was cake. The week after, she sent little Eliza into the country to a peasant and his wife, and then she told the king so many untrue things about the young princes that he gave himself no more trouble respecting them.

'Go out into the world and get your own living,' said the queen. 'Fly like great birds, who have no voice.' But she could not make them ugly as she wished, for they were turned into eleven beautiful wild swans. Then, with a strange cry, they flew through the windows of the palace, over the park, to the forest beyond. It was early morning when they passed the peasant's cottage, where their sister Eliza lay asleep in her room. They hovered over the roof, twisted their long necks and flapped their wings, but no one heard them or saw them, so they were at last obliged to fly away, high up in the clouds; and over the wide world they flew till they came to a thick, dark wood, which stretched far away to the seashore. Poor little Eliza was alone in her room playing with a green leaf, for she had no other playthings, and she pierced a hole through the leaf, and looked through it at the sun, and it was as if she saw her brothers' clear eyes, and when the warm sun shone on her cheeks, she thought of all the kisses they had given her. One day passed just like another; sometimes the winds rustled through the leaves of the rose-bush, and would whisper to the roses, 'Who can be more beautiful than you!' But the roses would shake their heads, and say, 'Eliza is.' And when the old woman sat at the cottage door on Sunday, and read her hymn-book, the wind would flutter the leaves, and say to the book, 'Who can be more pious than you?' and then the hymn-book would answer, 'Eliza.' And the roses and the hymn-book told the real truth. At fifteen she returned home, but when the queen saw how beautiful she was, she became full of spite and hatred towards her. Willingly would she have turned her into a swan, like her brothers, but she did not dare to do so yet, because the king wished to see his daughter. Early one morning the queen went into the bathroom; it was built of marble, and had soft cushions, trimmed with the most beautiful tapestry. She took three toads with her, and kissed them, and said to one, 'When Eliza comes to the bath, seat yourself upon her head, that she may become as stupid as you are.' Then she said to another, 'Place yourself on her forehead, that she may become as ugly as you are, and that her father may not know her.' 'Rest on her heart,' she whispered to the third, 'then she will have evil inclinations, and suffer in consequence.' So she put the toads into the clear water, and they turned green immediately. She next called Eliza, and helped her to undress and get into the bath. As Eliza dipped her head under the water, one of the toads sat on her hair, a second on her forehead and a third on her breast, but she did not seem to notice them, and when she rose out of the water, there were three red poppies floating upon it. Had not the creatures been venomous or been kissed by the witch, they would have been changed into red roses. At all events they became flowers, because they had rested on Eliza's head, and on her heart. She was too good and too innocent for witchcraft to have any power over her. When the wicked queen saw this, she rubbed her face with walnut-juice, so that she was quite brown; then she tangled her beautiful hair and smeared it with disgusting ointment, till it was quite impossible to recognise the beautiful Eliza.

When her father saw her, he was much shocked, and declared she was not his daughter. No one but the watch-dog and the swallows knew her; and they were only poor animals, and could say nothing. Then poor Eliza wept, and thought of her eleven brothers, who were all away. Sorrowfully, she stole away from the palace, and walked, the whole day, over fields and moors, till she came to the great forest. She knew not in what direction to go; but she was so unhappy, and longed so for her brothers, who had been, like herself, driven out into the world, that she was determined to seek them. She had been but a short time in the wood when night came on, and she quite lost the path; so she laid herself down on the soft moss, offered up her evening prayer, and leaned her head against the stump of a tree. All nature was still, and the soft, mild air fanned her forehead. The light of hundreds of glow-worms shone amidst the grass and the moss, like green fire; and if she touched a twig with her hand, ever so lightly, the brilliant insects fell down around her, like shooting-stars.

All night long she dreamt of her brothers. She and they were children again, playing together. She saw them writing with their diamond pencils on golden slates, while she looked at the beautiful picture-book which had cost half a kingdom. They were not writing lines and letters, as they used to do; but descriptions of the noble deeds they had performed, and of all they had discovered and seen. In the picture-book, too, everything was living. The birds sang, and the people came out of the book, and spoke to Eliza and her brothers; but, as the leaves turned over, they darted back again to their places, that all might be in order.

When she awoke, the sun was high in the heavens; yet she could not see him, for the lofty trees spread their branches thickly over her head; but his beams were glancing through the leaves here and there, like a golden mist. There was a sweet fragrance from the fresh green verdure, and the birds almost perched upon her shoulders. She heard water rippling from a number of springs, all flowing in a lake with golden sands. Bushes grew thickly round the lake, and at one spot an opening had been made by a deer, through which Eliza went down to the water. The lake was so clear that, had not the wind rustled the branches of the trees and the bushes, so that they moved, they would have appeared as if painted in the depths of the lake; for every leaf was reflected in the water, whether it stood in the shade or the sunshine. As soon as Eliza saw her own face, she was quite terrified at finding it so brown and ugly; but when she wetted her little hand, and rubbed her eyes and forehead, the white skin gleamed forth once more; and, after she had undressed, and dipped herself in the fresh water, a more beautiful king's daughter could not be found in the wide world. As soon as she had dressed herself again, and braided her long hair, she went to the bubbling spring, and drank some water out of the hollow of her hand. Then she wandered far into the forest, not knowing whither she went. She thought of her brothers, and felt sure that God would not forsake her. It is God who makes the wild apples grow in the wood, to satisfy the hungry, and He now led her to one of these trees, which was so loaded with fruit that the boughs bent beneath the weight. Here she held her noonday repast, placed props under the boughs, and then went into the gloomiest depths of the forest. It was so still that she could hear the sound of her own footsteps, as well as the rustling of every withered leaf which she crushed under her feet. Not a bird was to be seen, not a sunbeam could penetrate through the large, dark boughs of the trees. Their lofty trunks stood so close together, that, when she looked before her, it seemed as if she were enclosed within trellis-work. Such solitude she had never known before. The night was very dark. Not a single glow-worm glittered in the moss.

Sorrowfully she laid herself down to sleep; and, after a while, it seemed to her as if the branches of the trees parted over her head, and that the mild eyes of angels looked down upon her from heaven. When she awoke in the morning, she knew not whether she had dreamt this, or if it had really been so. Then she continued her wandering; but she had not gone many steps forward when she met an old woman with berries in her basket, and she gave her a few to eat. Then Eliza asked her if she had not seen eleven princes riding through the forest.

'No,' replied the old woman, 'but I saw yesterday eleven swans, with gold crowns on their heads, swimming on the river close by.' Then she led Eliza a little distance farther to a sloping bank, and at the foot of it wound a little river. The trees on its banks stretched their long leafy branches across the water towards each other, and where the growth prevented them from meeting naturally, the roots had torn themselves away from the ground, so that the branches might mingle their foliage as they hung over the water. Eliza bade the old woman farewell, and walked by the flowing river till she reached the shore of the open sea. And there, before the young maiden's eyes, lay the glorious ocean, but not a sail appeared on its surface, not even a boat could be seen. How was she to go farther? She noticed how the countless pebbles on the sea-shore had been smoothed and rounded by the action of the water. Glass, iron, stones, everything that lay there mingled together, had taken its shape from the same power, and felt as smooth, or even smoother than her own delicate hand. 'The water rolls on without weariness,' she said, 'till all that is hard becomes smooth; so will I be unwearied in my task. Thanks for your lessons, bright rolling waves; my heart tells me you will lead me to my dear brothers.' On the foam-covered sea-weeds lay eleven white swan feathers, which she gathered up and placed together. Drops of water lay upon them; whether they were dew-drops or tears no one could say. Lonely as it was on the sea-shore, she did not observe it, for the ever-moving sea showed more changes in a few hours than the most varying lake could produce during a whole year. If a black heavy cloud arose, it was as if the sea said, 'I can look dark and angry too;' and then the wind blew, and the waves turned to white foam as they rolled. When the wind slept, and the clouds glowed with the red sunlight, then the sea looked like a rose leaf. But however quietly its white glassy surface rested, there was still a motion on the shore, as its waves rose and fell like the breast of a sleeping child. When the sun was about to set, Eliza saw eleven white swans with golden crowns on their heads, flying towards the land, one behind the other, like a long white ribbon. Then Eliza went down the slope from the shore, and hid herself behind the bushes. The swans alighted quite close to her and flapped their great white wings. As soon as the sun had disappeared under the water, the feathers of the swans fell off, and eleven beautiful princes, Eliza's brothers, stood near her. She uttered a loud cry, for, although they were very much changed, she knew them immediately. She sprang into their arms, and called them each by name. Then, how happy the princes were at meeting their little sister again, for they recognised her, although she had grown so tall and beautiful. They laughed, and they wept, and very soon understood how wickedly their mother had acted to them all. 'We brothers,' said the eldest, 'fly about as wild swans, so long as the sun is in the sky; but as soon as it sinks behind the hills, we recover our human shape. Therefore must we always be near a resting place for our feet before sunset; for if we should be flying towards the clouds at the time we recovered our natural shape as men, we should sink deep into the sea. We do not dwell here, but in a land just as fair that lies beyond the ocean, which we have to cross for a long distance; there is no island in our passage upon which we could pass, the night; nothing but a little rock rising out of the sea, upon which we can scarcely stand with safety, even closely crowded together. If the sea is rough, the foam dashes over us, yet we thank God even for this rock; we have passed whole nights upon it, or we should never have reached our beloved fatherland, for our flight across the sea occupies two of the longest days in the year. We have permission to visit our home once in every year, and to remain eleven days, during which we fly across the forest to look once more at the palace where our father dwells, and where we were born, and at the church, where our mother lies buried. Here it seems as if the very trees and bushes were related to us. The wild horses leap over the plains as we have seen them in our childhood. The charcoal burners sing the old songs, to which we have danced as children. This is our fatherland, to which we are drawn by loving ties; and here we have found you, our dear little sister. Two days longer we can remain here, and then must we fly away to a beautiful land which is not our home; and how can we take you with us? We have neither ship nor boat.'

'How can I break this spell?' said their sister. And then she talked about it nearly the whole night, only slumbering for a few hours. Eliza was awakened by the rustling of the swans' wings as they soared above. Her brothers were again changed to swans, and they flew in circles wider and wider, till they were far away; but one of them, the youngest swan, remained behind, and laid his head in his sister's lap, while she stroked his wings; and they remained together the whole day. Towards evening, the rest came back, and as the sun went down they resumed their natural forms. 'Tomorrow,' said one, 'we shall fly away, not to return again till a whole year has passed. But we cannot leave you here. Have you courage to go with us? My arm is strong enough to carry you through the wood; and will not all our wings be strong enough to fly with you over the sea?'

'Yes, take me with you,' said Eliza. Then they spent the whole night in weaving a net with the pliant willow and rushes. It was very large and strong. Eliza laid herself down on the net, and when the sun rose, and her brothers again became wild swans, they took up the net with their beaks, and flew up to the clouds with their dear sister, who still slept. The sunbeams fell on her face, therefore one of the swans soared over her head, so that his broad wings might shade her. They were far from the land when Eliza woke. She thought she must still be dreaming, it seemed so strange to her to feel herself being carried so high in the air over the sea. By her side lay a branch full of beautiful ripe berries, and a bundle of sweet roots; the youngest of her brothers had gathered them for her, and placed them by her side. She smiled her thanks to him; she knew it was the same who had hovered over her to shade her with his wings. They were now so high that a large ship beneath them looked like a white seagull skimming the waves. A great cloud floating behind them appeared like a vast mountain, and upon it Eliza saw her own shadow and those of the eleven swans, looking gigantic in size.

Altogether it formed a more beautiful picture than she had ever seen; but as the sun rose higher, and the clouds were left behind, the shadowy picture vanished away. Onward the whole day they flew through the air like a winged arrow, yet more slowly than usual, for they had their sister to carry. The weather seemed inclined to be stormy, and Eliza watched the sinking sun with great anxiety, for the little rock in the ocean was not yet in sight. It appeared to her as if the swans were making great efforts with their wings. Alas! She was the cause of their not advancing more quickly. When the sun set, they would change to men, fall into the sea and be drowned. Then she offered a prayer from her inmost heart, but still no appearance of the rock. Dark clouds came nearer, the gusts of wind told of a coming storm, while from a thick, heavy mass of clouds the lightning burst forth flash after flash. The sun had reached the edge of the sea, when the swans darted down so swiftly, that Eliza's head trembled; she believed they were falling, but they again soared onward. Presently she caught sight of the rock just below them, and by this time the sun was half hidden by the waves. The rock did not appear larger than a seal's head thrust out of the water. They sunk so rapidly that at the moment their feet touched the rock, it shone only like a star, and at last disappeared like the last spark in a piece of burnt paper. Then she saw her brothers standing closely round her with their arms linked together. There was but just room enough for them, and not the smallest space to spare. The sea dashed against the rock, and covered them with spray. The heavens were lighted up with continual flashes, and peal after peal of thunder rolled. But the sister and brothers sat holding each other's hands, and singing hymns, from which they gained hope and courage. In the early dawn the air became calm and still, and at sunrise the swans flew away from the rock with Eliza. The sea was still rough, and from their high position in the air, the white foam on the dark green waves looked like millions of swans swimming on the water. As the sun rose higher, Eliza saw before her, floating on the air, a range of mountains, with shining masses of ice on their summits. In the centre rose a castle apparently a mile long, with rows of columns, rising one above another, while, around it, palm-trees waved and flowers bloomed as large as mill wheels. She asked if this was the land to which they were hastening. The swans shook their heads, for what she beheld were the beautiful ever-changing cloud palaces of the 'Fata Morgana', into which no mortal can enter. Eliza was still gazing at the scene, when mountains, forests, and castles melted away, and twenty stately churches rose in their stead, with high towers and pointed gothic windows. Eliza even fancied she could hear the tones of the organ, but it was the music of the murmuring sea which she heard. As they drew nearer to the churches, they also changed into a fleet of ships, which seemed to be sailing beneath her; but as she looked again, she found it was only a sea mist gliding over the ocean. So there continued to pass before her eyes a constant change of scene, till at last she saw the real land to which they were bound, with its blue mountains, its cedar forests, and its cities and palaces. Long before the sun went down, she sat on a rock, in front of a large cave, on the floor of which the overgrown yet delicate green creeping plants looked like an embroidered carpet. 'Now we shall expect to hear what you dream of tonight,' said the youngest brother, as he showed his sister her bedroom.

'Heaven grant that I may dream how to save you,' she replied. And this thought took such hold upon her mind that she prayed earnestly to God for help, and even in her sleep she continued to pray. Then it appeared to her as if she were flying high in the air, towards the cloudy palace of the 'Fata Morgana', and a fairy came out to meet her, radiant and beautiful in appearance, and yet very much like the old woman who had given her berries in the wood, and who had told her of the swans with golden crowns on their heads. 'Your brothers can be released,' said she, 'if you have only courage and perseverance. True, water is softer than your own delicate hands, and yet it polishes stones into shapes; it feels no pain as your fingers would feel, it has no soul, and cannot suffer such agony and torment as you will have to endure. Do you see the stinging nettle which I hold in my hand? Quantities of the same sort grow round the cave in which you sleep, but none will be of any use to you unless they grow upon the graves in a churchyard. These you must gather even while they burn blisters on your hands. Break them to pieces with your hands and feet, and they will become flax, from which you must spin and weave eleven coats with long sleeves; if these are then thrown over the eleven swans, the spell will be broken. But remember, that from the moment you commence your task until it is finished, even should it occupy years of your life, you must not speak. The first word you utter will pierce through the hearts of your brothers like a deadly dagger. Their lives hang upon your tongue. Remember all I have told you.' And as she finished speaking, she touched her hand lightly with the nettle, and a pain, as of burning fire, awoke Eliza.

It was broad daylight, and close by where she had been sleeping lay a nettle like the one she had seen in her dream. She fell on her knees and offered her thanks to God. Then she went forth from the cave to begin her work with her delicate hands. She groped in amongst the ugly nettles, which burnt great blisters on her hands and arms, but she determined to bear it gladly if she could only release her dear brothers. So she bruised the nettles with her bare feet and spun the flax. At sunset her brothers returned and were very much frightened when they found her dumb. They believed it to be some new sorcery of their wicked step-mother. But when they saw her hands they understood what she was doing on their behalf, and the youngest brother wept, and where his tears fell the pain ceased, and the burning blisters vanished. She kept to her work all night, for she could not rest till she had released her dear brothers. During the whole of the following day, while her brothers were absent, she sat in solitude, but never before had the time flown so quickly. One coat was already finished and she had begun the second, when she heard the huntsman's horn, and was struck with fear. The sound came nearer and nearer, she heard the dogs barking, and fled with terror into the cave. She hastily bound together the nettles she had gathered into a bundle and sat upon them. Immediately a great dog came bounding towards her out of the ravine, and then another and another; they barked loudly, ran back, and then came again. In a very few minutes all the huntsmen stood before the cave, and the handsomest of them was the king of the country. He advanced towards her, for he had never seen a more beautiful maiden.

'How did you come here, my sweet child?' he asked. But Eliza shook her head. She dared not speak, at the cost of her brothers' lives. And she hid her hands under her apron, so that the king might not see how she must be suffering.

'Come with me,' he said; 'here you cannot remain. If you are as good as you are beautiful, I will dress you in silk and velvet, I will place a golden crown upon your head, and you shall dwell, and rule, and make your home in my richest castle.' And then he lifted her on his horse. She wept and wrung her hands, but the king said, 'I wish only for your happiness. A time will come when you will thank me for this.' And then he galloped away over the mountains, holding her before him on this horse, and the hunters followed behind them. As the sun went down, they approached a fair royal city, with churches, and cupolas. On arriving at the castle the king led her into marble halls, where large fountains played, and where the walls and the ceilings were covered with rich paintings. But she had no eyes for all these glorious sights, she could only mourn and weep. Patiently she allowed the women to array her in royal robes, to weave pearls in her hair, and draw soft gloves over her blistered fingers. As she stood before them in all her rich dress, she looked so dazzlingly beautiful that the court bowed low in her presence. Then the king declared his intention of making her his bride, but the archbishop shook his head, and whispered that the fair young maiden was only a witch who had blinded the king's eyes and bewitched his heart. But the king would not listen to this; he ordered the music to sound, the daintiest dishes to be served, and the loveliest maidens to dance. Afterwards he led her through fragrant gardens and lofty halls, but not a smile appeared on her lips or sparkled in her eyes. She looked the very picture of grief. Then the king opened the door of a little chamber in which she was to sleep; it was adorned with rich green tapestry, and resembled the cave in which he had found her. On the floor lay the bundle of flax which she had spun from the nettles, and under the ceiling hung the coat she had made. These things had been brought away from the cave as curiosities by one of the huntsmen.

'Here you can dream yourself back again in the old home in the cave,' said the king; 'here is the work with which you employed yourself. It will amuse you now in the midst of all this splendour to think of that time.'

When Eliza saw all these things which lay so near her heart, a smile played around her mouth, and the crimson blood rushed to her cheeks. She thought of her brothers, and their release made her so joyful that she kissed the king's hand. Then he pressed her to his heart. Very soon the joyous church bells announced the marriage feast, and that the beautiful dumb girl out of the wood was to be made the queen of the country. Then the archbishop whispered wicked words in the king's ear, but they did not sink into his heart. The marriage was still to take place, and the archbishop himself had to place the crown on the bride's head; in his wicked spite, he pressed the narrow circlet so tightly on her forehead that it caused her pain. But a heavier weight encircled her heart – sorrow for her brothers. She felt not bodily pain. Her mouth was closed; a single word would cost the lives of her brothers. But she loved the kind, handsome king, who did everything to make her happy more and more each day; she loved him with all her heart, and her eyes beamed with the love she dared not speak. Oh! If she had only been able to confide in him and tell him of her grief. But dumb she must remain till her task was finished. Therefore at night she crept away into her little chamber, which had been decked out to look like the cave, and quickly wove one coat after another. But when she began the seventh she found she had no more flax. She knew that the nettles she wanted to use grew in the churchyard, and that she must pluck them herself. How should she get out there? 'Oh, what is the pain in my fingers to the torment which my heart endures?' said she. 'I must venture, I shall not be denied help from heaven.' Then with a trembling heart, as if she were about to perform a wicked deed, she crept into the garden in the broad moonlight, and passed through the narrow walks and the deserted streets, till she reached the churchyard. Then she saw on one of the broad tombstones a group of ghouls. These hideous creatures took off their rags, as if they intended to bathe, and then clawing open the fresh graves with their long, skinny fingers, pulled out the dead bodies and ate the flesh! Eliza had to pass close by them, and they fixed their wicked glances upon her, but she prayed silently, gathered the burning nettles, and carried them home with her to the castle. One person only had seen her, and that was the archbishop – he was awake while everybody was asleep. Now he thought his opinion was evidently correct. All was not right with the queen. She was a witch, and had bewitched the king and all the people. Secretly he told the king what he had seen and what he feared, and as the hard words came from his tongue, the carved images of the saints shook their heads as if they would say. 'It is not so. Eliza is innocent.'

But the archbishop interpreted it in another way; he believed that they witnessed against her, and were shaking their heads at her wickedness. Two large tears rolled down the king's cheeks, and he went home with doubt in his heart, and at night he pretended to sleep, but there came no real sleep to his eyes, for he saw Eliza get up every night and disappear in her own chamber. From day to day his brow became darker, and Eliza saw it and did not understand the reason, but it alarmed her and made her heart tremble for her brothers. Her hot tears glittered like pearls on the regal velvet and diamonds, while all who saw her were wishing they could be queens. In the mean time she had almost finished her task; only one coat of mail was wanting, but she had no flax left, and not a single nettle. Once more only, and for the last time, must she venture to the churchyard and pluck a few handfuls. She thought with terror of the solitary walk, and of the horrible ghouls, but her will was firm, as well as her trust in Providence. Eliza went, and the king and the archbishop followed her. They saw her vanish through the wicket gate into the churchyard, and when they came nearer they saw the ghouls sitting on the tombstone, as Eliza had seen them, and the king turned away his head, for he thought she was with them – she whose head had rested on his breast that very evening. 'The people must condemn her,' said he, and she was very quickly condemned by every one to suffer death by fire. Away from the gorgeous regal halls was she led to a dark, dreary cell, where the wind whistled through the iron bars. Instead of the velvet and silk dresses, they gave her the coats of mail which she had woven to cover her, and the bundle of nettles for a pillow; but nothing they could give her would have pleased her more. She continued her task with joy, and prayed for help, while the street-boys sang jeering songs about her, and not a soul comforted her with a kind word. Towards evening, she heard at the grating the flutter of a swan's wing, it was her youngest brother – he had found his sister, and she sobbed for joy, although she knew that very likely this would be the last night she would have to live. But still she could hope, for her task was almost finished, and her brothers were come. Then the archbishop arrived, to be with her during her last hours, as he had promised the king. But she shook her head, and begged him, by looks and gestures, not to stay; for in this night she knew she must finish her task, otherwise all her pain and tears and sleepless nights would have been suffered in vain. The archbishop withdrew, uttering bitter words against her; but poor Eliza knew that she was innocent, and diligently continued her work.

The little mice ran about the floor, they dragged the nettles to her feet, to help as well as they could; and the thrush sat outside the grating of the window, and sang to her the whole night long, as sweetly as possible, to keep up her spirits.

It was still twilight, and at least an hour before sunrise, when the eleven brothers stood at the castle gate, and demanded to be brought before the king. They were told it could not be, it was yet almost night, and as the king slept they dared not disturb him. They threatened, they entreated. Then the guard appeared, and even the king himself, inquiring what all the noise meant. At this moment the sun rose. The eleven brothers were seen no more, but eleven wild swans flew away over the castle.

And now all the people came streaming forth from the gates of the city, to see the witch burnt. An old horse drew the cart on which she sat. They had dressed her in a garment of coarse sackcloth. Her lovely hair hung loose on her shoulders, her cheeks were deadly pale, her lips moved silently, while her fingers still worked at the green flax. Even on the way to death, she would not give up her task. The ten coats of mail lay at her feet, she was working hard at the eleventh, while the mob jeered her and said, 'See the witch, how she mutters! She has no hymn-book in her hand. She sits there with her ugly sorcery. Let us tear it in a thousand pieces.'

And then they pressed towards her, and would have destroyed the coats of mail, but at the same moment eleven wild swans flew over her, and alighted on the cart. Then they flapped their large wings, and the crowd drew on one side in alarm.

'It is a sign from heaven that she is innocent,' whispered many of them; but they ventured not to say it aloud.

As the executioner seized her by the hand, to lift her out of the cart, she hastily threw the eleven coats of mail over the swans, and they immediately became eleven handsome princes; but the youngest had a swan's wing, instead of an arm; for she had not been able to finish the last sleeve of the coat.

'Now I may speak,' she exclaimed. 'I am innocent.'

Then the people, who saw what happened, bowed to her, as before a saint; but she sank lifeless in her brothers' arms, overcome with suspense, anguish and pain.

'Yes, she is innocent,' said the eldest brother; and then he related all that had taken place; and while he spoke there rose in the air a fragrance as from millions of roses. Every piece of faggot in the pile had taken root, and threw out branches, and appeared a thick hedge, large and high, covered with roses; while above all bloomed a white and shining flower that glittered like a star.

This flower the king plucked, and placed in Eliza's bosom, when she awoke from her swoon, with peace and happiness in her heart. And all the church bells rang of themselves, and the birds came in great troops. And a marriage procession returned to the castle, such as no king had ever before seen.

THE EMPEROR'S NEW SUIT

Many, many years ago lived an emperor, who thought so much of new clothes that he spent all his money in order to obtain them; his only ambition was to be always well dressed. He did not care for his soldiers, and the theatre did not amuse him; the only thing, in fact, he thought anything of was to drive out and show a new suit of clothes. He had a coat for every hour of the day; and as one would say of a king, 'He is in his cabinet,' so one could say of him, 'The emperor is in his dressing-room.'

The great city where he resided was very gay; every day many strangers from all parts of the globe arrived. One day two swindlers came to this city; they made people believe that they were weavers, and declared they could manufacture the finest cloth to be imagined. Their colours and patterns, they said, were not only exceptionally beautiful, but the clothes made of their material possessed the wonderful quality of being invisible to any man who was unfit for his office or unpardonably stupid.

'That must be wonderful cloth,' thought the emperor. 'If I were to be dressed in a suit made of this cloth I should be able to find out which men in my empire were unfit for their places, and I could distinguish the clever from the stupid. I must have this cloth woven for me without delay.' And he gave a large sum of money to the swindlers, in advance, that they should set to work without any loss of time. They set up two looms, and pretended to be very hard at work, but they did nothing whatever on the looms. They asked for the finest silk and the most precious gold-cloth; all they got they did away with, and worked at the empty looms till late at night.

'I should very much like to know how they are getting on with the cloth,' thought the emperor. But he felt rather uneasy when he remembered that he who was not fit for his office could not see it. Personally, he was of opinion that he had nothing to fear, yet he thought it advisable to send somebody else first to see how matters stood. Everybody in the town knew what a remarkable quality the stuff possessed, and all were anxious to see how bad or stupid their neighbours were.

'I shall send my honest old minister to the weavers,' thought the emperor. 'He can judge best how the stuff looks, for he is intelligent, and nobody understands his office better than he.'

The good old minister went into the room where the swindlers sat before the empty looms. 'Heaven preserve us!' he thought, and opened his eyes wide, 'I cannot see anything at all,' but he did not say so. Both swindlers requested him to come near, and asked him if he did not admire the exquisite pattern and the beautiful colours, pointing to the empty looms. The poor old minister tried his very best, but he could see nothing, for there was nothing to be seen. 'Oh dear,' he thought, 'can I be so stupid? I should never have thought so, and nobody must know it! Is it possible that I am not fit for my office? No, no, I cannot say that I was unable to see the cloth.'

'Now, have you got nothing to say?' said one of the swindlers, while he pretended to be busily weaving.

'Oh, it is very pretty, exceedingly beautiful,' replied the old minister looking through his glasses. 'What a beautiful pattern, what brilliant colours! I shall tell the emperor that I like the cloth very much.'

'We are pleased to hear that,' said the two weavers, and described to him the colours and explained the curious pattern. The old minister listened attentively, that he might relate to the emperor what they said; and so he did.

Now the swindlers asked for more money, silk and gold-cloth, which they required for weaving. They kept everything for themselves, and not a thread came near the loom, but they continued, as hitherto, to work at the empty looms.

Soon afterwards the emperor sent another honest courtier to the weavers to see how they were getting on, and if the cloth was nearly finished. Like the old minister, he looked and looked but could see nothing, as there was nothing to be seen.

'Is it not a beautiful piece of cloth?' asked the two swindlers, showing and explaining the magnificent pattern, which, however, did not exist.

'I am not stupid,' said the man. 'It is therefore my good appointment for which I am not fit. It is very strange, but I must not let anyone know it;' and he praised the cloth, which he did not see, and expressed his joy at the beautiful colours and the fine pattern. 'It is very excellent,' he said to the emperor.

Everybody in the whole town talked about the precious cloth. At last the emperor wished to see it himself, while it was still on the loom. With a number of courtiers, including the two who had already been there, he went to the two clever swindlers, who now worked as hard as they could, but without using any thread.

'Is it not magnificent?' said the two old statesmen who had been there before. 'Your Majesty must admire the colours and

THE EMPEROR'S NEW SUIT

the pattern.' And then they pointed to the empty looms, for they imagined the others could see the cloth.

'What is this?' thought the emperor. 'I do not see anything at all. That is terrible! Am I stupid? Am I unfit to be emperor? That would indeed be the most dreadful thing that could happen to me.'

'Really,' he said, turning to the weavers, 'your cloth has our most gracious approval;' and nodding contentedly he looked at the empty loom, for he did not like to say that he saw nothing. All his attendants, who were with him, looked and looked, and although they could not see anything more than the others, they said, like the emperor, 'It is very beautiful.' And all advised him to wear the new magnificent clothes at a great procession which was soon to take place. 'It is magnificent, beautiful, excellent,' one heard them say; everybody seemed to be delighted, and the emperor appointed the two swindlers 'Imperial Court weavers'.

The whole night previous to the day on which the procession was to take place, the swindlers pretended to work, and burned more than sixteen candles. People should see that they were busy to finish the emperor's new suit. They pretended to take the cloth from the loom, and worked about in the air with big scissors, and sewed with needles without thread, and said at last: 'The emperor's new suit is ready now.'

The emperor and all his barons then came to the hall; the swindlers held their arms up as if they held something in their hands and said: 'These are the trousers!' 'This is the coat!' and 'Here is the cloak!' and so on. 'They are all as light as a cobweb, and one must feel as if one had nothing at all upon the body; but that is just the beauty of them.'

'Indeed!' said all the courtiers; but they could not see anything, for there was nothing to be seen.

'Does it please your Majesty now to graciously undress,' said the swindlers, 'that we may assist your Majesty in putting on the new suit before the large looking-glass?'

The emperor undressed, and the swindlers pretended to put the new suit upon him, one piece after another; and the emperor looked at himself in the glass from every side.

'How well they look! How well they fit!' said all. 'What a beautiful pattern! What fine colours! That is a magnificent suit of clothes!'

The master of the ceremonies announced that the bearers of the canopy, which was to be carried in the procession, were ready.

'I am ready,' said the emperor. 'Does not my suit fit me marvellously?' Then he turned once more to the looking-glass, that people should think he admired his garments.

The chamberlains, who were to carry the train, stretched their hands to the ground as if they lifted up a train, and pretended to hold something in their hands; they did not like people to know that they could not see anything.

The emperor marched in the procession under the beautiful canopy, and all who saw him in the street and out of the windows exclaimed: 'Indeed, the emperor's new suit is incomparable! What a long train he has! How well it fits him!' Nobody wished to let others know he saw nothing, for then he would have been unfit for his office or too stupid. Never emperor's clothes were more admired.

'But he has nothing on at all,' said a little child at last. 'Good heavens! Listen to the voice of an innocent child,' said the father, and one whispered to the other what the child had said. 'But he has nothing on at all,' cried at last the whole people. That made a deep impression upon the emperor, for it seemed to him that they were right; but he thought to himself, 'Now I must bear up to the end.' And the chamberlains walked with still greater dignity, as if they carried the train which did not exist.

THE SWINEHERD

Once upon a time lived a poor prince; his kingdom was very small, but it was large enough to enable him to marry, and marry he would. It was rather bold of him that he went and asked the emperor's daughter: 'Will you marry me?' but he ventured to do so, for his name was known far and wide, and there were hundreds of princesses who would have gladly accepted him, but would she do so? Now we shall see.

On the grave of the prince's father grew a rose-tree, the most beautiful of its kind. It bloomed only once in five years, and then it had only one single rose upon it, but what a rose! It had such a sweet scent that one instantly forgot all sorrow and grief when one smelt it. He had also a nightingale, which could sing as if every sweet melody was in its throat. This rose and the nightingale he wished to give to the princess; and therefore both were put into big silver cases and sent to her.

The emperor ordered them to be carried into the great hall where the princess was just playing 'Visitors are coming' with her ladies-in-waiting; when she saw the large cases with the presents therein, she clapped her hands for joy.

'I wish it were a little pussy cat,' she said. But then the rose-tree with the beautiful rose was unpacked.

'Oh, how nicely it is made,' exclaimed the ladies.

'It is more than nice,' said the emperor, 'it is charming.'

The princess touched it and nearly began to cry.

'For shame, pa,' she said, 'it is not artificial, it is natural!'

'For shame, it is natural' repeated all her ladies.

'Let us first see what the other case contains before we are angry,' said the emperor; then the nightingale was taken out, and it sang so beautifully that no one could possibly say anything unkind about it.

'*Superbe, charmant,*' said the ladies of the court, for they all prattled French, one worse than the other.

'How much the bird reminds me of the musical box of the late lamented empress,' said an old courtier, 'it has exactly the same tone, the same execution.'

'You are right,' said the emperor, and began to cry like a little child.

'I hope it is not natural,' said the princess.

'Yes, certainly it is natural,' replied those who had brought the presents.

'Then let it fly,' said the princess, and refused to see the prince.

But the prince was not discouraged. He painted his face, put on common clothes, pulled his cap over his forehead, and came back.

'Good day, emperor,' he said, 'could you not give me some employment at the court?'

'There are so many,' replied the emperor, 'who apply for places, that for the present I have no vacancy, but I will remember you. But wait a moment; it just comes into my mind, I require somebody to look after my pigs, for I have a great many.'

Thus the prince was appointed imperial swineherd, and as such he lived in a wretchedly small room near the pigsty; there he worked all day long, and when it was night he had made a pretty little pot. There were little bells round the rim, and when the water began to boil in it, the bells began to play the old tune:

A jolly old sow once lived in a sty,
Three little piggies had she, &c.

But what was more wonderful was that, when one put a finger into the steam rising from the pot, one could at once smell what meals they were preparing on every fire in the whole town. That was indeed much more remarkable than the rose. When the princess with her ladies passed by and heard the tune, she stopped and looked quite pleased, for she also could play it – in fact, it was the only tune she could play, and she played it with one finger.

'That is the tune I know,' she exclaimed. 'He must be a well-educated swineherd. Go and ask him how much the instrument is.'

One of the ladies had to go and ask; but she put on pattens.

'What will you take for your pot?' asked the lady.

'I will have ten kisses from the princess,' said the swineherd.

'God forbid,' said the lady.

'Well, I cannot sell it for less,' replied the swineherd.

'What did he say?' said the princess.

'I really cannot tell you,' replied the lady.

'You can whisper it into my ear.'

'It is very naughty,' said the princess, and walked off.

But when she had gone a little distance, the bells rang again so sweetly:

A jolly old sow once lived in a sty,
Three little piggies had she, &c.

'Ask him,' said the princess, 'if he will be satisfied with ten kisses from one of my ladies.'

'No, thank you,' said the swineherd: 'ten kisses from the princess, or I keep my pot.'

'That is tiresome,' said the princess. 'But you must stand before me, so that nobody can see it.'

The ladies placed themselves in front of her and spread out their dresses, and she gave the swineherd ten kisses and received the pot.

That was a pleasure! Day and night the water in the pot was boiling; there was not a single fire in the whole town of which they did not know what was preparing on it, the chamberlain's as well as the shoemaker's. The ladies danced and clapped their hands for joy.

'We know who will eat soup and pancakes; we know who will eat porridge and cutlets; oh, how interesting!'

'Very interesting, indeed,' said the mistress of the household. 'But you must not betray me, for I am the emperor's daughter.'

'Of course not,' they all said.

The swineherd – that is to say, the prince, but they did not know otherwise than that he was a real swineherd – did not waste a single day without doing something; he made a rattle, which, when turned quickly round, played all the waltzes, gallops and polkas known since the creation of the world.

'But that is *superbe*,' said the princess passing by. 'I have never heard a more beautiful composition. Go down and ask him what the instrument costs; but I shall not kiss him again.'

'He will have a hundred kisses from the princess,' said the lady, who had gone down to ask him.

'I believe he is mad,' said the princess, and walked off, but soon she stopped. 'One must encourage art,' she said. 'I am the emperor's daughter! Tell him I will give him ten kisses, as I did the other day; the remainder one of my ladies can give him.'

'But we do not like to kiss him' said the ladies.

'That is nonsense,' said the princess; 'if I can kiss him, you can also do it. Remember that I give you food and employment.' And the lady had to go down once more.

'A hundred kisses from the princess,' said the swineherd, 'or everybody keeps his own.'

'Place yourselves before me,' said the princess then. They did as they were bidden, and the princess kissed him.

'I wonder what that crowd near the pigsty means!' said the emperor, who had just come out on his balcony. He rubbed his eyes and put his spectacles on.

'The ladies of the court are up to some mischief, I think. I shall have to go down and see.' He pulled up his shoes, for they were down at the heels, and he was very quick about it. When he had come down into the courtyard he walked quite softly, and the ladies were so busily engaged in counting the kisses, that all should be fair, that they did not notice the emperor. He raised himself on tiptoe.

'What does this mean?' he said, when he saw that his daughter was kissing the swineherd, and then hit their heads with his shoe just as the swineherd received the sixty-eighth kiss.

'Go out of my sight,' said the emperor, for he was very angry; and both the princess and the swineherd were banished from the empire. There she stood and cried, the swineherd scolded her, and the rain came down in torrents.

'Alas, unfortunate creature that I am!' said the princess, 'I wish I had accepted the prince. Oh, how wretched I am!'

The swineherd went behind a tree, wiped his face, threw off his poor attire and stepped forth in his princely garments; he looked so beautiful that the princess could not help bowing to him.

'I have now learnt to despise you,' he said. 'You refused an honest prince; you did not appreciate the rose and the nightingale; but you did not mind kissing a swineherd for his toys; you have no one but yourself to blame!'

And then he returned into his kingdom and left her behind. She could now sing at her leisure:

A jolly old sow once lived in a sty,
Three little piggies has she, &c.

THE SHEPHERDESS AND THE SWEEP

Have you ever seen an old wooden cupboard quite black with age, and ornamented with carved foliage and curious figures? Well, just such a cupboard stood in a parlour, and had been left to the family as a legacy by the great-grandmother. It was covered from top to bottom with carved roses and tulips; the most curious scrolls were drawn upon it, and out of them peeped little stags' heads, with antlers. In the middle of the cupboard door was the carved figure of a man most ridiculous to look at. He grinned at you, for no one could call it laughing. He had goat's legs, little horns on his head, and a long beard; the children in the room always called him 'Major-general-field-sergeant-commander Billy-goat's-legs'. It was certainly a very difficult name to pronounce, and there are very few who ever receive such a title, but then it seemed wonderful how he came to be carved at all; yet there he was, always looking at the table under the looking-glass, where stood a very pretty little shepherdess made of china. Her shoes were gilt, and her dress had a red rose or an ornament. She wore a hat, and carried a crook, that were both gilded, and looked very bright and pretty.

Close by her side stood a little chimney-sweep, as black as coal, and also made of china. He was, however, quite as clean and neat as any other china figure; he only represented a black chimney-sweep, and the china workers might just as well have made him a prince, had they felt inclined to do so. He stood holding his ladder quite handily, and his face was as fair and rosy as a girl's; indeed, that was rather a mistake, it should have had some black marks on it. He and the shepherdess had been placed close together, side by side; and, being so placed, they became engaged to each other, for they were very well suited, being both made of the same sort of china, and being equally fragile. Close to them stood another figure, three times as large as they were, and also made of china. He was an old Chinaman, who could nod his head, and used to pretend that he was the grandfather of the shepherdess, although he could not prove it. He however assumed authority over her, and therefore when 'Major-general-field-sergeant-commander Billy-goat's-legs' asked for the little shepherdess to be his wife, he nodded his head to show that he consented. 'You will have a husband,' said the old Chinaman to her, 'who I really believe is made of mahogany. He will make you a lady of Major-general-field-sergeant-commander Billy-goat's-legs. He has the whole cupboard full of silver plate, which he keeps locked up in secret drawers.'

'I won't go into the dark cupboard,' said the little shepherdess. 'I have heard that he has eleven china wives there already.'

'Then you shall be the twelfth,' said the old Chinaman. 'Tonight as soon as you hear a rattling in the old cupboard, you shall be married, as true as I am a Chinaman;' and then he nodded his head and fell asleep.

Then the little shepherdess cried, and looked at her sweetheart, the china chimney-sweep. 'I must entreat you,' said she, 'to go out with me into the wide world, for we cannot stay here.'

'I will do whatever you wish,' said the little chimney-sweep; 'let us go immediately: I think I shall be able to maintain you with my profession.'

'If we were but safely down from the table!' said she. 'I shall not be happy till we are really out in the world.'

Then he comforted her, and showed her how to place her little foot on the carved edge and gilt-leaf ornaments of the table. He brought his little ladder to help her, and so they contrived to reach the floor. But when they looked at the old cupboard, they saw it was all in an uproar. The carved stags pushed out their heads, raised their antlers, and twisted their necks. The major-general sprung up in the air; and cried out to the old Chinaman, 'They are running away! They are running away!' The two were rather frightened at this, so they jumped into the drawer of the window-seat. Here were three or four packs of cards not quite complete, and a doll's theatre, which had been built up very neatly. A comedy was being performed in it, and all the queens of diamonds, clubs, hearts and spades sat in the first row fanning themselves with tulips, and behind them stood all the knaves, showing that they had heads above and below as playing cards generally have. The play was about two lovers, who were not allowed to marry, and the shepherdess wept because it was so like her own story. 'I cannot bear it,' said she, 'I must get out of the drawer;' but when they reached the floor, and cast their eyes on the table, there was the old Chinaman awake and shaking his whole body, till all at once down he came on the floor, 'plump'. 'The old Chinaman is coming,' cried the little shepherdess in a fright, and down she fell on one knee.

'I have thought of something,' said the chimney-sweep; 'let us get into the great pot-pourri jar which stands in the corner; there we can lie on rose-leaves and lavender, and throw salt in his eyes if he comes near us.'

'No, that will never do,' said she, 'because I know that the

Chinaman and the pot-pourri jar were lovers once, and there always remains behind a feeling of good-will between those who have been so intimate as that. No, there is nothing left for us but to go out into the wide world.'

'Have you really courage enough to go out into the wide world with me?' said the chimney-sweep. 'Have you thought how large it is, and that we can never come back here again?'

'Yes, I have,' she replied.

When the chimney-sweep saw that she was quite firm, he said, 'My way is through the stove and up the chimney. Have you courage to creep with me through the fire-box, and the iron pipe? When we get to the chimney I shall know how to manage very well. We shall soon climb too high for anyone to reach us, and we shall come through a hole in the top out into the wide world.' So he led her to the door of the stove.

'It looks very dark,' said she; still she went in with him through the stove and through the pipe, where it was as dark as pitch.

'Now we are in the chimney,' said he; 'and look, there is a beautiful star shining above it.' It was a real star shining down upon them as if it would show them the way. So they clambered, and crept on, and a frightful steep place it was; but the chimney-sweep helped her and supported her, till they got higher and higher. He showed her the best places on which to set her little china foot, so at last they reached the top of the chimney, and sat themselves down, for they were very tired, as may be supposed. The sky, with all its stars, was over their heads, and below were the roofs of the town. They could see for a very long distance out into the wide world, and the poor little shepherdess leaned her head on her chimney-sweep's shoulder, and wept till she washed the gilt off her sash; the world was so different to what she expected. 'This is too much,' she said; 'I cannot bear it, the world is too large. Oh, I wish I were safe back on the table again, under the looking glass; I shall never be happy till I am safe back again. Now I have followed you out into the wide world, you will take me back, if you love me.'

Then the chimney-sweep tried to reason with her, and spoke of the old Chinaman, and of the Major-general-field-sergeant-commander Billy-goat's-legs; but she sobbed so bitterly, and kissed her little chimney-sweep till he was obliged to do all she asked, foolish as it was. And so, with a great deal of trouble, they climbed down the chimney, and then crept through the pipe and stove, which were certainly not very pleasant places. Then they stood in the dark fire-box, and listened behind the door, to hear what was going on in the room. As it was all quiet, they peeped out. Alas! There lay the old Chinaman on the floor; he had fallen down from the table as he attempted to run after them, and was broken into three pieces; his back had separated entirely, and his head had rolled into a corner of the room. The major-general stood in his old place, and appeared lost in thought.

'This is terrible,' said the little shepherdess. 'My poor old grandfather is broken to pieces, and it is our fault. I shall never live after this;' and she wrung her little hands.

'He can be riveted,' said the chimney-sweep; 'he can be riveted. Do not be so hasty. If they cement his back, and put a good rivet in it, he will be as good as new, and be able to say as many disagreeable things to us as ever.'

'Do you think so?' said she; and then they climbed up to the table, and stood in their old places.

'As we have done no good,' said the chimney-sweep, 'we might as well have remained here, instead of taking so much trouble.'

'I wish grandfather was riveted,' said the shepherdess. 'Will it cost much, I wonder?'

And she had her wish. The family had the Chinaman's back mended, and a strong rivet put through his neck; he looked as good as new, but he could no longer nod his head.

'You have become proud since your fall broke you to pieces,' said Major-general-field-sergeant-commander Billy-goat's-legs. 'You have no reason to give yourself such airs. Am I to have her or not?'

The chimney-sweep and the little shepherdess looked piteously at the old Chinaman, for they were afraid he might nod; but he was not able: besides, it was so tiresome to be always telling strangers he had a rivet in the back of his neck.

And so the little china people remained together, and were glad of the grandfather's rivet, and continued to love each other till they were broken to pieces.

THE UGLY DUCKLING

It was lovely summer weather in the country, and the golden corn, the green oats and the haystacks piled up in the meadows looked beautiful. The stork walking about on his long red legs chattered in the Egyptian language, which he had learnt from his mother. The corn-fields and meadows were surrounded by large forests, in the midst of which were deep pools. It was, indeed, delightful to walk about in the country. In a sunny spot stood a pleasant old farm-house close by a deep river, and from the house down to the water-side grew great burdock leaves, so high that under the tallest of them a little child could stand upright. The spot was as wild as the centre of a thick wood. In this snug retreat sat a duck on her nest, watching for her young brood to hatch; she was beginning to get tired of her task, for the little ones were a long time coming out of their shells, and she seldom had any visitors. The other ducks liked much better to swim about in the river than to climb the slippery banks and sit under a burdock leaf to have a gossip with her. At length one shell cracked, and then another, and from each egg came a living creature that lifted its head and cried, 'Peep, peep.' 'Quack, quack,' said the mother, and then they all quacked as well as they could, and looked about them on every side at the large green leaves. Their mother allowed them to look as much as they liked, because green is good for the eyes. 'How large the world is,' said the young ducks, when they found how much more room they now had than while they were inside the egg-shell. 'Do you imagine this is the whole world?' asked the mother; 'Wait till you have seen the garden; it stretches far beyond that to the parson's field, but I have never ventured to such a distance. Are you all out?' she continued, rising; 'No, I declare, the largest egg lies there still. I wonder how long this is to last, I am quite tired of it;' and she seated herself again on the nest.

'Well, how are you getting on?' asked an old duck, who paid her a visit.

'One egg is not hatched yet,' said the duck, 'it will not break. But just look at all the others, are they not the prettiest little ducklings you ever saw? They are the image of their father, who is so unkind, he never comes to see.'

'Let me see the egg that will not break,' said the duck; 'I have no doubt it is a turkey's egg. I was persuaded to hatch some once, and after all my care and trouble with the young ones, they were afraid of the water. I quacked and clucked, but all to no purpose. I could not get them to venture in. Let me look at the egg. Yes, that is a turkey's egg; take my advice, leave it where it is and teach the other children to swim.'

'I think I will sit on it a little while longer,' said the duck; 'as I have sat so long already, a few days will be nothing.'

'Please yourself,' said the old duck, and she went away.

At last the large egg broke, and a young one crept forth crying, 'Peep, peep.' It was very large and ugly. The duck stared at it and exclaimed, 'It is very large and not at all like the others. I wonder if it really is a turkey. We shall soon find it out, however, when we go to the water. It must go in, if I have to push it myself.'

On the next day the weather was delightful, and the sun shone brightly on the green burdock leaves, so the mother duck took her young brood down to the water, and jumped in with a splash. 'Quack, quack,' cried she, and one after another the little ducklings jumped in. The water closed over their heads, but they came up again in an instant, and swam about quite prettily with their legs paddling under them as easily as possible, and the ugly duckling was also in the water swimming with them.

'Oh,' said the mother, 'that is not a turkey; how well he uses his legs, and how upright he holds himself! He is my own child, and he is not so very ugly after all if you look at him properly. Quack, quack! Come with me now, I will take you into grand society, and introduce you to the farmyard, but you must keep close to me or you may be trodden upon; and, above all, beware of the cat.'

When they reached the farmyard, there was a great disturbance, two families were fighting for an eel's head, which, after all, was carried off by the cat. 'See, children, that is the way of the world,' said the mother duck, whetting her beak, for she would have liked the eel's head herself. 'Come, now, use your legs, and let me see how well you can behave. You must bow your heads prettily to that old duck yonder; she is the highest born of them all, and has Spanish blood, therefore, she is well off. Don't you see she has a red flag tied to her leg, which is something very grand, and a great honour for a duck; it shows that every one is anxious not to lose her, as she can be recognised both by man and beast. Come, now, don't turn your toes, a well-bred duckling spreads his feet wide apart, just like his father and mother, in this way; now bend your neck, and say "quack".'

The ducklings did as they were bid, but the other duck stared, and said, 'Look, here comes another brood, as if there were not enough of us already! And what a queer looking object one of them is; we don't want him here,' and then one flew out and bit him in the neck.

'Let him alone,' said the mother; 'he is not doing any harm.' 'Yes, but he is so big and ugly,' said the spiteful duck, 'and therefore he must be turned out.'

'The others are very pretty children,' said the old duck, with the rag on her leg, 'all but that one; I wish his mother could improve him a little.'

'That is impossible, your grace,' replied the mother; 'he is not pretty; but he has a very good disposition, and swims as well or even better than the others. I think he will grow up pretty, and perhaps be smaller; he has remained too long in the egg, and therefore his figure is not properly formed.' And then she stroked his neck and smoothed the feathers, saying, 'It is a drake, and therefore not of so much consequence. I think he will grow up strong, and able to take care of himself.'

'The other ducklings are graceful enough,' said the old duck. 'Now make yourself at home, and if you can find an eel's head, you can bring it to me.'

And so they made themselves comfortable; but the poor duckling who had crept out of his shell last of all, and looked so ugly, was bitten and pushed and made fun of, not only by the ducks, but by all the poultry. 'He is too big,' they all said, and the turkey cock, who had been born into the world with spurs, and fancied himself really an emperor, puffed himself out like a vessel in full sail, and flew at the duckling, and became quite red in the head with passion, so that the poor little thing did not know where to go, and was quite miserable because he was so ugly and laughed at by the whole farmyard. So it went on from day to day till it got worse and worse. The poor duckling was driven about by everyone; even his brothers and sisters were unkind to him, and would say, 'Ah, you ugly creature, I wish the cat would get you,' and his mother said she wished he had never been born. The ducks pecked him, the chickens beat him, and the girl who fed the poultry kicked him with her feet. So at last he ran away, frightening the little birds in the hedge as he flew over the palings.

'They are afraid of me because I am ugly,' he said. So he closed his eyes, and flew still farther, until he came out on a large moor, inhabited by wild ducks. Here he remained the whole night, feeling very tired and sorrowful.

In the morning, when the wild ducks rose in the air, they stared at their new comrade. 'What sort of a duck are you?' they all said, coming round him.

He bowed to them, and was as polite as he could be, but he did not reply to their question. 'You are exceedingly ugly,' said the wild ducks, 'but that will not matter if you do not want to marry one of our family.'

Poor thing! He had no thoughts of marriage; all he wanted was permission to lie among the rushes, and drink some of the water on the moor. After he had been on the moor two days, there came two wild geese, or rather goslings, for they had not been out of the egg long, and were very saucy. 'Listen, friend,' said one of them to the duckling, 'you are so ugly that we like you very well. Will you go with us, and become a bird of passage? Not far from here is another moor, in which there are some pretty wild geese, all unmarried. It is a chance for you to get a wife; you may be lucky, ugly as you are.'

'Pop, pop,' sounded in the air, and the two wild geese fell dead among the rushes, and the water was tinged with blood.

'Pop, pop,' echoed far and wide in the distance, and whole flocks of wild geese rose up from the rushes. The sound continued from every direction, for the sportsmen surrounded the moor, and some were even seated on branches of trees, overlooking the rushes. The blue smoke from the guns rose like clouds over the dark trees, and as it floated away across the water, a number of sporting dogs bounded in among the rushes, which bent beneath them wherever they went. How they terrified the poor duckling! He turned away his head to hide it under his wing, and at the same moment a large terrible dog passed quite near him. His jaws were open, his tongue hung from his mouth, and his eyes glared fearfully. He thrust his nose close to the duckling, showing his sharp teeth, and then, 'splash, splash,' he went into the water without touching him, 'Oh,' sighed the duckling, 'how thankful I am for being so ugly; even a dog will not bite me.' And so he lay quite still, while the shot rattled through the rushes, and gun after gun was fired over him. It was late in the day before all became quiet, but even then the poor young thing did not dare to move. He waited quietly for several hours, and then, after looking carefully around him, hastened away from the moor as fast as he could. He ran over field and meadow till a storm arose, and he could hardly struggle against it. Towards evening, he reached a poor little cottage that seemed ready to fall, and only remained standing because it could not decide on which side to fall first. The storm continued so violent that the duckling could go no farther; he sat down by the cottage, and then he noticed that the door was not quite closed in consequence of one of the hinges having given way. There was therefore a narrow opening near the bottom large enough for him to slip through, which he did very quietly, and got a shelter for the night. A woman, a tom cat and a hen lived in this cottage. The tom cat, whom the mistress called 'My little son', was a great favourite; he could raise his back, and purr, and could even throw out sparks from his fur if it were stroked the wrong way. The hen had very short legs, so she was called 'Chickie short legs'. She laid good eggs, and her mistress loved her as if she had been her own child. In the morning, the strange visitor was discovered, and the tom cat began to purr, and the hen to cluck.

'What is that noise about?' said the old woman, looking round the room, but her sight was not very good; therefore, when she saw the duckling she thought it must be a fat duck that had strayed from home. 'Oh what a prize!' she exclaimed, 'I hope it is not a drake, for then I shall have some duck's eggs. I must wait and see.' So the duckling was allowed to remain on trial for three weeks, but there were no eggs. Now the tom cat was the master of the house, and the hen was mistress, and they always said 'we and the world', for they believed themselves to be half the world, and the better half too. The duckling thought that others might hold a different opinion on the subject, but the hen would not listen to such doubts. 'Can you lay eggs?' she asked. 'No.' 'Then have the goodness to hold your tongue.' 'Can you raise your back, or purr, or throw out sparks?' said the tom cat. 'No.' 'Then you have no right to express an opinion when sensible people are speaking.' So the duckling sat in a corner, feeling very low-spirited, till the sunshine and the fresh air came into the room through the open door, and then he began to feel such a great longing for a swim on the water that he could not help telling the hen.

'What an absurd idea,' said the hen. 'You have nothing else to do, therefore you have foolish fancies. If you could purr or lay eggs, they would pass away.'

'But it is so delightful to swim about on the water,' said the duckling, 'and so refreshing to feel it close over your head, while you dive down to the bottom.'

'Delightful, indeed!' said the hen. 'Why you must be crazy! Ask the cat, he is the cleverest animal I know, ask him how he would like to swim about on the water, or to dive under it, for I will not speak of my own opinion; ask our mistress, the old woman – there is no one in the world more clever than she is. Do you think she would like to swim, or to let the water close over her head?'

'You don't understand me,' said the duckling.

'We don't understand you? Who can understand you, I wonder? Do you consider yourself more clever than the cat, or the old woman? I will say nothing of myself. Don't imagine such nonsense, child, and thank your good fortune that you have been received here. Are you not in a warm room, and in society from which you may learn something. But you are a chatterer, and your company is not very agreeable. Believe me, I speak only for your own good. I may tell you unpleasant truths, but that is a proof of my friendship. I advise you, therefore, to lay eggs, and learn to purr as quickly as possible.'

'I believe I must go out into the world again,' said the duckling.

'Yes, do,' said the hen. So the duckling left the cottage, and soon found water on which it could swim and dive, but was avoided by all other animals, because of its ugly appearance. Autumn came, and the leaves in the forest turned to orange and gold; then, as winter approached, the wind caught them as they fell and whirled them in the cold air. The clouds, heavy with hail and snow-flakes, hung low in the sky, and the raven stood on the ferns crying,

'Croak, croak.' It made one shiver with cold to look at him. All this was very sad for the poor little duckling. One evening, just as the sun set amid radiant clouds, there came a large flock of beautiful birds out of the bushes. The duckling had never seen any like them before. They were swans, and they curved their graceful necks, while their soft plumage shone with dazzling whiteness. They uttered a singular cry, as they spread their glorious wings and flew away from those cold regions to warmer countries across the sea. As they mounted higher and higher in the air, the ugly little duckling felt quite a strange sensation as he watched them. He whirled himself in the water like a wheel, stretched out his neck towards them, and uttered a cry so strange that it frightened himself. Could he ever forget those beautiful, happy birds. And when at last they were out of his sight, he dived under the water, and rose again almost beside himself with excitement. He knew not the names of these birds, nor where they had flown, but he felt towards them as he had never felt for any other bird in the world. He was not envious of these beautiful creatures, but wished to be as lovely as they. Poor ugly creature, how gladly he would have lived even with the ducks had they only given him encouragement. The winter grew colder and colder; he was obliged to swim about on the water to keep it from freezing, but every night the space on which he swam became smaller and smaller. At length it froze so hard that the ice in the water crackled as he moved, and the duckling had to paddle with his legs as well as he could, to keep the space from closing up. He became exhausted at last, and lay still and helpless, frozen fast in the ice.

Early in the morning, a peasant, who was passing by, saw what had happened. He broke the ice in pieces with his wooden shoe, and carried the duckling home to his wife. The warmth revived the poor little creature; but when the children wanted to play with him, the duckling thought they would do him some harm; so he started up in terror, fluttered into the milk-pan, and splashed the milk about the room. Then the woman clapped her hands, which frightened him still more. He flew first into the butter-cask, then into the meal-tub, and out again. What a condition he was in! The woman screamed, and struck at him with the tongs; the children laughed and screamed, and tumbled over each other in their efforts to catch him; but luckily he escaped. The door stood open; the poor creature could just manage to slip out among the bushes, and lie down quite exhausted in the newly fallen snow.

It would be very sad, were I to relate all the misery and privations which the poor little duckling endured during the hard winter; but when it had passed, he found himself lying one morning in a moor, amongst the rushes. He felt the warm sun shining, and heard the lark singing, and saw that all around was beautiful spring. Then the young bird felt that his wings were strong, as he flapped them against his sides, and rose high into the air. They bore him onwards, until he found himself in a large garden, before he well knew how it had happened. The apple-trees were in full blossom, and the fragrant elders bent their long green branches down to the stream which wound round a smooth lawn. Everything looked beautiful, in the freshness of early spring. From a thicket close by came three beautiful white swans, rustling their feathers, and swimming lightly over the smooth water. The duckling remembered the lovely birds, and felt more strangely unhappy than ever.

'I will fly to those royal birds,' he exclaimed, 'and they will kill me, because I am so ugly, and dare to approach them; but it does not matter: better be killed by them than pecked by the ducks, beaten by the hens, pushed about by the maiden who feeds the poultry, or starved with hunger in the winter.'

Then he flew to the water, and swam towards the beautiful swans. The moment they espied the stranger, they rushed to meet him with outstretched wings.

'Kill me,' said the poor bird; and he bent his head down to the surface of the water, and awaited death.

But what did he see in the clear stream below? His own image; no longer a dark, grey bird, ugly and disagreeable to look at, but a graceful and beautiful swan. To be born in a duck's nest, in a farmyard, is of no consequence to a bird, if it is hatched from a swan's egg. He now felt glad at having suffered sorrow and trouble, because it enabled him to enjoy so much better all the pleasure and happiness around him; for the great swans swam round the newcomer, and stroked his neck with their beaks, as a welcome.

Into the garden presently came some little children, and threw bread and cake into the water.

'See,' cried the youngest, 'there is a new one;' and the rest were delighted, and ran to their father and mother, dancing and clapping their hands, and shouting joyously, 'There is another swan come; a new one has arrived.'

Then they threw more bread and cake into the water, and said, 'The new one is the most beautiful of all; he is so young and pretty.' And the old swans bowed their heads before him.

Then he felt quite ashamed, and hid his head under his wing; for he did not know what to do, he was so happy, and yet not at all proud. He had been persecuted and despised for his ugliness, and now he heard them say he was the most beautiful of all the birds. Even the elder-tree bent down its bows into the water before him, and the sun shone warm and bright. Then he rustled his feathers, curved his slender neck, and cried joyfully, from the depths of his heart, 'I never dreamed of such happiness as this, while I was an ugly duckling.'

THE NAUGHTY BOY

Once upon a time there was an old poet, one of those right good old poets.

One evening, as he was sitting at home, there was a terrible storm going on outside; the rain was pouring down, but the old poet sat comfortably in his chimney-corner, where the fire was burning and the apples were roasting.

'There will not be a dry thread left on the poor people who are out in this weather,' he said.

'Oh, open the door! I am so cold and wet through,' called a little child outside. It was crying and knocking at the door, whilst the rain was pouring down and the wind was rattling all the windows.

'Poor creature!' said the poet, and got up and opened the door. Before him stood a little boy; he was naked, and the water flowed from his long, fair locks. He was shivering with cold; if he had not been let in, he would certainly have perished in the storm.

'Poor little thing!' said the poet, and took him by the hand. 'Come to me; I will soon warm you. You shall have some wine and an apple, for you are such a pretty boy.'

And he was, too. His eyes sparkled like two bright stars, and although the water flowed down from his fair locks, they still curled quite beautifully.

He looked like a little angel, but was pale with cold, and trembling all over. In his hand he held a splendid bow, but it had been entirely spoilt by the rain, and the colours of the pretty arrows had run into one another by getting wet.

The old man sat down by the fire, and taking the little boy on his knee, wrung the water out of his locks and warmed his hands in his own.

He then made him some hot spiced wine, which quickly revived him; so that with reddening cheeks, he sprang upon the floor and danced around the old man.

'You are a merry boy,' said the latter. 'What is your name?'

'My name is Cupid,' he answered. 'Don't you know me? There lies my bow. I shoot with that, you know. Look, the weather is getting fine again – the moon is shining.'

'But your bow is spoilt,' said the old poet.

'That would be unfortunate,' said the little boy, taking it up and looking at it. 'Oh, it's quite dry and isn't damaged at all. The string is quite tight; I'll try it.' So, drawing it back, he took an arrow, aimed and shot the good old poet right in the heart. 'Do you see now that my bow was not spoilt?' he said, and, loudly laughing, ran away. What a naughty boy to shoot the old poet like that, who had taken him into his warm room, had been so good to him, and had given him the nicest wine and the best apple!

The good old man lay upon the floor crying; he was really shot in the heart. 'Oh!' he cried. 'What a naughty boy this Cupid is! I shall tell all the good children about this, so that they take care never to play with him, lest he hurt them.'

And all good children, both girls and boys, whom he told about this, were on their guard against wicked Cupid; but he deceives them all the same, for he is very deep. When the students come out of class, he walks beside them with a book under his arm, and wearing a black coat. They cannot recognise him. And then, if they take him by the arm, believing him to be a student too, he sticks an arrow into their chest. And when the girls go to church to be confirmed, he is amongst them too. In fact, he is always after people. He sits in the large chandelier in the theatre and blazes away, so that people think it is a lamp; but they soon find out their mistake. He walks about in the castle garden and on the promenades. Yes, once he shot your father and your mother in the heart too. Just ask them, and you will hear what they say. Oh! He is a bad boy, this Cupid, and you must never have anything to do with him, for he is after everyone. Just think, he even shot an arrow at old grandmother; but that was a long time ago. The wound has long been healed, but such things are never forgotten.

Now you know what a bad boy this wicked Cupid is.

THE PRINCESS AND THE PEA

Once upon a time there was a prince who wanted to marry a princess; but she would have to be a real princess. He travelled all over the world to find one, but nowhere could he get what he wanted. There were princesses enough, but it was difficult to find out whether they were real ones. There was always something about them that was not as it should be. So he came home again and was sad, for he would have liked very much to have a real princess.

One evening a terrible storm came on; there was thunder and lightning, and the rain poured down in torrents. Suddenly a knocking was heard at the city gate, and the old king went to open it.

It was a princess standing out there in front of the gate. But, good gracious, what a sight the rain and the wind had made her look! The water ran down from her hair and clothes; it ran down into the toes of her shoes and out again at the heels. And yet she said that she was a real princess.

'Well, we'll soon find that out,' thought the old queen. But she said nothing, went into the bedroom, took all the bedding off the bedstead, and laid a pea on the bottom; then she took twenty mattresses and laid them on the pea, and then twenty eider-down beds on top of the mattresses.

On this the princess had to lie all night. In the morning she was asked how she had slept.

'Oh, very badly!' said she. 'I have scarcely closed my eyes all night. Heaven only knows what was in the bed, but I was lying on something hard, so that I am black and blue all over my body. It's horrible!'

Now they knew that she was a real princess because she had felt the pea right through the twenty mattresses and the twenty eider-down beds.

Nobody but a real princess could be as sensitive as that.

So the prince took her for his wife, for now he knew that he had a real princess; and the pea was put in the museum, where it may still be seen, if no one has stolen it.

There, that is a true story.

THE BRAVE TIN SOLDIER

There were once five-and-twenty tin soldiers, who were all brothers, for they had been made out of the same old tin spoon. They shouldered arms and looked straight before them, and wore a splendid uniform, red and blue. The first thing in the world they ever heard were the words 'Tin soldiers!' uttered by a little boy, who clapped his hands with delight when the lid of the box, in which they lay, was taken off. They were given him for a birthday present, and he stood at the table to set them up. The soldiers were all exactly alike, excepting one, who had only one leg; he had been left to the last, and then there was not enough of the melted tin to finish him, so they made him to stand firmly on one leg, and this caused him to be very remarkable.

The table on which the tin soldiers stood was covered with other playthings, but the most attractive to the eye was a pretty little paper castle. Through the small windows the rooms could be seen. In front of the castle a number of little trees surrounded a piece of looking-glass, which was intended to represent a transparent lake. Swans, made of wax, swam on the lake, and were reflected in it. All this was very pretty, but the prettiest of all was a tiny little lady, who stood at the open door of the castle; she, also, was made of paper, and she wore a dress of clear muslin, with a narrow blue ribbon over her shoulders just like a scarf. In front of these was fixed a glittering tinsel rose, as large as her whole face. The little lady was a dancer, and she stretched out both her arms, and raised one of her legs so high that the tin soldier could not see it at all, and he thought that she, like himself, had only one leg. 'That is the wife for me,' he thought; 'but she is too grand, and lives in a castle, while I have only a box to live in, five-and-twenty of us altogether, that is no place for her. Still I must try and make her acquaintance.' Then he laid himself at full length on the table behind a snuff-box that stood upon it, so that he could peep at the little delicate lady, who continued to stand on one leg without losing her balance. When evening came, the other tin soldiers were all placed in the box, and the people of the house went to bed. Then the playthings began to have their own games together, to pay visits, to have sham fights, and to give balls. The tin soldiers rattled in their box; they wanted to get out and join the amusements, but they could not open the lid. The nut-crackers played at leap-frog, and the pencil jumped about the table. There was such a noise that the canary woke up and began to talk, and in poetry too. Only the tin soldier and the dancer remained in their places. She stood on tiptoe, with her legs stretched out, as firmly as he did on his one leg. He never took his eyes from her for even a moment. The clock struck twelve, and, with a bounce, up sprang the lid of the snuff-box; but, instead of snuff, there jumped up a little black goblin; for the snuff-box was a toy puzzle.

'Tin soldier,' said the goblin, 'don't wish for what does not belong to you.'

But the tin soldier pretended not to hear.

'Very well; wait till tomorrow, then,' said the goblin.

When the children came in the next morning, they placed the tin soldier in the window. Now, whether it was the goblin who did it, or the draught, is not known, but the window flew open,

THE BRAVE TIN SOLDIER

and out fell the tin soldier, heels over head, from the third story, into the street beneath. It was a terrible fall; for he came head downwards, his helmet and his bayonet stuck in between the flagstones, and his one leg up in the air. The servant maid and the little boy went down stairs directly to look for him; but he was nowhere to be seen, although once they nearly trod upon him. If he had called out, 'Here I am,' it would have been all right, but he was too proud to cry out for help while he wore a uniform.

Presently it began to rain, and the drops fell faster and faster, till there was a heavy shower. When it was over, two boys happened to pass by, and one of them said, 'Look, there is a tin soldier. He ought to have a boat to sail in.'

So they made a boat out of a newspaper, and placed the tin soldier in it, and sent him sailing down the gutter, while the two boys ran by the side of it, and clapped their hands. Good gracious, what large waves arose in that gutter! And how fast the stream rolled on! For the rain had been very heavy. The paper boat rocked up and down, and turned itself round sometimes so quickly that the tin soldier trembled; yet he remained firm; his countenance did not change; he looked straight before him, and shouldered his musket. Suddenly the boat shot under a bridge which formed a part of a drain, and then it was as dark as the tin soldier's box.

'Where am I going now?' thought he. 'This is the black goblin's fault, I am sure. Ah, well, if the little lady were only here with me in the boat, I should not care for any darkness.'

Suddenly there appeared a great water-rat, who lived in the drain.

'Have you a passport?' asked the rat. 'Give it to me at once.' But the tin soldier remained silent and held his musket tighter than ever. The boat sailed on and the rat followed it. How he did gnash his teeth and cry out to the bits of wood and straw, 'Stop him, stop him; he has not paid toll, and has not shown his pass.' But the stream rushed on stronger and stronger. The tin soldier could already see daylight shining where the arch ended. Then he heard a roaring sound quite terrible enough to frighten the bravest man. At the end of the tunnel the drain fell into a large canal over a steep place, which made it as dangerous for him as a waterfall would be to us. He was too close to it to stop, so the boat rushed on, and the poor tin soldier could only hold himself as stiffly as possible, without moving an eyelid, to show that he was not afraid. The boat whirled round three or four times, and then filled with water to the very edge; nothing could save it from sinking. He now stood up to his neck in water, while deeper and deeper sank the boat, and the paper became soft and loose with the wet, till at last the water closed over the soldier's head. He thought of the elegant little dancer whom he should never see again, and the words of the song sounded in his ears –

Farewell, warrior! ever brave,
Drifting onward to thy grave.

Then the paper boat fell to pieces, and the soldier sank into the water and immediately afterwards was swallowed up by a great fish. Oh how dark it was inside the fish! A great deal darker than in the tunnel, and narrower too, but the tin soldier continued firm, and lay at full length shouldering his musket. The fish swam to and fro, making the most wonderful movements, but at last he became quite still. After a while, a flash of lightning seemed to pass through him, and then the daylight approached, and a voice cried out, 'I declare here is the tin soldier.' The fish had been caught, taken to the market and sold to the cook, who took him into the kitchen and cut him open with a large knife. She picked up the soldier and held him by the waist between her finger and thumb, and carried him into the room. They were all anxious to see this wonderful soldier who had travelled about inside a fish; but he was not at all proud. They placed him on the table, and – how many curious things do happen in the world! – there he was in the very same room from the window of which he had fallen, there were the same children, the same playthings, standing on the table, and the pretty castle with the elegant little dancer at the door; she still balanced herself on one leg, and held up the other, so she was as firm as himself. It touched the tin soldier so much to see her that he almost wept tin tears, but he kept them back. He only looked at her and they both remained silent. Presently one of the little boys took up the tin soldier, and threw him into the stove. He had no reason for doing so, therefore it must have been the fault of the black goblin who lived in the snuff-box. The flames lighted up the tin soldier, as he stood, the heat was very terrible, but whether it proceeded from the real fire or from the fire of love he could not tell. Then he could see that the bright colours were faded from his uniform, but whether they had been washed off during his journey or from the effects of his sorrow, no one could say. He looked at the little lady, and she looked at him. He felt himself melting away, but he still remained firm with his gun on his shoulder. Suddenly the door of the room flew open and the draught of air caught up the little dancer, she fluttered like a sylph right into the stove by the side of the tin soldier, and was instantly in flames and was gone. The tin soldier melted down into a lump, and the next morning, when the maid servant took the ashes out of the stove, she found him in the shape of a little tin heart. But of the little dancer nothing remained but the tinsel rose, which was burnt black as a cinder.

LITTLE CLAUS AND BIG CLAUS

In a village there once lived two men who had the same name. They were both called Claus. One of them had four horses, but the other had only one; so to distinguish them, people called the owner of the four horses, 'Big Claus', and he who had only one 'Little Claus'. Now we shall hear what happened to them, for this is a true story.

Through the whole week, Little Claus was obliged to plough for Big Claus, and lend him his one horse; and once a week, on a Sunday, Big Claus lent him all his four horses. Then how Little Claus would smack his whip over all five horses, they were as good as his own on that one day. The sun shone brightly, and the church bells were ringing merrily as the people passed by, dressed in their best clothes, with their prayer-books under their arms. They were going to hear the clergyman preach. They looked at Little Claus ploughing with his five horses, and he was so proud that he smacked his whip, and said, 'Gee-up, my five horses.'

'You must not say that,' said Big Claus; 'for only one of them belongs to you.' But Little Claus soon forgot what he ought to say, and when anyone passed he would call out, 'Gee-up, my five horses!'

'Now I must beg you not to say that again,' said Big Claus; 'for if you do, I shall hit your horse on the head, so that he will drop dead on the spot, and there will be an end of him.'

'I promise you I will not say it any more,' said the other; but as soon as people came by, nodding to him, and wishing him 'Good day,' he became so pleased, and thought how grand it looked to have five horses ploughing in his field, that he cried out again, 'Gee-up, all my horses!'

'I'll gee-up your horses for you,' said Big Claus; and seizing a hammer, he struck the one horse of Little Claus on the head, and he fell dead instantly.

'Oh, now I have no horse at all,' said Little Claus, weeping. But after a while he took off the dead horse's skin, and hung the hide to dry in the wind. Then he put the dry skin into a bag, and, placing it over his shoulder, went out into the next town to sell the horse's skin. He had a very long way to go, and had to pass through a dark, gloomy forest. Presently a storm arose, and he lost his way, and before he discovered the right path, evening came on, and it was still a long way to the town, and too far to return home before night. Near the road stood a large farmhouse. The shutters outside the windows were closed, but lights shone through the crevices at the top. 'I might get permission to stay here for the night,' thought Little Claus; so he went up to the door and knocked. The farmer's wife opened the door; but when she heard what he wanted, she told him to go away, as her husband would not allow her to admit strangers. 'Then I shall be obliged to lie out here,' said Little Claus to himself, as the farmer's wife shut the door in his face. Near to the farmhouse stood a large haystack, and between it and the house was a small shed, with a thatched roof. 'I can lie up there,' said Little Claus, as he saw the roof; 'it will make a famous bed, but I hope the stork will not fly down and bite my legs;' for on it stood a living stork, whose nest was in the roof. So Little Claus climbed to the roof of the shed, and while he turned himself to get comfortable, he discovered that the wooden shutters, which were closed, did not reach to the tops of the windows of the farmhouse, so that he could see into a room, in which a large table was laid out with wine, roast meat and a splendid fish. The farmer's wife and the sexton were sitting at the table together; and she filled his glass, and helped him plenteously to fish, which appeared to be his favourite dish. 'If I could only get some, too,' thought Little Claus; and then, as he stretched his neck towards the window he spied a large, beautiful pie – indeed they had a glorious feast before them.

At this moment he heard someone riding down the road, towards the farmhouse. It was the farmer returning home. He was a good man, but still he had a very strange prejudice – he could not bear the sight of a sexton. If one appeared before him, he would put himself in a terrible rage. In consequence of this dislike, the sexton had gone to visit the farmer's wife during her husband's absence from home, and the good woman had placed before him the best she had in the house to eat. When she heard the farmer coming she was frightened, and begged the sexton to hide himself in a large empty chest that stood in the room. He did so, for he knew her husband could not endure the sight of a sexton. The woman then quickly put away the wine, and hid all the rest of the nice things in the oven; for if her husband had seen them he would have asked what they were brought out for.

'Oh, dear,' sighed Little Claus from the top of the shed, as he saw all the good things disappear.

'Is anyone up there?' asked the farmer, looking up and discovering Little Claus. 'Why are you lying up there? Come down, and come into the house with me.' So Little Claus came down and told the farmer how he had lost his way and begged for a night's lodging.

'All right,' said the farmer; 'but we must have something to eat first.'

The woman received them both very kindly, laid the cloth on a large table, and placed before them a dish of porridge. The farmer was very hungry, and ate his porridge with a good appetite, but Little Claus could not help thinking of the nice roast meat, fish and pies, which he knew were in the oven. Under the table, at his feet, lay the sack containing the horse's skin, which he intended to sell at the next town. Now Little Claus did not relish the porridge at all, so he trod with his foot on the sack under the table, and the dry skin squeaked quite loud. 'Hush!' said Little Claus to his sack, at the same time treading upon it again, till it squeaked louder than before.

'Hello! What have you got in your sack?' asked the farmer.

'Oh, it is a conjuror,' said Little Claus; 'and he says we need not eat porridge, for he has conjured the oven full of roast meat, fish and pie.'

'Wonderful!' cried the farmer, starting up and opening the oven door; and there lay all the nice things hidden by the farmer's wife, but which he supposed had been conjured there by the wizard under the table. The woman dared not say anything; so she placed the things before them, and they both ate of the fish, the meat and the pastry.

Then Little Claus trod again upon his sack, and it squeaked as before. 'What does he say now?' asked the farmer.

'He says,' replied Little Claus, 'that there are three bottles of wine for us, standing in the corner, by the oven.'

So the woman was obliged to bring out the wine also, which she had hidden, and the farmer drank it till he became quite merry. He would have liked such a conjuror as Little Claus carried in his sack. 'Could he conjure up the evil one?' asked the farmer. 'I should like to see him now, while I am so merry.'

'Oh, yes!' replied Little Claus. 'My conjuror can do anything I ask him – can you not?' he asked, treading at the same time on the sack till it squeaked. 'Do you hear? He answers, "Yes," but he fears that we shall not like to look at him.'

'Oh, I am not afraid. What will he be like?'

'Well, he is very much like a sexton.'

'Ha!' said the farmer. 'Then he must be ugly. Do you know I cannot endure the sight of a sexton? However, that doesn't matter, I shall know who it is; so I shall not mind. Now then, I have got up my courage, but don't let him come too near me.'

'Stop, I must ask the conjuror,' said Little Claus; so he trod on the bag, and stooped his ear down to listen.

'What does he say?'

'He says that you must go and open that large chest which stands in the corner, and you will see the evil one crouching down inside; but you must hold the lid firmly, that he may not slip out.'

'Will you come and help me hold it?' said the farmer, going towards the chest in which his wife had hidden the sexton, who now lay inside, very much frightened. The farmer opened the lid a very little way, and peeped in.

'Oh,' cried he, springing backwards, 'I saw him, and he is exactly like our sexton. How dreadful it is!' So after that he was obliged to drink again, and they sat and drank till far into the night.

'You must sell your conjuror to me,' said the farmer; 'ask as much as you like, I will pay it; indeed I would give you directly a whole bushel of gold.'

'No, indeed, I cannot,' said Little Claus; 'only think how much profit I could make out of this conjuror.'

'But I should like to have him,' said the farmer, still continuing his entreaties.

'Well,' said Little Claus at length, 'you have been so good as to give me a night's lodging, I will not refuse you; you shall have the conjuror for a bushel of money, but I will have quite full measure.'

'So you shall,' said the farmer; 'but you must take away the chest as well. I would not have it in the house another hour; there is no knowing if he may not be still there.'

So Little Claus gave the farmer the sack containing the dried horse's skin, and received in exchange a bushel of money – full measure. The farmer also gave him a wheelbarrow on which to carry away the chest and the gold.

'Farewell,' said Little Claus, as he went off with his money and the great chest, in which the sexton lay still concealed. On one side of the forest was a broad, deep river, the water flowed so rapidly that very few were able to swim against the stream. A new bridge had lately been built across it, and in the middle of this bridge Little Claus stopped, and said, loud enough to be heard by the sexton, 'Now what shall I do with this stupid chest; it is as heavy as if it were full of stones: I shall be tired if I roll it any farther, so I may as well throw it in the river; if it swims after me to my house, well and good, and if not, it will not much matter.'

So he seized the chest in his hand and lifted it up a little, as if he were going to throw it into the water.

'No, leave it alone,' cried the sexton from within the chest; 'let me out first.'

'Oh,' exclaimed Little Claus, pretending to be frightened, 'he is in there still, is he? I must throw him into the river, that he may be drowned.'

'Oh, no; oh, no,' cried the sexton; 'I will give you a whole bushel full of money if you will let me go.'

'Why, that is another matter,' said Little Claus, opening the chest. The sexton crept out, pushed the empty chest into the water, and went to his house, then he measured out a whole bushel full of gold for Little Claus, who had already received one from the farmer, so that now he had a barrow full.

'I have been well paid for my horse,' said he to himself when he reached home, entered his own room, and emptied all his money into a heap on the floor. 'How vexed Big Claus will be when he finds out how rich I have become all through my one horse; but I shall not tell him exactly how it all happened.' Then he sent a boy to Big Claus to borrow a bushel measure.

'What can he want it for?' thought Big Claus; so he smeared the bottom of the measure with tar, that some of whatever was put into it might stick there and remain. And so it happened; for when the measure returned, three new silver florins were sticking to it.

'What does this mean?' said Big Claus; so he ran off directly to Little Claus, and asked, 'Where did you get so much money?'

'Oh, for my horse's skin, I sold it yesterday.'

'It was certainly well paid for then,' said Big Claus; and he ran home to his house, seized a hatchet, and knocked all his four horses on the head, flayed off their skins, and took them to the town to sell. 'Skins, skins, who'll buy skins?' he cried, as he went through the streets. All the shoemakers and tanners came running, and asked how much he wanted for them.

'A bushel of money, for each,' replied Big Claus.

'Are you mad?' they all cried. 'Do you think we have money to spend by the bushel?'

'Skins, skins,' he cried again, 'who'll buy skins?' but to all who inquired the price, his answer was, 'A bushel of money.'

'He is making fools of us,' said they all; then the shoemakers took their straps, and the tanners their leather aprons, and began to beat Big Claus.

'Skins, skins!' they cried, mocking him; 'Yes, we'll mark your skin for you, till it is black and blue.'

'Out of the town with him,' said they. And Big Claus was obliged to run as fast as he could, he had never before been so thoroughly beaten.

'Ah,' said he, as he came to his house; 'Little Claus shall pay me for this; I will beat him to death.'

Meanwhile the old grandmother of Little Claus died. She had been cross, unkind and really spiteful to him; but he was very sorry, and took the dead woman and laid her in his warm bed to see if he could bring her to life again. There he determined that she should lie the whole night, while he seated himself in a chair in a corner of the room as he had often done before. During the night, as he sat there, the door opened, and in came Big Claus with a hatchet. He knew well where Little Claus's bed stood; so he went right up to it, and struck the old grandmother on the head, thinking it must be Little Claus.

'There,' cried he, 'now you cannot make a fool of me again;' and then he went home.

'That is a very wicked man,' thought Little Claus; 'he meant to kill me. It is a good thing for my old grandmother that she was already dead, or he would have taken her life.' Then he dressed his old grandmother in her best clothes, borrowed a horse of his neighbour, and harnessed it to a cart. Then he placed the old woman on the back seat, so that she might not fall out as he drove, and rode away through the wood. By sunrise they reached a large inn, where Little Claus stopped and went to get something to eat. The landlord was a rich man, and a good man too; but as passionate as if he had been made of pepper and snuff.

'Good morning,' said he to Little Claus; 'you are come betimes today.'

'Yes,' said Little Claus; 'I am going to the town with my old grandmother; she is sitting at the back of the wagon, but I cannot bring her into the room. Will you take her a glass of mead? But you must speak very loud, for she cannot hear well.'

'Yes, certainly I will,' replied the landlord; and, pouring out a glass of mead, he carried it out to the dead grandmother, who sat upright in the cart. 'Here is a glass of mead from your grandson,' said the landlord. The dead woman did not answer a word, but sat quite still. 'Do you not hear?' cried the landlord as loud as he could; 'Here is a glass of mead from your grandson.'

Again and again he bawled it out, but as she did not stir he flew into a passion, and threw the glass of mead in her face; it struck her on the nose, and she fell backwards out of the cart, for she was only seated there, not tied in.

'Hello!' cried Little Claus, rushing out of the door, and seizing hold of the landlord by the throat; 'You have killed my grandmother; see, here is a great hole in her forehead.'

'Oh, how unfortunate,' said the landlord, wringing his hands. 'This all comes of my fiery temper. Dear Little Claus, I will give you a bushel of money; I will bury your grandmother as if she were my own; only keep silent, or else they will cut off my head, and that would be disagreeable.'

So it happened that Little Claus received another bushel of money, and the landlord buried his old grandmother as if she had been his own. When Little Claus reached home again, he immediately sent a boy to Big Claus, requesting him to lend him a bushel measure. 'How is this?' thought Big Claus; 'Did I not kill him? I must go and see for myself.' So he went to Little Claus, and took the bushel measure with him. 'How did you get all this money?' asked Big Claus, staring with wide open eyes at his neighbour's treasures.

'You killed my grandmother instead of me,' said Little Claus; 'so I have sold her for a bushel of money.'

'That is a good price at all events,' said Big Claus. So he went home, took a hatchet, and killed his old grandmother with one blow. Then he placed her on a cart, and drove into the town to the apothecary, and asked him if he would buy a dead body.

'Whose is it, and where did you get it?' asked the apothecary.

'It is my grandmother,' he replied; 'I killed her with a blow, that I might get a bushel of money for her.'

'Heaven preserve us!' cried the apothecary. 'You are out of your mind. Don't say such things, or you will lose your head.' And then he talked to him seriously about the wicked deed he had done, and told him that such a wicked man would surely be punished. Big Claus got so frightened that he rushed out of the surgery, jumped into the cart, whipped up his horses, and drove home quickly. The apothecary and all the people thought him mad, and let him drive where he liked.

'You shall pay for this,' said Big Claus, as soon as he got into the high-road, 'that you shall, Little Claus.' So as soon as he reached home he took the largest sack he could find and went over to Little Claus. 'You have played me another trick,' said he. 'First, I killed all my horses, and then my old grandmother, and it is all your fault; but you shall not make a fool of me any more.' So he laid hold of Little Claus round the body, and pushed him into the sack, which he took on his shoulders, saying, 'Now I'm going to drown you in the river.'

He had a long way to go before he reached the river, and Little Claus was not a very light weight to carry. The road led by the church, and as they passed he could hear the organ playing and the people singing beautifully. Big Claus put down the sack close to the church-door, and thought he might as well go in and hear a psalm before he went any farther. Little Claus could not possibly get out of the sack, and all the people were in church; so in he went.

'Oh dear, oh dear,' sighed Little Claus in the sack, as he turned and twisted about; but he found he could not loosen the string with which it was tied. Presently an old cattle driver, with snowy hair, passed by, carrying a large staff in his hand, with which he drove a large herd of cows and oxen before him. They stumbled against the sack in which lay Little Claus, and turned it over. 'Oh dear,' sighed Little Claus, 'I am very young, yet I am soon going to heaven.'

'And I, poor fellow,' said the drover, 'I who am so old already cannot get there.'

'Open the sack,' cried Little Claus; 'creep into it instead of me, and you will soon be there.'

'With all my heart,' replied the drover, opening the sack, from which sprung Little Claus as quickly as possible. 'Will you take care of my cattle?' said the old man, as he crept into the bag.

'Yes,' said Little Claus, and he tied up the sack, and then walked off with all the cows and oxen.

When Big Claus came out of church, he took up the sack, and placed it on his shoulders. It appeared to have become lighter, for the old drover was not half so heavy as Little Claus.

'How light he seems now,' said he. 'Ah, it is because I have been to a church.' So he walked on to the river, which was deep and broad, and threw the sack containing the old drover into the water, believing it to be Little Claus. 'There you may lie!' he exclaimed. 'You will play me no more tricks now.' Then he turned to go home, but when he came to a place where two roads crossed, there was Little Claus driving the cattle. 'How is this?' said Big Claus. 'Did I not drown you just now?'

'Yes,' said Little Claus; 'you threw me into the river about half an hour ago.'

'But wherever did you get all these fine beasts?' asked Big Claus.

'These beasts are sea-cattle,' replied Little Claus. 'I'll tell you the whole story, and thank you for drowning me; I am above you now, I am really very rich. I was frightened, to be sure, while I lay tied up in the sack, and the wind whistled in my ears when you threw me into the river from the bridge, and I sank to the bottom immediately; but I did not hurt myself, for I fell upon beautifully soft grass which grows down there; and in a moment, the sack opened, and the sweetest little maiden came towards me. She had snow-white robes, and a wreath of green leaves on her wet hair. She took me by the hand, and said, 'So you are come, Little Claus, and here are some cattle for you to begin with. About a mile farther on the road, there is another herd for you.' Then I saw that the river formed a great highway for the people who live in the sea. They were walking and driving here and there from the sea to the land at the spot where the river terminates. The bed of the river was covered with the loveliest flowers and sweet fresh grass. The fish swam past me as rapidly as the birds do here in the air. How handsome all the people were, and what fine cattle were grazing on the hills and in the valleys!'

'But why did you come up again,' said Big Claus, 'if it was all so beautiful down there? I should not have done so!'

'Well,' said Little Claus, 'it was good policy on my part; you heard me say just now that I was told by the sea-maiden to go a mile farther on the road, and I should find a whole herd of cattle. By the road she meant the river, for she could not travel any other way; but I knew the winding of the river, and how it bends, sometimes to the right and sometimes to the left, and it seemed a long way, so I chose a shorter one; and, by coming up to the land, and then driving across the fields back again to the river, I shall save half a mile, and get all my cattle more quickly.'

'What a lucky fellow you are!' exclaimed Big Claus. 'Do you think I should get any sea-cattle if I went down to the bottom of the river?'

'Yes, I think so,' said Little Claus; 'but I cannot carry you there in a sack, you are too heavy. However if you will go there first, and then creep into a sack, I will throw you in with the greatest pleasure.'

'Thank you,' said Big Claus; 'but remember, if I do not get any sea-cattle down there I shall come up again and give you a good thrashing.'

'No, now, don't be too fierce about it!' said Little Claus, as they walked on towards the river. When they approached it, the cattle, who were very thirsty, saw the stream, and ran down to drink.

'See what a hurry they are in,' said Little Claus, 'they are longing to get down again,'

'Come, help me, make haste,' said Big Claus; 'or you'll get beaten.' So he crept into a large sack, which had been lying across the back of one of the oxen.

'Put in a stone,' said Big Claus, 'or I may not sink.'

'Oh, there's not much fear of that,' he replied; still he put a large stone into the bag, and then tied it tightly, and gave it a push.

'Plump!' In went Big Claus, and immediately sank to the bottom of the river.

'I'm afraid he will not find any cattle,' said Little Claus, and then he drove his own beasts homewards.

THE WICKED PRINCE

There lived once upon a time a wicked prince whose heart and mind were set upon conquering all the countries of the world, and on frightening the people; he devastated their countries with fire and sword, and his soldiers trod down the crops in the fields and destroyed the peasants' huts by fire, so that the flames licked the green leaves off the branches, and the fruit hung dried up on the singed black trees. Many a poor mother fled, her naked baby in her arms, behind the still-smoking walls of her cottage; but also there the soldiers followed her, and when they found her, she served as new nourishment to their diabolical enjoyments; demons could not possibly have done worse things than these soldiers! The prince was of opinion that all this was right, and that it was only the natural course which things ought to take. His power increased day by day, his name was feared by all, and fortune favoured his deeds.

He brought enormous wealth home from the conquered towns, and gradually accumulated in his residence riches which could nowhere be equalled. He erected magnificent palaces, churches and halls, and all who saw these splendid buildings and great treasures exclaimed admiringly: 'What a mighty prince!' But they did not know what endless misery he had brought upon other countries, nor did they hear the sighs and lamentations which rose up from the debris of the destroyed cities.

The prince often looked with delight upon his gold and his magnificent edifices, and thought, like the crowd: 'What a mighty prince! But I must have more – much more. No power on earth must equal mine, far less exceed it.'

He made war with all his neighbours, and defeated them. The conquered kings were chained up with golden fetters to his chariot when he drove through the streets of his city. These kings had to kneel at his and his courtiers' feet when they sat at table, and live on the morsels which they left. At last the prince had his own statue erected on the public places and fixed on the royal palaces; nay, he even wished it to be placed in the churches, on the altars, but in this the priests opposed him, saying: 'Prince, you are mighty indeed, but God's power is much greater than yours; we dare not obey your orders.'

'Well,' said the prince, 'then I will conquer God too.' And in his haughtiness and foolish presumption he ordered a magnificent ship to be constructed, with which he could sail through the air; it was gorgeously fitted out and of many colours; like the tail of a peacock, it was covered with thousands of eyes, but each eye was the barrel of a gun. The prince sat in the centre of the ship, and had only to touch a spring in order to make thousands of bullets fly out in all directions, while the guns were at once loaded again. Hundreds of eagles were attached to this ship, and it rose with the swiftness of an arrow up towards the sun. The earth was soon left far below, and looked, with its mountains and woods, like a cornfield where the plough had made furrows which separated green meadows; soon it looked only like a map with indistinct lines upon it; and at last it entirely disappeared in mist and clouds. Higher and higher rose the eagles up into the air; then God sent one of his numberless angels against the ship. The wicked prince showered thousands of bullets upon him, but they rebounded from his shining wings and fell down like ordinary hailstones. One drop of blood, one single drop, came out of the white feathers of the angel's wings and fell upon the ship in which the prince sat, burnt into it, and weighed upon it like thousands of hundredweights, dragging it rapidly down to the earth again; the strong wings of the eagles gave way, the wind roared round the prince's head, and the clouds around – were they formed by the smoke rising up from the burnt cities? – took strange shapes, like crabs many, many miles long, which stretched their claws out after him, and rose up like enormous rocks, from which rolling masses dashed down, and became fire-spitting dragons.

The prince was lying half-dead in his ship, when it sank at last with a terrible shock into the branches of a large tree in the wood.

'I will conquer God!' said the prince. 'I have sworn it: my will must be done!'

And he spent seven years in the construction of wonderful ships to sail through the air, and had darts cast from the hardest steel to break the walls of heaven with. He gathered warriors from all countries, so many that when they were placed side by side they covered the space of several miles. They entered the ships and the prince was approaching his own, when God sent a swarm of gnats – one swarm of little gnats. They buzzed round the prince and stung his face and hands; angrily he drew his sword and brandished it, but he only touched the air and did not hit the gnats. Then he ordered his servants to bring costly coverings and wrap him in them, that the gnats might no longer be able to reach him. The servants carried out his orders, but one single gnat had placed itself inside one of the coverings, crept into the prince's ear and stung him. The place burnt like fire, and the poison entered into his blood. Mad with pain, he tore off the coverings and his clothes too, flinging them far away, and danced about before the eyes of his ferocious soldiers, who now mocked at him, the mad prince, who wished to make war with God, and was overcome by a single little gnat.

THE PHOENIX BIRD

In the Garden of Paradise, beneath the Tree of Knowledge, bloomed a rose-bush. Here, in the first rose, a bird was born. His flight was like the flashing of light, his plumage was beauteous, and his song ravishing. But when Eve plucked the fruit of the tree of knowledge of good and evil, when she and Adam were driven from Paradise, there fell from the flaming sword of the cherub a spark into the nest of the bird, which blazed up forthwith. The bird perished in the flames; but from the red egg in the nest there fluttered aloft a new one – the one solitary Phoenix bird. The fable tells that he dwells in Arabia, and that every hundred years, he burns himself to death in his nest; but each time a new Phoenix, the only one in the world, rises up from the red egg.

The bird flutters round us, swift as light, beauteous in colour, charming in song. When a mother sits by her infant's cradle, he stands on the pillow, and, with his wings, forms a glory around the infant's head. He flies through the chamber of content, and brings sunshine into it, and the violets on the humble table smell doubly sweet.

But the Phoenix is not the bird of Arabia alone. He wings his way in the glimmer of the Northern Lights over the plains of Lapland, and hops among the yellow flowers in the short Greenland summer. Beneath the copper mountains of Fablun, and England's coal mines, he flies, in the shape of a dusty moth, over the hymn-book that rests on the knees of the pious miner. On a lotus leaf he floats down the sacred waters of the Ganges, and the eye of the Hindoo maid gleams bright when she beholds him.

The Phoenix bird, dost thou not know him? The Bird of Paradise, the holy swan of song! On the car of Thespis he sat in the guise of a chattering raven, and flapped his black wings, smeared with the lees of wine; over the sounding harp of Iceland swept the swan's red beak; on Shakspeare's shoulder he sat in the guise of Odin's raven, and whispered in the poet's ear, 'Immortality!' and at the minstrels' feast he fluttered through the halls of the Wartburg.

The Phoenix bird, dost thou not know him? He sang to thee the Marseillaise, and thou kissedst the pen that fell from his wing; he came in the radiance of Paradise, and perchance thou didst turn away from him towards the sparrow who sat with tinsel on his wings.

The Bird of Paradise – renewed each century – born in flame, ending in flame! Thy picture, in a golden frame, hangs in the halls of the rich, but thou thyself often fliest around, lonely and disregarded, a myth – 'The Phoenix of Arabia'.

In Paradise, when thou wert born in the first rose, beneath the Tree of Knowledge, thou receivedst a kiss, and thy right name was given thee – thy name, Poetry.

LITTLE IDA'S FLOWERS

'My poor flowers are quite dead,' said little Ida, 'they were so pretty yesterday evening, and now all the leaves are hanging down quite withered. What do they do that for?' she asked, of the student who sat on the sofa; she liked him very much, he could tell the most amusing stories, and cut out the prettiest pictures: hearts, and ladies dancing, castles with doors that opened, as well as flowers; he was a delightful student. 'Why do the flowers look so faded today?' she asked again, and pointed to her nosegay, which was quite withered.

'Don't you know what is the matter with them?' said the student. 'The flowers were at a ball last night, and therefore, it is no wonder they hang their heads.'

'But flowers cannot dance?' cried little Ida.

'Yes indeed, they can,' replied the student. 'When it grows dark, and everybody is asleep, they jump about quite merrily. They have a ball almost every night.'

'Can children go to these balls?'

'Yes,' said the student, 'little daisies and lilies of the valley.'

'Where do the beautiful flowers dance?' asked little Ida.

'Have you not often seen the large castle outside the gates of the town, where the king lives in summer, and where the beautiful garden is full of flowers? And have you not fed the swans with bread when they swam towards you? Well, the flowers have capital balls there, believe me.'

'I was in the garden out there yesterday with my mother,' said Ida, 'but all the leaves were off the trees, and there was not a single flower left. Where are they? I used to see so many in the summer.'

'They are in the castle,' replied the student. 'You must know that as soon as the king and all the court are gone into the town, the flowers run out of the garden into the castle, and you should see how merry they are. The two most beautiful roses seat themselves on the throne, and are called the king and queen, then all the red cockscombs range themselves on each side, and bow; these are the lords-in-waiting. After that the pretty flowers come in, and there is a grand ball. The blue violets represent little naval cadets, and dance with hyacinths and crocuses which they call young ladies. The tulips and tiger-lilies are the old ladies who sit and watch the dancing, so that everything may be conducted with order and propriety.'

'But,' said little Ida, 'is there no one there to hurt the flowers for dancing in the king's castle?'

'No one knows anything about it,' said the student. 'The old steward of the castle, who has to watch there at night, sometimes comes in; but he carries a great bunch of keys, and as soon as the flowers hear the keys rattle, they run and hide themselves behind the long curtains, and stand quite still, just peeping their heads out. Then the old steward says, "I smell flowers here," but he cannot see them.'

'Oh how capital,' said little Ida, clapping her hands. 'Should I be able to see these flowers?'

'Yes,' said the student, 'mind you think of it the next time you go out, no doubt you will see them, if you peep through the window. I did so today, and I saw a long yellow lily lying stretched out on the sofa. She was a court lady.'

'Can the flowers from the Botanical Gardens go to these balls?' asked Ida. 'It is such a distance!'

'Oh yes,' said the student 'whenever they like, for they can fly. Have you not seen those beautiful red, white and yellow butterflies that look like flowers? They were flowers once. They have flown off their stalks into the air, and flap their leaves as if they were little wings to make them fly. Then, if they behave well, they obtain permission to fly about during the day, instead of being obliged to sit still on their stems at home, and so in time their leaves become real wings. It may be, however, that the flowers in the Botanical Gardens have never been to the king's palace, and, therefore, they know nothing of the merry doings at night, which take place there. I will tell you what to do, and the botanical professor, who lives close by here, will be so surprised. You know him very well, do you not? Well, next time you go into his garden, you must tell one of the flowers that there is going to be a grand ball at the castle, then that flower will tell all the others, and they will fly away to the castle as soon as possible. And when the professor walks into his garden, there will not be a single flower left. How he will wonder what has become of them!'

'But how can one flower tell another? Flowers cannot speak?'

'No, certainly not,' replied the student; 'but they can make signs. Have you not often seen that when the wind blows they nod at one another, and rustle all their green leaves?'

'Can the professor understand the signs?' asked Ida.

'Yes, to be sure he can. He went one morning into his garden, and saw a stinging nettle making signs with its leaves to a beautiful red carnation. It was saying, 'You are so pretty, I like you very much.' But the professor did not approve of such nonsense, so he clapped his hands on the nettle to stop it. Then the leaves, which are its fingers, stung him so sharply that he has never ventured to touch a nettle since.'

'Oh how funny!' said Ida, and she laughed.

'How can anyone put such notions into a child's head?' said a tiresome lawyer, who had come to pay a visit and sat on the sofa. He did not like the student, and would grumble when he saw him cutting out droll or amusing pictures. Sometimes it would be a man hanging on a gibbet and holding a heart in his hand as if he had been stealing hearts. Sometimes it was an old witch riding through the air on a broom and carrying her husband on her nose. But the lawyer did not like such jokes, and he would say as he had just said, 'How can anyone put such nonsense into a child's head! What absurd fancies there are!'

But to little Ida, all these stories which the student told her about the flowers seemed very droll, and she thought over them a great deal. The flowers did hang their heads, because they had been dancing all night, and were very tired, and most likely they were ill. Then she took them into the room where a number of toys lay on a pretty little table, and the whole of the table drawer besides was full of beautiful things. Her doll Sophy lay in the doll's bed asleep, and little Ida said to her, 'You must really get up Sophy, and be content to lie in the drawer tonight; the poor flowers are ill, and they must lie in your bed, then perhaps they will get well again.' So she took the doll out, who looked quite cross, and said not a single word, for she was angry at being turned out of her bed. Ida placed the flowers in the doll's bed, and drew the quilt over them. Then she told them to lie quite still and be good, while she made some tea for them, so that they might be quite well and able to get up the next morning.

And she drew the curtains close round the little bed, so that the sun might not shine in their eyes. During the whole evening she could not help thinking of what the student had told her. And before she went to bed herself, she was obliged to peep behind the curtains into the garden where all her mother's beautiful flowers grew, hyacinths and tulips, and many others. Then she whispered to them quite softly, 'I know you are going to a ball tonight.' But the flowers appeared as if they did not understand, and not a leaf moved; still Ida felt quite sure she knew all about it. She lay awake a long time after she was in bed, thinking how pretty it must be to see all the beautiful flowers dancing in the king's garden. 'I wonder if my flowers have really been there,' she said to herself, and then she fell asleep. In the night she awoke; she had been dreaming of the flowers and of the student, as well as of the tiresome lawyer who found fault with him. It was quite still in Ida's bedroom; the night-lamp burnt on the table, and her father and mother were asleep. 'I wonder if my flowers are still lying in Sophy's bed,' she thought to herself; 'how much I should like to know.' She raised herself a little, and glanced at the door of the room where all her flowers and playthings lay; it was partly open, and as she listened, it seemed as if someone in the room was playing the piano, but softly and more prettily than she had ever before heard it. 'Now all the flowers are certainly dancing in there,' she thought, 'oh how much I should like to see them,' but she did not dare move for fear of disturbing her father and mother. 'If they would only come in here,' she thought; but they did not come, and the music continued to play so beautifully, and was so pretty, that she could resist no longer. She crept out of her little bed, went softly to the door and looked into the room. Oh what a splendid sight there was to be sure! There was no night-lamp burning, but the room appeared quite light, for the moon shone through the window upon the floor, and made it almost like day. All the hyacinths and tulips stood in two long rows down the room, not a single flower remained in the window, and the flower-pots were all empty. The flowers were dancing gracefully on the floor, making turns and holding each other by their long green leaves as they swung round. At the piano sat a large yellow lily which little Ida was sure she had seen in the summer, for she remembered the student saying she was very much like Miss Lina, one of Ida's friends. They all laughed at him then, but now it seemed to little Ida as if the tall, yellow flower was really like the young lady. She had just the same manners while playing, bending her long yellow face from side to side, and nodding in time to the beautiful music. Then she saw a large purple crocus jump into the middle of the table where the playthings stood, go up to the doll's bedstead and draw back the curtains; there lay the sick flowers, but they got up directly, and nodded to the others as a sign that they wished to dance with them. The old rough doll, with the broken mouth, stood up and bowed to the pretty flowers. They did not look ill at all now, but jumped about and were very merry, yet none of them noticed little Ida. Presently it seemed as if something fell from the table. Ida looked that way, and saw a slight carnival rod jumping down among the flowers as if it belonged to them; it was, however, very smooth and neat, and a little wax doll with a broad brimmed hat on her head, like the one worn by the lawyer, sat upon it. The carnival rod hopped about among the flowers on its three red stilted feet, and stamped quite loud when it danced the Mazurka; the flowers could not perform this dance, they were too light to stamp in that manner.

LITTLE IDA'S FLOWERS

All at once the wax doll which rode on the carnival rod seemed to grow larger and taller, and it turned round and said to the paper flowers, 'How can you put such things in a child's head? They are all foolish fancies;' and then the doll was exactly like the lawyer with the broad-brimmed hat, and looked as yellow and as cross as he did; but the paper dolls struck him on his thin legs, and he shrunk up again and became quite a little wax doll. This was very amusing, and Ida could not help laughing. The carnival rod went on dancing, and the lawyer was obliged to dance also. It was no use, he might make himself great and tall, or remain a little wax doll with a large black hat; still he must dance. Then at last the other flowers interceded for him, especially those who had lain in the doll's bed, and the carnival rod gave up his dancing. At the same moment a loud knocking was heard in the drawer where Ida's doll Sophy lay with many other toys. Then the rough doll ran to the end of the table, laid himself flat down upon it, and began to pull the drawer out a little way.

Then Sophy raised herself, and looked round quite astonished, 'There must be a ball here tonight,' said Sophy. 'Why did not somebody tell me?'

'Will you dance with me?' said the rough doll.

'You are the right sort to dance with, certainly,' said she, turning her back upon him.

Then she seated herself on the edge of the drawer, and thought that perhaps one of the flowers would ask her to dance; but none of them came. Then she coughed, 'Hem, hem, a-hem;' but for all that not one came. The shabby doll now danced quite alone, and not very badly, after all. As none of the flowers seemed to notice Sophy, she let herself down from the drawer to the floor, so as to make a very great noise. All the flowers came round her directly, and asked if she had hurt herself, especially those who had lain in her bed. But she was not hurt at all, and Ida's flowers thanked her for the use of the nice bed, and were very kind to her. They led her into the middle of the room, where the moon shone, and danced with her, while all the other flowers formed a circle round them. Then Sophy was very happy, and said they might keep her bed; she did not mind lying in the drawer at all. But the flowers thanked her very much, and said –

'We cannot live long. Tomorrow morning we shall be quite dead; and you must tell little Ida to bury us in the garden, near to the grave of the canary; then, in the summer we shall wake up and be more beautiful than ever.'

'No, you must not die,' said Sophy, as she kissed the flowers.

Then the door of the room opened, and a number of beautiful flowers danced in. Ida could not imagine where they could come from, unless they were the flowers from the king's garden. First came two lovely roses, with little golden crowns on their heads; these were the king and queen. Beautiful stocks and carnations followed, bowing to everyone present. They had also music with them. Large poppies and peonies had pea-shells for instruments, and blew into them till they were quite red in the face. The bunches of blue hyacinths and the little white snowdrops jingled their bell-like flowers, as if they were real bells. Then came many more flowers: blue violets, purple heart's-ease, daisies and lilies of the valley, and they all danced together, and kissed each other. It was very beautiful to behold.

At last the flowers wished each other good-night. Then little Ida crept back into her bed again, and dreamt of all she had seen. When she arose the next morning, she went quickly to the little table, to see if the flowers were still there. She drew aside the curtains of the little bed. There they all lay, but quite faded; much more so than the day before. Sophy was lying in the drawer where Ida had placed her; but she looked very sleepy.

'Do you remember what the flowers told you to say to me?' said little Ida. But Sophy looked quite stupid, and said not a single word.

'You are not kind at all,' said Ida; 'and yet they all danced with you.'

Then she took a little paper box, on which were painted beautiful birds, and laid the dead flowers in it.

'This shall be your pretty coffin,' she said; 'and by and by, when my cousins come to visit me, they shall help me to bury you out in the garden; so that next summer you may grow up again more beautiful than ever.'

Her cousins were two good-tempered boys, whose names were James and Adolphus. Their father had given them each a bow and arrow, and they had brought them to show Ida. She told them about the poor flowers which were dead; and as soon as they obtained permission, they went with her to bury them. The two boys walked first, with their crossbows on their shoulders, and little Ida followed, carrying the pretty box containing the dead flowers. They dug a little grave in the garden. Ida kissed her flowers and then laid them, with the box, in the earth. James and Adolphus then fired their crossbows over the grave, as they had neither guns nor cannons.

THE BUCKWHEAT

Very often, after a violent thunder-storm, a field of buckwheat appears blackened and singed, as if a flame of fire had passed over it. The country people say that this appearance is caused by lightning; but I will tell you what the sparrow says, and the sparrow heard it from an old willow-tree which grew near a field of buckwheat, and is there still. It is a large venerable tree, though a little crippled by age. The trunk has been split, and out of the crevice grass and brambles grow. The tree bends forward slightly, and the branches hang quite down to the ground just like green hair. Corn grows in the surrounding fields, not only rye and barley, but oats – pretty oats that, when ripe, look like a number of little golden canary-birds sitting on a bough. The corn has a smiling look and the heaviest and richest ears bend their heads low as if in pious humility. Once there was also a field of buckwheat, and this field was exactly opposite to old willow-tree. The buckwheat did not bend like the other grain, but erected its head proudly and stiffly on the stem. 'I am as valuable as any other corn,' said he, 'and I am much handsomer; my flowers are as beautiful as the bloom of the apple blossom, and it is a pleasure to look at us. Do you know of anything prettier than we are, you old willow-tree?'

And the willow-tree nodded his head, as if he would say, 'Indeed I do.'

But the buckwheat spread itself out with pride, and said, 'Stupid tree; he is so old that grass grows out of his body.'

There arose a very terrible storm. All the field-flowers folded their leaves together, or bowed their little heads, while the storm passed over them, but the buckwheat stood erect in its pride. 'Bend your head as we do,' said the flowers.

'I have no occasion to do so,' replied the buckwheat.

'Bend your head as we do,' cried the ears of corn; 'the angel of the storm is coming; his wings spread from the sky above to the earth beneath. He will strike you down before you can cry for mercy.'

'But I will not bend my head,' said the buckwheat.

'Close your flowers and bend your leaves,' said the old willow-tree. 'Do not look at the lightning when the cloud bursts; even men cannot do that. In a flash of lightning heaven opens, and we can look in; but the sight will strike even human beings blind. What then must happen to us, who only grow out of the earth, and are so inferior to them, if we venture to do so?'

'Inferior, indeed!' said the buckwheat. 'Now I intend to have a peep into heaven.' Proudly and boldly he looked up, while the lightning flashed across the sky as if the whole world were in flames.

When the dreadful storm had passed, the flowers and the corn raised their drooping heads in the pure still air, refreshed by the rain, but the buckwheat lay like a weed in the field, burnt to blackness by the lightning. The branches of the old willow-tree rustled in the wind, and large water-drops fell from his green leaves as if the old willow were weeping. Then the sparrows asked why he was weeping, when all around him seemed so cheerful. 'See,' they said, 'how the sun shines, and the clouds float in the blue sky. Do you not smell the sweet perfume from flower and bush? Wherefore do you weep, old willow-tree?' Then the willow told them of the haughty pride of the buckwheat, and of the punishment which followed in consequence.

This is the story told me by the sparrows one evening when I begged them to relate some tale to me.

OLE-LUK-OIE, THE DREAM GOD

There is nobody in the world who knows so many stories as Ole-Luk-Oie, or who can relate them so nicely. In the evening, while the children are seated at the table or in their little chairs, he comes up the stairs very softly, for he walks in his socks, then he opens the doors without the slightest noise, and throws a small quantity of very fine dust in their eyes, just enough to prevent them from keeping them open, and so they do not see him. Then he creeps behind them, and blows softly upon their necks, till their heads begin to droop. But Ole-Luk-Oie does not wish to hurt them, for he is very fond of children, and only wants them to be quiet that he may relate to them pretty stories, and they never are quiet until they are in bed and asleep. As soon as they are asleep, Ole-Luk-Oie seats himself upon the bed. He is nicely dressed; his coat is made of silken stuff; it is impossible to say of what colour, for it changes from green to red, and from red to blue as he turns from side to side. Under each arm he carries an umbrella; one of them, with pictures on the inside, he spreads over the good children, and then they dream the most beautiful stories the whole night. But the other umbrella has no pictures, and this he holds over the naughty children so that they sleep heavily, and wake in the morning without having dreamed at all.

Now we shall hear how Ole-Luk-Oie came every night during a whole week to the little boy named Hjalmar, and what he told him. There were seven stories, as there are seven days in the week.

MONDAY

'Now pay attention,' said Ole-Luk-Oie, in the evening, when Hjalmar was in bed, 'and I will decorate the room.'

Immediately all the flowers in the flower-pots became large trees, with long branches reaching to the ceiling, and stretching along the walls, so that the whole room was like a greenhouse. All the branches were loaded with flowers, each flower as beautiful and as fragrant as a rose; and, had anyone tasted them, he would have found them sweeter even than jam. The fruit glittered like gold, and there were cakes so full of plums that they were nearly bursting. It was incomparably beautiful. At the same time sounded dismal moans from the table-drawer in which lay Hjalmar's school books.

'What can that be now?' said Ole-Luk-Oie, going to the table and pulling out the drawer.

It was a slate, in such distress because of a false number in the sum that it had almost broken itself to pieces. The pencil pulled and tugged at its string as if it were a little dog that wanted to help, but could not.

And then came a moan from Hjalmar's copy-book. Oh, it was quite terrible to hear! On each leaf stood a row of capital letters, every one having a small letter by its side. This formed a copy; under these were other letters, which Hjalmar had written: they fancied they looked like the copy, but they were mistaken; for they were leaning on one side as if they intended to fall over the pencil-lines.

'See, this is the way you should hold yourselves,' said the copy. 'Look here, you should slope thus, with a graceful curve.'

'Oh, we are very willing to do so, but we cannot,' said Hjalmar's letters; 'we are so wretchedly made.'

'You must be scratched out, then,' said Ole-Luk-Oie.

'Oh, no!' they cried, and then they stood up so gracefully it was quite a pleasure to look at them.

'Now we must give up our stories, and exercise these letters,' said Ole-Luk-Oie; 'One, two – one, two – ' So he drilled them till they stood up gracefully, and looked as beautiful as a copy could look. But after Ole-Luk-Oie was gone, and Hjalmar looked at them in the morning, they were as wretched and as awkward as ever.

TUESDAY

As soon as Hjalmar was in bed, Ole-Luk-Oie touched, with his little magic wand, all the furniture in the room, which immediately began to chatter, and each article only talked of itself.

Over the chest of drawers hung a large picture in a gilt frame, representing a landscape, with fine old trees, flowers in the grass and a broad stream, which flowed through the wood, past several castles, far out into the wild ocean. Ole-Luk-Oie touched the picture with his magic wand, and immediately the birds commenced singing, the branches of the trees rustled, and the clouds moved across the sky, casting their shadows on the landscape beneath them. Then Ole-Luk-Oie lifted little Hjalmar up to the frame, and placed his feet in the picture, just on the high grass, and there he stood with the sun shining down upon him through the branches of the trees. He ran to the water, and seated himself in a little boat which lay there, and which was painted red and white. The sails glittered like silver, and six swans, each with a golden circlet round its neck, and a bright blue star on its forehead, drew the boat past the green wood, where the trees talked of robbers and witches, and the flowers of beautiful little elves and fairies, whose histories the butterflies had related to them. Brilliant fish, with scales like silver and gold, swam after the boat, sometimes making a spring and splashing the water round them, while birds, red and blue, small and great, flew after him in two long lines. The gnats danced round them, and the cockchafers cried 'Buzz, buzz'. They all wanted to follow Hjalmar, and all had some story to tell him. It was a most pleasant sail. Sometimes the forests were thick and dark, sometimes like a beautiful garden, gay with sunshine and flowers; then he passed great palaces of glass and of marble, and on the balconies stood princesses, whose faces were those of little girls whom Hjalmar knew well, and had often played with. One of them held out her hand, in which was a heart made of sugar, more beautiful than any confectioner ever sold. As Hjalmar sailed by, he caught hold of one side of the sugar heart, and held it fast, and the princess held fast also, so that it broke in two pieces. Hjalmar had one piece, and the princess the other, but Hjalmar's was the largest. At each castle stood little princes acting as sentinels. They presented arms, and had golden swords, and made it rain plums and tin soldiers, so that they must have been real princes.

Hjalmar continued to sail, sometimes through woods, sometimes as it were through large halls, and then by large cities. At last he came to the town where his nurse lived, who had carried him in her arms when he was a very little boy, and had always been kind to him. She nodded and beckoned to him, and then sang the little verses she had herself composed and set to him:

How oft my memory turns to thee,
My own Hjalmar, ever dear!
When I could watch thy infant glee,
Or kiss away a pearly tear.
'Twas in my arms thy lisping tongue
First spoke the half-remembered word,
While o'er thy tottering steps I hung,
My fond protection to afford.
Farewell! I pray the Heavenly Power
To keep thee till thy dying hour.

And all the birds sang the same tune, the flowers danced on their stems, and the old trees nodded as if Ole-Luk-Oie had been telling them stories as well.

WEDNESDAY

How the rain did pour down! Hjalmar could hear it in his sleep; and when Ole-Luk-Oie opened the window, the water flowed quite up to the window-sill. It had the appearance of a large lake outside, and a beautiful ship lay close to the house.

'Wilt thou sail with me tonight, little Hjalmar?' said Ole-Luk-Oie. 'Then we shall see foreign countries, and thou shalt return here in the morning.'

All in a moment, there stood Hjalmar, in his best clothes, on the deck of the noble ship; and immediately the weather became fine. They sailed through the streets, round by the church, and on every side rolled the wide, great sea. They sailed till the land disappeared, and then they saw a flock of storks, who had left their own country, and were travelling to warmer climates. The storks flew one behind the other, and had already been a long, long time on the wing. One of them seemed so tired that his wings could scarcely carry him. He was the last of the row, and was soon left very far behind. At length he sunk lower and lower, with outstretched wings, flapping them in vain, till his feet touched the rigging of the ship, and he slided from the sails to the deck, and stood before them. Then a sailor-boy caught him, and put him in the hen-house, with the fowls, the ducks and the turkeys, while the poor stork stood quite bewildered amongst them.

'Just look at that fellow,' said the chickens.

Then the turkey-cock puffed himself out as large as he could, and inquired who he was; and the ducks waddled backwards, crying, 'Quack, quack.'

Then the stork told them all about warm Africa, of the pyramids, and of the ostrich, which, like a wild horse, runs across the desert. But the ducks did not understand what he said, and quacked amongst themselves, 'We are all of the same opinion; namely, that he is stupid.'

'Yes, to be sure, he is stupid,' said the turkey-cock; and gobbled.

Then the stork remained quite silent, and thought of his home in Africa.

'Those are handsome thin legs of yours,' said the turkey-cock. 'What do they cost a yard?'

'Quack, quack, quack,' grinned the ducks; but the stork pretended not to hear.

'You may as well laugh,' said the turkey; 'for that remark was rather witty, or perhaps it was above you. Ah, ah, is he not clever? He will be a great amusement to us while he remains here.' And then he gobbled, and the ducks quacked, 'Gobble, gobble; Quack, quack.'

What a terrible uproar they made, while they were having such fun among themselves!

Then Hjalmar went to the hen-house; and, opening the door, called to the stork. Then he hopped out on the deck. He had rested himself now, and he looked happy, and seemed as if he nodded to Hjalmar, as if to thank him. Then he spread his wings, and flew away to warmer countries, while the hens clucked, the ducks quacked, and the turkey-cock turned quite scarlet in the head.

'Tomorrow you shall be made into soup,' said Hjalmar to the fowls; and then he awoke, and found himself lying in his little bed.

It was a wonderful journey which Ole-Luk-Oie had made him take this night.

THURSDAY

'What do you think I have got here?' said Ole-Luk-Oie, 'Do not be frightened, and you shall see a little mouse.' And then he held out his hand to him, in which lay a lovely little creature. 'It has come to invite you to a wedding. Two little mice are going to enter into the marriage state tonight. They reside under the floor of your mother's store-room, and that must be a fine dwelling-place.'

'But how can I get through the little mouse-hole in the floor?' asked Hjalmar.

'Leave me to manage that,' said Ole-Luk-Oie. 'I will soon make you small enough.' And then he touched Hjalmar with his magic wand, whereupon he became less and less, until at last he was not longer than a little finger. 'Now you can borrow the dress of the tin soldier. I think it will just fit you. It looks well to wear a uniform when you go into company.'

'Yes, certainly,' said Hjalmar; and in a moment he was dressed as neatly as the neatest of all tin soldiers.

'Will you be so good as to seat yourself in your mamma's thimble,' said the little mouse, 'that I may have the pleasure of drawing you to the wedding.'

'Will you really take so much trouble, young lady?' said Hjalmar. And so in this way he rode to the mouse's wedding.

First they went under the floor, and then passed through a long passage, which was scarcely high enough to allow the thimble to drive under, and the whole passage was lit up with the phosphorescent light of rotten wood.

'Does it not smell delicious?' asked the mouse, as she drew him along. 'The wall and the floor have been smeared with bacon-rind; nothing can be nicer.'

Very soon they arrived at the bridal hall. On the right stood all the little lady-mice, whispering and giggling, as if they were making game of each other. To the left were the gentlemen-mice, stroking their whiskers with their fore-paws; and in the centre of the hall could be seen the bridal pair, standing side by side, in a hollow cheese-rind, and kissing each other, while all eyes were upon them; for they had already been betrothed, and were soon to be married. More and more friends kept arriving, till the mice were nearly treading each other to death; for the bridal pair now stood in the doorway, and none could pass in or out.

The room had been rubbed over with bacon-rind, like the passage, which was all the refreshment offered to the guests. But for dessert they produced a pea, on which a mouse belonging to the bridal pair had bitten the first letters of their names. This was something quite uncommon. All the mice said it was a very beautiful wedding, and that they had been very agreeably entertained.

After this, Hjalmar returned home. He had certainly been in grand society; but he had been obliged to creep under a room, and to make himself small enough to wear the uniform of a tin soldier.

FRIDAY

'It is incredible how many old people there are who would be glad to have me at night,' said Ole-Luk-Oie, 'especially those who have done something wrong. "Good little Ole," say they to me, "we cannot close our eyes, and we lie awake the whole night and see all our evil deeds sitting on our beds like little imps, and sprinkling us with hot water. Will you come and drive them away, that we may have a good night's rest?" and then they sigh so deeply and say, "We would gladly pay you for it. Good-night, Ole-Luk, the money lies on the window." But I never do anything for gold.' 'What shall we do tonight?' asked Hjalmar. 'I do not know whether you would care to go to another wedding,' he replied, 'although it is quite a different affair to the one we saw last night. Your sister's large doll, that is dressed like a man, and is called Herman, intends to marry the doll Bertha. It is also the dolls' birthday, and they will receive many presents.'

'Yes, I know that already,' said Hjalmar, 'my sister always allows her dolls to keep their birthdays or to have a wedding when they require new clothes; that has happened already a hundred times, I am quite sure.'

'Yes, so it may; but tonight is the hundred and first wedding, and when that has taken place it must be the last, therefore this is to be extremely beautiful. Only look.'

Hjalmar looked at the table, and there stood the little cardboard doll's house, with lights in all the windows, and drawn up before it were the tin soldiers presenting arms. The bridal pair were seated on the floor, leaning against the leg of the table, looking very thoughtful, and with good reason. Then Ole-Luk-Oie, dressed up in grandmother's black gown, married them.

As soon as the ceremony was concluded, all the furniture in the room joined in singing a beautiful song, which had been composed by the lead pencil, and which went to the melody of a military tattoo.

What merry sounds are on the wind,
As marriage rites together bind
A quiet and a loving pair,
Though formed of kid, yet smooth and fair!

Hurrah! If they are deaf and blind,
We'll sing, though weather prove unkind.

And now came the present; but the bridal pair had nothing to eat, for love was to be their food.

'Shall we go to a country house, or travel?' asked the bridegroom.

Then they consulted the swallow who had travelled so far, and the old hen in the yard, who had brought up five broods of chickens.

And the swallow talked to them of warm countries, where the grapes hang in large clusters on the vines, and the air is soft and mild, and about the mountains glowing with colours more beautiful than we can think of.

'But they have no red cabbage like we have,' said the hen, 'I was once in the country with my chickens for a whole summer, there was a large sand-pit, in which we could walk about and scratch as we liked. Then we got into a garden in which grew red cabbage; oh, how nice it was, I cannot think of anything more delicious.'

'But one cabbage stalk is exactly like another,' said the swallow; 'and here we have often bad weather.'

'Yes, but we are accustomed to it,' said the hen.

'But it is so cold here, and freezes sometimes.'

'Cold weather is good for cabbages,' said the hen; 'besides we do have it warm here sometimes. Four years ago, we had a summer that lasted more than five weeks, and it was so hot one could scarcely breathe. And then in this country we have no poisonous animals, and we are free from robbers. He must be wicked who does not consider our country the finest of all lands.

He ought not to be allowed to live here.' And then the hen wept very much and said, 'I have also travelled. I once went twelve miles in a coop, and it was not pleasant travelling at all.'

'The hen is a sensible woman,' said the doll Bertha. 'I don't care for travelling over mountains, just to go up and come down again. No, let us go to the sand-pit in front of the gate, and then take a walk in the cabbage garden.'

And so they settled it.

SATURDAY

'Am I to hear any more stories?' asked little Hjalmar, as soon as Ole-Luk-Oie had sent him to sleep.

'We shall have no time this evening,' said he, spreading out his prettiest umbrella over the child. 'Look at these Chinese,' and then the whole umbrella appeared like a large china bowl, with blue trees and pointed bridges, upon which stood little Chinamen nodding their heads. 'We must make all the world beautiful for tomorrow morning,' said Ole-Luk-Oie, 'for it will be a holiday, it is Sunday. I must now go to the church steeple and see if the little sprites who live there have polished the bells, so that they may sound sweetly. Then I must go into the fields and see if the wind has blown the dust from the grass and the leaves, and the most difficult task of all which I have to do, is to take down all the stars and brighten them up. I have to number them first before I put them in my apron, and also to number the places from which I take them, so that they may go back into the right holes, or else they would not remain, and we should have a number of falling stars, for they would all tumble down one after the other.'

'Hark ye! Mr Luk-Oie,' said an old portrait which hung on the wall of Hjalmar's bedroom. 'Do you know me? I am Hjalmar's great-grandfather. I thank you for telling the boy stories, but you must not confuse his ideas. The stars cannot be taken down from the sky and polished; they are spheres like our earth, which is a good thing for them.'

'Thank you, old great-grandfather,' said Ole-Luk-Oie. 'I thank you; you may be the head of the family, as no doubt you are, but I am older than you. I am an ancient heathen. The old Romans and Greeks named me the Dream-god. I have visited the noblest houses, and continue to do so; still I know how to conduct myself both to high and low, and now you may tell the stories yourself:' and so Ole-Luk-Oie walked off, taking his umbrellas with him.

'Well, well, one is never to give an opinion, I suppose,' grumbled the portrait. And it woke Hjalmar.

SUNDAY

'Good evening,' said Ole-Luk-Oie.

Hjalmar nodded, and then sprang out of bed, and turned his great-grandfather's portrait to the wall, so that it might not interrupt them as it had done yesterday. 'Now,' said he, 'you must tell me some stories about five green peas that lived in one pod; or of the chickseed that courted the chickweed; or of the darning needle, who acted so proudly because she fancied herself an embroidery needle.'

'You may have too much of a good thing,' said Ole-Luk-Oie. 'You know that I like best to show you something, so I will show you my brother. He is also called Ole-Luk-Oie but he never visits any one but once, and when he does come, he takes him away on his horse, and tells him stories as they ride along. He knows only two stories. One of these is so wonderfully beautiful that no one in the world can imagine anything at all like it; but the other is just as ugly and frightful, so that it would be impossible to describe it.' Then Ole-Luk-Oie lifted Hjalmar up to the window. 'There now, you can see my brother, the other Ole-Luk-Oie; he is also called Death. You perceive he is not so bad as they represent him in picture books; there he is a skeleton, but now his coat is embroidered with silver, and he wears the splendid uniform of a hussar, and a mantle of black velvet flies behind him, over the horse. Look, how he gallops along.' Hjalmar saw that as this Ole-Luk-Oie rode on, he lifted up old and young, and carried them away on his horse. Some he seated in front of him, and some behind, but always inquired first, 'How stands the mark-book?'

'Good,' they all answered.

'Yes, but let me see for myself,' he replied; and they were obliged to give him the books. Then all those who had 'Very good' or 'Exceedingly good' came in front of the horse, and heard the beautiful story; while those who had 'Middling' or 'Tolerably good' in their books, were obliged to sit behind, and listen to the frightful tale. They trembled and cried, and wanted to jump down from the horse, but they could not get free, for they seemed fastened to the seat.

'Why, Death is a most splendid Luk-Oie,' said Hjalmar. 'I am not in the least afraid of him.'

'You need have no fear of him,' said Ole-Luk-Oie, 'if you take care and keep a good conduct book.'

'Now I call that very instructive,' murmured the great-grandfather's portrait. 'It is useful sometimes to express an opinion;' so he was quite satisfied.

These are some of the doings and sayings of Ole-Luk-Oie. I hope he may visit you himself this evening, and relate some more.

THE TOP AND BALL

A whipping top and a little ball lay together in a box, among other toys, and the top said to the ball, 'Shall we be married, as we live in the same box?'

But the ball, which wore a dress of morocco leather, and thought as much of herself as any other young lady, would not even condescend to reply.

The next day came the little boy to whom the playthings belonged, and he painted the top red and yellow, and drove a brass-headed nail into the middle, so that while the top was spinning round it looked splendid.

'Look at me,' said the top to the ball. 'What do you say now? Shall we be engaged to each other? We should suit so well; you spring, and I dance. No one could be happier than we should be.'

'Indeed! Do you think so? Perhaps you do not know that my father and mother were morocco slippers, and that I have a Spanish cork in my body.'

'Yes; but I am made of mahogany,' said the top. 'The major himself turned me. He has a turning lathe of his own, and it is a great amusement to him.'

'Can I believe it?' asked the ball.

'May I never be whipped again,' said the top, 'if I am not telling you the truth.'

'You certainly know how to speak for yourself very well,' said the ball; 'but I cannot accept your proposal. I am almost engaged to a swallow. Every time I fly up in the air, he puts his head out of the nest, and says, "Will you?" and I have said, "Yes," to myself silently, and that is as good as being half engaged; but I will promise never to forget you.'

'Much good that will be to me,' said the top; and they spoke to each other no more.

Next day the ball was taken out by the boy. The top saw it flying high in the air, like a bird, till it would go quite out of sight. Each time it came back, as it touched the earth, it gave a higher leap than before, either because it longed to fly upwards, or from having a Spanish cork in its body. But the ninth time it rose in the air, it remained away, and did not return. The boy searched everywhere for it, but he searched in vain, for it could not be found; it was gone.

'I know very well where she is,' sighed the top; 'she is in the swallow's nest, and has married the swallow.'

The more the top thought of this, the more he longed for the ball. His love increased the more, just because he could not get her; and that she should have been won by another, was the worst of all. The top still twirled about and hummed, but he continued to think of the ball; and the more he thought of her, the more beautiful she seemed to his fancy.

Thus several years passed by, and his love became quite old. The top, also, was no longer young; but there came a day when he looked handsomer than ever; for he was gilded all over. He was now a golden top, and whirled and danced about till he hummed quite loud, and was something worth looking at; but one day he leaped too high, and then he, also, was gone. They searched everywhere, even in the cellar, but he was nowhere to be found. Where could he be? He had jumped into the dust-bin, where all sorts of rubbish were lying: cabbage-stalks, dust and rain-droppings that had fallen down from the gutter under the roof.

'Now I am in a nice place,' said he; 'my gilding will soon be washed off here. Oh dear, what a set of rabble I have got amongst!' And then he glanced at a curious round thing like an old apple, which lay near a long, leafless cabbage-stalk. It was, however, not an apple, but an old ball, which had lain for years in the gutter, and was soaked through with water.

'Thank goodness, here comes one of my own class, with whom I can talk,' said the ball, examining the gilded top. 'I am made of morocco,' she said. 'I was sewn together by a young lady, and I have a Spanish cork in my body; but no one would think it, to look at me now. I was once engaged to a swallow; but I fell in here from the gutter under the roof, and I have lain here more than five years, and have been thoroughly drenched. Believe me, it is a long time for a young maiden.'

The top said nothing, but he thought of his old love; and the more she said, the more clear it became to him that this was the same ball.

The servant then came to clean out the dust-bin.

'Ah,' she exclaimed, 'here is a gilt top.' So the top was brought again to notice and honour, but nothing more was heard of the little ball. He spoke not a word about his old love; for that soon died away. When the beloved object has lain for five years in a gutter, and has been drenched through, no one cares to know her again on meeting her in a dust-bin.

THE FIR-TREE

Far down in the forest, where the warm sun and the fresh air made a sweet resting-place, grew a pretty little fir-tree; and yet it was not happy, it wished so much to be tall like its companions – the pines and firs which grew around it. The sun shone, and the soft air fluttered its leaves, and the little peasant children passed by, prattling merrily, but the fir-tree heeded them not. Sometimes the children would bring a large basket of raspberries or strawberries, wreathed on a straw, and seat themselves near the fir-tree, and say, 'Is it not a pretty little tree?' which made it feel more unhappy than before. And yet all this while the tree grew a notch or joint taller every year; for by the number of joints in the stem of a fir-tree we can discover its age. Still, as it grew, it complained, 'Oh! How I wish I were as tall as the other trees, then I would spread out my branches on every side, and my top would over-look the wide world. I should have the birds building their nests on my boughs, and when the wind blew, I should bow with stately dignity like my tall companions.' The tree was so discontented that it took no pleasure in the warm sunshine, the birds or the rosy clouds that floated over it morning and evening. Sometimes, in winter, when the snow lay white and glittering on the ground, a hare would come springing along, and jump right over the little tree; and then how mortified it would feel! Two winters passed, and when the third arrived, the tree had grown so tall that the hare was obliged to run round it. Yet it remained unsatisfied, and would exclaim, 'Oh, if I could but keep on growing tall and old! There is nothing else worth caring for in the world!' In the autumn, as usual, the woodcutters came and cut down several of the tallest trees, and the young fir-tree, which was now grown to its full height, shuddered as the noble trees fell to the earth with a crash. After the branches were lopped off, the trunks looked so slender and bare, that they could scarcely be recognised. Then they were placed upon wagons, and drawn by horses out of the forest. 'Where were they going? What would become of them?' The young fir-tree wished very much to know; so in the spring, when the swallows and the storks came, it asked, 'Do you know where those trees were taken? Did you meet them?'

The swallows knew nothing, but the stork, after a little reflection, nodded his head, and said, 'Yes, I think I do. I met several new ships when I flew from Egypt, and they had fine masts that smelt like fir. I think these must have been the trees; I assure you they were stately, very stately.'

'Oh, how I wish I were tall enough to go on the sea,' said the fir-tree. 'What is the sea, and what does it look like?'

'It would take too much time to explain,' said the stork, flying quickly away.

'Rejoice in thy youth,' said the sunbeam; 'rejoice in thy fresh growth, and the young life that is in thee.'

And the wind kissed the tree, and the dew watered it with tears; but the fir-tree regarded them not.

Christmas-time drew near, and many young trees were cut down, some even smaller and younger than the fir-tree who enjoyed neither rest nor peace with longing to leave its forest home. These young trees, which were chosen for their beauty, kept their branches, and were also laid on wagons and drawn by horses out of the forest.

'Where are they going?' asked the fir-tree. 'They are not taller than I am: indeed, one is much less; and why are the branches not cut off? Where are they going?'

'We know, we know,' sang the sparrows; 'we have looked in at the windows of the houses in the town, and we know what is done with them. They are dressed up in the most splendid manner. We have seen them standing in the middle of a warm room, and adorned with all sorts of beautiful things – honey cakes, gilded apples, playthings and many hundreds of wax tapers.'

'And then,' asked the fir-tree, trembling through all its branches, 'and then what happens?'

'We did not see any more,' said the sparrows; 'but this was enough for us.'

'I wonder whether anything so brilliant will ever happen to me,' thought the fir-tree. 'It would be much better than crossing the sea. I long for it almost with pain. Oh! When will Christmas be here? I am now as tall and well grown as those which were taken away last year. Oh! That I were now laid on the wagon, or standing in the warm room, with all that brightness and splendour around me! Something better and more beautiful is to come after, or the trees would not be so decked out. Yes, what follows will be grander and more splendid. What can it be? I am weary with longing. I scarcely know how I feel.'

'Rejoice with us,' said the air and the sunlight. 'Enjoy thine own bright life in the fresh air.'

But the tree would not rejoice, though it grew taller every day; and, winter and summer, its dark-green foliage might be seen in the forest, while passers-by would say, 'What a beautiful tree!'

A short time before Christmas, the discontented fir-tree was the first to fall. As the axe cut through the stem, and divided the pith, the tree fell with a groan to the earth, conscious of pain and faintness, and forgetting all its anticipations of happiness, in sorrow at leaving its home in the forest. It knew that it should never again see its dear old companions, the trees, nor the little bushes and many-coloured flowers that had grown by its side; perhaps not even the birds. Neither was the journey at all pleasant. The tree first recovered itself while being unpacked in the courtyard of a house, with several other trees; and it heard a man say, 'We only want one, and this is the prettiest.'

Then came two servants in grand livery, and carried the fir-tree into a large and beautiful apartment. On the walls hung pictures, and near the great stove stood great china vases, with lions on the lids. There were rocking chairs, silken sofas, large tables, covered with pictures, books and playthings, worth a great deal of money – at least, the children said so. Then the fir-tree was placed in a large tub, full of sand; but green baize hung all around it, so that no one could see it was a tub, and it stood on a very handsome carpet. How the fir-tree trembled! 'What was going to happen to him now?' Some young ladies came, and the servants helped them to adorn the tree. On one branch they hung little bags cut out of coloured paper, and each bag was filled with sweetmeats; from other branches hung gilded apples and walnuts, as if they had grown there; and above, and all round, were hundreds of red, blue and white tapers, which were fastened on the branches. Dolls, exactly like real babies, were placed under the green leaves – the tree had never seen such things before – and at the very top was fastened a glittering star, made of tinsel. Oh, it was very beautiful!

'This evening,' they all exclaimed, 'how bright it will be!' 'Oh, that the evening were come,' thought the tree, 'and the tapers lighted! then I shall know what else is going to happen. Will the trees of the forest come to see me? I wonder if the sparrows will peep in at the windows as they fly? Shall I grow faster here, and keep on all these ornaments summer and winter?' But guessing was of very little use; it made his bark ache, and this pain is as bad for a slender fir-tree, as headache is for us. At last the tapers were lighted, and then what a glistening blaze of light the tree presented! It trembled so with joy in all its branches, that one of the candles fell among the green leaves and burnt some of them. 'Help! Help!' exclaimed the young ladies, but there was no danger, for they quickly extinguished the fire. After this, the tree tried not to tremble at all, though the fire frightened him; he was so anxious not to hurt any of the beautiful ornaments, even while their brilliancy dazzled him. And now the folding doors were thrown open, and a troop of children rushed in as if they intended to upset the tree; they were followed more silently by their elders. For a moment the little ones stood silent with astonishment, and then they shouted for joy, till the room rang, and they danced merrily round the tree, while one present after another was taken from it.

'What are they doing? What will happen next?' thought the fir. At last the candles burnt down to the branches and were put out. Then the children received permission to plunder the tree.

Oh, how they rushed upon it, till the branches cracked, and had it not been fastened with the glistening star to the ceiling, it must have been thrown down. The children then danced about with their pretty toys, and no one noticed the tree, except the children's maid who came and peeped among the branches to see if an apple or a fig had been forgotten.

'A story, a story,' cried the children, pulling a little fat man towards the tree.

'Now we shall be in the green shade,' said the man, as he seated himself under it, 'and the tree will have the pleasure of hearing also, but I shall only relate one story; what shall it be? Ivede-Avede, or Humpty Dumpty, who fell down stairs, but soon got up again, and at last married a princess.'

'Ivede-Avede,' cried some. 'Humpty Dumpty,' cried others, and there was a fine shouting and crying out. But the fir-tree remained quite still, and thought to himself, 'Shall I have anything to do with all this?' but he had already amused them as much as they wished. Then the old man told them the story of Humpty Dumpty, how he fell down stairs, and was raised up again, and married a princess. And the children clapped their hands and cried, 'Tell another, tell another,' for they wanted to hear the story of 'Ivede-Avede'; but they only had 'Humpty Dumpty'. After this the fir-tree became quite silent and thoughtful; never had the birds in the forest told such tales as 'Humpty Dumpty', who fell down stairs, and yet married a princess.

'Ah! Yes, so it happens in the world,' thought the fir-tree; he believed it all, because it was related by such a nice man. 'Ah! Well,' he thought, 'who knows? Perhaps I may fall down too, and marry a princess;' and he looked forward joyfully to the next evening, expecting to be again decked out with lights and playthings, gold and fruit. 'Tomorrow I will not tremble,' thought he; 'I will enjoy all my splendour, and I shall hear the story of Humpty Dumpty again, and perhaps Ivede-Avede.' And the tree remained quiet and thoughtful all night. In the morning the servants and the housemaid came in. 'Now,' thought the fir, 'all my splendour is going to begin again.' But they dragged him out of the room and upstairs to the garret, and threw him on the floor, in a dark corner, where no daylight shone, and there they left him. 'What does this mean?' thought the tree, 'What am I to do here? I can hear nothing in a place like this,' and he had time enough to think, for days and nights passed and no one came near him, and when at last somebody did come, it was only to put away large boxes in a corner. So the tree was completely hidden from sight as if it had never existed. 'It is winter now,' thought the tree, 'the ground is hard and covered with snow, so that people cannot plant me. I shall be sheltered here, I dare say, until spring comes. How thoughtful and kind everybody is to me! Still I wish this place were not so dark, as well as lonely, with not even a little hare to look at. How pleasant it was out in the forest while the snow lay on the ground, when the hare would run by, yes, and jump over me too, although I did not like it then. Oh! It is terrible lonely here.'

'Squeak, squeak,' said a little mouse, creeping cautiously towards the tree; then came another; and they both sniffed at the fir-tree and crept between the branches.

'Oh, it is very cold,' said the little mouse, 'or else we should be so comfortable here, shouldn't we, you old fir-tree?'

'I am not old,' said the fir-tree, 'there are many who are older than I am.'

'Where do you come from? And what do you know?' asked the mice, who were full of curiosity. 'Have you seen the most beautiful places in the world, and can you tell us all about them? And have you been in the storeroom, where cheeses lie on the shelf, and hams hang from the ceiling? One can run about on tallow candles there, and go in thin and come out fat.'

'I know nothing of that place,' said the fir-tree, 'but I know the wood where the sun shines and the birds sing.' And then the tree told the little mice all about its youth. They had never heard such an account in their lives; and after they had listened to it attentively, they said, 'What a number of things you have seen? You must have been very happy.'

'Happy!' exclaimed the fir-tree, and then as he reflected upon what he had been telling them, he said, 'Ah, yes! After all those were happy days.' But when he went on and related all about Christmas-eve, and how he had been dressed up with cakes and lights, the mice said, 'How happy you must have been, you old fir-tree.'

'I am not old at all,' replied the tree, 'I only came from the forest this winter, I am now checked in my growth.'

'What splendid stories you can relate,' said the little mice. And the next night four other mice came with them to hear what the tree had to tell. The more he talked the more he remembered, and then he thought to himself, 'Those were happy days, but they may come again. Humpty Dumpty fell down stairs, and yet he married the princess; perhaps I may marry a princess too.' And the fir-tree thought of the pretty little birch-tree that grew in the forest, which was to him a real beautiful princess.

'Who is Humpty Dumpty?' asked the little mice. And then the tree related the whole story; he could remember every single word, and the little mice was so delighted with it that they were ready to jump to the top of the tree. The next night a great many more mice made their appearance, and on Sunday two rats came with them; but they said, it was not a pretty story at all, and the little mice were very sorry, for it made them also think less of it.

'Do you know only one story?' asked the rats.

'Only one,' replied the fir-tree; 'I heard it on the happiest evening of my life; but I did not know I was so happy at the time.'

'We think it is a very miserable story,' said the rats. 'Don't you know any story about bacon, or tallow in the storeroom.'

'No,' replied the tree.

'Many thanks to you then,' replied the rats, and they marched off.

The little mice also kept away after this, and the tree sighed, and said, 'It was very pleasant when the merry little mice sat round me and listened while I talked. Now that is all passed too. However, I shall consider myself happy when someone comes to take me out of this place.' But would this ever happen? Yes; one morning people came to clear out the garret, the boxes were packed away, and the tree was pulled out of the corner, and thrown roughly on the garret floor; then the servant dragged it out upon the staircase where the daylight shone. 'Now life is beginning again,' said the tree, rejoicing in the sunshine and fresh air. Then it was carried downstairs and taken into the courtyard so quickly that it forgot to think of itself, and could only look about, there was so much to be seen. The court was close to a garden, where everything looked blooming. Fresh and fragrant roses hung over the little palings. The linden-trees were in blossom; while the swallows flew here and there, crying, 'Twit, twit, twit, my mate is coming,' – but it was not the fir-tree they meant. 'Now I shall live,' cried the tree, joyfully spreading out its branches; but alas, they were all withered and yellow, and it lay in a corner amongst weeds and nettles. The star of gold paper still stuck in the top of the tree and glittered in the sunshine. In the same courtyard two of the merry children were playing who had danced round the tree at Christmas, and had been so happy.

The youngest saw the gilded star, and ran and pulled it off the tree. 'Look what is sticking to the ugly old fir-tree,' said the child, treading on the branches till they crackled under his boots. And the tree saw all the fresh bright flowers in the garden, and then looked at itself, and wished it had remained in the dark corner of the garret. It thought of its fresh youth in the forest, of the merry Christmas evening, and of the little mice who had listened to the story of 'Humpty Dumpty'. 'Past! Past!' said the old tree; 'Oh, had I but enjoyed myself while I could have done so! But now it is too late.' Then a lad came and chopped the tree into small pieces, till a large bundle lay in a heap on the ground. The pieces were placed in a fire under the copper, and they quickly blazed up brightly, while the tree sighed so deeply that each sigh was like a pistol-shot. Then the children, who were at play, came and seated themselves in front of the fire, and looked at it and cried, 'Pop, pop.' But at each 'pop', which was a deep sigh, the tree was thinking of a summer day in the forest; and of Christmas evening, and of 'Humpty Dumpty', the only story it had ever heard or knew how to relate, till at last it was consumed. The boys still played in the garden, and the youngest wore the golden star on his breast, with which the tree had been adorned during the happiest evening of its existence. Now all was past; the tree's life was past, and the story also – for all stories must come to an end at last.

THE DARNING-NEEDLE

There was once a darning-needle who thought herself so fine that she fancied she must be fit for embroidery. 'Hold me tight,' she would say to the fingers, when they took her up, 'don't let me fall; if you do I shall never be found again, I am so very fine.'

'That is your opinion, is it?' said the fingers, as they seized her round the body.

'See, I am coming with a train,' said the darning-needle, drawing a long thread after her; but there was no knot in the thread.

The fingers then placed the point of the needle against the cook's slipper. There was a crack in the upper leather, which had to be sewn together.

'What coarse work!' said the darning-needle, 'I shall never get through. I shall break! – I am breaking!' And sure enough she broke. 'Did I not say so?' said the darning-needle, 'I know I am too fine for such work as that.'

'This needle is quite useless for sewing now,' said the fingers; but they still held it fast, and the cook dropped some sealing-wax on the needle, and fastened her handkerchief with it in front.

'So now I am a breast-pin,' said the darning-needle; 'I knew very well I should come to honour some day: merit is sure to rise;' and she laughed, quietly to herself, for of course no one ever saw a darning-needle laugh. And there she sat as proudly as if she were in a state coach, and looked all around her. 'May I be allowed to ask if you are made of gold?' she inquired of her neighbour, a pin. 'You have a very pretty appearance, and a curious head, although you are rather small. You must take pains to grow, for it is not everyone who has sealing-wax dropped upon him;' and as she spoke, the darning-needle drew herself up so proudly that she fell out of the handkerchief right into the sink, which the cook was cleaning. 'Now I am going on a journey,' said the needle, as she floated away with the dirty water, 'I do hope I shall not be lost.' But she really was lost in a gutter. 'I am too fine for this world,' said the darning-needle, as she lay in the gutter; 'but I know who I am, and that is always some comfort.' So the darning-needle kept up her proud behaviour, and did not lose her good humour. Then there floated over her all sorts of things – chips and straws, and pieces of old newspaper. 'See how they sail,' said the darning-needle; 'they do not know what is under them. I am here, and here I shall stick. See, there goes a chip, thinking of nothing in the world but himself – only a chip. There's a straw going by now; how he turns and twists about! Don't be thinking too much of yourself, or you may chance to run against a stone. There swims a piece of newspaper; what is written upon it has been forgotten long ago, and yet it gives itself airs. I sit here patiently and quietly. I know who I am, so I shall not move.'

One day something lying close to the darning-needle glittered so splendidly that she thought it was a diamond; yet it was only a piece of broken bottle. The darning-needle spoke to it, because it sparkled, and represented herself as a breast-pin. 'I suppose you are really a diamond?' she said.

'Why yes, something of the kind,' he replied; and so each believed the other to be very valuable, and then they began to talk about the world, and the conceited people in it.

'I have been in a lady's work-box,' said the darning-needle. 'And this lady was the cook. She had on each hand five fingers, and anything so conceited as these five fingers I have never seen; and yet they were only employed to take me out of the box and to put me back again.'

'Were they not high-born?'

'High-born!' said the darning-needle, 'no indeed, but so haughty. They were five brothers, all born fingers; they kept very proudly together, though they were of different lengths. The one who stood first in the rank was named the thumb, he was short and thick, and had only one joint in his back, and could therefore make but one bow; but he said that if he were cut off from a man's hand, that man would be unfit for a soldier. Sweet-tooth, his neighbour, dipped himself into sweet or sour, pointed to the sun and moon, and formed the letters when the fingers wrote. Longman, the middle finger, looked over the heads of all the others. Gold-band, the next finger, wore a golden circle round his waist. And little Playman did nothing at all, and seemed proud of it. They were boasters, and boasters they will remain; and therefore I left them.'

'And now we sit here and glitter,' said the piece of broken bottle.

At the same moment more water streamed into the gutter, so that it overflowed, and the piece of bottle was carried away.

'So he is promoted,' said the darning-needle, 'while I remain here; I am too fine, but that is my pride, and what do I care?' And so she sat there in her pride, and had many such thoughts as these – 'I could almost fancy that I came from a sunbeam, I am so fine. It seems as if the sunbeams were always looking for me under the water. Ah! I am so fine that even my mother cannot find me. Had I still my old eye, which was broken off, I believe I should weep; but no, I would not do that, it is not genteel to cry.'

One day a couple of street boys were paddling in the gutter, for they sometimes found old nails, farthings and other treasures. It was dirty work, but they took great pleasure in it. 'Hello!' cried one, as he pricked himself with the darning-needle. 'Here's a fellow for you.'

'I am not a fellow, I am a young lady,' said the darning-needle; but no one heard her.

The sealing-wax had come off, and she was quite black; but black makes a person look slender, so she thought herself even finer than before.

'Here comes an egg-shell sailing along,' said one of the boys; so they stuck the darning-needle into the egg-shell.

'White walls, and I am black myself,' said the darning-needle, 'that looks well; now I can be seen, but I hope I shall not be sea-sick, or I shall break again.' She was not sea-sick, and she did not break. 'It is a good thing against sea-sickness to have a steel stomach, and not to forget one's own importance. Now my sea-sickness has past: delicate people can bear a great deal.'

Crack went the egg-shell, as a waggon passed over it. 'Good heavens, how it crushes!' said the darning-needle. 'I shall be sick now. I am breaking!' but she did not break, though the waggon went over her as she lay at full length; and there let her lie.

THE LITTLE MATCH-SELLER

It was terribly cold and nearly dark on the last evening of the old year, and the snow was falling fast. In the cold and the darkness, a poor little girl, with bare head and naked feet, roamed through the streets. It is true she had on a pair of slippers when she left home, but they were not of much use. They were very large, so large, indeed, that they had belonged to her mother, and the poor little creature had lost them in running across the street to avoid two carriages that were rolling along at a terrible rate. One of the slippers she could not find, and a boy seized upon the other and ran away with it, saying that he could use it as a cradle, when he had children of his own. So the little girl went on with her little naked feet, which were quite red and blue with the cold. In an old apron she carried a number of matches, and had a bundle of them in her hands. No one had bought anything of her the whole day, nor had anyone given her even a penny. Shivering with cold and hunger, she crept along; poor little child, she looked the picture of misery. The snowflakes fell on her long, fair hair, which hung in curls on her shoulders, but she regarded them not.

Lights were shining from every window, and there was a savoury smell of roast goose, for it was New Year's eve – yes, she remembered that. In a corner, between two houses, one of which projected beyond the other, she sank down and huddled herself together. She had drawn her little feet under her, but she could not keep off the cold; and she dared not go home, for she had sold no matches, and could not take home even a penny of money. Her father would certainly beat her; besides, it was almost as cold at home as here, for they had only the roof to cover them, through which the wind howled, although the largest holes had been stopped up with straw and rags. Her little hands were almost frozen with the cold. Ah! Perhaps a burning match might be some good, if she could draw it from the bundle and strike it against the wall, just to warm her fingers. She drew one out – 'Scratch!' how it sputtered as it burnt! It gave a warm, bright light, like a little candle, as she held her hand over it. It was really a wonderful light. It seemed to the little girl that she was sitting by a large iron stove, with polished brass feet and a brass ornament. How the fire burned! And seemed so beautifully warm that the child stretched out her feet as if to warm them, when, lo, the flame of the match went out, the stove vanished, and she had only the remains of the half-burnt match in her hand.

She rubbed another match on the wall. It burst into a flame, and where its light fell upon the wall it became as transparent as a veil, and she could see into the room. The table was covered with a snowy white table-cloth, on which stood a splendid dinner service and a steaming roast goose, stuffed with apples and dried plums. And what was still more wonderful, the goose jumped down from the dish and waddled across the floor, with a knife and fork in its breast, to the little girl. Then the match went out, and there remained nothing but the thick, damp, cold wall before her.

She lighted another match, and then she found herself sitting under a beautiful Christmas-tree. It was larger and more beautifully decorated than the one which she had seen through the glass door at the rich merchant's. Thousands of tapers were burning upon the green branches, and coloured pictures, like those she had seen in the show-windows, looked down upon it all. The little one stretched out her hand towards them, and the match went out.

The Christmas lights rose higher and higher, till they looked to her like the stars in the sky. Then she saw a star fall, leaving behind it a bright streak of fire. 'Someone is dying,' thought the little girl, for her old grandmother, the only one who had ever loved her, and who was now dead, had told her that when a star falls, a soul was going up to God.

She again rubbed a match on the wall, and the light shone round her; in the brightness stood her old grandmother, clear and shining, yet mild and loving in her appearance. 'Grandmother,' cried the little one, 'O take me with you; I know you will go away when the match burns out; you will vanish like the warm stove, the roast goose, and the large, glorious Christmas-tree.' And she made haste to light the whole bundle of matches, for she wished to keep her grandmother there. And the matches glowed with a light that was brighter than the noonday, and her grandmother had never appeared so large or so beautiful. She took the little girl in her arms, and they both flew upwards in brightness and joy far above the earth, where there was neither cold nor hunger nor pain, for they were with God.

In the dawn of morning there lay the poor little one, with pale cheeks and smiling mouth, leaning against the wall; she had been frozen to death on the last evening of the year; and the New Year's sun rose and shone upon a little corpse! The child still sat, in the stiffness of death, holding the matches in her hand, one bundle of which was burnt. 'She tried to warm herself,' said some. No one imagined what beautiful things she had seen, nor into what glory she had entered with her grandmother, on New Year's Day.

THE SHADOW

In very hot climates, where the heat of the sun has great power, people are usually as brown as mahogany; and in the hottest countries they are negroes, with black skins. A learned man once travelled into one of these warm climates, from the cold regions of the north, and thought he would roam about as he did at home; but he soon had to change his opinion. He found that, like all sensible people, he must remain in the house during the whole day, with every window and door closed, so that it looked as if all in the house were asleep or absent. The houses of the narrow street in which he lived were so lofty that the sun shone upon them from morning till evening, and it became quite unbearable. This learned man from the cold regions was young as well as clever; but it seemed to him as if he were sitting in an oven, and he became quite exhausted and weak, and grew so thin that his shadow shrivelled up, and became much smaller than it had been at home. The sun took away even what was left of it, and he saw nothing of it till the evening, after sunset. It was really a pleasure, as soon as the lights were brought into the room, to see the shadow stretch itself against the wall, even to the ceiling, so tall was it; and it really wanted a good stretch to recover its strength. The learned man would sometimes go out into the balcony to stretch himself also; and as soon as the stars came forth in the clear, beautiful sky, he felt revived. People at this hour began to make their appearance in all the balconies in the street; for in warm climates every window has a balcony, in which they can breathe the fresh evening air, which is very necessary, even to those who are used to a heat that makes them as brown as mahogany; so that the street presented a very lively appearance. Here were shoemakers, and tailors, and all sorts of people sitting. In the street beneath, they brought out tables and chairs, lighted candles by hundreds, talked and sang, and were very merry. There were people walking, carriages driving and mules trotting along, with their bells on the harness, 'tingle, tingle,' as they went. Then the dead were carried to the grave with the sound of solemn music, and the tolling of the church bells. It was indeed a scene of varied life in the street. One house only, which was just opposite to the one in which the foreign learned man lived, formed a contrast to all this, for it was quite still; and yet somebody dwelt there, for flowers stood in the balcony, blooming beautifully in the hot sun; and this could not have been unless they had been watered carefully. Therefore someone must be in the house to do this. The doors leading to the balcony were half opened in the evening; and although in the front room all was dark, music could be heard from the interior of the house. The foreign learned man considered this music very delightful; but perhaps he fancied it; for everything in these warm countries pleased him, excepting the heat of the sun. The foreign landlord said he did not know who had taken the opposite house – nobody was to be seen there; and as to the music, he thought it seemed very tedious, to him most uncommonly so.

'It is just as if someone was practising a piece that he could not manage; it is always the same piece. He thinks, I suppose, that he will be able to manage it at last; but I do not think so, however long he may play it.'

Once the foreigner woke in the night. He slept with the door open which led to the balcony; the wind had raised the curtain before it, and there appeared a wonderful brightness over all in the balcony of the opposite house. The flowers seemed like flames of the most gorgeous colours, and among the flowers stood a beautiful slender maiden. It was to him as if light streamed from her, and dazzled his eyes; but then he had only just opened them, as he awoke from his sleep. With one spring he was out of bed, and crept softly behind the curtain. But she was gone – the brightness had disappeared; the flowers no longer appeared like flames, although still as beautiful as ever. The door stood ajar, and from an inner room sounded music so sweet and so lovely, that it produced the most enchanting thoughts, and acted on the senses with magic power. Who could live there? Where was the real entrance? For, both in the street and in the lane at the side, the whole ground floor was a continuation of shops; and people could not always be passing through them.

One evening the foreigner sat in the balcony. A light was burning in his own room, just behind him. It was quite natural, therefore, that his shadow should fall on the wall of the opposite house; so that, as he sat amongst the flowers on his balcony, when he moved, his shadow moved also.

'I think my shadow is the only living thing to be seen opposite,' said the learned man; 'see how pleasantly it sits among the flowers. The door is only ajar; the shadow ought to be clever enough to step in and look about him, and then to come back and tell me what he has seen. You could make yourself useful in this way,' said he, jokingly; 'be so good as to step in now, will you?' and then he nodded to the shadow, and the shadow nodded in return. 'Now go, but don't stay away altogether.'

Then the foreigner stood up, and the shadow on the opposite balcony stood up also; the foreigner turned round, the shadow turned; and if anyone had observed, they might have seen it go straight into the half-opened door of the opposite balcony, as the learned man re-entered his own room, and let the curtain fall. The next morning he went out to take his coffee and read the newspapers.

'How is this?' he exclaimed, as he stood in the sunshine. 'I have lost my shadow. So it really did go away yesterday evening, and it has not returned. This is very annoying.'

And it certainly did vex him, not so much because the shadow was gone, but because he knew there was a story of a man without a shadow. All the people at home, in his country, knew this story; and when he returned, and related his own adventures, they would say it was only an imitation; and he had no desire for such things to be said of him. So he decided not to speak of it at all, which was a very sensible determination.

In the evening he went out again on his balcony, taking care to place the light behind him; for he knew that a shadow always wants his master for a screen; but he could not entice him out. He made himself little, and he made himself tall; but there was no shadow, and no shadow came. He said, 'Hem, a-hem;' but it was all useless. That was very vexatious; but in warm countries everything grows very quickly; and, after a week had passed, he saw, to his great joy, that a new shadow was growing from his feet, when he walked in the sunshine; so that the root must have remained. After three weeks, he had quite a respectable shadow, which, during his return journey to northern lands, continued to grow, and became at last so large that he might very well have spared half of it. When this learned man arrived at home, he wrote books about the true, the good, and the beautiful, which are to be found in this world; and so days and years passed – many, many years.

One evening, as he sat in his study, a very gentle tap was heard at the door. 'Come in,' said he; but no one came. He opened the door, and there stood before him a man so remarkably thin that he felt seriously troubled at his appearance. He was, however, very well dressed, and looked like a gentleman. 'To whom have I the honour of speaking?' said he.

'Ah, I hoped you would recognise me,' said the elegant stranger; 'I have gained so much that I have a body of flesh, and clothes to wear. You never expected to see me in such a condition. Do you not recognise your old shadow? Ah, you never expected that I should return to you again. All has been prosperous with me since I was with you last; I have become rich in every way, and, were I inclined to purchase my freedom from service, I could easily do so.' And as he spoke he rattled between his fingers a number of costly trinkets which hung on a thick gold watch-chain he wore round his neck. Diamond rings sparkled on his fingers, and it was all real.

'I cannot recover from my astonishment,' said the learned man. 'What does all this mean?'

'Something rather unusual,' said the shadow; 'but you are yourself an uncommon man, and you know very well that I have followed in your footsteps ever since your childhood. As soon as you found that I have travelled enough to be trusted alone, I went my own way, and I am now in the most brilliant circumstances. But I felt a kind of longing to see you once more before you die, and I wanted to see this place again, for there is always a clinging to the land of one's birth. I know that you have now another shadow; do I owe you anything? If so, have the goodness to say what it is.'

'No! Is it really you?' said the learned man. 'Well, this is most remarkable; I never supposed it possible that a man's old shadow could become a human being.'

'Just tell me what I owe you,' said the shadow, 'for I do not like to be in debt to any man.'

'How can you talk in that manner?' said the learned man. 'What question of debt can there be between us? You are as free as anyone. I rejoice exceedingly to hear of your good fortune. Sit down, old friend, and tell me a little of how it happened, and what you saw in the house opposite to me while we were in those hot climates.'

'Yes, I will tell you all about it,' said the shadow, sitting down; 'but then you must promise me never to tell in this city, wherever you may meet me, that I have been your shadow. I am thinking of being married, for I have more than sufficient to support a family.'

'Make yourself quite easy,' said the learned man; 'I will tell no one who you really are. Here is my hand – I promise, and a word is sufficient between man and man.'

'Between man and a shadow,' said the shadow; for he could not help saying so.

It was really most remarkable how very much he had become a man in appearance. He was dressed in a suit of the very finest black cloth, polished boots, and an opera crush hat, which could be folded together so that nothing could be seen but the crown and the rim, besides the trinkets, the gold chain and the diamond rings already spoken of. The shadow was, in fact, very well dressed, and this made a man of him. 'Now I will relate to you what you wish to know,' said the shadow, placing his foot with the polished leather boot as firmly as possible on the arm of the new shadow of the learned man, which lay at his feet like a poodle dog. This was done, it might be from pride, or perhaps that the new shadow might cling to him, but the prostrate shadow remained quite quiet and at rest, in order that it might listen, for it wanted to know how a shadow could be sent away by its master, and become a man itself. 'Do you know,' said the shadow, 'that in the house opposite to you lived the most glorious creature in the world? It was poetry. I remained there three weeks, and it was more like three thousand years, for I read all that has ever been written in poetry or prose; and I may say, in truth, that I saw and learnt everything.'

'Poetry!' exclaimed the learned man. 'Yes, she lives as a hermit in great cities. Poetry! Well, I saw her once for a very short moment, while sleep weighed down my eyelids. She flashed upon me from the balcony like the radiant aurora borealis, surrounded with flowers like flames of fire. Tell me, you were on the balcony that evening; you went through the door, and what did you see?'

'I found myself in an ante-room,' said the shadow. 'You still sat opposite to me, looking into the room. There was no light, or at least it seemed in partial darkness, for the door of a whole suite of rooms stood open, and they were brilliantly lighted. The blaze of light would have killed me, had I approached too near the maiden myself, but I was cautious, and took time, which is what everyone ought to do.'

'And what didst thou see?' asked the learned man.

'I saw everything, as you shall hear. But – it really is not pride on my part, as a free man and possessing the knowledge that I do, besides my position, not to speak of my wealth – I wish you would say you to me instead of thou.'

'I beg your pardon,' said the learned man; 'it is an old habit, which it is difficult to break. You are quite right; I will try to think of it. But now tell me everything that you saw.'

'Everything,' said the shadow; 'for I saw and know everything.'

'What was the appearance of the inner rooms?' asked the scholar. 'Was it there like a cool grove, or like a holy temple? Were the chambers like a starry sky seen from the top of a high mountain?'

'It was all that you describe,' said the shadow; 'but I did not go quite in – I remained in the twilight of the ante-room – but I was in a very good position – I could see and hear all that was going on in the court of poetry.'

'But what did you see? Did the gods of ancient times pass through the rooms? Did old heroes fight their battles over again? Were there lovely children at play, who related their dreams?'

'I tell you I have been there, and therefore you may be sure that I saw everything that was to be seen. If you had gone there, you would not have remained a human being, whereas I became one; and at the same moment I became aware of my inner being, my inborn affinity to the nature of poetry. It is true I did not think much about it while I was with you, but you will remember that I was always much larger at sunrise and sunset, and in the moonlight even more visible than yourself, but I did not then understand my inner existence. In the ante-room it was revealed to me. I became a man; I came out in full maturity. But you had left the warm countries. As a man, I felt ashamed to go about without boots or clothes, and that exterior finish by which man is known. So I went my own way; I can tell you, for you will not put it in a book. I hid myself under the cloak of a cake woman, but she little thought who she concealed. It was not till evening that I ventured out. I ran about the streets in the moonlight. I drew myself up to my full height upon the walls, which tickled my back very pleasantly. I ran here and there, looked through the highest windows into the rooms, and over the roofs. I looked in, and saw what nobody else could see, or indeed ought to see; in fact, it is a bad world, and I would not care to be a man, but that men are of some importance. I saw the most miserable things going on between husbands and wives, parents and children – sweet, incomparable children. I have seen what no human being has the power of knowing, although they would all be very glad to know – the evil conduct of their neighbours. Had I written a newspaper, how eagerly it would have been read! Instead of which, I wrote directly to the persons themselves, and great alarm arose in all the town I visited. They had so much fear of me, and yet how dearly they loved me. The professor made me a professor. The tailor gave me new clothes; I am well provided for in that way. The overseer of the mint struck coins for me. The women declared that I was handsome, and so I became the man you now see me. And now I must say adieu. Here is my card. I live on the sunny side of the street, and always stay at home in rainy weather.' And the shadow departed.

'This is all very remarkable,' said the learned man.

Years passed, days and years went by, and the shadow came again. 'How are you going on now?' he asked.

'Ah!' said the learned man; 'I am writing about the true, the beautiful and the good; but no one cares to hear anything about it. I am quite in despair, for I take it to heart very much.'

'That is what I never do,' said the shadow; 'I am growing quite fat and stout, which everyone ought to be. You do not understand the world; you will make yourself ill about it; you ought to travel; I am going on a journey in the summer, will you go with me? I should like a travelling companion; will you travel with me as my shadow? It would give me great pleasure, and I will pay all expenses.'

'Are you going to travel far?' asked the learned man.

'That is a matter of opinion,' replied the shadow. 'At all events, a journey will do you good, and if you will be my shadow, then all your journey shall be paid.'

'It appears to me very absurd,' said the learned man.

'But it is the way of the world,' replied the shadow, 'and always will be.' Then he went away.

Everything went wrong with the learned man. Sorrow and trouble pursued him, and what he said about the good, the beautiful and the true was of as much value to most people as a nutmeg would be to a cow. At length he fell ill. 'You really look like a shadow,' people said to him, and then a cold shudder would pass over him, for he had his own thoughts on the subject.

'You really ought to go to some watering-place,' said the shadow on his next visit. 'There is no other chance for you. I will take you with me, for the sake of old acquaintance. I will pay the expenses of your journey, and you shall write a description of it to amuse us by the way. I should like to go to a watering-place; my beard does not grow as it ought, which is from weakness, and I must have a beard. Now do be sensible and accept my proposal; we shall travel as intimate friends.'

And at last they started together. The shadow was master now, and the master became the shadow. They drove together, and rode and walked in company with each other, side by side, or one in front and the other behind, according to the position of the sun.

The shadow always knew when to take the place of honour, but the learned man took no notice of it, for he had a good heart, and was exceedingly mild and friendly.

One day the master said to the shadow, 'We have grown up together from our childhood, and now that we have become travelling companions, shall we not drink to our good fellowship, and say thee and thou to each other?'

'What you say is very straightforward and kindly meant,' said the shadow, who was now really master. 'I will be equally kind and straightforward. You are a learned man, and know how wonderful human nature is. There are some men who cannot endure the smell of brown paper; it makes them ill. Others will feel a shuddering sensation to their very marrow, if a nail is scratched on a pane of glass. I myself have a similar kind of feeling when I hear anyone say thou to me. I feel crushed by it, as I used to feel in my former position with you. You will perceive that this is a matter of feeling, not pride. I cannot allow you to say thou to me; I will gladly say it to you, and therefore your wish will be half fulfilled.' Then the shadow addressed his former master as thou.

'It is going rather too far,' said the latter, 'that I am to say you when I speak to him, and he is to say thou to me.' However, he was obliged to submit.

They arrived at length at the baths, where there were many strangers, and among them a beautiful princess, whose real disease consisted in being too sharp-sighted, which made everyone very uneasy. She saw at once that the newcomer was very different to everyone else. 'They say he is here to make his beard grow,' she thought; 'but I know the real cause, he is unable to cast a shadow.' Then she became very curious on the matter, and one day, while on the promenade, she entered into conversation with the strange gentleman. Being a princess, she was not obliged to stand upon much ceremony, so she said to him without hesitation, 'Your illness consists in not being able to cast a shadow.'

'Your royal highness must be on the high road to recovery from your illness,' said he. 'I know your complaint arose from being too sharp-sighted, and in this case it has entirely failed. I happen to have a most unusual shadow. Have you not seen a person who is always at my side? Persons often give their servants finer cloth for their liveries than for their own clothes, and so I have dressed out my shadow like a man; nay, you may observe that I have even given him a shadow of his own; it is rather expensive, but I like to have things about me that are peculiar.'

'How is this?' thought the princess. 'Am I really cured? This must be the best watering-place in existence. Water in our times has certainly wonderful power. But I will not leave this place yet, just as it begins to be amusing. This foreign prince – for he must be a prince – pleases me above all things. I only hope his beard won't grow, or he will leave at once.'

In the evening, the princess and the shadow danced together in the large assembly rooms. She was light, but he was lighter still; she had never seen such a dancer before. She told him from what country she had come, and found he knew it and had been there, but not while she was at home. He had looked into the windows of her father's palace, both the upper and the lower windows; he had seen many things, and could therefore answer the princess, and make allusions which quite astonished her. She thought he must be the cleverest man in all the world, and felt the greatest respect for his knowledge. When she danced with him again she fell in love with him, which the shadow quickly discovered, for she had with her eyes looked him through and through. They danced once more, and she was nearly telling him, but she had some discretion; she thought of her country, her kingdom and the number of people over whom she would one day have to rule. 'He is a clever man,' she thought to herself, 'which is a good thing, and he dances admirably, which is also good. But has he well-grounded knowledge? That is an important question, and I must try him.' Then she asked him a most difficult question, she herself could not have answered it, and the shadow made a most unaccountable grimace.

'You cannot answer that,' said the princess.

'I learnt something about it in my childhood,' he replied; 'and believe that even my very shadow, standing over there by the door, could answer it.'

'Your shadow,' said the princess; 'indeed that would be very remarkable.'

'I do not say so positively,' observed the shadow; 'but I am inclined to believe that he can do so. He has followed me for so many years, and has heard so much from me, that I think it is very likely. But your royal highness must allow me to observe that he is very proud of being considered a man, and to put him in a good humour, so that he may answer correctly, he must be treated as a man.'

'I shall be very pleased to do so,' said the princess. So she walked up to the learned man, who stood in the doorway, and spoke to him of the sun and the moon, of the green forests, and of people near home and far off; and the learned man conversed with her pleasantly and sensibly.

'What a wonderful man he must be, to have such a clever shadow!' thought she. 'If I were to choose him it would be a real blessing to my country and my subjects, and I will do it.' So the princess and the shadow were soon engaged to each other, but no one was to be told a word about it, till she returned to her kingdom.

'No one shall know,' said the shadow; 'not even my own shadow;' and he had very particular reasons for saying so.

After a time, the princess returned to the land over which she reigned, and the shadow accompanied her.

'Listen my friend,' said the shadow to the learned man; 'now that I am as fortunate and as powerful as any man can be, I will do something unusually good for you. You shall live in my palace, drive with me in the royal carriage, and have a hundred thousand dollars a year; but you must allow everyone to call you a shadow, and never venture to say that you have been a man. And once a year, when I sit in my balcony in the sunshine, you must lie at my feet as becomes a shadow to do; for I must tell you I am going to marry the princess, and our wedding will take place this evening.'

'Now, really, this is too ridiculous,' said the learned man. 'I cannot, and will not, submit to such folly. It would be cheating the whole country, and the princess also. I will disclose everything, and say that I am the man, and that you are only a shadow dressed up in men's clothes.'

'No one would believe you,' said the shadow; 'be reasonable, now, or I will call the guards.'

'I will go straight to the princess,' said the learned man.

'But I shall be there first,' replied the shadow, 'and you will be sent to prison.' And so it turned out, for the guards readily obeyed him, as they knew he was going to marry the king's daughter.

'You tremble,' said the princess, when the shadow appeared before her. 'Has anything happened? You must not be ill today, for this evening our wedding will take place.'

'I have gone through the most terrible affair that could possibly happen,' said the shadow; 'only imagine, my shadow has gone mad; I suppose such a poor, shallow brain, could not bear much; he fancies that he has become a real man, and that I am his shadow.'

'How very terrible,' cried the princess; 'is he locked up?'

'Oh yes, certainly; for I fear he will never recover.'

'Poor shadow!' said the princess. 'It is very unfortunate for him; it would really be a good deed to free him from his frail existence; and, indeed, when I think how often people take the part of the lower class against the higher, in these days, it would be policy to put him out of the way quietly.'

'It is certainly rather hard upon him, for he was a faithful servant,' said the shadow; and he pretended to sigh.

'Yours is a noble character,' said the princess, and bowed herself before him.

In the evening the whole town was illuminated, and cannons fired 'boom', and the soldiers presented arms. It was indeed a grand wedding. The princess and the shadow stepped out on the balcony to show themselves, and to receive one cheer more. But the learned man heard nothing of all these festivities, for he had already been executed.

THE OLD HOUSE

A very old house stood once in a street with several that were quite new and clean. The date of its erection had been carved on one of the beams, and surrounded by scrolls formed of tulips and hop-tendrils; by this date it could be seen that the old house was nearly three hundred years old. Verses too were written over the windows in old-fashioned letters, and grotesque faces, curiously carved, grinned at you from under the cornices. One story projected a long way over the other, and under the roof ran a leaden gutter, with a dragon's head at the end. The rain was intended to pour out at the dragon's mouth, but it ran out of his body instead, for there was a hole in the gutter. The other houses in the street were new and well built, with large window panes and smooth walls. Any one could see they had nothing to do with the old house. Perhaps they thought, 'How long will that heap of rubbish remain here to be a disgrace to the whole street? The parapet projects so far forward that no one can see out of our windows what is going on in that direction. The stairs are as broad as the staircase of a castle, and as steep as if they led to a church-tower. The iron railing looks like the gate of a cemetery, and there are brass knobs upon it. It is really too ridiculous.'

Opposite to the old house were more nice new houses, which had just the same opinion as their neighbours.

At the window of one of them sat a little boy with fresh rosy cheeks and clear sparkling eyes, who was very fond of the old house, in sunshine or in moonlight. He would sit and look at the wall from which the plaster had in some places fallen off, and fancy all sorts of scenes which had been in former times. How the street must have looked when the houses had all gable roofs, open staircases and gutters with dragons at the spout. He could even see soldiers walking about with halberds. Certainly it was a very good house to look at for amusement.

An old man lived in it, who wore knee-breeches, a coat with large brass buttons, and a wig, which anyone could see was a real wig. Every morning an old man came to clean the rooms, and to wait upon him, otherwise the old man in the knee-breeches would have been quite alone in the house. Sometimes he came to one of the windows and looked out; then the little boy nodded to him, and the old man nodded back again, till they became acquainted, and were friends, although they had never spoken to each other; but that was of no consequence.

The little boy one day heard his parents say, 'The old man opposite is very well off, but is terribly lonely.' The next Sunday morning the little boy wrapped something in a piece of paper and took it to the door of the old house, and said to the attendant who waited upon the old man, 'Will you please give this from me to the gentleman who lives here; I have two tin soldiers, and this is one of them, and he shall have it, because I know he is terribly lonely.'

And the old attendant nodded and looked very pleased, and then he carried the tin soldier into the house.

Afterwards he was sent over to ask the little boy if he would not like to pay a visit himself. His parents gave him permission, and so it was that he gained admission to the old house.

The brassy knobs on the railings shone more brightly than ever, as if they had been polished on account of his visit; and on the door were carved trumpeters standing in tulips, and it seemed as if they were blowing with all their might, their cheeks were so puffed out. 'Tanta-ra-ra, the little boy is coming; Tanta-ra-ra, the little boy is coming.'

Then the door opened. All round the hall hung old portraits of knights in armour, and ladies in silk gowns; and the armour rattled, and the silk dresses rustled. Then came a staircase which went up a long way, and then came down a little way and led to a balcony, which was in a very ruinous state. There were large holes and long cracks, out of which grew grass and leaves, indeed the whole balcony, the courtyard and the walls were so overgrown with green that they looked like a garden. In the balcony stood flower-pots, on which were heads having asses' ears, but the flowers in them grew just as they pleased. In one pot pinks were growing all over the sides, at least the green leaves were shooting forth stalk and stem, and saying as plainly as they could speak, 'The air has fanned me, the sun has kissed me, and I am promised a little flower for next Sunday – really for next Sunday.'

Then they entered a room in which the walls were covered with leather, and the leather had golden flowers stamped upon it.

'Gilding will fade in damp weather,
To endure, there is nothing like leather,'

said the walls. Chairs handsomely carved, with elbows on each side, and with very high backs, stood in the room, and as they creaked they seemed to say, 'Sit down. Oh dear, how I am creaking. I shall certainly have the gout like the old cupboard. Gout in my back, ugh.'

And then the little boy entered the room where the old man sat.

'Thank you for the tin soldier, my little friend,' said the old man, 'and thank you also for coming to see me.'

'Thanks, thanks,' or 'Creak, creak,' said all the furniture.

There was so much that the pieces of furniture stood in each other's way to get a sight of the little boy.

On the wall near the centre of the room hung the picture of a beautiful lady, young and gay, dressed in the fashion of the olden times, with powdered hair and a full, stiff skirt. She said neither 'thanks' nor 'creak', but she looked down upon the little boy with her mild eyes; and then he said to the old man, 'Where did you get that picture?'

'From the shop opposite,' he replied. 'Many portraits hang there that none seem to trouble themselves about. The persons they represent have been dead and buried long since. But I knew this lady many years ago, and she has been dead nearly half a century.'

Under a glass beneath the picture hung a nosegay of withered flowers, which were no doubt half a century old too, at least they appeared so.

And the pendulum of the old clock went to and fro, and the hands turned round; and as time passed on, everything in the room grew older, but no one seemed to notice it.

'They say at home,' said the little boy, 'that you are very lonely.'

'Oh,' replied the old man, 'I have pleasant thoughts of all that has passed, recalled by memory; and now you are come to visit me, and that is very pleasant.'

Then he took from the book-case a book full of pictures representing long processions of wonderful coaches, such as are never seen at the present time. Soldiers like the knave of clubs, and citizens with waving banners. The tailors had a flag with a pair of scissors supported by two lions, and on the shoemakers' flag there were not boots, but an eagle with two heads, for the shoemakers must have everything arranged so that they can say, 'This is a pair.' What a picture-book it was; and then the old man went into another room to fetch apples and nuts. It was very pleasant, certainly, to be in that old house.

'I cannot endure it,' said the tin soldier, who stood on a shelf, 'it is so lonely and dull here. I have been accustomed to live in a family, and I cannot get used to this life. I cannot bear it. The whole day is long enough, but the evening is longer. It is not here like it was in your house opposite, when your father and mother talked so cheerfully together, while you and all the dear children made such a delightful noise. No, it is all lonely in the old man's house. Do you think he gets any kisses? Do you think he ever has friendly looks, or a Christmas tree? He will have nothing now but the grave. Oh, I cannot bear it.'

'You must not look only on the sorrowful side,' said the little boy; 'I think everything in this house is beautiful, and all the old pleasant thoughts come back here to pay visits.'

'Ah, but I never see any, and I don't know them,' said the tin soldier, 'and I cannot bear it.'

'You must bear it,' said the little boy. Then the old man came back with a pleasant face; and brought with him beautiful preserved fruits, as well as apples and nuts; and the little boy thought no more of the tin soldier. How happy and delighted the little boy was; and after he returned home, and while days and weeks passed, a great deal of nodding took place from one house to the other, and then the little boy went to pay another visit. The carved trumpeters blew 'Tanta-ra-ra. There is the little boy. Tanta-ra-ra.' The swords and armour on the old knight's pictures rattled. The silk dresses rustled, the leather repeated its rhyme, and the old chairs had the gout in their backs, and cried, 'Creak;' it was all exactly like the first time; for in that house, one day and one hour were just like another. 'I cannot bear it any longer,' said the tin soldier; 'I have wept tears of tin, it is so melancholy here. Let me go to the wars, and lose an arm or a leg, that would be some change; I cannot bear it. Now I know what it is to have visits from one's old recollections, and all they bring with them. I have had visits from mine, and you may believe me it is not altogether pleasant. I was very nearly jumping from the shelf. I saw you all in your house opposite, as if you were really present. It was Sunday morning, and you children stood round the table, singing the hymn that you sing every morning. You were standing quietly, with your hands folded, and your father and mother were looking just as serious, when the door opened, and your little sister Maria, who is not two years old, was brought into the room. You know she always dances when she hears music and singing of any sort; so she began to dance immediately, although she ought not to have done so, but she could not get into the right time because the tune was so slow; so she stood first on one leg and then on the other, and bent her head very low, but it would not suit the music. You all stood looking very grave, although it was very difficult to do so, but I laughed so to myself that I fell down from the table, and got a bruise, which is there still; I know it was not right to laugh. So all this, and everything else that I have seen, keeps running in my head, and these must be the old recollections that bring so many thoughts with them. Tell me whether you still sing on Sundays, and tell me about your little sister Maria, and how my old comrade is, the other tin soldier. Ah, really he must be very happy; I cannot endure this life.'

'You are given away,' said the little boy; 'you must stay. Don't you see that?' Then the old man came in, with a box containing many curious things to show him. Rouge-pots, scent-boxes, and old cards, so large and so richly gilded that none are ever seen like them in these days. And there were smaller boxes to look at, and the piano was opened, and inside the lid were painted landscapes. But when the old man played, the piano sounded quite out of tune. Then he looked at the picture he had bought at the broker's, and his eyes sparkled brightly as he nodded at it, and said, 'Ah, she could sing that tune.'

'I will go to the wars! I will go to the wars!' cried the tin soldier as loud as he could, and threw himself down on the floor. Where could he have fallen? The old man searched, and the little boy searched, but he was gone, and could not be found. 'I shall find him again,' said the old man, but he did not find him. The boards of the floor were open and full of holes. The tin soldier had fallen through a crack between the boards, and lay there now in an open grave. The day went by, and the little boy returned home; the week passed, and many more weeks. It was winter, and the windows were quite frozen, so the little boy was obliged to breathe on the panes, and rub a hole to peep through at the old house. Snow drifts were lying in all the scrolls and on the inscriptions, and the steps were covered with snow as if no one were at home. And indeed nobody was home, for the old man was dead. In the evening, a hearse stopped at the door, and the old man in his coffin was placed in it. He was to be taken to the country to be buried there in his own grave; so they carried him away; no one followed him, for all his friends were dead; and the little boy kissed his hand to the coffin as the hearse moved away with it. A few days after, there was an auction at the old house, and from his window the little boy saw the people carrying away the pictures of old knights and ladies, the flower-pots with the long ears, the old chairs and the cupboards. Some were taken one way, some another. Her portrait, which had been bought at the picture dealer's, went back again to his shop, and there it remained, for no one seemed to know her, or to care for the old picture. In the spring, they began to pull the house itself down; people called it complete rubbish. From the street could be seen the room in which the walls were covered with leather, ragged and torn, and the green in the balcony hung straggling over the beams; they pulled it down quickly, for it looked ready to fall, and at last it was cleared away altogether. 'What a good riddance,' said the neighbours' houses. Very shortly, a fine new house was built farther back from the road; it had lofty windows and smooth walls, but in front, on the spot where the old house really stood, a little garden was planted, and wild vines grew up over the neighbouring walls; in front of the garden were large iron railings and a great gate, which looked very stately. People used to stop and peep through the railings. The sparrows assembled in dozens upon the wild vines, and chattered all together as loud as they could, but not about the old house; none of them could remember it, for many years had passed by, so many indeed that the little boy was now a man, and a really good man too, and his parents were very proud of him. He was just married, and had come, with his young wife, to reside in the new house with the garden in front of it, and now he stood there by her side while she planted a field flower that she thought very pretty. She was planting it herself with her little hands, and pressing down the earth with her fingers. 'Oh dear, what was that?' she exclaimed, as something pricked her. Out of the soft earth something was sticking up. It was – only think! – it was really the tin soldier, the very same which had been lost up in the old man's room, and had been hidden among old wood and rubbish for a long time, till it sunk into the earth, where it must have been for many years. And the young wife wiped the soldier, first with a green leaf, and then with her fine pocket-handkerchief that smelt of such beautiful perfume. And the tin soldier felt as if he was recovering from a fainting fit. 'Let me see him,' said the young man, and then he smiled and shook his head, and said, 'It can scarcely be the same, but it reminds me of something that happened to one of my tin soldiers when I was a little boy.' And then he told his wife about the old house and the old man, and of the tin soldier which he had sent across, because he thought the old man was lonely; and he related the story so clearly that tears came into the eyes of the young wife for the old house and the old man. 'It is very likely that this is really the same soldier,' said she, and I will take care of him, and always remember what you have told me; but some day you must show me the old man's grave.'

'I don't know where it is,' he replied; 'no one knows. All his friends are dead; no one took care of him, and I was only a little boy.'

'Oh, how dreadfully lonely he must have been,' said she.

'Yes, terribly lonely,' cried the tin soldier; 'still it is delightful not to be forgotten.'

'Delightful indeed,' cried a voice quite near to them; no one but the tin soldier saw that it came from a rag of the leather which hung in tatters; it had lost all its gilding, and looked like wet earth, but it had an opinion, and it spoke it thus: –

> *'Gilding will fade in damp weather,*
> *To endure, there is nothing like leather.'*

But the tin soldier did not believe any such thing.

THE HAPPY FAMILY

The largest green leaf in this country is certainly the burdock-leaf. If you hold it in front of you, it is large enough for an apron; and if you hold it over your head, it is almost as good as an umbrella, it is so wonderfully large. A burdock never grows alone; where it grows, there are many more, and it is a splendid sight; and all this splendour is good for snails. The great white snails, which grand people in olden times used to have made into fricassees; and when they had eaten them, they would say, 'O, what a delicious dish!' For these people really thought them good; and these snails lived on burdock-leaves, and for them the burdock was planted.

There was once an old estate where no one now lived to require snails; indeed, the owners had all died out, but the burdock still flourished; it grew over all the beds and walks of the garden – its growth had no check – till it became at last quite a forest of burdocks. Here and there stood an apple or a plum-tree; but for this, nobody would have thought the place had ever been a garden. It was burdock from one end to the other; and here lived the last two surviving snails. They knew not themselves how old they were; but they could remember the time when there were a great many more of them, and that they were descended from a family which came from foreign lands, and that the whole forest had been planted for them and theirs. They had never been away from the garden; but they knew that another place once existed in the world, called the Duke's Palace Castle, in which some of their relations had been boiled till they became black, and were then laid on a silver dish; but what was done afterwards they did not know. Besides, they could not imagine exactly how it felt to be boiled and placed on a silver dish; but no doubt it was something very fine and highly genteel. Neither the cockchafer, nor the toad, nor the earth-worm, whom they questioned about it, would give them the least information; for none of their relations had ever been cooked or served on a silver dish. The old white snails were the most aristocratic race in the world – they knew that. The forest had been planted for them, and the nobleman's castle had been built entirely that they might be cooked and laid on silver dishes.

They lived quite retired and very happily; and as they had no children of their own, they had adopted a little common snail, which they brought up as their own child. The little one would not grow, for he was only a common snail; but the old people, particularly the mother snail, declared that she could easily see how he grew; and when the father said he could not perceive it, she begged him to feel the little snail's shell, and he did so, and found that the mother was right.

One day it rained very fast. 'Listen, what a drumming there is on the burdock-leaves; turn, turn, turn; turn, turn, turn,' said the father snail.

'There come the drops,' said the mother; 'they are trickling down the stalks. We shall have it very wet here presently. I am very glad we have such good houses, and that the little one has one of his own. There has been really more done for us than for any other creature; it is quite plain that we are the most noble people in the world. We have houses from our birth, and the burdock forest has been planted for us. I should very much like to know how far it extends, and what lies beyond it.'

'There can be nothing better than we have here,' said the father snail; 'I wish for nothing more.'

'Yes, but I do,' said the mother; 'I should like to be taken to the palace, and boiled, and laid upon a silver dish, as was done to all our ancestors; and you may be sure it must be something very uncommon.'

'The nobleman's castle, perhaps, has fallen to decay,' said the snail-father, 'or the burdock wood may have grown out. You need not be in a hurry; you are always so impatient, and the youngster is getting just the same. He has been three days creeping to the top of that stalk. I feel quite giddy when I look at him.'

'You must not scold him,' said the mother snail; 'he creeps so very carefully. He will be the joy of our home; and we old folks have nothing else to live for. But have you ever thought where we are to get a wife for him? Do you think that farther out in the wood there may be others of our race?'

'There may be black snails, no doubt,' said the old snail; 'black snails without houses; but they are so vulgar and conceited too. But we can give the ants a commission; they run here and there, as if they all had so much business to get through. They, most likely, will know of a wife for our youngster.'

'I certainly know a most beautiful bride,' said one of the ants; 'but I fear it would not do, for she is a queen.'

'That does not matter,' said the old snail; 'has she a house?'

'She has a palace,' replied the ant – 'a most beautiful ant-palace with seven hundred passages.'

'Thank you,' said the mother snail; 'but our boy shall not go to live in an ant-hill. If you know of nothing better, we will give the commission to the white gnats; they fly about in rain and sunshine; they know the burdock wood from one end to the other.'

'We have a wife for him,' said the gnats; 'a hundred man-steps from here there is a little snail with a house, sitting on a gooseberry-bush; she is quite alone, and old enough to be married. It is only a hundred man-steps from here.'

'Then let her come to him,' said the old people. 'He has the whole burdock forest; she has only a bush.'

So they brought the little lady-snail. She took eight days to perform the journey; but that was just as it ought to be; for it showed her to be one of the right breeding. And then they had a wedding. Six glow-worms gave as much light as they could; but in other respects it was all very quiet; for the old snails could not bear festivities or a crowd. But a beautiful speech was made by the mother snail. The father could not speak; he was too much overcome. Then they gave the whole burdock forest to the young snails as an inheritance, and repeated what they had so often said, that it was the finest place in the world, and that if they led upright and honourable lives, and their family increased, they and their children might some day be taken to the nobleman's palace, to be boiled black, and laid on a silver dish. And when they had finished speaking, the old couple crept into their houses, and came out no more; for they slept.

The young snail pair now ruled in the forest, and had a numerous progeny. But as the young ones were never boiled or laid in silver dishes, they concluded that the castle had fallen into decay, and that all the people in the world were dead; and as nobody contradicted them, they thought they must be right. And the rain fell upon the burdock-leaves, to play the drum for them, and the sun shone to paint colours on the burdock forest for them, and they were very happy; the whole family were entirely and perfectly happy.